PEGASUS
TO
PARADISE

Michael Tappenden

MICHAEL
TAPPENDEN

Copyright © Michael Tappenden 2013

Published by Acorn Independent Press, 2013.

The right of Michael Tappenden to be identified as the Author of the Work has been asserted by him in accordance with the Copyright, Designs and Patents Act 1988.

This book is sold subject to the condition it shall not, by way of trade or otherwise be circulated in any form or by any means, electronic or otherwise without the publisher's prior consent.

Set in 10.5 pt Minion Pro

ISBN 978-1-909121-31-7

www.acornindependentpress.com

For Ted, Florrie, Michael and Barry

This book is dedicated to all those veterans and their families - past, present and future - who gave and continue to give so much.

Special thanks to fellow writers Jacqueline Andrews and Steve Hayward for their help and encouragement and to all those behind the scenes.

Special acknowledgement to the Veterans Charity (www.veteranscharity.org.uk) for their tireless support of servicemen and servicewomen in need.
It takes words and deeds.

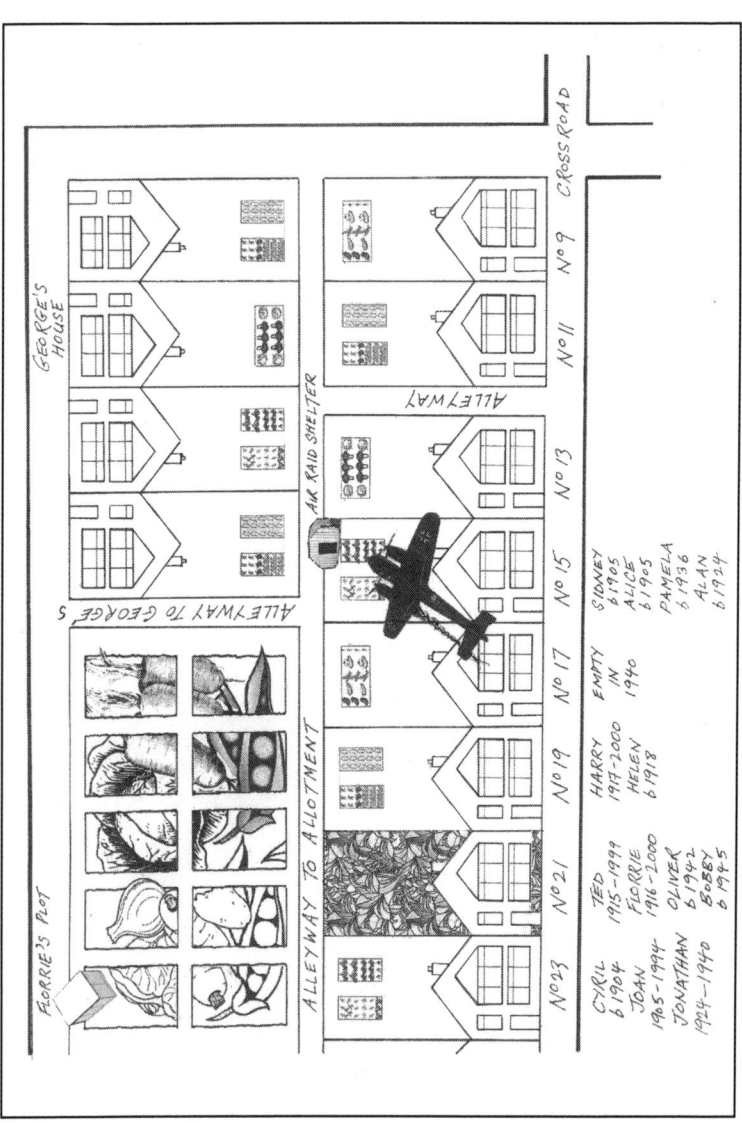

ONE

In the Beginning: On the Hill and a Hurled Pepper Pot

*'I stood upon the hills, when heaven's wide arch
Was glorious with the sun's returning march,
And words were brightened, and soft gales
Went forth to kiss the sun glad vales.'*

Henry Wadsworth Longfellow

'Marry when June roses grow, over land and sea you'll go.'

Anon

'It's a girl.'

A thousand alien suns blinded her and her throat, mouth and nose full of the soupy swamp from which she had come, bubbled and sucked desperately.

'She's struggling!'

She could taste her mother and her mother's mother and, at that moment, countless generations locked in her cells cried out. Urging. Encouraging. Insisting.

'Don't give up. Never give up.'

From far away, other sounds swirled into her mind. Shouts – the shouts of men in battle, their voices edged with terror and exultation. And cries – desperate cries of those tumbling helplessly into a cold and hungry sea, their last words bubbling soundlessly towards the surface.

'Don't give up. Never give up.'

She raged. Flushed crimson. Fingers and toes curled in frustration and then like a broadside, a tiny voice exploded from her.

'She's OK now.'

'What a performance. Bound for the stage this one,' smiled the midwife turning towards old Mrs Partridge, there to help, from number sixty nine just down the road.

Later, clean and calm, the newborn baby lay on her back, wondering at the blur of colour around her. A shaft of sunshine slipped through the bedroom window, narrowing her eyes but covering her in a soft, natural warmth, as if her ancestors, rejoicing, were bathing her in a golden light. Inside, she smiled peacefully.

It was the 9th May, 1916; a great sea battle was reverberating off the coast of Jutland, British Summer Time was being introduced and Florrie was born. Like planets and stars, all three fell into a conjunction.

Florrie grew up between two World Wars, on top of the Hill. Below she could see the criss-cross of roads and the regular patchwork of dark red roof tiles that could glow in the sun or be dulled by the rain; and the wilful river undulating through it all and off out of sight, changing like a chameleon in the fickle Medway light. From the edges of the town, broad brush strokes of greens and browns faded into the horizon.

The Hill was long and steep and arduous; climbing it preyed mercilessly on your limbs and lungs and spirit. You could stop and rest but you could never give in, if you wanted to achieve its summit.

Before she was thirty, Florrie had climbed many such Hills. The Hills of Destruction, of Death, of Fear, of Loss and, at long last, of Victory. There were times, when she had trembled with fear and pain and felt she simply wouldn't make it, but somehow, she always managed to put her dread and suffering to one side and place one leaden step in front of the other.

Climbing the Hill to Victory had been exhausting and demanding and its very name had trembled uncertainly on peoples' lips. The peak was so often hidden by the black shadows of death and uncertainty and violent storms and desperate avalanches threatened to sweep hope away. Many had fallen.

Florrie, like everyone else, had struggled and faltered along the way, but finally, with fire in her heart, she had rushed the final distance to the top and had stood there, looking around, tasting the sweetest joy. And best of all, a miracle had happened: Ted had joined her, coming home from the War alive and unharmed and she had been overwhelmed with happiness. It had been pure and wondrous – a black and white moment, good over evil, right over wrong, freedom over tyranny and the elation she felt etched itself deeply into her soul forever. This, she knew, would have to be defended and celebrated for the rest of her life.

She was not to know how many more of such Hills were to stretch before her into the hazy distance of her life – maybe that was just as well.

She had four sisters and three brothers, one of whom never survived to see a single candle flickering on a birthday cake and another, a self-employed coal carman died aged fifteen, from a disease that destroyed his young lungs. And so there were five. But such tragedies were common.

Her father, John Henry, traded as a hawker, buying and selling this and that. As a young man, he had waited grim-faced as the bayonets of the Prussian Guard advanced toward him, glinting terribly in the Flanders' light – Hun steel seeking British gut and he had fought for his life. Later, in that same sodden slaughterhouse, he had choked on poison gas but again, somehow, had found the will to survive as his ancestors whispered urgently.

He carried that experience with him for the rest of his life in more ways than one. Every year in March he would burn with fever, as pieces of German shrapnel forced themselves through his scarred flesh and out, like some awful harvest.

At Christmas, full of whisky, it was nightmares that escaped. In front of his family.

'Come on Dad, not now.'

But his words wept. Each stained peace and goodwill. Terrible words that thankfully were soon lost in a slur of alcoholic sadness.

Florrie's mother, Sarah Jane, always known as Sally, was like a little bird; a tiny, slight, but never fragile jenny wren, hopping from place to place. Maybe it was the malnutrition of Southern Ireland that had stunted her growth, for she had fled with her family from the poverty and hopelessness of County Cork for the poverty and possibilities of the East End of London.

Later, one September, she met her husband-to-be in the green tranquil hop fields of Kent; they had married nearby.

Sarah Jane's tiny frame never ever increased, as if in a living protest to the sorrow of her homeland, despite frequent visits to the Tam O' Shanter, just down the Hill, where she sat, enjoying many glasses of black creamy stout. There, solicitors rubbed shoulders with horse dealers, doctors with thieves, landlords with labourers and scrap merchants with magistrates. She knew them all and they, in turn, regularly helped her home – unsteadily back up the Hill.

It was a noisy, chaotic, happy, argumentative household ruled firmly but benignly by John Henry who was determined that his daughters should become ladies and that his remaining son become successful. There was one exception – Florrie. Florrie had decided to be a boy.

A fighting, wrestling, yelling, running, scrumping, black-eyed, grazing-your-knees, getting-into-scrapes sort of boy. A tree-climbing, football-kicking, pipe-smoking, roller-skating, cigarette-card-collecting, conker-smashing, rebellious sort of boy – and she was always in trouble.

'Florence!'

'Yes Mother?'

'Mrs Jenkins has been in.'

'Oh yes?'

'Yes! Why did you punch her Samuel on the nose? There was blood all over his new shirt.'

'It was his fault.'

'How was it his fault?'

'He shouldn't call me Flo. Nobody calls me Flo and gets away with it. I warned him.'

'Oh Florence.'

And then she met Ted.

Ted also lived on the Hill, but higher up, in the bay-fronted house called Fairview and on the other side of the brown ribbon of road that struggled upwards and sped downwards. For generations, Ted's ancestors had toiled the fields of Kent and he had inherited their quiet mental and physical strength. He was tall and athletic with a wave of fair hair that flopped above his laughing blue eyes. Ted was a keen sportsman who played football well enough to represent his town as an amateur inheriting his skill from his father, Mick who had played professionally just after the Great War. A skilful and hard tackling centre half, Mick had been prone to weight problems due to his liking for Irish Stout, and surely enough, his sporting career had been very short. Undeterred he continued to drink the profits from his bookmaking business despite the rages of his wife Edith, who would occasionally, in sheer frustration, beat him with a poker taken from the fireplace. He would grin – drunkenly, infuriatingly – at every blow. Ted, the young onlooker, vowed never to touch the stuff and, apart from the occasional sherry, never did.

Ted and Florrie had of course known of each other, living as they did, close by on the Hill. It was difficult not to be aware of Florrie's escapades and Ted's tall physique and handsome looks certainly turned female heads, although he was quite unaware of his appeal. To Florrie, however, he seemed too quiet, not exciting, almost boring and she looked away.

Occasionally, Ted called in to see John Henry to buy domestic items for his mother: a pot or a pan or shoe polish or candles. He was always polite and often embarrassed by the giggles of Florrie's sisters as they peeked at him from around doorways. He hardly ever spoke to Florrie, not really, not until the day of the summer market.

John Henry worked hard at his business, an activity for which he possessed a natural flair and strong business acumen, despite the fact he could neither read nor write, and his tiny wife had to read the local papers to him.

'Just the interesting bits, Sally. What are the politicians doing? Need to keep an eye on the bastards. Anyone local died?'

His interest in any local demise was not usually out of neighbourly concern but because of the opportunity for a house clearance. He may not be able to read or write, but he could certainly count.

Sometimes Florrie would help him, calling out the wares at their stall and aping the cries of the other market people. He appreciated her help, but was always aware that occasionally the steely personalities of father and teenage daughter would collide with a terrible ringing clash. On this day, however, the sun smiled warmly from an endless depth of blue and looking skywards John Henry rubbed his hands. It was a perfect day for selling; nothing could go wrong.

It was not easy for a young woman to compete against the counterpoint of loud tenor, baritone and bass voices as well as the general chatter and bustle of the summer market. All around her she could hear men's voices calling out their wares.

'Juicy Jaffas. Get yer juicy Jaffas 'ere. Come on girls when they've gone, they've gone.'

'Lovely caulis. 'Ave yer seen one that big darlin'? No! Wot yer laughing at then?'

'Come on ladies, this is your lucky day. A lovely new iron. Make yer old man look a treat. Wot yer ain't got one? See me after darlin'. Right naw. Ten bob in the shops. But today, not ten bob, not eight bob, not even seven and six. For you darlin' six shillings. Yes, six bob. Can't even believe it meself. Hurry now, just a few left. One over there Jack.'

People strolling between the canvas-covered stalls would be intrigued to come across a young woman competing so enthusiastically.

'Quality brushes. The very best. Get your brushes here. Come on now, you all need brushes.'

Florrie thrust a pair of green boot brushes under the noses of a passing middle-aged couple. They stopped and looked at each other uncertainly, waiting for the other to take the initiative.

'No thank you my dear,' smiled the man, obviously enjoying taking in Florrie's dark curls and blue eyes while his wife shifted uneasily.

Florrie was not going to be deterred.

'Everybody needs brushes.'

Despite the pull on his arm, the man took one of the brushes from

Florrie and turned it over in his large hands. There was something wrong.

'Why are they painted?'

Yes, of course, Florrie thought to herself, *brushes are never painted, are they? Stained or varnished but never... and dark green, where have I seen that before?* Thoughts showered like meteorites through her mind.

'To protect them of course.'

'Come on Jim, let's go dear.'

'There's something dodgy about those.'

'We have to be at my sister's soon,' the woman chipped in with a strained smile.

'They're definitely dodgy,' scratching at the paint with a cracked fingernail.

'Oi enough of that. If you don't want the goods…' John Henry moved towards the man growling like an old bear.

The couple turned away, the woman pulling at the arm of her husband, anxious to leave; the man turning occasionally, looking back. John Henry slipped the brush into his pocket.

'They're the same colour as our front door.'

'Can't waste good paint.'

'What are you up…?'

Florrie jumped as something cold and wet rubbed against her hand.

'Good morning, John. Good morning, Florence.'

Neither had noticed the small man that now stood next to them, waiting his turn, not wanting to interrupt their conversation. He wore a white collarless shirt, baggy trousers and had thick dark hair brushed backwards from his brow so that it sloped up like a strange curly crown. He had been very careful to call Florrie by her full name. Didn't want *her* shouting at him. A large black greyhound stood beside him. Taut and streamlined, the dog's body curved backwards from the white blaze on his deep chest to the tip of his upturned tail. The dog was less reserved than his owner and looked up at Florrie, smiling, hoping for a hug.

'Ketchup, how are you boy?' she said kneeling to fondle his ears while Ketchup, straining at his leash, grinned, tail swishing and attempted to lick her nose.

John Henry gave Ketchup a perfunctory pat on his sleek head and the dog, sensing his indifference, ignored him completely. It was true that John Henry ordinarily had no interest in dogs, seeing them as yet another mouth to feed, but for Ketchup he made an exception. This dog won races and with that came prize money. He considered whether he should get a greyhound for himself. They needed a lot of training and exercise of course, but he did have that plot of land outside town. The trouble was that Florrie and the others would turn him into a pet – a lap dog. Soft, the lot of them.

'Hello Fred. How's the dog?'

'Well he's no Mick the Miller, but we just won a steeplechase cup at Haringey.'

'Good money?'

'Not bad, John. Not bad.' Fred dropped his head slightly to one side and nodded slowly. He continued the conversation more confidently. 'So John, how's business? Did you shift those old brushes, you know the ones that… you know…' and his head nodded more vigorously now and his eyebrows rose conspiratorially.

Florrie stood up abruptly.

'What old brushes?'

Fred missed the edge in Florrie's voice.

'You know,' Fred whispered. 'The ones with the worm.'

John Henry, still pondering greyhound glory, heard the words escape like the scream of a German shell arriving too close. Far too close.

'Florrie, can you look after the stall while Fred and me go…?'

'What worm?'

The shell exploded.

'Shh, for goodness sake!'

Both men quickly crowded around Florrie to stop the shrapnel spraying any further, but she had already turned, snatched up a brush and was vigorously scratching away a layer of green paint.

'Don't do that Florrie!'

She turned away, ignoring her father.

Hidden by the paint were woodworm holes filled with hardened putty.

'You can't sell these,' she hissed, blue eyes flashing. 'You can't cheat people. You...'

She suddenly paused as realisation swept over her.

'You got me to sell them,' she gasped. 'You used me!'

'Oh Florrie, that's ridiculous,'

But the fuse was lit now and travelling at unstoppable speed towards the powder keg and both men instinctively winced as she exploded with a terrible cry and flung the brush to the ground with such force that it broke in half. Furiously, she turned and strode off. Fred muttered weak apologies. Ketchup strained and barked loudly and John Henry picked up the two halves and wondered if he could still sell them as nailbrushes.

Florrie's anger bounced her several miles through the town and halfway up the Hill before realising where she was and how breathless and exhausted she'd become. She stopped. She didn't want to stop. It angered her to stop. She wanted to walk on forever, across the land and out into the sea – then they'd be sorry. But her legs burned with fatigue and her heart pounded in her chest and ears and so, reluctantly, she stopped and bent forward, hands on her knees. A couple passing by on the other side looked across at her, concerned.

'Are you alright miss?'

Florrie half smiled and waved in their direction.

See, they care, she thought to herself, *even if nobody else does.*

She stood up. Hands now on hips. Looked around. *What am I doing? Why do I behave like this? Oh God. What's happening to me? They're only silly brushes. I don't understand. I don't understand.*

Often she would feel ecstatic, wound up like a happy spring, ready to whirl through life and grab it in great golden handfuls, but sometimes, her feelings became tinder dry and any spark could quickly turn them into a raging fire, charring her reason and filling her nose and eyes with an acrid anger. Afterwards, she would feel exhausted and empty and she could feel herself begin to slide, without moving, over an edge, as if a sheer chasm had opened up in front of her. She tried to stop herself from falling, gripping hard by the fingertips of her mind because, despite the daylight around her, she could feel the freezing darkness of a moonless winter night far below.

She hitched up her skirt, sat on a concrete step and put her head in her hands. The step soon felt cold and uncomfortable – that was good, like a punishment.

Eventually, when she had calmed down, she looked up to find, to her surprise, that she was sitting opposite her own home. Had she made her way there instinctively looking for refuge or for somewhere to hide? Either way she wasn't sure, but now she half hoped somebody would see her through a window and call out to her, *'Florrie, what are you doing there? What's the matter?'* But the windows stared back empty and cold and the dark green front door appeared to shake its head slowly at her.

Inside, her mother would be preparing tea; laying the table; loading it with sandwiches, angel cake and fruit cake; and clattering spoons into cups and saucers, but Florrie wasn't hungry, at least not for food.

If she tried to talk to her mother, she knew what Sally would say – what she always said, she would support her husband. She would remind her young daughter that her father had to feed and clothe and be responsible for eight people and how lucky she was not to know hunger and cold, like they had. She always said that – every time.

Sally knew of the regular clashes between John Henry and their fiery daughter, they happened all the time, but never lasted long. They would soon make up. That's how it was. She never thought to look any deeper and Florrie never knew how to begin to talk about something that she didn't understand. And then there was the fear that her parents wouldn't understand either, leaving her quite alone. Then what would she do?

Sally would always try to lighten the situation.

'Come on now. Let's have a tiny treat,' knowing that Florrie would be forced to smile at the thought of what was coming.

Her mother always did this. It really was an excuse for self-indulgence, but what a performance. It was always very difficult not to smile.

'Sure it's a filthy habit and one you mustn't copy. You promise me,' she would say and look up at her daughter, concern in her watery eyes as she would take a small metal tin from a drawer and carefully open it. Florrie would shake her head and say, 'No of course not, Mother'. But she had already secretly tried it and was in no hurry to repeat the explosive experience. But it was that knowledge that made what would come next even more compelling. Every time, it was like watching a balloon being blown up and up – bigger and tighter, impossibly bigger, impossibly tighter; stretching and stretching; until... *Bang!*

Sally would take a pinch of powder from the tin, place some into each nostril and inhale long sniffs. This would always be followed by a pause, a long pause and then suddenly, something would grip her in an anguish that would turn her body rigid and stop her breathing.

Florrie would watch and, in some strange state of sympathy, would also hold her breath, as she felt her chest tighten. Come on. Come on. The tension would climb and climb. The room would seem to rumble and shudder, and then, Sally's eyes would stare wide open as if sighting the Dullahan itself. Then at last. Aahshoo! – a mighty explosion, then, another, and another and yet another enormous sneeze that rocked her tiny frame and would almost lift her entire body off the floor.

Slowly, slowly the suspense would ebb away and her mother would emerge from behind a large white cotton handkerchief, stained brown, smiling shyly like a naughty child, wiping tears and residue snuff away. Around them the air would prickle with pepper. It was always difficult to remain angry after such theatrics.

On the other side of the road, Florrie smiled weakly, but today she was in no mood for such antics. She needed to walk again – to where she didn't know, just walk and think, and think and walk. She stood up and strode further up the Hill looking fixedly at the grey pavement. Lost in thought, it was hardly surprising that she failed to see the figure in front of her. She stopped abruptly and looked up angrily at this person who had disrupted her wretchedness.

It was Ted.

'Hallo Florrie.'

She looked sullenly back at him. She wanted desperately to walk on.

'Are you alright?'

'Yes,' she pouted and then, to her horror, a solitary tear escaped and rolled its story slowly down her pale cheek. She brushed it away, angrily, like an annoying fly.

'Are you sure?' he asked softly.

'No.'

And she stood there, arms folded across her.

They sat on a wooden bench in the grounds of the nearby church and Florrie related the story of the brushes and of her anger and frustration, no more than that. She couldn't believe she was telling him this. They had hardly spoken before but she realised how comfortable and relaxed she was with him; how different this was from the endless chatter, noise and argument of her home.

Ted said nothing, but listened carefully.

He had always felt nervous and shy about the opposite sex with their secret smiles and long lingering looks. He didn't understand them and, at times, he felt almost hunted. It was the way he had been brought up he supposed: he never had a sister, just a brother. But Florrie was different because she really was different and not afraid to show it. He knew that some disliked her for that – just for being herself really – but he admired it. He wished he could be more like that. His mind wandered for a moment from Florrie's words, and suddenly a strange thought ticked in his mind, without permission. *I hope my children don't grow up like me.* Children! What *was* he thinking about? Embarrassed, he swept the thought away. It had taken less than a breath.

Finally he spoke. And, without interrupting, Florrie listened.

'He does work very hard you know. In fact, they both take their responsibilities very seriously and although they never really talk about it, they've both had very hard lives. Your Dad during the First War – that must have been terrible and having no work afterwards and your mother and her family facing famine in Ireland. Do you know he once told me he was so hungry he went into a field and pulled a turnip to eat? The farmer caught him but could see how starving he was and let him go. He could have called the police or given him a beating, but he took pity on him. Imagine that. They just want to make sure that never happens to you, that's all.'

Florrie tried to feel the terror of hot metal slicing into her and the endless gnawing pain of starvation, but she couldn't. But for the first time she wanted to.

'How do you know all that? He never told me.'

'Well of course not.' He paused and looked away for a moment. 'People tell me things. I suppose because they know I'll listen.'

'And they trust you.'

Florrie watched this man and realised there was so much more to him if you bothered to look beyond his handsome appearance, and she had never bothered to look. He was not a fizzing firework that glittered and showered for some short-lived glorious moment and then turned into empty blackness, he was much more than that. He was, well... he was like his position on the pitch. She liked football and had played with the boys, charging after the ball like a lunatic. The boys knew of Ted and admired his skills on the field. She realised Ted was not a flashy winger, taking the crowd's excited cheers or the goalkeeper, the last line of dogged defence. He was the centre half, the heart of the team, both thwarting the plans of the opposition and planning and delivering decisive attacks in return. That was him, right in the middle; solid, dependable, all seeing. Suddenly, she felt strangely safe and secure.

They both paused and thought about the words that had been spoken. Ted smiled.

'Did I ever tell you about the football boots?'

Florrie turned and shook her head.

'Well, I did a small job for your father. Can't remember what now, but when I'd finished he said he couldn't pay me,' and he smiled again.

Florrie turned, concerned.

'No it's OK, I didn't expect any payment. It was a favour really. Anyway, he said he had several pairs of football boots in his big shed and I was welcome to take a pair.'

Ted chuckled at the thought of what was coming next.

'Oh no, what did he do?'

'Well, they were there alright, all hanging neatly in pairs, but when I got them down and looked at them more closely, guess what?'

Florrie buried her head in her hands for a moment, and then looked sideways.

'Go on, tell me.'

Ted laughed again.

'Every single boot was left-footed.'

'*No*. He knew that. The old devil knew that.'

'Yes, but it was OK.'

'No it wasn't. He cheated you.'

'No,' he paused and smiled at her, 'I took all the laces instead.'

Florrie laughed and asked, 'What did he do? Wasn't he angry?'

'No, he just gave me a long look and smiled.'

They had been sitting on the bench for at least twenty minutes, but to Florrie it had passed in a flash. Thoughts and emotions raced through her mind, too many and too fast to make any attempt to comprehend, let alone dare to articulate and it felt as if she had suddenly and mysteriously grown up.

Inside her the fire that could scorch her veins was now reduced to a warm comforting glow, and she felt calm and steady but at the same time her body trembled and she tucked her hands between her legs in case he should notice them shaking.

A tiny black spider toiled upwards along the ploughed landscape of Florrie's cardigan sleeve. Ted placed his finger gently in its path; Florrie felt his soft touch. It thrilled her. He leant forward and let the creature move safely onto a blade of grass and they both watched it disappear. Florrie and Ted turned their heads, smiled shyly at each other and then turned away. Between them an electrical storm shivered.

Slowly he put his arm around her slim shoulders. She did not object, it seemed to be the most natural thing in the world.

***

They were married inside the very same church, St Augustine's. It stood calm and strong on the very summit of the Hill, its pale stone walls textured with dark patterns of cut flint standing out like punctuation marks across open ecclesiastical pages. The church was like an island, in a sea of bright green grass, surrounded by a low wall with black iron railings and a dark green privet hedge. The entrance to the grounds was through an ornamental double iron gate, and, once inside and away from the grey-brown bustle, it offered a sense of sanctuary and solemnity that hushed even the voices of non-believers. It had seen generation after generation from the Hill: family and friends in their Sunday best, uncomfortable in new collars and shoes, thrilling in flowers and frills, arriving through its large church doors and sitting quietly on the same hard wooden pews in the solemn company of each other.

Florrie stood in her bedroom before a full-length mirror. In just under an hour she would arrive at the church and marry Ted.

'Florrie you do look lovely.'

Alice, one of the three bridesmaids, stopped making adjustments to Florrie's Tudor style headdress and allowed the long embroidered tulle veil to drop across her shoulders and float downwards to below her waist. She looked over Florrie's shoulder. Eyes sparkling, Florrie gazed curiously at her own reflection and saw before her a young woman wearing a long white satin dress that folded around her throat and shoulders and shimmering, dropped straight, following her slim shape. She cocked her head slightly to one side. Her dark hair had been cut short and wavy, in contrast to the smooth whiteness of the satin. Lifting one arm, she could see the folds of material fall from her shoulder to swell like a trumpet at her wrist. The bridesmaids watched spellbound.

'I could do with a fag.'

'Oh Florrie. Not now.'

'And a whisky mac, a large one.'

Her mind drifted two hundred yards up the Hill. She wondered what Ted was doing right now. How he was feeling? Were his palms damp and were the butterflies skipping in his stomach? Probably not – strong, dependable Ted. He always took everything in his stride and her love for him welled up inside her.

'Come on, the car's waiting,' a voice called out from somewhere below.

'Oh no. Quick. Florrie, one last look in the mirror – for luck.'

And Florrie turned and saw herself as a single woman for the final time.

'Come on.'

They scooped up their hems in handfuls and clumped carefully down the staircase in their new white satin shoes to collect their bouquets. Three dozen pink roses with a long, trailing fern for Florrie and carnations and freesias for the bridesmaids. They were ready.

Outside, an Austin 20 Landaulette sat waiting patiently, its white and black bodywork, silver headlights and glass windows gleaming from a vigorous polishing. From each of the two outside mirrors, a white satin ribbon descended firmly in a V shape towards the radiator, where its fixing was hidden by a small garland of white artificial flowers. At the wheel sat the driver, resplendent in his dark suit, glossy peaked cap and black leather gloves. He had been up very early making sure that everything was spotless.

He tried to recall how many brides he had taken to how many churches, but gave up. The most important thing was how much he enjoyed sharing in the excitement of the occasion. He always spoke calmly to them, like a father. He tried to make them less nervous. Didn't have a daughter of his own, just boys.

The driver smiled to himself and smoothed his thick moustache while looking straight ahead. He didn't want to appear too chatty with the excited crowd of friends and neighbours now growing at a deferential distance around the car – mainly women and children. They were always mainly women and children, waiting for a first look at the bride. What men there were, seemed more interested in the gleaming Austin.

'Gawd what a beauty. Ain't seen one of those before, 'ave you Alf?'

'Can't say I 'ave Sid. Can't say I 'ave.'

A young boy suddenly climbed onto the running board and stared silently at the driver, as if he had just descended from the moon.

'Git down. Git your mucky fingers orf that car.'

A large woman in a startling floral dress, partly obscured by an apron, grabbed the boy and pulled him back into the crowd, back to where he belonged and from where he continued to gawp silently.

Two middle-aged housewives stood together, arms folded, speaking straight ahead.

'Lovely man that Ted.'

'Oh *yes*.'

'Wouldn't mind being in his bed tonight.'

'Mavis, you are terrible. What would your Jack say?'

'Wouldn't tell 'im.'

Both women sniggered, then paused.

'Mind you, bet she'll be a handful, even for him, that Florrie.'

'Yeh, you never know do you, you just never know.'

Both women looked wistfully away, lost for a moment in their own thoughts.

'Here they come. Oh, isn't she lovely.'

With much waving and cheering, the limousine purred gently away down the Hill, chased for a while by small boys. Unusually it drove away from the church, on a roundabout journey to ensure that the maximum number of local people also enjoyed the splendour of the moment, and, to ensure value for money.

'I am *not* spending that sort of cash just to drive two hundred yards,' John Henry had insisted. 'You might as well walk, that's what I'm going to do.'

'Well we'll drive to Margate and back first if that pleases you,' Florrie had retorted.

John Henry just shrugged.

Eventually, the car whispered to a halt outside the church. The driver got out and gently helped Florrie step down from its shady grey-leather interior into the June sunshine. Her fussing bridesmaids followed. Slowly and elegantly, Florrie walked into the cool entrance of the musty whispery church and took the arm of John Henry. A gold chain stretched across the waistcoat of his dark suit, but this elegance was in stark contrast to the brutally short haircut which had been administered to him by Sally standing on a wooden box with a pair of hand clippers.

Ahead, down the long aisle, stood Ted. Around him, the organ burbled. It felt comfortable, as if the organist was just playing for himself – practising, on his own, in an empty church. Below the notes was another sound. It had started quietly, as guests and friends met at the entrance, but now it had grown and spread and filled the pews. *Prickling. Tinkling.*

At his side, Ted felt Lionel shuffling nervously. He turned to smile at his best man and reassure him, but Lionel was staring straight ahead, face slightly flushed, silently mouthing his speech.

Ted looked away and down at the grey stones beneath him and thought about the promises he had to make. He had memorised them and his head moved slightly as he wrote each sentence across the floor in his mind. Some words he underlined. They were important. He had been surprised at how complete the promises were despite their simplicity. He had sat alone in his room and he had repeated them, word for word, stopping and considering. There was nothing to add.

He looked up and breathed in deeply. Behind him, friends and family sat quietly now, knowing the ceremony was about to begin. Around them stood generation after generation, invisible to the eye, but Ted felt their presence and a shiver of history trembled through him. He was about to make a sacred vow. He was ready.

Suddenly from high up, the organ called out to them.

Here she comes. Here comes the bride.

A ripple of expectation blew like a warm breeze down the spine of the church and outwards, filling each wooden pew. The congregation stood in an excited rustle and those nearest the aisle, looked intently ahead, straining for the tiniest sound of the bridal procession approaching: the faint rustle of fabric, the light tread of satin shoes, the heavier sound of leather on flagstone. Nostrils twitched for a tiny wisp of perfume or the fragrance of flowers. Some, unable to resist the temptation, turned and smiled their delight. Others peered from the corners of their eyes at the group as they slowly passed. And around everyone, clusters of notes marched from the organ, rich and reverberating they swept on, swelling every heart.

Children, sensing the majesty of the occasion, smiled up at their parents. Grandmothers wept silently into tiny lace-edged handkerchiefs.

The organ released its final notes. Hand in hand, they merged into a tumultuous chord that swept over and around the congregation, before finally fading away. The atmosphere vibrated with a resounding silence. The ceremony trembled, anxious to begin.

The vicar smiled, and all eyes turned upon him. He bent slightly towards Ted and Florrie. Silent nods and encouraging whispers as if to intonate it will be fine, now…

'We are gathered here today…'

For Ted and Florrie, there began a dizzying whirl of words and sounds.

'All things bright and beau-ti-ful, all creatures great and small…'

They glanced at each other almost shyly.

'He gave us eyes to see them, and lips that we might tell…'

They stood side by side; anxious to savour every booming heartbeat and every last morsel. Lost together in a magical landscape, filled with soft tumbles of sweetness and rainbow swirls.

'Repeat after me.'

The congregation stood in silence. Somewhere a small child called out.

Both of their voices rang loud and clear as their promises drifted upwards, entwining in each other's words…

'To have and to hold from this day forward…'

'For better, for worse…'

'For richer, for poorer…'

Sunny yellow for Florrie…

'In sickness and in health.'

Dark blue for Ted…

'To love and to cherish.'

… mingling into a vivid green lovers' knot.

'Til death us do part.'

'With this ring I thee wed; with my body I thee honour; and all my worldly goods with thee I share. In the name of the Father, the Son and the Holy Ghost.'

I will. I will. I will.

Ted and Florrie walked together, arm in arm, surrounded by the thick, vibrant chords of Mendelssohn. They moved slowly from the cool dark sanctuary of the church towards the dazzling light of a beautiful summer's day. They had been swept along, almost helplessly, tossed like corks on this warm matrimonial sea and, apart from their vows, they had not spoken to each other since the previous day. Ted was now very anxious to do so. He turned towards his new wife.

'You alright love? You look wonderful.'

Florrie turned and smiled, her blue eyes flashing with an intensity he had never seen before.

'I'm so happy Ted, so happy.'

'Me too love,' he said with moist eyes.

Friends and family followed steadily and quietly as if to hurry would be disrespectful. They smiled politely at each other and also at those they did not know. Today, everybody was a friend. Soon the throng outside buzzed with chatter. Through it came a loud voice. It was Uncle Charlie, the self-appointed photographer, anxious to get his shots before the mood slipped away.

'Right, bride and groom and parents only. No, not you dear. Bridesmaids later. OK, now move closer, that's it, be friendly, you're all family now. OK that's good, now… smile, say cheese. That's it. Come on, smile Mick, it's a wedding not a funeral, good, that's better. Now, hold it.'

Click.

Soon people drifted away and strolled across the lawn in twos and threes. They stopped occasionally to use their box cameras, anxious to have their own personal record of the day. Much, much later they would pass their black and white snaps around and chuckle or sigh at the images they had captured. Some would write a comment or the date on the back of the photographs before placing them in a drawer, or an old shoebox, where they would lie quietly, still smiling, still young and hopeful for decade after decade. They never reached the exalted position of a wedding album, because there never was one. Instead, a few days later, Ted, Florrie, the best man and the three bridesmaids, dressed once more for the wedding would visit the local photographic studio. There, they would pose against heavy drapes: the ladies sitting on ornate throne-like chairs, the men standing proudly at slight angles behind them. They would stare outwards, self-consciously, smiles fixed, into the camera lens. The result was ornately framed in a deckle-edged mount with the photographer's name written delicately in pencil below and positioned proudly on the mantelpiece or sideboard for all to see; forever.

The wedding guests now moved slowly towards a black painted wooden building with a corrugated roof that stood nearby. Some waited in the shade of its verandah for as long as possible and through the open windows they heard the sound of a gramophone and the slightly scratched tones of Bing Crosby.

A light tepid breeze, gently moved the white lace curtains at each window.

'Please take your seats everybody,' Ted's father, Mick, called out loudly, and the music stopped abruptly.

The trestle tables were covered with plain white tablecloths and had been placed together to form two long rows that ran the length of the building. A further row had been placed at right angles to them right across one end – the top table. Their brilliant appearance complemented the white painted walls and ceiling, giving a feeling of coolness and space. Silver plated cutlery and white napkins had been laid out along every side and small glass vases broke up the formal discipline at intervals each containing a splash of colour with their patterns of freshly cut flowers. To one side, the metal grill protecting a bar had already rattled upwards and two barmen in white shirts, black ties and trousers held drinking glasses up to their critical eyes and then rubbed an additional sparkle for good luck.

The room quickly filled with people politely bobbing around each other as they tried to read the names on the small, white cards positioned at the head of each set of cutlery.

'You're over here Fred, with your missus, next to Uncle Jim.'

'Gawd got to put up with 'im 'ave I.'

'Worse for me,' retorted Jim, standing close by. 'I've got to put up with you.'

Everybody laughed at the silliness, even though they had heard it all before.

Soon, everybody was seated. Ted sat quietly while Florrie chattered brightly, smiled and raised her eyebrows as a silent welcome to those she had not already met. The ladies had removed their hats and the men their jackets, which they placed on the backs of chairs. Uncle Charlie was still taking photos with his Kodak Retina, and the caterers were fretting as the lettuce began to wilt and the ham began to dry, despite cellophane covering.

John Henry slowly stood up. He placed his thumbs in his waistcoat pockets and looked around.

Mothers shushed children, men sat up and all the guests looked expectantly as the laughter and chatter quickly died away. John Henry was a well-respected figure on the Hill. He coughed, seeming unusually nervous.

'Thank you all for coming.'

The words burst out as if they had been queuing anxiously all day.

'Today... To Ted and Florrie's wedding.'

He paused, uncertain as to what to say next, and glanced down at Sally sitting beside him. She smiled back.

'Err... I hope you enjoy the grub.' He paused again. 'Should do, it cost enough.'

Laughter rippled around the room and guests looked at each other knowingly as he abruptly sat down. Being thrifty had made him a successful businessman. He begrudged every penny he had to spend and would undercut his suppliers and competitors ruthlessly.

'Well done John,' a man's voice called out.

'Mean old bugger,' somebody said under their breath.

'Is that it?' queried another. 'Thought he had to make the speech later?'

But that was all he had to say.

This was the sign the caterers had been waiting for. Waitresses, dressed in a variety of black tops, skirts and small white aprons, shot forward like greyhounds out of their traps, and scurried intently back and forth, delivering plates of food. The ladies sipped sherry;

the children drank R. White's lemonade or Tizer and the men quaffed pints and thought about the whisky to follow.

'Great beef this,' Fred called out to nobody in particular.

Around him heads nodded silently as the chatter was replaced by the tinkling of knives and forks on plates and then spoons in glass bowls.

Uncle Charlie pushed away his empty bowl. An excess of food, warm weather and several pints of Guinness caused him to slump back into his chair, and mop his shiny face and balding head with a large white handkerchief. His braces were curving tightly over his rotund belly, and peeked out from beneath his black waistcoat. His suit jacket had now partially slipped off the back of his chair and was hanging by only one shoulder. He tapped his right-hand trouser pocket and felt the reassuring shape of the roll of film he had taken from his camera, the camera which now lay snapped shut on the table in front of him. *Mustn't lose that – very important.* His feet, encased in heavy black leather shoes, ached a bit, but apart from that he was enjoying himself. *Don't get out much these days, not since the old girl went.*

He took another large gulp from his half-empty pint glass, wiped his mouth on the back of his sleeve, looked around, grinned and nodded. At that moment, Lionel, the best man, raised his short figure upwards, picked up a nearby spoon and rang it against a glass. The chatter and laughter, assisted by a number of cries of 'Hush' and 'Shh', slowly spluttered into a sort of silence. Lionel smiled, waiting patiently for the noise to die away. He drew in a deep breath and, at that moment, a voice roared out.

'Good old Lionel.'

It was Charlie. A sense of occasion had never been Charlie's strong point and now, what little there was, had been swept away by an onslaught of alcohol and food.

A few sniggered; some looked annoyed at his interruption, remembering his attempts at herding them for photographs outside the church.

'Save it Charlie,' somebody called out.

Charlie grinned, waved a pudgy hand vaguely in some direction, picked up his glass, drank the last drops and looked around for more.

Lionel, privately relieved at the interruption and reassured by the wave of sympathy that had swept back from the guests, smiled and launched into his speech.

He had thought long and hard about how to address his audience today. Obviously they were a mixture of friends and family and even a few strangers, but to address them separately seemed rather formal and Lionel hated formality. Even his suit, new shoes, collar and tie felt formally oppressive. He would much rather have been pottering around his greenhouse in old baggy trousers, a collarless shirt and wellington boots rolled down at the tops, but duty was duty.

'Friends.'

He paused for dramatic effect and looked around to see if anybody objected. Everybody was waiting intently.

'It's turned out nice again.'

They all chuckled at the well-known catch phrase. He smiled back at them, feeling more confident.

'I have known Ted and Florrie since I was this big,' he said holding his hand just above the trestle table top.

'Well you ain't much bigger now,' a voice called out.

Spontaneous, good-natured laughter rang around the room. People looked from one to the other, smiles on their faces. Some of the ladies, fanning themselves with their order of service, uttered an 'Ahh' and looked as if they could quite happily hold the little man to their bosoms.

Charlie, grinning wildly, banged on the table, slopping his latest pint over podgy fingers.

Lionel, unabashed, held up a hand for silence, a smile on his lips.

'Maybe,' he paused, 'but I'm big enough to be Ted's best man.'

Cheers, applause and a solitary whistle rang out.

Slightly pink in the face, Lionel continued. 'I want to tell you about Ted.'

A low rumble grinned around the room.

'I remember when Ted was playing for the Chats one Saturday. Centre half wasn't it Ted?

Ted nodded and smiled to himself, looking down at the table, knowing what was coming next.

'Yes, centre half, against Maidstone. Right, Ted?'

'Reserves. Maidstone Reserves.'

'Right. Reserves. You were there that day Mick?'

Mick nodded and grinned as everybody turned and looked in his direction.

'Anyway, Ted was having problems with one of their supporters. Sitting on the wall he was, at the cemetery end. You know, the big wall at the far end.'

Everybody nodded even if they had no idea, eager to hear the story. The ladies continued fanning themselves. Charlie undid his tie and belched.

'Well this bloke was barracking Ted, kept calling him Blondie. You know, because of his fair hair. Every time he got the ball. "Blondie, Blondie," he called out. So do you know what Ted did? Do you know what he did? Well, he turned and kicked the ball straight at him. Flew like an arrow. Straight at him. Hit him full in the chest and knocked him clean over the wall, straight into the cemetery. Never saw him again.'

'Probably still there,' somebody called out as laughter broke out once more.

The two men smiled at each other; best man and groom.

As the noise slowly subsided, Lionel took advantage of the lull and mopped his face. He felt very pleased with the way it had gone. He had been quite nervous, but everybody seemed to enjoy it. All he had to do now was to introduce Ted, then he could sit down and moisten his dry mouth with the pint of mild and bitter that sat waiting on the table before him. He held up his hand once more and waited patiently.

'Ladies and gentlemen.'

There was now complete silence. Lionel paused, amazed at his power. He turned slightly and held out his hand.

'Ted.'

The room erupted as Ted slowly stood and tugged his grey waistcoat back down into position. He smiled shyly.

'Good ol' Ted. Good ol' Blondie.'

'Shut up Charlie. Shut up.'

Cousin Ethel, who was sitting opposite, leant forward and hissed urgently whilst stealing anxious glances towards the top table.

'Tell him to shut up,' she whispered to Charlie's neighbour.

'Shut up you silly old fool.'

His neighbour nudged him with an elbow, spilling even more beer onto the tablecloth where it sat in a brown pool, gradually soaking into Charlie's once white shirtsleeve. Charlie took another large gulp and gave out a satisfied, 'Ahh...' He smacked his thick lips and seemed quite oblivious to the trickle that had missed his mouth and now dripped onto his waistcoat. His eyes were beginning to drown under the lake of Guinness and a scarlet glow was gradually creeping up from his neck like an early sunrise.

'Thank you all very much for being here...'

Florrie looked up at her husband with undisguised affection and admiration.

'...and for all the cards and presents and greetings you have so kindly given us and which are still arriving,' Ted added, holding up a handful of large, golden coloured envelopes containing telegrams.

'Good ol' Ted. Good ol' Blondie. Blondeee.'

Ethel hid her face in her hands. Some of the ladies looked from one to the other in dismay and a small child pointed an enquiring finger towards Uncle Charlie. Ted looked sternly towards Charlie who was now slowly sliding towards the floor. Lionel looked up at Ted, waiting for orders. Edith seemed to be on the point of tears and others visualised Charlie sitting on the wall at the cemetery end and could only begin to imagine his fate.

Florrie glared daggers of blue.

Oblivious, Charlie, eyes half closed, started again.

'Good ol' ...'

Florrie leapt to her feet, face fierce, picked up the nearest object and flung it at Uncle Charlie. She had spent many hours with the boys on the Hill perfecting the skill of throwing, so those present should not have been surprised to see a silver pepper pot – thankfully slightly closer to her than a large vase of flowers – fly with accuracy, and some force, and bounce off the top of Charlie's head with a noticeable clonk, then clatter across the floor and disappear under a table.

There was a gasp, then silence.

The unexpected shock of the flying pepper pot seemed to revive Charlie. He looked around somewhat bewildered and ruefully rubbed the top of his head.

'Ahh, oo did 'at?'

The words came out thickly.

'Come on Charlie,' muttered the man sitting next to him who had ducked from the flying missile and now stood and took Charlie's left arm.

'Woz 'at you?' Charlie asked looking up at him.

'No it was Florrie and you don't want to tangle with her. Not today.'

'Florrie! Well you know wot 'ey say, don't yer?' his words slurred. 'Yer know wot 'ey say. A June bride will be impet… impetu and… and somefing or other. Can't member the rest. Wot's a rest?'

'Come on Uncle Charlie, let's get a breath of fresh air.'

Charlie was slowly helped outside, leaving his jacket and camera behind, still muttering to himself.

'Gawd 'elp us. Bleedin' women. Gawd 'elp us.'

Inside the tension was bubbling.

'Well, he deserved it, silly old codger. He was ruining it; upsetting them – Ted and Florrie – on their big day.'

'Yes, but to throw a salt pot at him, an old man, at a wedding.'

'It was a pepper pot, not a salt pot.'

'So a pepper pot is better is it? Lighter?'

'George, why are you always so contrary? Always have been.'

'Me? Contrary? That's a…'

'Shh, Ted's trying to speak.'

Ted's voice cut through the atmosphere.

'Please.'

The bubbling in the room dropped to a light simmer.

'There are many people to thank today, but there is one person in particular. That is the person who will always stand by you and defend and support you. The person who will speak up for you when you don't have the words, the person who will fight for you when you don't have the strength, a very special person. So, please, lift your glasses.'

People looked at each other with some surprise at the passion and eloquence of his words. This was not the Ted they normally knew, the strong silent type, the Gary Cooper of the Hill.

'To Florrie.'

'To Florrie,' a roar of voices echoed and Charlie was forgotten.

And so the reception returned to normal, and continued its gentle progress. Ted and Florrie stood close to each other, hands gripping the knife that cut through the pristine brittle icing and plunged into the soft, dark interior. Florrie took the two small plaster figures that stood together on the top tier and slid them into Ted's pocket. She would place them on a bookcase shelf in the front room of their new home where they would stand together forever.

Later, after they had danced close together to smiles and nods, they left the bustle and noise behind them, walked out onto the green lawn and stood, feeling the soft warmth of the early evening. Ted slipped his hand into that of his new wife and they looked together into the flawless blue sky that surrounded them.

At the same time, hundreds of miles away, a young Rhinelander dropped his Bücker Bü 180 trainer aircraft out of the same blue sky onto the grassy flatness of an airfield, taxied to a bumpy halt and switched off the engine. He sat for a while in silence and then, in the distance, thought he heard the low rumble of thunder. It sounded for a moment like a giant army, marching and assembling, a long way off. It was June 1937.

TWO

Called Up: A Letter from Home and the Boxing Booth

'If I should die, think only this of me:
That there's some corner of a foreign field
That is for ever England. There shall be
In that rich earth a richer dust concealed;
A dust whom England bore, shaped, made aware,
Gave, once, her flowers to love, her ways to roam,
A body of England's, breathing English air,
Washed by the rivers, blest by suns of home.'

Rupert Brooke

The room smelt of Woodbines and boot polish.

'Wot bleedin' day is it?'

Billy Kite looked up sharply. He sat on the edge of his bed, his left hand tucked inside an army boot and his right holding a duster stained with black polish. Next to him a jam jar lid held a cigarette whose smoke drifted languidly upwards adding to the haze that was beginning to obscure the barrack ceiling. He turned his shaven head slightly to one side and spoke over a bony shoulder to those behind him.

'Wot… bleedin'… *day*… is it?'

His dark doggy eyes darted around the room. Nobody answered him. Nobody normally wanted to have a conversation with Billy. Those who did, often found themselves mesmerised like rabbits caught in Deptford headlights and loaned him their last cigarette or shilling. They rarely got them back.

'When I get paid, mate. As soon as I get paid. I promise… bit short this week mate. Can you wait a bit?'

They often gave up.

'Oi Darkie. Do *you* know wot day it is?'

'No Billy.'

The answer came back quickly, too quickly and Billy knew it.

'Course yer don't know. Don't s'pose yer 'ad calendars in yer bleedin' caravan. Too busy eating bleedin' 'edgeogs and tellin' fuckin' fortunes. Jesus.'

Darkie said nothing. The words gave a prickle of annoyance, but at the same time amused him. That was the trouble with Billy – he was always ignoring how slippery the tightrope was between the advantages of friendship and being just downright offensive. No wonder he was always falling off into the mire; always. Mind you, while he was down there he would probably try and sell it to somebody. That was Billy. Black and white Billy.

Darkie stopped for a moment. Maybe it had been a mistake to tell his new mates his nickname? Mind you it wasn't really a nickname. It was what he was known as, always had been, for as long as he could remember. Somebody at some time had called him Darkie. He couldn't remember who or when. But it must have been done with some affection because it always felt right, felt like him. He did have a real Christian name, but when he thought about it, he didn't know who that person was. Had never said it aloud and nor had anybody else, ever. There'd been no parents to call *him* in from playing in any childhood garden.

His surname had already been lost, long ago; stolen from him and owned by others – those in charge.

'Mace. Stop shivering lad. It's not cold.'

'Mace. Don't look at me like that, lad. That's dumb insolence.'

Mace. Mace. Mace. Cold muffled echoes.

And now it was happening again, in the army.

'Mace. Get your bleedin' hair cut.'

'Mace. Where did you get those bleedin' ears?'

'Mace. You are a horrible, scruffy, little man.'

So he kept his head down and mouth shut. That's how he'd survived the empty institutions of his childhood. That's how he would survive the army. They could do what they liked with his surname, but he had kept Darkie for himself... until now. Now he realised he had a chance to belong, maybe even have a friend, and the thought kicked sharply in his stomach. He'd had a friend once, in the children's home. He'd been pale and thin, his friend. Well, weren't they all? Well, thin at least. Maybe that's where his nickname had started – from some remark about his dark complexion. His friend had coughed a lot; was always coughing. Then, one day, he was sent to a hospital. Never came back. Since then, Darkie had been very cautious. But maybe with this small group of men, all thrown together in a war. Could he...?

He had his Romany family of course, but they weren't everyday – just in the background. So he had told them.

'My name is Darkie.'

'Darkie! Wot sorta bleedin' name is that? You out the fuckin' jungle?'

'No Billy,' he had replied hotly. 'I'm from a gypsy family.'

'A gypsy! Fu-ckinell. Watch out for yer gear lads, we got a bleedin' didicoy wiv us.'

Billy swore with fluent ease, peppering every sentence. The other men selected expletives according to their mood or the situation, but for Billy, like other Londoners, it was part of his lexicon and on special occasions he would turn to his favourite three syllables – which he would modulate and express according to levels of annoyance, dismay or surprise – with the skills of an accomplished actor.

Darkie had ignored Billy then, and as much as possible since, but the other men accepted him as Darkie, no questions. They also helped him with his uniform, and that felt good.

It was true the army had had trouble fitting him into a uniform. Not that they had bothered much. A sergeant had taken one look at him, called out a size and he had staggered off under a weight of ill-fitting clothing and strange equipment. So now his too baggy serge trousers were dependent on the braces that stretched tightly over his too large khaki shirt and the dark hair that had camouflaged his ears was now gone, leaving them protruding like open car doors.

He stopped for a moment to reflect on his situation, and then dipped his duster into the tap water that filled the upturned lid of the polish tin and continued rubbing small circles onto his boot toecap, even though it already shone like black glass.

'Ted my son, wot day is it?'

Billy turned towards Ted, but his attitude had softened. Instinctively he always sensed the strengths and weaknesses of all he met, looking for a chink, an advantage. He knew that despite Ted's reserved nature, he should not be underestimated. Like a street wolf, he smelled the steel in his backbone.

Ted also sat on his bed. He sat as close as he could to the edge, not wanting to disrupt the grey blanket stretched taut as a drum skin over the single mattress and sliced with immaculate hospital corners. Tomorrow it would be inspected again and anything less than perfect would result in a lot of shouting. For a moment he thought it might be better not to sleep in it tonight, assuming there would be any time left to sleep, although the alternative would be on the floor.

From his position near the end of the long room, he could see two rows of identical beds facing each other and, at his feet, the bed legs reflected in the polished surface of the wooden floor. The same taut blanket with perfect corners and a neatly boxed blanket at its head covered each mattress. Beside each bed rested a tall metal locker, and in the centre of the room, a cold, black coal stove and shiny bucket waited patiently for the army to determine when winter would start, regardless of any freezing temperatures that might inconveniently occur beforehand. The room was straight lines and right angles, and he knew every item was in exactly the same regulation place and distance from every other.

He stopped bulling his boots and looked down at his feet, which were covered in thick, grey woollen socks. A wave of tiredness swept over him. He pushed it away and carried on. Everything had to be perfect, nothing less than perfect.

Around his neck swung one red and one green disc that had been issued by a lance corporal who had barked at them and ticked off their names.

'Right. Listen in. Right. When I call out your names, you will collect your cold meat tickets. You *will* wear them at all times.' He spoke like a set of regulations.

'What's a cold meat ticket, corporal?' a voice dared.

'Right. These are discs. Identification. One. This one 'ere will be taken away so we know you're dead, and not just skiving, and this one will be left with your miserable cold body. Get it? Right. Anderson. Where are you Anderson? Come on. Jildi.'

Ted slipped the discs around his neck, not knowing they would remain there for the next six years. Not knowing that for most of the men now sitting and chatting around him, they would be gathered in far earlier.

He rubbed his hand over the bristles of his shaved head. It had been like shearing sheep. They were held firmly by the army and shorn with little dignity, feeling their former lives tumble to the floor, lock by lock, curl by curl to be swept up and disposed of. They had felt cold and vulnerable, but it had gathered them together. A new flock: a new start. Nobody liked to think where it might end. Ted felt the exposed boniness of his skull and shivered.

The past weeks had been hard, harder than anything he had ever experienced. He had been pushed relentlessly day after day without a break. Long forced marches, mile after long mile, the weight of their packs and rifles dragging down on breaking backs; legs stabbing with spasms of pain; lungs rasping; mouths barren and speechless and feet covered in blisters which burst and bled red raw as they marched. They drowned in their own sweat. Froze in gasping winds. They climbed and jumped and ran and lifted and then lay motionless in pools of mud, peering into the silent darkness, icy rain dripping from the rims of their steel helmets. They charged and screamed and thrust bayonets savagely into dummy enemies, wishing it was those who forced them on and on. Those who shouted and demanded and ordered and who, at that moment, they hated. *Good. Hate is good. Hate more.* They slept little and never ate enough. Men befuddled with lack of sleep and riddled with exhaustion, collapsed. They heaved them to their feet. And when they weren't training, they were cleaning or drilling. There were endless drill parades. They listened to the unintelligible screech of the drill sergeant and learned to react instantly to commands.

'Lef', right. Lef', right. Lef', right. Le...hhf. Keep those arms up. Sharper now. Lef', right. Lef', right. Lef', right. Le...hhf. Eyeees... *right.* Eyeees... *front.* Lef', right. Lef', right. Lef', right. Le...hhf. Right wheeel *forw'd.* Lef', right. Lef', right. Lef', right. Le...hhf. Abaart... *tun.* Lef', right. Lef', right. Lef', right. Le...hhf. Squaaad... *howt.* Tup three. Stand still. Don't move. *You.* Yes *you.* Don't look at me you little worm. Keep your eyes to the front. Are you paralysed laddy? Don't speak to me! Move your right arm faster. Cut it in to your side. Like this. Cut it!' *Dark glinting eyes. Face inches away. Specks of spittle on a brisk black moustache.*

'If you don't laddie, I will tear it off... and beat you to death with the soggy end. QUIET! Who gave you permission to laugh? You will not laugh. You will not breathe. You will not fart. You will not even shag the missus unless I say so. Do you understand?'

'Yes sergeant.'

'DO YOU UNDERSTAND?'

'YES SERGEANT.'

'Right... By the Lef'. Queeek march. Lef', right. Lef', right. Lef', right. Le...hhf. That's better my lads. Give it some swank. Give it some pride. Lef', right. Lef', right. Lef', right. Le...hhf.'

But Ted never gave up. It just wasn't in him and slowly his body and mind, once soft and comfortable, changed into a lean, hard machine. And he was learning just how determined and stubborn and proud he was. Where had that come from? Maybe it was for Florrie? *I am fighting for you, love. I will not let these Jerry bastards harm you. Never.*

He missed her so much.

Like tens of thousands of others who now found themselves in this alien world, he had been called up. He thought about that use of words, "called up". It was hardly a calling, like a doctor or an artist. It was most definitely an order: you will or else. On the other hand he supposed that his country was calling him to help defend itself from an enemy, a call to arms. Put like that it seemed more reasonable, more important, more patriotic, although he had never thought of himself as a patriot. He had just jogged along like everybody else getting on with life. But now he had to think about his King and country. That's what he was told he was going to fight for: on the radio, in the newspapers, from his officers. But he found the words difficult to comprehend. What did country mean? He had a vague sense of hills and woods. But it was more than that. What about nation? His nation. That made more sense. It was all the people who lived on it like Billy and Darkie and the other men and their families and homes. And the King? Well, he had never met the King or his family, but then he had never met Billy and Darkie before, or millions of others who lived in his Nation and why should somebody try to take all that away, take away their lives, their freedom? Bastards. Yes, that was worth fighting for.

He had already been issued with piles of equipment – a chilling reminder of his new predicament. Hanging from his locker door, he could see his battledress blouse, cleaned, pressed and waiting to be inspected. Only the army could be so insensitive as to remind the wearer of his fate. Battledress – battle. Could be worse, he supposed. It could be called This-is-what-I-will-be-wearing-when-I-am-blown-into-small-bloody-pieces-dress. And then there was his gas mask, tin helmet, field dressings, bayonet, identification discs – of course – as well as his greatcoat, webbing, gaiters, forage cap, packs and mess tins, plus a host of items aimed at one of the army's major preoccupations alongside shouting, drilling and inflicting fatigue – cleaning.

Cleaning, it seemed, was a major skill required of the successful soldier, far more than he had ever realised and it soon became very clear that every single part of this mighty military machine required a great deal of cleaning, washing, painting, sweeping, trimming, dusting, pressing, pulling through, oiling and above all, polishing. Polishing was extremely popular. He had been issued with a button stick, brushes and a housewife containing sewing items plus orders to buy dusters, blanco and tins of Bluebell metal polish from his meagre two shillings a day pay. He also knew that this had to be taken very seriously, remembering the words of his platoon sergeant who had made it quite clear that failure to achieve perfect results would be taken as a personal insult, and that terrible consequences would result. He hadn't used those exact words. His had been far more colourful and it had to be said, far more imaginative, but everybody seemed to understand immediately.

'Ted?'

Billy roused him back to his question.

'Er sorry Billy. What day is it? Sunday, Billy. It's Sunday.'

Billy took in a short sharp breath.

'Sunday… SUNDAY! Gordon Bennett! We shouldn't be 'ere. Not on a fuckin' Sunday. It's a day of rest. The bastards. We shouldn't be 'ere; we should be at bleedin' church or summink. Not ere. Bullin' bleedin' boots. Fuck me what a bleedin' liberty.'

A ripple of smiles lit up the bare room at the thought of Billy Kite in a church, unless it was on the roof, nicking lead.

'Big inspection tomorrow Billy.'

'Fuck that.'

Billy spat viciously onto his boot and continued to rub angrily.

The men had enjoyed the passion of Billy's impossible tirade. They had already learned the power and satisfaction of complaining, of moaning, of rumour and counter rumour. It was a glue that held them all together and a punch bag against which they could unleash flurries of words that helped ease their frustration, fatigue or fear. Now their feelings, salved by Billy's outburst, settled back into a reverie of cleaning.

The barrack door burst open and the figure of the platoon corporal strode into the sparse room, his ammo boots clattering. He stood at ease and looked around balefully. Every face turned towards him, cleaning suspended. Now what?

'Post for you lot. Anderson, Smith, Dawson, Hennessey, Turner, Johnson, Tappenden, Dawson again. Somebody must love you Dawson. Christ knows why… Dean, Bell.' He stopped. 'Here, Bell you hand them out,' and, with that, he clattered out.

A wave of excitement swept through the room and each looked up expectantly as Private Bell collected the precious pile and had the pleasure of distributing the letters as if they were personal presents.

'One for you Paddy. Nothing today Sid, sorry mate. Dixie. Ted. Here you are Ted.'

'Thanks Tinker.'

Letters from home were the greatest joy. They coated each reader with warmth and colour that, for a while, shut out the harshness and solitude of their khaki world.

Some men tore open their envelopes and read greedily, smiles coming and going as they absorbed their news. Others held their letters with a reverence, fingers stroking the paper as if to feel the words within. Some held them under their nose, trying to remember the perfume of a girlfriend or the smells of their homes. Some hid them away, waiting for a private moment. Those that had nothing looked on enviously, carried on with their preparation, looked up occasionally, and shared others' smiles.

'Come on Paddy, read it out.'

'Bollocks.'

'Alright keep yer ginger wig on. That's a fine way to talk to a mate.'

'Here, listen to this. My missus says that the censor had a go at my last letter home. Blacked out a bit. I told her we was going to the ranges, you know to practise shooting. He crossed it out. Must have thought it was a place or a mountain or something. Sillee sod.'

The men grinned and shook their heads, confident in their superior knowledge and reassured that the establishment that held them in its grip was once again seen to be incompetent. Their brotherhood drew tighter around them.

Florrie wrote to Ted nearly every day even though there wasn't always a lot to say. She told him about the neighbours and their good luck or ailments, about their pets and what was growing in the garden, about both of their parents and the weather, but her everyday words filled him with reassurance and hope and love. But today, he did not recognise this letter and opening it carefully, he saw the untidy pencil scrawl and many corrections of his father's handwriting. There was no date.

Dear Ted

Just a line, hoping you are fit and well, as I trust you will be, all A1 soldiers are generally fit. Do not think that you are ever out of my thoughts because you never will be. When you went to "School," I have always told you to say, God save your "Mother and Father." Those Days you were only a Boy. Times make a change in one's lifetime. You are now fighting for the freedom of your Wife, for your "Mum and Dad" and also for the best Country on God Earth "Lovely England." The best Country in the World. This is the first war in my lifetime that any such war has been fought for Freedom of the working classes; all other wars have been different. They have been for "Money." To get down to the less serious side of things, do not think I am getting old and "morbid" but "facts are facts." When you come out of the army, which I hope and pray to God that some day you will, Hold your head high and say I have fought for everything in life worthwhile God made living for. "Wife" "Parents" and "Freedom."

Do not think that I am getting to sentimental "oh no" but there are times when I am "Sober" I do think that I have been reformed due to Financial Cramp. I sit at home and hold your mother's hand sipping a grapefruit through a straw. "Beer I hate it" because of one thing, not because it is

> *Bitter, not because it makes you "Fill Hill" (Jack Warner) but because of the price of the stuff.*
> *Well keep your pecker up. All will be well. Cheerio. "Best of Luck." Dad.*

He had never received a letter from his father before and he knew how difficult it would have been for him to write it. The gentle giant, so big and yet so weak. He smiled at the thought of his father in the Tam O' Shanter, buying pints for everybody and loudly regaling them with his son's military deeds.

'Fit as a fiddle Ted you know. Fit as a fiddle,' without realising that could also mean a death sentence.

Perfectly fit. No desk job. Not unfit for duty. Straight to the front line.

Suddenly, unexpectedly, he felt his stomach move. For a second it was like the tide slapping quietly and thickly against the jetty wall at Southend, where he used to cycle with Florrie on sunny Sundays, before the war. He felt confused and surprised as a dark brown feeling spread upwards from the pit of his stomach, across his chest and flooded into his cheeks prickling his eyes. It was a forgotten feeling from childhood that had escaped and caught him unawares. Damn. He slowly placed the letter face down on his bed and went back to his boot. *Small circles. Small circles.* He looked carefully around at the others but they were too engrossed to notice him. *Small circles. Small circles. Small circles,* until he felt the dark brown fade away. He picked up the letter and read it again. The grey pencil marks seemed so uncertain, the mistakes so evident, the heavier darker corrections almost anguished and he pictured his father, Mick, sitting at the kitchen table, sleeves rolled up, the tip of his tongue protruding between his lips, aware of his lack of education, struggling to compose the letter, talking the words out loud, trying to reassure himself that they were right and were just what he had to say to his son at war. Ted folded the letter very carefully, returned it gently to its envelope and placed it safely in his locker.

***

The men had done well and with the other platoons and companies on the camp were awarded their first forty-eight hour pass. The majority, having collected their rail passes, had left to spend every precious moment with their families. Of the rest, a few had to remain on duty and one or two men who had no families also stayed. The camp felt eerily quiet and empty.

Ted's pass was delayed because he was placed on night telephone duty. Although he was eager to return to Florrie, he was pleased that the skills and responsibilities that he had acquired working in the family business were recognised and that the men had begun to respect him and even saw him as a potential NCO.

'Don't forget us poor bloody footsloggers Ted, when you're made up, will you?'

Ted simply smiled.

The duty officer, a young second lieutenant, arrived at the company office. His brisk manner was in keeping with the newness of his rank. This is how one should speak to the men – all the other officers did. His curtness might also have been because of the young woman's bed that would otherwise have awaited him. Still, duty was duty.

'Everything OK?'

'Yes, sir.'

'Good.'

'Jeep ready?'

'Yes, sir. Tank full and I have the keys here,' Ted said pointing to the desk before him.

'Good. Well done. OK…' The officer paused, wondering if he had missed anything.

Ted stood silently to attention.

'OK. Well you know where I am if there are any problems.'

Ted heard the question in the young man's voice and replied, 'Yes, sir.'

'In the mess.'

'Yes sir, I know where to find you.'

'Good. OK. Well. OK. Carry on.'

'Yes, sir,'

The officer swung just as briskly out of the office and headed for the solitude of the officers' mess and the solace of a large gin.

It was 2303 hours when the phone rang. Ted picked it up.

'Hallo. *Hallo*. Is that the camp? D Company **SMASH...** This is **CRASH...** andlord **ROAR** SevenStar **COME ON THEN...** One of **BASTARD** men **SHOUT** a fight **SMASH** quickly.'

The line went dead. Ted sat for a moment, uncertain as to what to do. He knew that the message was about the Seven Stars and that it wasn't unusual to find trouble there. It *had* been a sleepy country pub, frequented by a few farm workers and the occasional passing salesman and it had been heavily reliant on weekend trade. But, when the nearby military camp had reopened just before war was declared, it had suddenly filled with thirsty soldiers. It was far enough from the main town that the local constabulary turned a blind eye, happy that the army was contained at arm's length and the landlord, relishing his new customers cheerfully amended the licensing hours, grinning broadly every time the till rang and ignoring the occasional misdemeanour and the raucous sounds of soldiers swaying their way back to their beds, only stopping to vomit into the hedgerow.

Ted knew what he *should* do. He *should* report this to the duty officer who would then inform the provost sergeant or the military police. He knew this was one of the lads in trouble and that the military would simply arrest him once he had recovered from a possible beating, but if he dealt with it himself, he would have to leave his post and for that he would be charged and disciplined and any hope of promotion would vanish. Maybe he would even lose his pass to see Florrie. He agonised for a moment. There was no one around to cover for him. Everyone was either on duty or off the camp – and there wasn't time anyway. In his head he heard the words of the old sweats – the old soldiers who knew the score. You always looked out for each other; never left anyone behind. If it came to it, you risked your life for your mates.

He had no choice.

Outside the company office, he stood for a moment in the darkness and listened. Somewhere in the distance a radio was playing music and the night breeze rustled the trees nearby. There was no sign of anybody and the peace was at odds with the adrenalin pumping through his body and the violence that was occurring just two miles down the empty road. He started to walk, briskly at first, until the walk turned into a run and he clattered along the roadways towards his barrack hut in the hope of reinforcements. As he approached, he could see lights blazing although no sound or movement came from within. He burst through the door and quickly looked around. Damn – nobody. Then a movement made him look again. There, stretched out on his bed lay the slim shape of Darkie, reading a copy of the Dandy. He looked up, surprised.

'Hallo Ted. What you doing here?'

Ted groaned inwardly. Shit. He was hoping to find somebody bigger, more intimidating. No time now.

'Darkie, quick! One of the lads is in trouble.'

Darkie jumped from his bed, slid into his boots, grabbed his battledress and hobbled after Ted, struggling to get into his tunic, his untied laces whipping the floor.

The jeep drove quickly along the black country lane until its headlights swept coldly across the front of the Seven Stars. Bumping off the road, they came to a halt and sat in silence. Everything was in darkness except for the light that poured through the etched windows of the public bar. There was no sound save for the mechanical ticking of the hot engine.

'Come on.'

Ted's voice was low, intent.

'Maybe it's all over Ted, maybe they've gone,' but as the words whispered out, they both saw a distorted shadow glide across the lit window and vanish.

A narrow dark corridor that smelled of stale beer faced them and, at its end, light pierced the window of a side door. Ted opened it and stepped inside. In front of him stood three soldiers each wearing a dark green-tinged battledress with the word *Canada* in white flashed across their shoulders. Between their threatening shapes, Ted could see Billy Kite pressed hard against the bar corner behind a barricade of upturned chairs and a table. In his hand he held a broken bottle by its neck, which he moved menacingly toward his adversaries.

'Come on yer Canuck bastards. Who wants it then? What yer waitin' for, the bleedin' Mounties?'

His words hid his desperation. This time he *was* in trouble, big trouble.

Ted's boots crunched on broken glass in the beer-soaked carpet.

'Well about bleedin' time. Wot kept yer lads?'

'Shut up Billy.'

The nearest Canadian turned. The others continued to stare silent and unblinking at Billy, their bodies wound tight as springs, like mountain lions surrounding a trapped prey. They waited for the merest twitch of weakness or opportunity before launching themselves at his throat. A hot flush of anger and alcohol spread across the face of the Canadian facing Ted and dissolved into the roots of his close cropped ginger hair. He looked deeply, fiercely, at Ted and Darkie. All he could see was one loud-mouthed cockney bastard who deserved a beating, one tall athletic-looking Englishman who could be a problem and a runt. The fire in the Canadian's belly did not subside.

'Keep out of this eh.'

'We've come for our mate.'

'I said keep out of it buddy. He deserves what's coming to him.'

Ted felt the tension in his face and his heart pounded but he couldn't show it. He stared unblinkingly back at the Canadian and spoke quietly and firmly.

'No, we're taking him back. Now.'

For a second there was no sound other than the ticking of the bar clock. *Tick tock tick tock tick...* Suddenly the ginger-haired Canadian bared his teeth and made to move, fists clenched, face contorted, eyes molten with violence and then... inexplicably, he doubled over and let out an astonished yelp of air. Nobody saw the first punch, for it was an explosive blur that slammed the Canadian's solar plexus against his spine. The second blow was already streaking – a short right hook to the point of the jaw, which moved the Canadian lurching already unconscious into the man behind him and the final, a left uppercut lifted the third man off his feet before the other two had crashed onto a table, which splintered and dropped them in a heap onto the bar floor. Left, right, left. No pauses. Two seconds of controlled, accurate, awful power in perfect symmetry.

Nobody moved.

'Fu–ckinell.'

Ted and Billy looked at Darkie, astonished.

'Where the fuck did you learn that?'

'On the road Billy, in the booths. Been doing it all my life. It's in the family. Goes back generations.'

'But yer such a skinny sod.'

'I fought as a bantamweight.'

'There's nuffin of yer.'

'Up to eight stone and six pounds, Billy. Sometimes had as many as fifteen bouts a day, at the fairs and places like that. Often big blokes – miners and the like. No more than three rounds though. Knocked most of them out,' he declared as he gave his knuckles a professional inspection.

'I'm not bleedin' surprised,' said Billy as he dropped his broken bottle onto the heap of bodies and climbed out of the tangle of broken furniture.

'Right, that's settled. Nah 'ow abart one fer the road lads. Oose round is it?'

'Outside, Billy. NOW!'

Ted grabbed his tunic and pulled him spluttering to the waiting jeep.

They returned to the camp, past the same bored guard at the main gate who had let them out.

'You ain't seen us, Dixie. Alright?'

'Alright mate.'

It was still as quiet as when they left, quieter for the radio had been switched off and the breeze had dropped. In the officers' mess, the second lieutenant dozed in a large armchair and the company telephone lay silent. Ted took them to the company office, where Darkie made them all a mug of tea. Billy was unusually quiet.

'Sugar Billy?'
'Two spoons please mate.'
'Ted?'
'Same please, Darkie.'
Billy slowly stirred his tea.
'Fanks fer wot yer did Darkie. You're a good mate.'

Darkie grinned, realising this was Billy's apology for his regular verbal abuse, which would return soon enough. That was Billy, he couldn't help it. But he also knew it would never be the same again. In future they would just be words, no more than that and he felt at last as if he belonged.

'Don't thank me, Billy. It's Ted you need to thank. He risked getting into a lot of trouble to help you and don't you forget it. Just think what would have happened if the duty officer had rung while he was saving your sorry skin? Just imagine. Let's just hope he didn't and he's not on his way here right now.'

Billy turned towards Ted.

'Thanks Ted. I owe you one,' he said as the telephone let out an urgent metallic ring.

The three men stopped and looked from one to the other. *Oh shit.*

Ted picked up the receiver.

'Hallo. D Company.'

There was a long silence.

'Yes sir... Yes... OK... Thank you sir... Goodnight.'

Slowly Ted replaced the receiver. Billy and Darkie looked in anguish at Ted's face.

'Well... Ted?'

Ted paused. Stony faced. Then grinned.

'Wrong number.'

'Fu–ckinell.'

THREE

Sunday Dinner, the Flying Pencil and Charred Beans

15 September 1940

'Keep calm and carry on.'

Ministry of Information 1939

'No one can say how far Herr Hitler's empire will extend before this war is over, but I have no doubt it will pass away perhaps more swiftly than Napoleon's empire, and without its glory. The British spirit and temperament, bred in freedom, will prove more enduring and resilient than the most efficient mechanical discipline.'

Winston Churchill

Florrie lowered the newspaper into her lap, looked through the dining room window and thought about the Prime Minister's words.

I'm sure Winston's right. He doesn't make it sound easy though.

She sat alone in her terraced house. The women who were her neighbours on either side were probably also sitting, certainly alone. They formed a long row of terraced aloneness, which stretched across the nation.

She folded the paper and placed it on the mahogany table – a wedding present from Mick and Edie – and thought about their wedding day. Such a long time ago – well, only three years but in another world, another time, and she stroked the cool polished wood with a mixture of affection and sadness.

Right. Come on Florrie. It's almost time to go.

She moved to the window, parted the net curtains and peered out. The radio had crackled of it being cloudy but dry with sunny intervals and that seemed to match her patch of weather.

Think I'll leave my mac behind.

Nothing worse than having to wear something that made you too warm or that constantly slid off your shoulder when you wanted to walk briskly and swing your arms, even if you did happen to be carrying an old saucepan.

A saucepan may have seemed a strange companion, but she didn't care. These weren't normal times and Edie had asked her to save her one from being salvaged, after she had taken her other spare pots and pans to the dump. When was that? Last Wednesday? She had smiled at the thought of the sign chalked on a large blackboard that had greeted her.

"Out of the frying pan into the (Spit) fire."

'Thanks love,' the workman had said as she handed them over. 'It all 'elps. Do you know, somebody even brought in an old racing car? Yeah, a racing car and, better than that, some geezer brought in an artificial leg. Would you believe it, an artificial leg? Must 'ave 'opped 'ome,' he said with a wheezing laugh.

Florrie smiled back. Around her there was always lots of humour. It was defiance really: two fingers to the Nazi enemy, and it made you feel better.

She stopped and checked her appearance in the long mirror that hung in the hallway. Light poured in through the frosted panels at the top of the front door and, for a moment, she imagined Ted standing behind her, as he often did, smiling, hands gently on her shoulders, warm, reassuring.

She smiled back, but he was gone and her smile felt like an imposter.

Bloody war.

When would she see him again? Would she ever see him again? *No. Don't.* She shook the thoughts vigorously away like a wet dog coming out of the sea. *None of that.* She pulled herself upright. *That's it. Shoulders back. Chin up. One last check. You'll do.* She turned, opened the front door and stepped outside.

'Morning Florrie. How are you? How's Ted? Have you heard?'

The words came out quickly.

'Morning Joan. He's fine thanks.'

Well she supposed he was. She often wondered what he was doing, but his letters said so little. Not allowed to say much more, she supposed. Perhaps he had the day off today. Well it was Sunday after all. Did the army work on Sundays? Surely not. Everybody needs a day off. Well at least he was safe, for now anyway.

'How's Cyril?'

Joan rested on the soft broom she had been using to sweep the front path. She was short and slim with sharp features that gave her a rather bony appearance, but men found her attractive. The outbreak of war and the absence of her husband who was a serving sailor had allowed her unexpected freedom. She missed him of course, but he was a bit old fashioned and, after all, she was still only in her mid thirties. It hadn't been easy to collect all the make-up she needed – all she saw in the magazines and on the silver screen every Saturday. But she had managed it and it had transformed her appearance into a new warmness. Her thick eyebrows had been changed, with the help of tweezers and a brown-black pencil into clear well defined arches that, together with mascara and curled lashes, now accentuated her large brown eyes. Her cheeks glowed red and rosy and her full sensual lips were always coated in true red lipstick. 'Just being patriotic,' she would say.

She now exuded a glamorous softness, even when sweeping the front path in an apron. Men looked twice and smiled at her. The local women, however, stood in groups of two or three and whispered to each other. She had tried her new look on Ted before he went away, but had been met with polite coolness and she certainly didn't want to cross Florrie. Nowadays you needed your friends and neighbours like never before.

'He's well, I think. Got a letter from him last Wednesday. He's probably in the Med. Says it's nice and warm wherever he is.'

Both women paused and looked away for a moment. They both had awful fears that were never spoken of, certainly not in public.

'Still, I do have Jonathan for company. He's a good boy. Yes. So are you off to visit your mother-in-law?'

Florrie smiled. 'Yes, I try to see Edith every Sunday. She worries a lot and I need to give her this,' waving the saucepan.

'Must be very difficult for her. Still she's got her husband with her.'

Florrie nodded, silently thinking how useless he was.

'Well, Florrie, can't stay nattering. I'm off to church this morning. Just got to get my hat and coat on. Hope there are no raids. Ended up in the crypt last week.'

She laughed nervously and Florrie saw the worry in her well made-up eyes and knew the solace that the shrapnel-pocked church gave her.

'I can't stop either. Must go. Bye.'

Florrie opened and closed the green wooden front gate with a click and set off, looking up at the clouds and hoping for some blue sky.

***

A few hundred miles away, Wendell Schmitt sat in the briefing room at Cambrai, half listening to his instructions for that day's bombing raid on London. He felt unusually restless and constantly looked through the windows of the small room that was crammed full of flying crew. In the distance, he could see the dark shapes of the waiting Dornier aircraft and, beyond them, the September weather that he hoped would shield him from the murderous attacks of the Royal Air Force. Other less operational things, however, distracted his mind. He had been a pilot since his youth in Kaiserslautern and he had visited England just before the war, cycling around the leafy lanes of Kent, the same lanes that flashed below his aircraft on every mission. Today, he found himself thinking of the people he had met, who, like him, were now transformed by this bitter struggle and the demands of duty. He tried to shake the thoughts from his head and concentrate on his target. Despite the warmth of the room, a shiver ran through him.

***

Florrie's journey led her downwards, past the long rows of identical terraced houses, until she reached the park that sat like a green carpet on the chalky soil, overlooking the river below. She had been told the whiteness of the soft chalk shone upwards and gave the grass a silvery hue, but she had never noticed it. What she *could* clearly see, however, was the bandstand. An old friend, it stood strong, dressed in its green ornamental ironwork, waiting patiently for the brassy notes of Elgar and Sousa to return and the sunny striped deckchairs and gentle snoozing murmurs of Sunday afternoons. It was amazing what she missed, what everybody missed. She shivered. The warm shawl of Englishness was being pulled from her shoulders leaving them cold and unprotected.

For a moment she was tempted to delay her journey and sit in the peace of the gardens and to let tensions drift away into the big sky. She always felt comfortable and reassured there. She felt a sense of time and place and history. Victoria Gardens had been named after an empress.

She tried to imagine the ordinary people, way back then, in Victorian times, just like her. She thought that they must have struggled too having fought foreign armies like the Zulus, the Boers and the Afghans. They overcame adversity, of course they did. Winston was right: The British spirit *was* bred in freedom; and in that moment, a warm pride pushed away the chilliness of the day.

But she couldn't stop now. Edith would already be stealing glances at the brown mantle clock.

There were few people about and a single car passed. The town felt deserted; the buildings tense, waiting anxiously and her footsteps dared to echo through the stillness.

Soon she arrived at the Hill and began the long climb. The Hill recognised her, smiled, whispered in her ear, and a small breeze ran towards her, toying with her dark curls in greeting. She ran her hand along the rough concrete wall that bordered the road and touched the small smooth pebbles embedded there. Each one felt like a nugget of memory to be opened by her fingertips. Whirls of colour and laughter, scraps of smiles, dashes of hopes and dreams, sweet tastes and heady smells, and the chatter of words and sounds. All of them ran scampering around her mind. But the Hill also growled of darker and difficult memories, of unhappy times and a sad parting that made her set her jaw and stare at the cold, hard pavement beneath her feet and move on.

She passed familiar houses, now often full of strangers, but still with the ghosts of the past lingering nearby, reluctant to leave. Both her family and Ted's had lived on the Hill for generations, never straying far, keeping their story together.

Here, a cat curled tight against the autumn weather, stirred, lifted a drowsy head and looked up at her. There, a small dog wagged his tail and pushed his wet nose under a wooden garden gate.

Soon she reached the bay-fronted house that stood high above the roadway. A little further on, she could just see the church in which she had married Ted. The fine gateway and metal railings that had surrounded it had gone for scrap. It felt strange that part of a church would now become a tank track or a naval gun or a bomb to be dropped from a high flying bomber onto another land, another people. Maybe the church railings and gateway would be separated and only used for peaceful, helpful purposes.

No, most unlikely. We really are all in this together.

The thick hedge which had helped give the church grounds its sanctuary had also gone, leaving only the small supporting wall, open and bare with black squares in the stone like a row of rotten teeth where the metal uprights had been cut away. She sighed. She knew things had to change. That was the order of things, but this – this was so desperate.

At the top of the wide steps leading up from the main road to the house she stopped for a moment to catch her breath and look back across the town nestling below, retracing in her mind the journey she had just taken. She could still see the criss-crossing roads and the red tiles of roofs and she could almost see her house – her and Ted's new house, bought the year they were married. Not on the Hill anymore, but not so far away. She could also see the river – dull silver in the distance. Back then it had simply disappeared from her sight. Now she was aware of how it flowed to the sea and beyond; that its waters touched other lands torn by war, not so far away. Her hand touched her breast as she knew that men would die today and tomorrow and the next day in its chilly embrace.

She turned away and adjusted the black beret she wore on the side of her head, patted her curly black hair, smoothed the polka dot scarf inside her light jumper and tightened the leather belt around her narrow waist. Her long skirt stopped just above her ankles, below which she wore white ankle socks and white shoes. Sunday visiting meant Sunday best. Satisfied, she moved to the side of the house and opened the creosoted gate. The clatter of the latch alerted Edie.

'Hallo Florrie. How are you dear? My, you do look nice.'

'Hallo Edie. Thank you. Oh this is for you,' she said as she handed her the saucepan.

'Thanks very much dear, that'll come in very handy.'

From inside the house the sound of a radio crackled intermittently, but not enough to disguise the velvet voice of Vera Lynn.

"*... and when the shadows fall behind you,*
There'll come another day..."

'She has such a lovely voice. Don't you think so, Florrie?'

"*... and then together in sunny weather,*
We'll wander hand in hand..."

'I'll turn her off for now though.'

The radio clicked into silence.

'There, that's better. I thought we could have a cup of tea in the garden later if the weather's fine enough. I've laid a table.'

She paused and then asked the question that filled her every hour.

'Heard from Ted?'

She asked the question cheerfully, as casually as she could manage, but it wasn't difficult to catch the tremor in her voice.

'He's very well Edie, very well.'

She nodded and smiled and looked for something to do.

Edith was tall, like her son, much taller than her daughter-in-law and she loved pearls. It was their lustre and feel and, when the moment was right, she would wear them as a necklace or earrings, but not now. Now she covered herself from neck to wrist to ankle in simple black and white. Her country was at war again. Times were austere and uncertain and wearing jewellery and colour seemed to her to be disrespectful.

She might have been mistaken for being in mourning, and maybe in her mind she was, with her son away, maybe never to return and her husband spending so much time in the pub. That's where he was now.

Her grey hair was pulled back from her face into a tight bun, but within the severity of her appearance, her eyes were soft and anxious.

'Table looks nice.'

Florrie pointed down the garden.

'Thank you dear. Why don't you have a little walk? I've just got a few more things to do.'

The garden was long and narrow and walled with red brick on all sides. A small concrete yard faced the back door and within it stood an outside toilet that had been painted dark green with a brass handle, tarnished dark by the weather. Nearby, a trellised archway of grey rough wood stood forlorn, waiting for red roses to clamber cheerfully over it again and beyond it, empty flowerbeds sat around a rectangular lawn.

Dominating the garden was the forbidding shape of an Anderson shelter dug into the lawn. Its metal was dark and rusted in places like some awful skin disease and it brooded like a corrugated segment from a giant insect. Florrie shivered and hoped she wouldn't have to enter its metal gut. Nearby was a small wooden table. Its delicately carved legs were partly covered by a pure white, perfectly ironed, embroidered tablecloth, hanging with exact precision around each side. Edith always did things so exactly. The autumn breeze moved it gently.

'Do you want to come in now dear? It's a bit chilly isn't it? I've managed to get some nice pork sausages for Sunday dinner this week. I know how much you enjoy them.'

While Edie disappeared into the kitchen to finish preparing the meal, Florrie sat in the adjoining dining room, picked up the local newspaper and scoured the front page for news. She knew before she started there would be scant information on the progress of the war, other than its local impact and even that would be heavily censored. The paper bore no headlines and only half a dozen or so small photographs stared out at her: the fuzzy faces of men who were killed in action, missing or taken prisoner. They often smiled out as if nothing had happened. For some, it was as if their young hearts were still beating, as if they would be coming home on leave that weekend. *Please God* she would never see Ted smiling back at her like that and her blue eyes moistened. She shook herself and concentrated once again on the forest of type in front of her. The paper was designed in many columns, each full to bursting with words. Sometimes boxes crossed two columns to break up the mass and more space and larger letters drew her eye.

'A programme of music by the band of the Corps of Royal Engineers in the park at Canterbury Street last Saturday. Pity I missed that, although the weather was not so good,' she mused.

'Ahh, war damage.'

She read aloud and quickly as the item was important to her. '"Claims under the government compensation scheme prepared in respect of property, furniture and stock… In the event of damage the possession of an independent valuation and inventory will secure a quick settlement of any claim." Now that's something I need to remember. You never know…' her voice trailed off as she turned her attention to something else.

'"Building Society… Sheerness and Gillingham Permanent Building Society… reducing their interest rates to three per cent for share accounts and two and a half for deposit accounts, free of liability to income tax." Not surprising really when you think about all that's going on.'

Her attention now changed to a column headed "Public Notices". She wanted to do her bit and help the war effort and also earn an income if she could. Ted sent home what he could but it wasn't enough to live on and she relied heavily on her family. Sometimes she went hungry.

'Let's see. Borough of Chatham,' she mumbled to herself. '"Tenders required for the erection of three brick surface shelters… require three heavy cart horses for Corporation work…" No don't think so. Hey…' and her attention sharpened. "Applications are required for the temporary appointments of persons (male or female) not liable for military service, who have a thorough experience of bookkeeping and accounts. The salary offered will depend upon experience, but will approximate £3.3s per week." Mmm maybe, not sure I have the experience though.'

As she was about to turn over, she noticed two small items at the bottom of the page, which made her smile as she read them.

'Edith, listen to this,' she started to read out loudly and slowly. '"Pills in about twenty containers picked up in a south-western area were analysed and found to contain tapioca starch. It is believed they were dropped from German raiding planes. Tapioca starch is frequently taken as an antidote to excessive nervousness."'

A snort from the direction of the kitchen indicated Edith had heard.

'They'll need more than starch when we've finished with them,' retorted Florrie.

'Certainly will,' said Edith, returning with a jingling tray of cutlery and condiments. 'Mind you, they're selling Bisma-Rex at the local store now. Said to be good for wartime indigestion and dyspepsia. Thought I might try some,' she said and the worry again sounded in her voice.

Edith sat next to Florrie.

'Won't be long.' She paused. 'I found this,' she said warmly. 'It's you and Ted, before the war,' she said producing a much-fingered black and white studio photograph. 'Always thought that you both looked so nice in this.'

Florrie took the photo and smiled as she recognised the slim young woman and the dark coloured plus-fours she was wearing above her tartan socks and cycling shoes.

'Oh I remember that cycling top and that jumper with the crew neck.'

'And that black beret. You still wear that beret Florrie. How old were you there?'

'I don't know, about eighteen.'

She slowly turned it over. On the other side, written clearly in pencil, "Sunday morning. 7th October 1934". The words caught at the back of her throat. October 1934 seemed like only yesterday and yet so long ago. A Sunday morning like this, but one of unruffled peace, and with Ted. She felt her eyes prickle, but she steadied herself – not in front of Edie.

'Ted looked nice too,' smiled Edie.

'Oh yes. Look at him.'

Standing close beside her, he was much taller – partly because of the large flat hat he was wearing at a jaunty angle. His dress was identical except for a grey roll neck jumper and the round badge of the cycling club they had belonged to fixed to the left breast of his jacket.

'You used to ride all the way to Southend and back. Don't you remember Florrie?'

Florrie smiled.

'On our old tandem. Never let us down.'

Together. A team. Cycling together. Feeling the exhilaration of their speed, their togetherness. Ted in front. Powerful. Never letting her down.

Florrie put the photo down. The hope and expectation shining in their young faces was too much to bear.

'Tea, Florrie?'

Edie poured some milk from a small jug into two white cups. Both cups and saucers were rimmed with a single gold band, which was scratched in places. She moved one cup and saucer and it rattled slightly as her hand trembled.

'We'll just wait for the tea to mash dear.'

The teapot, brown and crazed after a lifetime of service, sat warmly under a beige tea cosy.

'Help yourself to sugar dear.'

A round white bowl contained a small amount of sugar. In it was a small spoon decorated at the end with a coat of arms and the word "London".

'Oh just half a spoon, thank you.'

Rationed to just eight ounces a week for each adult, sugar was only offered to those you could trust with its scarcity.

Edie smiled thankfully.

'Any other stories? Anything a bit happier?'

Although Edie always bought the local paper, she never read it, afraid of what it might contain.

'Well, this is amusing. Listen, "A novel job is being done by the tenth Acton Boy Scouts. They have undertaken to be 'listeners' at the local church. The Scouts' job will be to listen for sirens during the singing of hymns, when other members of the congregation may not hear."'

They both smiled to themselves at the thought of the congregation singing so loudly for comfort.

'What's on at the pictures?' asked Edith.

'Would you like to go?'

'Oh I haven't been for years. Shall I pour?'

Florrie turned noisily to the relevant pages. Perhaps she could persuade her mother-in-law to go with her. It would get her out of the house. It would do her good – do them both good really.

'Well, there is a lot of choice.'

Florrie spoke slowly as she concentrated on the pages.

'Err, let's see, Rita Hayworth is on at the Ritz and Ronald Reagan at the Plaza. *Pinocchio* is on at the Palace and also at the Majestic, but you won't want to see that.'

'Is there nothing romantic? I do like a good love story.'

'Well how about Margaret Lockwood? Now you like her. She's on at the Regent with Rex Harrison.'

'Ooh, that sounds nice dear. What's the film called?'

'Night Train to Munich.'

'Munich? Isn't that in Germany? Oh no I couldn't see that. Wouldn't be right.'

'No of course not,' and Florrie tried to hide her amusement in the newspaper pages.

'Well, there are eight films showing at the Grand this week. Spencer Tracy and Hedy Lamarr. Vincent Price in The Invisible Man Returns.' She looked up hopefully and then looked down again. 'Ginger Rogers and Joel McCrea, or… we could go to the Royal Hippodrome and see Show a Leg – "The wonder revue of 1940 presented by Jack Sonn. Sixteen glamorous and glittering scenes including Jimmy Bryant *Funny and how*, Freason and Renova *Music sweet and hot,* Four smart girls *And how smart,* Ten show a leg girls, *Beautiful dames,* Percival Ponsonby, Jacob Rogers and Billy Shenton and his company in Cairo Capers."' She finished breathlessly. 'Prices sixpence to half a crown.'

'Oh no dear. I don't think so. Doesn't sound very proper, does it?'

'No s'pose not. *I know*,' said Florrie brightly. 'Why don't you have your hair done? You always enjoy that.'

'Oh no dear. Not with all these bombs dropping. Imagine if one dropped on me and they found me with rollers in, that would be dreadful.'

Florrie laughed at the thought of the Nazi war machine stopping so that Edith could take her rollers out.

'No, it's alright now. Listen to this,' and she turned back to the paper. '"The West End Hairdressing Salons. High Street. Accommodate you with emergency Air Raid Shelters. Expressly fitted for hairdressing during Air Raids. We carry on as usual. Come in between the raids. Service assured. Machineless Permanent Waving. No Electricity. No Wires. Other Moderate Perms completed in two hours."'

'I think I'll wait a little longer' said Edith, quite unconvinced. 'Dinner won't be long dear,' she said softly and squinted upwards through the dining room windows at an unexpected patch of pale sky that had appeared through the September clouds. 'I think it's getting a bit brighter.'

It was a strange sight, these two women, dressed for a special occasion, making an effort and carrying on as normal. Around them, street names resounded with the history of a glorious past: Shakespeare, Byron, Milton and Imperial – the road on which Edith's own house stood. Less than a hundred miles away, Europe was in darkness and here, Britain itself was again in grave danger.

***

Six thousand feet above where Florrie and Edie sipped their tea, Wendell Schmitt was limping back in his Dornier Do 17 bomber. His fast, nimble aircraft had done well in the early part of the war, especially during the invasion of Poland and before that, during the Spanish Civil War where it had been successful against the Republican fighters. However, now against the formidable opposition of Fighter Command, it was a very different matter. Today they had been shocked by the number of British fighters that had attacked them, breaking up their formations, leaving them so vulnerable.

'Mein Gott, I thought the RAF was finished.'

'We won't make our target. Ditch the bombs.'

Their deadly payload whistled down onto the streets of South London. The bomber, free of its heavy load, leaped upwards, anxious to return.

'Let's get out of here'

A thrill ran through the stomachs of each of the four airmen.

The squadron of Hurricanes had fallen upon them from out of the September cloud, slicing through the sky like falcons upon a flock of pigeons, breaking their nerve, scattering them and moving in for the kill, razor-taloned. Wendell heard the chatter of a machine gun and knew that Heinrich was fighting back. Heinrich was good – the best, if anybody could... The bomber juddered as bullets ripped through the port wing, instantly turning the engine into a useless mess of torn metal and spewing oil.

'Scheisse.'

All the bomber's machine guns were now firing defiantly. Beside him Otto punctuated each burst with a string of foul expletives. Despite their danger, this often made him smile, but not today as he pulled the ailing aircraft downwards into a bank of approaching cloud and disappeared into the grey veil. The plane flew on, invisible, muffled.

'Everybody OK? Good. Keep your eyes peeled.'

The order was hardly necessary. Inside the eerie swirling mass they strained to see the dark shapes of their enemy. They stared until their eyes ached and ran.

'Pray God this cloud continues until we are well over the Channel.'

***

In the dining room, both women heard the drone of an aircraft engine. It was a sound they had learned to recognise only too well as German bombers passed overhead on their way to attack London and other targets, but this sounded low, very low. They turned and looked at each other, concerned. Suddenly, above them, in the same blue sky that Florrie and Edie were enjoying, was an exposed German aircraft and below, gunners saw their chance and prepared to open fire. The air split open as shells exploded and both women's teacups rattled.

'Come on Edith.'

They ran into the garden. There before them, very clearly, the lone bomber was buffeted by deadly and accurate anti-aircraft fire.

'It's a Dornier,' said Florrie. 'A flying pencil.'

The two women said nothing. As each shell burst black smudges on the blue, Edith flinched but still she watched, face eager in the hope that as each explosion crept nearer, spewing red hot shards of metal, this bringer of death and destruction would itself be destroyed.

'Look, it's the RAF. It's one of ours.'

An RAF fighter suddenly appeared out of the clouds, skimming at high speed across the Dornier's tail. They clearly heard the rapid burst of fire before it swooped swiftly away. The bomber seemed to almost stop and buckle in the sky, like a boxer receiving a knockout blow.

***

Inside the stricken aircraft Wendell grappled with the controls and felt the plane shudder and heave in its death throes like a maddened animal tormented by its wounds. The craft shook so violently that he was amazed it didn't simply collapse, fold in the air and fall to earth like a spinning leaf. But it flew on.

'Hurricane. Hurricane,' a voice shouted into his ear and the bomber juddered under the force of machine gun fire and seemed to hesitate again.

'Get out,' screamed Wendell. 'Bail out.'

'We're too low.'

'Get out *now!*'

The crew tumbled into the sky, falling like soft black stones towards the hard roofs just below them, their eyes closed in terror. Suddenly each chute opened, jolting their bodies and leaving them hanging, breathless and exhausted.

Inside the empty plane, Wendell continued to wrestle with the controls that shook so violently that he could barely grip them. He knew it was too late to get out.

'I must keep the nose up.'

He pulled with all his strength, features distorted with the effort, sweat running down his face, wind howling at him through the shattered cockpit and the aircraft engine screaming in dying torment. Ahead of him, through the window, sped a patch of green amongst the mass of English houses: an allotment. He could clearly see the neat rows and patches and autumn colours, and for a moment his heart leaped. But around him tiled rooftops and chimneys flashed and closed in on him at breakneck speed. If he could only clear them.

***

'It's going down,' said Edie excitedly as the stricken bomber stalled, heeled over and fell from the sky into the town below them, sending up a plume of thick, black smoke.

'We got it. We got it Florrie!'

The two women cheered and hugged each other.

Florrie stopped and turned back towards the pall of smoke. Fingers of icy fear suddenly clutched at her and both women stood, eyes wide with horror.

'Oh Florrie.'

'That's my home!' shouted Florrie. 'That's my home. I've got to go.'

She bounded through the side gate, tears welling in her eyes, scuttled down the steps, heart pounding, and began to run down the long Hill as a sickening feeling grew inside her. This time the Hill helped her. No time for memories now. At the bottom she was forced to stop, gasping for breath, and face the gradual incline towards the ever-growing plume of smoke. She now walked rapidly, talking to herself, telling herself to keep calm and be more rational. Still panic crept in; tears welled.

What will I do? What can I save? Where will I live? Oh Ted, where are you? Why aren't you here? She controlled her thoughts *No. Come on. Be strong. Be strong.*

She passed familiar landmarks that signposted her route: past the railway arches, straight on, past the railway station, past the park and the bandstand. Now running, now walking determinedly. At last she reached the final long road. Her mouth was dry. Past the endless rows of terraced houses. Her lungs ached as she thought. *At the end of this road is my home, the devastated, destroyed, burning pile of rubble that is my HOME.*

***

In his crippled aircraft, Wendell froze in horror, and waited to die as the plane smashed into a roof, sending tiles and bricks and splinters of timber flying in all directions. Then it somersaulted into the back gardens, breaking in two with a tearing scream of metal and sliding to a halt. Suddenly there was no noise. To his amazement, the pilot found himself hanging upside down in his harness and still alive. Blood from a large cut on his chin ran down his face and began to fill his flying goggles and he wrenched them away. Around him a thick dust cloud made visibility impossible, but the smell of aviation fuel was everywhere and with it already drifted a thick, choking smoke.

***

Nearby, in the same garden, four occupants had huddled inside a gloomy Anderson shelter since the first air raid warning, unaware of the drama playing out in the sky above them. Waited patiently for the sound of the all-clear. In the distance they could hear the rhythmic and comforting pounding of anti-aircraft fire and, within the iron and heaped earth that protected them, the faint sound of aircraft engines. Two teenage boys looked up towards the sky and tried to make light of the situation.

'Glad we're in here Jon. Safe in here,' Alan spoke quietly, uncertainly.

His mother, Alice, held her small daughter tightly on her knee.

'Don't worry love, it'll be all over soon.'

'You alright, Pammy?' Alan smiled at his sister.

The little girl shook her head silently from side to side, eyes wide.

The explosion of sound as Wendell's bomber hit the roofs shocked them with its sudden violence. Showers of bricks and tiles and debris thudded down and bounced around them. The ground shook and heaved, and earth fell down on them from the shelter roof as the Dornier crashed down, broke up, metal howling and rending, and slid towards them, spewing out dust and fuel. In the shelter Pammy cried out in fear and, as she did so, a finger of fire found the fuel-sodden ground and rushed towards them, billowing flame and smoke.

The two boys looked at each other and at the heavy choking smoke that was beginning to drift through the shelter's open front entrance.

'Quick Jon! Out through the back door.'

They crowded across the woman and child, and attempted to wrench the back door open. It was locked. Already, the smoke was thickening and the heat was increasing rapidly.

'We've got to get out and get help. Hold your breath and just run through it.'

They looked at each other for a second, and then Alan took a deep breath and ran for his life through the choking smoke and burning heat. Jonathan followed, but as he did so an explosion of fire sent a wave of flame over his running body and he staggered through it and collapsed choking, his body blackened and smoking.

***

Three doors away, Harry Smith could see the terrible drama unfolding before him and heard Alan scream for help.

'It's locked. They can't get out. Quickly. Help us! Help!' before he too collapsed blackened and exhausted.

Harry snatched up a pickaxe and proceeded to hurdle the garden fences with a skill and determination that surprised him. As he approached the back of the shelter, he could feel the tremendous heat and his eyes and lungs smarted from the black smoke that enveloped him. Kneeling down, he could see smoke coming from inside the shelter and could hear a child screaming. For a second, a tremor of fear went through him as he imagined what he might find. Trembling, he quickly wrenched the back door open and reached inside.

'Quickly!'

He grabbed an arm and pulled. Two figures emerged covered in black soot, choking and spluttering.

***

Ahead of her, Florrie heard the sound of alarm bells from fire engines and ambulances and the intense buzz and flow of people. As she strode along the road, people came out of their houses, some grim-faced, some chattering at the drama of it all. She wanted to tell them that it was her house that had been destroyed, but she was afraid they might delay her and, in any case, she was uncertain of her emotions. She must be strong – Ted would expect that. All around her small boys ran, weaving in and out of the adults, anxious to get there quickly, anxious to find souvenirs.

The smell of acrid smoke filled her nostrils and perspiration covered her. She stopped for a moment and tried to mop her hot face with a small handkerchief, which was soon smeared with black smudges. As she turned into her street, a crowd of people held back by a police cordon met her. For a while she couldn't see above the crowd of shocked onlookers, and she ran from one to another, looking for a gap. Suddenly she saw it: the terrible damage to the roofs of two houses. Rubble, tiles and pieces of wreckage were everywhere and flames and smoke drifted around the buildings. Here and there small boys attempted to pick up ragged pieces of metal, some still too hot to handle and were shouted at and chased off by angry firemen. For a moment, she failed to grasp the enormity of the scene before her and then she realised. The bomber had missed her house – just.

'Unlucky for some,' she heard a man say. 'Hit number fifteen and the one next door. Think there's casualties though. Bastards.'

The bomber had missed her home by two houses – just two houses. Thank God. She sat on a nearby wall and quietly shook.

Later she identified herself to the nearest policeman and was escorted through the buzz of people and the shouted orders of the Air Raid Precautions and Auxiliary Fire Service men. She made her way over the lines of now limp hoses and puddles of water, past the ambulances and fire engines and back to the green wooden gate she had clicked shut just a few hours before.

Inside the house she quickly moved from room to room, but there was no serious damage other than ornaments that now lay on the floor and a bathroom mirror that had cracked under the shock. The back garden, however, was a different matter. The air reeked of smoke and dust and fuel, and her wooden fence, although doused by a fireman's hose, still smouldered black and charred. Wreckage and debris was strewn everywhere. Looking around, she recognised a large piece of red chimney pot lying like a wound amongst the dark green cauliflowers and, nearby, a sliver of tile, razor sharp, was embedded in the trunk of an apple tree. Small sections of metal, dull and crumpled lay at her feet and she bent down and picked up a piece. It felt strange to the touch and was warm, but as she held it, it gradually became cool and still as it died. To her left the view that she knew so well was blocked by the carcass of the upturned bomber – laying there, still smouldering, like some obscene black insect swatted from a nightmare. The mark of the swastika was still visible on its tail, punctured by machine gun bullets and shrapnel. The sight of the riddled symbol gave her hope. The thought of it still being whole, proud, and sneering would have been too much to bear.

She walked around in silence, still dazed, trying, but failing to make sense of it.

'The bastards,' she said grimly. 'The bastards have destroyed my runner beans.'

She returned to the kitchen, put the kettle on and gathered as many cups as she could find. A lot of people would be in need of a cup of tea.

***

Helen Smith knocked gently on the front door. It did not seem right to knock loudly and besides, she was still pale and shaken.

'Are you alright Florrie?'

The two young women sat in the dining room sipping hot tea and reassuring each other.

'Is Harry alright, Helen?'

'Oh yes, he's fine. You know Harry.'

She made no mention of his courage that day. Courage like that happened every day, unsung.

'No, it's Jon.'

'Jon?'

'Yes Jonathan – Joan's boy, Jonathan.'

Helen put down her tea for fear of spilling it.

'He was visiting Alan when the siren went. They were in the shelter with Alice and little Pamela when… They're both burnt, Jonathan very badly I think. Harry saw him being put into the ambulance. Saw his face. Said it looked like it had… melted.'

Both women felt the tears welling; both pushed them away.

Florrie visited the hospital the following day and sat with Joan, in silence, around her son's bed. She tried hard not to retch at the smell of his decaying body but finally was forced to hold a handkerchief to her nose.

Joan sat there, appearing not to notice. She wore no fresh make-up. She was still sitting there six days later when he died. He was sixteen.

Florrie returned to her home, cleared up the wreckage in her garden, replaced the ornaments and made a note in the calendar that hung on the dining room wall to buy more bean seed for next year.

FOUR

Pegasus Bridge, 0016hrs, June 6th 1944

'I see you stand like greyhounds in the slips,
Straining upon the start. The game's afoot:
Follow your spirit, and, upon this charge
Cry, "God for Harry! England and Saint George!"'

Henry V by William Shakespeare

Ted stood up in the semi darkness. He didn't really know where he was. Somewhere in Southern England. He knew that much. Around him, men spoke quietly: sometimes they laughed and occasionally they cursed. He looked up at the night sky thick with cloud and felt a keen breeze on his cheek. His stomach churned. Suddenly he felt alone and anxious.

They had arrived yesterday in covered lorries into a sealed camp surrounded with barbed wire with signs saying "Top Secret" and "No Entry". The men had looked at each other knowingly. This had to be something big.

The briefings had happened soon after their arrival. The major had outlined the Allied Invasion Plan. His voice had been calm, determined, as if the outcome had already been decided.

'The sixth Airborne Division will land here on the left flank of the British beach landings and two American Airborne Divisions will land on the right flank of *their* seaborne landings.' He circled a large section of the map of Normandy with his stick, 'Sixth Airborne will hold this area and prevent enemy reinforcements.' He paused and looked intently at his silent audience. 'D Company along with two platoons of B Company have been selected for a special mission.'

There was a low groan. D Company was always being selected for something. D Company was always the best, the major made sure of that. So this was the reward for all that intense, relentless training.

The major smiled for a second and then looked at his men fiercely.

'I cannot emphasise enough the importance of our mission.' He moved and unrolled another map, this time from a large aerial photograph. 'Here and here,' he pointed, 'just inland from the coast, are the two bridges crossing the Caen Canal and the River Orne. D Company plus a section of Royal Engineers, will land in six gliders, three per bridge, twenty-eight men per glider, ahead of the main invasion, capture the bridges intact and hold them against the enemy until relieved by Five Para Brigade who will be landing here. A company of Seven Para will make their way directly to us. We will be the first Allied troops in action.'

The groan changed into a buzz.

'The bridges will be vital crossing points for our own troops and equipment coming up from the beaches. They are also vital for enemy armour to cross to attack the beachhead. This we cannot allow.' He paused for emphasis. 'Intelligence tells us that two panzer divisions have recently moved into this area. Any questions so far?'

'Yes, sir.'

'Corporal Kite.'

'Do you know what divisions they are sir?'

'Yes. The twenty-first and the twelfth SS Hitlerjugend.'

There was a murmur and the men turned to each other.

'Anything else?'

'Yes sir.'

'Corporal Kite.'

'How many men is that sir? And tanks. How many tanks sir?'

'Approximately thirty thousand men and three hundred tanks.'

'And how far from the bridges, sir?'

'They are based in the area of Caen here. About five miles away.'

'Fu–ckinell.'

The major smiled. He had such admiration for these tough men and their irrepressible spirit, and their respect for him was boundless.

'That's OK Billy,' somebody called out, 'that's less than two tanks each.'

'You can have mine mate.'

'OK.' The major's voice demanded their attention. 'Remember you are an elite. You are the most highly trained infantry company in the British Army. We have prepared long and hard together for this one operation. You will attack with speed and deadly force. You are a coup-de-main unit.'

'Coo de bleedin' what?' a voice whispered.

After the briefing, Ted moved with the others into smaller platoon and section groups to study a scale model of the bridges' area. They were amazed both at the degree of detail and that the model was updated every day with new information from aerial reconnaissance and the French Resistance, right down to newly broken windows. Soon every man would know every bush, every ditch, every stone, just as they would know their own job and the job of every other man.

Ted sat with the platoon radio operators he had trained. Yet again, he ran through the signal codes that he would have to send. Everybody had to know them, just in case something happened to Ted.

'OK, at the canal bridge it's "Ham" if we capture it intact and "Jack" if we don't. At the river bridge it's "Jam" if we capture it intact and "Lard" if we don't. So what do we want to hear?'

'Ham and Jam, Corporal.'

'That's right.'

'And who are we sending it to?'

'Brigade Commander Five Para Brigade.'

'Right again.'

Ted was awestruck by the scale of the operation, the detailed planning and complete preparation. He also felt a pride that they had been chosen to lead the assault on Occupied Europe. How the hell had that happened? One minute he was minding his own business on Chatham Hill and the next, he was an elite warrior. Suddenly he wanted to tell Florrie – tell her how important he was and what he had achieved. You simply won't believe this love, this is really amazing. But he saw her face crumple. Oh don't worry love. We can do it. The lads can do it. We'll be fine. And he gave her a big hug while over her shoulder, where she couldn't see. *Can we do it? There are so many things that could go wrong. Will I make it? Will I come back?*

'When do we go, sir?'

'We are waiting on the weather.'

Ted stood up in the semi darkness. Beside him loomed the massive black shape of a Horsa glider, his glider. He wanted to touch it and be reassured, even though he knew how flimsy it was – simply fabric stretched over plywood. He wondered about those who had built it. Had they known its purpose? Had they put every effort into making it strong and safe for him? He wasn't to know among its builders were coffin makers from the Co-op.

He did know it certainly wouldn't stop anything, certainly not a bullet. It was so vulnerable. He also knew he couldn't touch it – that might be misconstrued as a weakness by the other men around him. They all needed each other for a common strength right now, not that any of them would admit it. Now they were all chatting and laughing and joking as if this was just another exercise.

Ahead, down the runway, he could see the outline of the Halifax bomber that would tug them into the air and a faint glimmer of light on the tow cable that attached them like an umbilical cord. But this mother would abandon them high over France. He thought about Florrie and little Oliver, his son, whose birth he had missed nearly two years and two months ago, warmly asleep and safe and he beat away the spasm of fear that trembled his stomach. *I will see you again. I will.*

'Hallo Ted. You OK?'

Out of the gloom stepped a familiar figure, already loaded with equipment. For once Darkie, now wearing combat dress, didn't have to be parade smart, but he still managed to look scruffy. The whites of his eyes glinted out of his blackened camouflaged face.

Ted smiled.

'Hallo Darkie. I'm fine. How are you mate?'

'Oh OK. Well, a bit nervous really. Wouldn't admit it to the others. Bit of a suicide job this, isn't it?'

'It'll be fine Darkie. If the major says we can do it, we *will* do it. Jerry's in for a hell of a surprise. Who was it said, "Jerry's like the June bride. Knows he's going to get it, just doesn't know how big it'll be."'

Darkie laughed.

'And you'll be our ears and voice, eh Ted?'

'Yes. Company HQ. The major's wireless operator. Where he goes, I go.'

'So you're in Glider Number One?'

'Yes. First up and first to land at the canal bridge,' he said with the slightest quaver in his voice.

'I'll be right behind you, Ted.'

'Not too close mate.'

Both men smiled. They knew full well the danger of a heavily laden glider landing at ninety miles per hour and crashing into the one in front.

'Hang on Ted, something's happening.'

A jeep was arriving at speed. It stopped abruptly. The passenger stood up and they all recognised the major.

'OK men. Enplane.'

The words cut clearly through the night air.

Ted and Darkie shook hands.

'Good luck mate.'

'Good luck.'

Ted pulled himself up into the glider with difficulty. Like everybody else, he was carrying a mass of equipment. His Mark II 38 radio set, additional batteries and a canvas carrier containing the four-foot aerial rods weighed twenty-two pounds alone. On top of that there was ammunition, grenades, mortar bombs, weapons, food, water, medical equipment, spare clothing and a steel helmet – even an escape map.

Each man and his equipment had already been weighed – there was a maximum of two hundred and fifty pounds to ensure the gliders would not be overloaded. Even so, many had then added more ammunition, knowing they would have to fight with what they could carry. It was not surprising that some had to be helped into the gliders, as the weight they carried pushed them to their knees.

'Thank God we 'aven't got to carry a bleedin' parachute as well,' somebody moaned.

Ted sat on the starboard side, near the front, close to the major, almost opposite the port door. To his right he could see the two pilots preparing for take-off, talking to the tug pilot along the radio cable that formed part of the tow wire.

God I hope you two make it tonight, and glide this beast through the darkness and put us down in as much of one piece as you can.

He strapped himself in and looked at his watch. It was almost twenty to eleven. He could feel sweat trickling down his back and chest and he moved uncomfortably on the hard wooden bench. He looked back along the glider at the men facing inwards at each other. There was Billy chattering away, nineteen to the dozen, helmet pushed towards the back of his head and chinstrap hanging unfastened. How did he manage it?

Oh come on, let's go if we're going to. Ted's thoughts panicked.

Suddenly, out of the darkness came coughs and splutters as the four Halifax engines burst into life, followed by a growing roar that deafened the men and made the glider tremble. They sat in silence, alone with their thoughts.

With a sudden jerk the glider started to roll forward. Ted's stomach somersaulted. The man to his left turned and shouted something into his ear, but in the din he couldn't hear him properly. It could have been, 'Here we go Ted.' He simply nodded. It didn't matter.

The rumbling of wheels on tarmac grew louder and faster, then stopped and the glider swayed slightly. They all knew what that meant: they were airborne. Ted relaxed. They were on their way, no turning back now.

Right let's get on with it.

The Halifax climbed steadily over the darkened sleeping countryside. A few vigilant eyes would have looked upwards at the noise; maybe even caught a glimpse as the moon slipped between the clouds and wondered what was happening.

Thousands of feet above, it was very uncomfortable. The bomber's engines had settled to a steady roar. The wind whistled around and inside the glider, which pitched and rolled and jerked as the tow cable took up the slack. Ted's role as company clerk sometimes excluded him from some of the glider training, but he had done enough to know that men were often airsick, but not tonight. The men sang, loosened their kit, shuffled on the wooden seats and thought about what was to come. Ted looked at his watch – the hands appeared to have stopped moving and he knew it would take an hour just to get to the French coast. A long hour. *Come on. Come on.* He looked up, smiled and nodded at the other men. Then a stab of panic grabbed him and he looked away and rehearsed his role over and over again in his mind.

The six bombers and their gliders moved together in formation. From below an enemy might have seen twelve large aircraft heading to bomb Caen. Later, they might have cheered as six fell from the sky.

'Coast coming up.'

At last.

'OK. Remove doors. Quiet now. Quiet.'

From his seat Ted could see, beyond the pilots, the flash of exploding flak and white lines of tracer lighting the night sky in the distance. *Pray God we won't meet that.* They had no protection against pieces of jagged metal slicing through their fragile craft and soft bodies. But he knew they were headed for a gap in the flak over Cabourg on the coast. *Let's hope Jerry hasn't closed it.* They flew on. *Not long now.* The men began to do up their equipment in readiness.

Then the noise changed. Ted grasped his seat. They were dropping out of the sky, at speed, alone. They had been cast off. The glider could only go one way now and that was down, at a hundred miles an hour, in virtual silence.

This is it, thought Ted. *This is it.*

In front of him the pilot levelled off and made the first turn, sweeping the glider silently like some huge bat over the French countryside. Desperately, they searched for a landmark but there were none.

'Turn now' called the co-pilot measuring their progress with a stopwatch. They turned on his calculation for the final approach, knowing they could not go around again – it was certain they would be seen and fired at.

'Where is it? Where's the bloody canal? Can you see it?' the pilot called out anxiously.

'There. There it is. And the bridge.'

'Thank Christ.'

'Link arms.'

Ted linked his arms tightly through those of his neighbours and lifted his legs, knowing that the floor and his feet could disintegrate with the impact.

The glider hit the ground at ninety miles an hour and bounced back into the air. Inside, the men were lifted from their seats and crashed back. Through the open door, Ted could see silhouettes of trees flash past at a hair-raising speed. The pilots called to each other.

'We're going too fast. We'll hit the bloody bridge at this rate. Stream. Stream the chute.'

The brake parachute deployed and slowed them slightly. The glider hit the ground again, the wheels tore off and the glider bounced and slewed wildly across the ground, sparks flashing off the stony ground, and then they slammed into the barbed wire defences exactly as planned, just fifty yards from the bridge. The pilots still strapped into their seats, crashed through the crumpled remains of the glider's nose and landed unconscious in the darkness outside.

Inside the wreckage of the glider it was still and silent. Ted could smell freshly churned earth and crushed grass, but couldn't move and nor could anyone else. He thought he was back in the Seven Stars having taken a clubbing right hook to the head. But that hadn't happened, had it? Stunned, he wondered why he appeared to be lower than those opposite him. Outside, the glider sat with its port wing pointing into the air like a crippled bird.

Around them the other two gliders landed: one crashed into marshland and broke in half, trapping the men. And as Ted desperately struggled to recover, one of those men began to drown.

Come on Ted. Stay here and die. Get up. Get out.

It had only been seconds.

He stumbled to his feet. Where was the door? It was just wreckage. Men smashed through the glider and clambered out, their supreme fitness and training now taking over. Where was the major?

Outside it felt cool and quiet and he knew exactly where he was. Thank God they still had the element of surprise.

On the bridge, the two sentries had been walking up and down in the darkness, from one end to the middle. They would meet, turn around and repeat. They had been doing this for an hour, not even speaking now, just looking forward to a warm bed.

'Did you hear that? That crash?' The youngest whispered.

'Yes.'

'What was it?'

In the distance they could hear the dull thunder of bombs exploding and see searchlights hunting the sky and tracer flying upwards. The night was flickering with flame as Caen burned.

'One piece of the RAF that won't be going home.'

'What should we do about it Hans?'

'Nothing, unless you enjoy writing out reports.'

The sixteen year old deferred to his fellow sentry. After all, not only was Hans four years older, but he was also German. The youngster hadn't asked to be here, he had been conscripted from Alsace and like so many others in Occupied Europe, he hated Germans.

Around the two sentries men slipped silently through the darkness into their positions. Ted moved to the bank of the canal, squatted beside the major and automatically began to set up the radio. He felt calm and alert.

There was a moment's pause as men crept forward like shadows. Suddenly the silence was ripped open by the crump of their grenades exploding inside the concrete pillbox that defended the bridge, slicing and smearing the enemy inside. Immediately came the shouts of Englishmen launching themselves into battle with a terrifying violence, their boots thudding across the metal bridge, voices screaming battle cries, hunting and killing their enemy. Determined. Ferocious. Clinical. *Cry Havoc.*

The teenager turned in horror. His blood froze and he ran panic-stricken; shrieking.

'Paratroopers! Paratroopers!'

Hans pulled a flare pistol and fired it into the night sky covering everything in a strange flickering light. A burst of Sten gun fire cut him down. The air was now rent with a savage cacophony of shouts and screams, firings and explosions, as the men charged across the bridge and their stunned enemy attempted to fight back. From the far side of the bridge, a German machine gun opened fire and was answered by a long burst from a Bren gun, which raked the position and silenced it. Grenades exploded and men screamed as jagged metal tore into them. A British platoon officer leading the charge pitched forward, his body torn open by enemy bullets. Around him young German conscripts shocked by the ferocity of the attack either fled or died for the Fatherland. There was no alternative. From the bank opposite, Ted came under rifle fire and heard the bullets zip past his head. He ignored them, slipped on his headphones and waited, immersed only in the hiss of his radio set and its familiar smell of rubber and lacquer.

Out of the darkness a figure approached him from the bridge. Ted drew his pistol, cocked it and pointed at the middle of the shape.

'Halt.'

The figure stopped.

Ted spoke. 'V.'

'For Victory,' came the quiet reply.

'OK. Approach.'

The figure materialised, crouched before them and spoke to the major.

'Report from the Royal Engineers, sir. The bridge has been prepared for demolition but there are no explosives. It's safe.'

'Excellent. Well done.'

'Radio message sir.' Ted spoke calmly. 'It's Ham. The Germans are running. The canal bridge has been taken.'

'Any news from the river bridge?'

'No not yet sir.'

'OK. Keep trying.'

An eerie silence had now settled over the battle and smoke and the acrid smell of explosives drifted across the canal. From somewhere a man moaned.

'Message from the river bridge, sir. It's Jam. It's Jam sir.'

The two men looked at each other. Speechless for a second. Unable to grasp the enormity of the simple message.

'My God we've done it. We've bloody done it.'

The radio crackled again in Ted's ear.

'Casualty report sir. From the canal bridge. One platoon officer killed. The rest wounded.'

'Damn. Damn,' the major cried and punched into the earth, but he knew the senior NCOs would automatically take command. That's what he had trained them to do. 'OK. Send the success signal. Seven Para will be jumping now and they need to know the bridges are captured intact if they are to get here quickly.'

Ted checked the radio and started to transmit.

'Hallo Four Dog. Ham and Jam. Hallo Four Dog. Ham and Jam. Over.'

The radio remained silent.

'Hallo Four Dog. Ham and Jam. Hallo Four Dog. Ham and Jam. Over.'

Nothing.

'Come on. Come on.'

Around Ted, runners arrived with further messages. One glider had not landed at the river bridge. Nobody knew where it was but the bridge had been undefended. The major reorganised his company, checked casualties and distributed ammunition. Two men had been killed and several wounded, some on landing. He prepared his defensive positions against counter attack and looked into the sky. It was still dark but he knew as soon as dawn appeared they would be very vulnerable. Hopefully before then reinforcements would arrive. He touched Ted on his shoulder.

'Any luck?'

'Not yet, sir.'

'OK. Keep trying.'

'Hallo Four Dog. Ham and Jam. Ham and Jam. Hallo Four Dog. Ham and Jam Over. Hallo Four Dog. Ham and Jam. Ham and Jam. Hallo Four Dog… Ham and Bloody Jam! Where the hell are you?' Ted shouted into the indifferent night.

Ted stopped to readjust the radio. He had felt so calm during the battle, concentrating solely on his own duties. Any dark, uncertain thoughts had been swept away as soon as he had set foot on French soil and now they had done it! The lads had done it! Against all the odds, and so quickly – it was all over so quickly. All that training had paid off. They had never experienced combat before, but had dealt with the enemy efficiently, ruthlessly. They had slashed a severe wound in the enemy's side and he felt an immense pride. He wanted Florrie and Mick and Edie to know, just in case he would never get the chance to tell them. Now he wanted to see it through to the end. Pray God he made it.

He returned to transmitting, his voice confident.

'Hallo Four Dog. Ham and Jam. Ham and Jam. Over. Hallo Four Dog. Ham and Jam. Ham and Jam. Ham and Jam. Over.'

Just outside Caen, Panzer commanders waited impatiently. Their men and tanks were on full alert as reports came in of British troops in action around the Caen canal and river Orne bridges. Was this the invasion, or a commando raid, or even a feint to draw them away? They knew they had to move now in total darkness. At daybreak their tanks would be easy targets for naval shelling and the Allied aircraft that dominated the skies. But only Adolf Hitler could make that decision. Only Hitler could order the tanks into battle and he was asleep and nobody wanted to wake him.

At the bridge, the men pulled the mangled bloody remains of German soldiers from their trenches, fortified the positions, took their places, checked their own weapons and waited in the darkness, listening for the slightest sound. Those nearest could hear Ted's muffled voice still transmitting.

'Hallo Four Dog. Ham and Jam. Ham and Jam. Over.'

His voice pinpointed him as a target but he kept sending. He had been doing it for almost an hour now.

Nearby lay the body of the platoon officer, his boots protruding from beneath a groundsheet laid over him. Ted stopped for a moment and looked at them. They had only just been kicking a football. Ted had joined in the game. 'When was that?' he thought. 'Yesterday. Christ, was it only yesterday?' To Ted it felt like another lifetime. He felt a wave of intense sorrow sweep over him as if the man lying cold and still was his brother.

'Hallo Four Dog. Ham and Jam. Ham and Jam. Over.'

Less than two miles away, a young British wireless operator from 5 Para Brigade lay dead and unnoticed in a dark field, his chute half covering him. His 38 radio set had not been switched on. Ted's message never arrived.

As dawn broke, Ted carefully lifted his head and peered along the bridge. A tank attached to the local German force sat burnt out at the other end. The men had destroyed it in the night as it probed their defences. It had exploded with an enormous flash of light and sound sending ammunition spraying in all directions. Around him Ted heard the men whoop with satisfaction and relief. The tank driver lost both legs.

Ted thought about the others – Billy and Darkie and wondered how they had done. He let his mind wander for a moment.

He checked his radio for the umpteenth time as, around him, the battle continued to rage. Shells dropped incessantly and he knew they were surrounded.

Even though the men of 7 Para had arrived during the night, their hold was still precarious and they were running out of ammunition. What then? They would fight with fists and bottles and bricks. Just like a Saturday night in Deptford.

'We're going to move to the pill box,' the major declared.

Ted gathered up his radio and equipment.

'OK?'

Ted nodded.

'Let's go. On the double.'

The major ran, crouched over, with Ted right behind. A bullet hissed past Ted's face and thwacked into the ground just beyond him.

'Shit. Sniper!'

He ran as fast as he could, fear frantically pumping his legs as he waited for the next bullet to slap him to the ground like a moving target at a fun fair. Ping! Gone.

Both men reached safety.

'Christ that was close.'

'You alright?'

'Yes, sir.' Ted replied, breathing heavily.

Inside the pillbox it was gloomy and heavy with the metallic putrid stench of blood and gore. The bodies of three German soldiers lay stiffly, a dark stain around them and spattered across the concrete walls. Flies buzzed.

'OK. Grab his ankles.'

Ted looked down. The German lay on his back, his arms drawn up in front of his chest. Maybe this was his last desperate act to protect himself before the grenades exploded. His right cheek had been scooped out and his right eye was almost closed. His left eye looked at Ted from a dead white face, empty. His intestines had tumbled from a tear in his body and lay in a jumbled twisted heap in his lap, their juices soaking thickly into his uniform. Ted pulled the body outside. As he did so, the intestines moved and began to slip onto the ground. He felt sick. The major joined him, pulling a second body. Around them, the violent battering of explosions and crack of firing constantly filled their ears and minds.

Suddenly, somewhere outside of that, a strange wailing sound pierced Ted's brain.

'What's that sir?'

'What?'

'That sir. Listen.'

The sound started to skirl.

'That's bagpipes.'

From the other side of the canal came the sound of cheering and a long line of soldiers appeared led by a piper.

'It's the Commandos – from the beaches. At bloody last!'

From a nearby trench two bedraggled figures emerged, the taller man with a child's face punched the air with his rifle and whooped. The shorter man approached Ted.

'We done it Ted. We done it!'

It was Darkie, tears of joy running from bloodshot eyes down his grimy face, teeth gleaming in a wild grin. 'Me and Tinker were almost out of ammo, but we done it.'

The three men hugged each other, clumsily, but with love.

Ted felt hugely weary. He hadn't slept since the day before the briefing and now his strength, sustained by adrenalin and will power, ebbed away. He sat down.

The men slept and ate and listened to rumours.

'Be going home soon, surely? We're the coo de man. Must be other bleedin' bridges to attack. You heard anything Ted?'

'No mate. Major doesn't confide in me.'

Later that day they were ordered to advance towards the small villages just a few miles from the bridges using a farm cart to carry the heavy equipment, but with no horse – it had either bolted or lay dead and bloated in a nearby field. They arrived in darkness, cautiously moving silently through empty streets to their new positions, seeing dead paratroopers hanging from the buildings.

The German counter attack was vicious. Shells and mortar bombs rained down constantly upon them, shattering the buildings they sheltered in, making the earth shake and heave as they crouched helplessly in trenches with clods of earth and stones falling upon them. Tanks and infantry followed. They desperately fought them off. No longer did they have the element of surprise. No longer could they shock an unsuspecting enemy. They now soaked up this awful punishment. Now attacking. Now withdrawing. Day after day. Night after night. Killing and dying. Their casualties mounted terribly.

'Tinker.'

'Yes, Ted.'

'Come on mate, we've got a job to do.'

Tinker Bell's baby face looked up from the comparative safety of his trench. He had joined up when he was fifteen – lied about his age.

Now he really didn't want to move. Not out there. Inside, his body and mind jumped at every sound.

'Come on, we've got to get some supplies. We're taking the jeep.'

'We going by the crossroads, Ted?'

'Of course. Come on.'

'Yes, corporal.'

The men's hearing had become acutely sensitive to every noise around them. They could recognise the different sound that every weapon and every vehicle made, both their own and the enemy. They knew their enemy could do the same – they could certainly hear the distinctive sound of a jeep approaching and would know when it would arrive in the centre of a crossroads. They also knew how to drop a mortar bomb exactly in that centre.

'Crossroads coming up, Ted.'

Ted kept driving.

'Put your foot down, Ted.'

The jeep surged forward flat out, engine screaming. Tinker gripped the side of the open vehicle.

The first mortar bomb arrived six seconds too early and exploded in front of them. Ted slammed on the brakes and pulled the jeep off the road. It slewed round, hit the verge with a huge jolt and stopped. Both men leaped from the jeep as the next bomb was still in the air.

'Under the jeep, Tinker!'

Ted flung himself into the ditch and grasped the ground to him, desperate to pull it over his body. Around him explosions tore the air apart and metal sliced through tree trunks and branches above his head. Ted's thoughts raced with fear. *Please God don't let one fall on me. It will go straight through me and explode inside. No. Don't think. Florrie. Florrie. I love you Florrie.*

Suddenly there was silence. Ted raised his head slightly and listened: nothing. He turned over onto his back and looked upwards. Above him he could see the clouds moving, ignorant of the carnage below. It was so peaceful now that Ted felt he could be in his garden. He got to his knees and peered out of the ditch. The jeep seemed to be still in one piece – *Amazing.*

'Tinker. You OK? Tinker?'

There was no reply. Nothing except for a sound that froze his skin. The sound of an animal in torment.

Tinker lay next to the jeep. Unharmed by the attack but curled up like a baby, his hands between his thighs. The sound came from within him. Pitch-black pain from somewhere so deep, poured out of him. The sinews of his young mind had stretched and stretched until they had torn.

Ted pulled Tinker towards him, felt Tinker's body shaking violently and saw the tears and snot soaking on his face; looked into his dead eyes; heard his howl; held him like a father holds a helpless son.

'It's alright Tinker. It's alright.'

But Tinker was lost. They were all lost.

***

It was September when the exhausted ragged remains of D Company were relieved. The order came through to withdraw at night under the cover of darkness and Ted sat in his trench watching the seconds hand on his watch sweeping onwards: tick tick, tick tick. If he put his ear close, he could hear it ticking like his pulse, a bit faster maybe, although sometimes… He looked at the time: twelve thirty-three. Twenty-seven minutes to go. *Please God they will still both be ticking then. Please God I get out of here.*

The men returned to England, back to the barracks where it had all started. Ted opened the barrack room door and stepped inside. It was just as they had left it: clean, polished, immaculate, cold, silent and empty. He sat on the edge of his bed, exactly where he had sat bulling his boots with the others. *Small circles. Small circles.* Trying to recall the chatter and laughter, the smell of cigarette smoke, but the memory had been seared away.

The other men sat or lay on their beds. Nobody spoke. For every one bed that felt their weight and warmth, four felt nothing – just empty, their hospital corners still immaculate. Blankets still stretched as taut as drum skins, identical, impersonal, simply waiting for a fresh occupant.

No Billy – wounded and in hospital, and no Tinker – locked away, mind screaming silently. And all those others: gone. There would be few letters from home now.

'I'm going to the Naafi.' Ted stood up. 'Anybody coming?'

They walked together, close to each other.

***

On leave, Ted and Florrie made love passionately, frantically, until they were exhausted, making up for lost time, thinking this may be the last time, ever. Ted walked around carrying Oliver, talking endlessly to him; confiding in him, whispering.

'Sorry mate I have to go back soon. Might not see you again. You be a good boy. Look after your Mum, OK?'

'Let's take a photo of you both. No, outside in your uniform and with your beret on.'

Florrie knew the significance of the maroon beret and the Pegasus flash and glider badge on his arm and of the pride with which they were worn. She also wanted a photograph of them together, just in case.

When he left, she smiled bravely and waved Oliver's tiny arm goodbye.

'Bye Daddy. See you soon.'

Back at the barracks, new faces arrived and the training continued as hard as ever, but now the old hands never complained, not even Billy who returned with a livid scar across his skull.

'What's this all leading up to Ted? We attacking another bridge?'

'Don't know Billy. Got to be something big. Looks like we're going back again.'

***

Hundreds of gliders and tug planes filled the sky. In the daytime haze below them, the river Rhine glinted dully as they crossed it.

The glider pilot peered into the haze and said, 'Casting off. Can't see a bloody thing.'

Ted's glider fell earthwards and then lurched, buffeted by heavy anti-aircraft fire. This time there would be no surprise; no darkness to hide them. This time the enemy would be waiting. Through the open door he saw large tears suddenly appear in the glider's wing and the fabric start to rip away. Above his head, bullets ripped through the fragile craft and out the other side. He grabbed at his seat as the glider staggered through the explosions, feeling totally helpless.

Please God. Not up here. I don't want to die up here.

The glider hit the ground, bounced and slid to a halt.

'Get out! Get out!' Frantically they scrambled clear and an instant later, a German machine gunner raked the glider. The man beside Ted fell, a bullet through his eye.

'Look out, Ted!'

As Ted ran for cover, he stopped and looked up. Around him a thick smokescreen mixed with shell bursts and burning gliders choked him. Bullets hissed across the landing ground and men shouted and screamed. Gliders were still landing. Some in flames from end to end, hit by incendiary bullets. Others broke up in the air and torn bodies fell and slammed to the ground around him, smashing bone and skull and brain.

'Fu–ckinell Ted. Look at this.'

It was Billy. Before them a fully laden glider had smashed through a heavy barbed wire emplacement, like a cheese slice. Inside arms and hands and legs, torsos and heads lay in a bloody jumbled heap. The two men looked at each other in horror.

'Christ isn't that Jacko's head? Poor bastards. It's like a bleedin' butcher's shop.'

'Come on Billy. Need to catch up with the major.'

But yet another white hot image had been branded into Ted's soul forever.

FIVE

Ted, Russian Vodka and an Unexpected Return

> *'Who made the Law that men should die in meadows?*
> *Who spake the word that blood should splash in lanes?*
> *Who gave it forth that gardens should be boneyards?*
> *Who spread the hills with flesh, and blood, and brains?*
> *Who made the Law?'*
>
> Leslie Coulson

Ted found himself walking up the Hill purposefully and unsettled. It wasn't meant to be like this. Yesterday he had been at Bad Kleinen arranging duty rosters and watching the Russian soldiers camped across the river. They had met in a great clash of joy and dancing and vodka – a lot of vodka. Now they watched each other, coolly, suspiciously.

The message that his father was dying had been acted upon immediately.

'Ted there's a plane leaving Lüneburg in an hour. Leave everything. There's a jeep outside. You need to go *now*.'

The major held out his hand for Ted to grasp.

'Good luck. We'll see you back in England.'

'Thank you, sir.'

They saluted each other. Not an act of regulation but with respect and love.

And so Ted left his military family, but it wasn't right. He should be returning with the lads – those that were left – back again to the barracks where this had all started, together.

He knew there had been little hope of surviving, he had known that from D plus one. The bridges had been captured so quickly, but after that all hell had broken out: fierce brutal fighting, house to house, room by room, inch by inch. And then the terrible price paid in men's lives for punching across the Rhine into the enemy homeland.

Somehow he had been so lucky. A German bullet had smashed into his radio set and lodged there, inches from his flesh. He had picked it out – his bullet. It was meant for him. He had weighed it in his hand and then thrown it far away, as far as he could, with a laugh – triumph hiding fear.

'Jammy Ted. Bleedin' jammy.'

But there were many more angry lead hornets looking for him, he knew that. So far, they hadn't found him and he was still with the lads.

There was also the problem of the German staff car he had acquired and would have to leave behind. The Mercedes was in good condition apart from the bullet holes through which the wind whistled at speed and threatened to remove the entire windscreen. The interior had been immaculate when he had ambushed it, but now it was smeared with local mud and the odd fragment of bone although Ted had done his best to clean away the blood and brains of the German army driver. Locked in the glove compartment was a treasure.

''ere Ted, can I 'ave those nylons if yer don't make it?'

'For Christ sake Billy, you don't have to tell every bugger.'

'Sorry mate. Mum's the word.'

***

Ted looked down and saw the shadow of the aircraft taking him home skimming over the landscape, undulating, as if trying to smooth the tortured world below. It was so different from above. From here, meadow stretched into meadow, forest merged with forest, hill rolled into hill – green to brown to green to blue to purple. There was no separation. Below, streams whispered their long liquid messages towards throaty rivers and trees, rustled by breezes, chattered their meaning. Nature knew no national frontiers, no hate, no horror. But that was not Ted's experience. He had marched and fought across this land as part of the Allied spearhead. He had fought from the blood-soaked Rhine Crossing to the Baltic, some three hundred miles, one hard step after another. He knew that there, way below, every tree, every ditch, every wall, every building, every blade of grass was smeared with the congealed stain of fear and death; was marked with a thousand moments of oblivion; strewn with the final moments of men, but he felt little. He was alive and that was all that mattered.

Once he reached Victoria, the train had been held for him and the guard placed his hand on Ted's shoulder.

'Come on mate. Been waiting for you. On yer get.'

As the train steamed out of battered London, he knew he had to make his way directly to his parents' home to see if his father was still alive. But he also wanted to phone Florrie, to let her know and to hear her voice, her surprise. And he wanted to see his boys, especially Robert, born in the last year of the war and whom he had never seen. He had Florrie's photos of him, of course, and proudly showed the lads, but that wasn't the same. He took his beret off, sat back in his seat and tried to relax, but his mind twitched and jumped.

When they discovered that he was returning, the lads had crowded round him, shaken his hand and wished him good luck.

'Lucky bugger, Ted. Back to Blighty eh?'

But somehow he still felt as if he was letting them down by leaving them behind. Why was that? After all, his father was terminally ill, was going to die, and Ted never thought he would ever see his family again.

He wondered what his father was dying of – the telegram hadn't said. He tried to picture Mick's face but it kept moving and changing into Florrie's and Oliver's and Edith's and the major's. He wondered what Robert looked like. Life had been so simple up to now: kill the enemy, stay alive, but now his head reeled.

He looked out of the smeary window, trying to concentrate on where he was, and gradually he began to recognise places that he had known. He knew them alright, but now they seemed so insignificant, like places he had known once in a dream a long, long time ago.

When he arrived at his station, he moved quickly along the platform with the smell of coal in his nostrils, and bounded up the stone metal-lipped steps. Outside he moved to the nearest phone box, opened the heavy door and took out a handful of coins and notes. Damn it was all useless money, of course. He pounded his fist against the coin box in frustration. He had no choice but to walk.

He marched briskly through the town and soon began to climb the Hill, purposefully and unsettled. At the bay-fronted house, he clicked open the side gate and strode across the small concrete yard. From inside the dining room Edith saw the movement of khaki and the flash of maroon and her heart cried out.

They met in the kitchen, stopped and faced each other. Her face was pale and drawn, not daring to believe, but her dark eyes gleamed.

'Ted, oh Ted.'

She held him and wept.

'Hallo Mum.'

'You're home. You're not going...'

'No, Mum. The war's over. I won't be going back. The battalion will be following soon. So I'll be demobbed here. So, home for good.'

'Oh Ted.' She held him – her little boy – close at last.

He took her thin shoulders and gently moved her back. 'How's Dad?'

She gasped and her body slumped. 'He died yesterday, dear. Cancer. It was very peaceful.' She studied his face, but it betrayed nothing.

Another man dead. He had watched his comrades and his enemy die: suddenly, violently, slowly and in agony. Had watched their light slip away leaving empty ragged shells and he had waited for his turn. He had hoped it would be quick, but he had missed the last moments of his own father – Big Mick.

'When's the funeral?'

'Next week dear. The Co-op's doing it. You remember that Mr Hobbs. Such a nice man... I'm so sorry Ted... Now, sit down dear. Oh dear look at me. I must look a mess. Are you hungry? I wish you had let me know. I would have got something in – something you like. Would you like some toast dear and a nice cup of tea? Oh dear. I don't have any butter. Oh if only you had let me know. Ah but I do have some nice strawberry jam. You like that...' She paused, as if beyond her joy, she sensed something. 'Are you alright dear?'

He smiled. 'Toast and tea is fine, Mum.'

Ted moved into the dining room, removed his maroon beret with the silver hunting horn badge and rubbed the red weal out of his forehead. He loosened his tunic, sat in one of the two armchairs and looked around the room. The room looked back, small and dark and uncertain about this stranger. He had spent so much of his life in this room and he knew it to be full of memories and familiar things. Those memories should be flooding back, smiling at him, so pleased to see him. Isn't that what's supposed to happen? But they hid from him, they were wary of this man, this other man, this other Ted who still reeked of horror. He felt a quick shock of alarm. Maybe he should go back, back to the other world, the one he had been in only yesterday. Only yesterday. Back to the world of destruction where he felt more comfortable. He had become so skilled at dealing destruction out.

Don't be so ridiculous. You're home now. Home.

He just felt so strange being so divided. He closed his eyes and listened to the heavy silence that was broken only by the tiny sounds of Edith weeping in the kitchen and the ticking of the mantel clock. He knew he must phone Florrie but he fell asleep, exhausted.

He slept only for seconds, a minute maybe. It was a twitching sleep with half a brain alert as he had become used to. Yet he had dreamed.

He saw himself in the same room, much younger and he was looking for something hidden in an untidy drawer full of mementoes, something placed there by Edith. A child's school books and scraps of drawings, a tarnished christening spoon, football medals and beneath it all, a blue teething ring. He picked it up, turning it over and then balancing it in the palm of his hand. It had been his, Edith had told him with a smile. He had once held it between tiny fingers and placed it between his sore gums. He knew that for certain, but, of course, he had no memory. It was of a different time, a different world, a different Ted, but it had been real. He knew that and felt reassured.

The warm smell of toasted bread, of family breakfasts, drifted into his brain and woke him. Too late a stubborn switch flicked before he could stop it, and released a warm, dark brown wave that spread from his stomach, slipped over his chest like an old familiar pullover and stroked his face and eyes. The shock made him jump.

Come on Ted, it's OK, you're home now mate.

But something was wrong, something was missing. Where was it? He could not find the fear and terror that had kept him alive. His mind screamed within him.

No Ted, it's over. All over… Yeah? So where are the healing tears eh? Where are they? Christ they dried up long before I crossed the Rhine and watched gliders explode in the air, in flames from end to end, full of my mates. Watched them fall, their bodies torn and burning, thudding onto the hard ground too far below. Christ that sound, I still hear it. And that glider that crashed through barbed wire, into pieces, men and glider, just pieces. I never want to think about it. Never. But it comes at night when no one else is around. And I can't stop it. And I watched all this, grim and stony and only wanted to kill the enemy before they killed me. And I did.

He sat for a moment and then reached for the phone. He knew he had to call Florrie. It was a shock when he realised he couldn't remember the number.

***

Florrie flung herself at him with a force that made him step backwards. She pressed frantically against him, trying to merge into his body and to make the two of them one again. Her mouth sought every part of his face and neck leaving a feverish rash of lip prints.

'I never thought I would see you again.'

Tears softened her eyes, turning the sapphires into warm salty blue lagoons. Behind her stood Oliver, watching quietly, unaware of the moment.

'Hey, who is this?'

Ted crouched, smiling and held out his arms. His son moved uncertainly towards him and was swept upwards. *Oh at last. At last.* Ted thought as he felt his son's tiny body and for a moment he closed his eyes.

'This is Daddy. Your Daddy. He's come back for you.' Tears ran unashamedly down Florrie's face.

Oliver looked at the man holding him, turned towards Florrie and held out his arms for his mother.

They both laughed.

'He'll get used to you, Ted.'

'And where's Robert?'

'Asleep in his pram. Don't wake him up.'

Ted looked down at his baby son. He was so tiny, so vulnerable. Everything was now complete. Nothing could possibly go wrong.

***

That night he lay staring at the dark ceiling while Florrie clung to him, soaking him up. She slid her hand inside the gap in his pyjama trousers, wanting him, but found only a still soft bud.

'Sorry, I'm very tired.'

'Of course. Go to sleep my love.'

He turned and she followed his shape, arms wrapped around him. It was OK, she knew they would soon get back to normal and she drifted away across a warm blissful sea.

Ted stared at the luminous dial on the bedside clock and watched it move, slowly, on and on into the empty night.

SIX

Number 21 a Teddy Boy and Apple Pie

'That will live with you through all your tomorrows.'

The Best Years of Our Lives (1946)

Saturday

The young sun began to warm one side of the red tiled roof. Soon, with no hampering bumps of cloud, it would slide easily across the flat blue sky and nudge the shadows away from the little terraced house, revealing its green and cream brightness. Green and cream, always green and cream, ever since Ted had first painted it on after the war, and carefully, lovingly, every year that followed. It was their statement to passers-by and it spoke of rebirth, eternal hope, richness of spirit, although never of money.

Silver coloured numbers – two and one – shone from the front door which had already been unlocked by Ted. He did it automatically each morning and placed it on the latch, ready for the day's callers. There was never an assumption there might not be any.

Curtains were drawn with a sudden swish, leaving windows surprised and blinking in the bright sunshine and beads of dew hanging in neat rows on the wooden window ledges, twinkled before disappearing in the rising warmth. The back door unlocked with a metallic rattle while at the front, full milk bottles arrived with a solid chunk-chink. The empties, having had their rolled messages read and noted, were whisked away into crates with a clatter. On nearby branches, sparrows and the occasional blue tit sat waiting for a safe moment to pierce the silver foil and breakfast on the creamy tops.

Somewhere inside, muffled voices could be heard talking, calling and laughing. The house sighed to itself. All houses recognise those who live within them. They know those who treat them badly, those who slam the doors, knock the woodwork and those who sweep and polish and repair and carefully paint on another smart layer every spring.

The house had been conceived two decades or more before. The foundations had been established in a very different time. Then, every house knew its place in society and behaved accordingly. Here, these houses might be terraced, but this was no sprawling estate, no lower working class street, no stilted cul-de-sac. These were neat new homes with their own front and back gardens, garages to rent, telephones, inside toilets and were on a bus route – they even had a crossroad. They may not be detached or even semi, but their owners had still earned the right to treat their homes as their castles – the war had seen to that. They treated them with respect, with reserve and even with a little aloofness. They pulled up their drawbridges – nothing wrong with that.

The house also knew about those who visited. They should open and close the front gate carefully, walk directly to the front door, knock twice – not too loudly, not too aggressively, not too softly – and then take one step back and wait patiently. But to leave the front door on the latch? To encourage people to push it ajar? To just walk in and call out 'Coo-ee. Anybody there?' – oh dear.

It was the weekend now, and Ted was preparing breakfast like he always did. No work today; no catching the bus to the offices in the Dockyard.

The Dockyard had not been planned. He had returned to the family bookmaking business after the war, but in a moment of cruel irony, jockey Tommy Lowrey had steered the grey, Airborne, first past the post by a length in the 1946 Derby. The horse, with no form at all, had caught the imagination of the public who remembered the exploits of the Airborne Forces in World War Two, including of course Ted and had backed it in droves. It had won at fifty-to-one and half the bookmakers in Britain went bust, including the family business.

Nonetheless, Ted felt comfortable in his new clerical job. It wasn't so different from the family business or D company's office and he was surrounded by men and women, many of whom had served during the war and knew the score. It hadn't been easy after the war to get work and, working in a naval dockyard, most of his new workmates had been in the Royal Navy and spoke a strange nautical language.

'So Brownjob, eh Ted?'

'Pardon?'

'You know. Pongo. Army.'

'Oh. Yes. Yes. Army. What about you?'

'I was in the Andrew mate. Destroyers. Out of Chats. Right here.'

'Sounds rough.'

Ted could talk to this man, share a tiny bit.

'Had its moments Ted… anyway you'll probably feel a bit adrift now you've gone outside. Think we all felt that, but you'll soon get your bearings. Good men here. Most of them just wanna quietly get on with it, you know. Just watch out for the Ruperts.'

'Ruperts?'

'Yes, naval officers. Well ex-navy now. Picking up all the plum management jobs of course and still barking out orders as if we're dodging U-boats in the Atlantic. They'll learn.'

So nothing's changed much, thought Ted ruefully. Maybe in a year or two he would start looking elsewhere, somewhere with more opportunity, a more senior post, but for now he was home safe and he had Florrie, Oliver and now little Bobby.

They had always wanted a companion for Oliver – a brother or sister. On leave after D-Day, their lovemaking became mechanical and frantic; pleasure was sacrificed for propagation. Neither spoke of their fears, but afterwards they had held each other silently. They both knew Ted would be sent straight back.

He had missed their births. 'I was a bit busy,' he used to say, but now he would pick them both up, feel their innocence and look at them in sheer wonderment. They gave him some hope. Just when the world was in darkness and tearing itself apart, they had arrived. He vowed to do everything in his power to give them a good life. Now that he was home, he would work as hard as he could, even if he was surrounded by ex-matelots.

He remembered at the end of the war, the lads had often talked about getting home. What they would do once demobbed.

'First thing, I'm going darn me local boozer an' drink it bleedin' dry. For a week. Wot about you Billy?'

'First fing? Nah. Soon as I see me missus, second fing I'm gonna do is put me bags darn.'

Nobody had thought for a moment there might be a problem in changing overnight from a programmed killing machine into a normal sane civilian.

As head of the house, he was always up first. In winter there was no heating unless you made some. The alarm would shake Ted awake, body warmly cocooned, face frosted. 'Just five minutes more,' he would tell himself over the tick tock of the alarm. 'Come on. Up you get,' he would insist. Then came his shivery rush into a thick dressing gown. He would tie the cord tight and wait for the warmth to wrap around, slippers on, feet already chilling.

Downstairs, the dining room fireplace waited, cold and anxious. The grate was already laid with newspaper and sticks and nuggets of coal. Kneeling, he'd scrape a match, so loud in the morning stillness, and fill his nostrils with the sulphur fumes. He would carry the fragile yellow flame carefully, slowly, between large fingers, protecting it with his other hand and offer it to the crumpled paper. Sentences would char and writhe silently as the flame moved across them. Blackened paragraphs and fragments of yesterday's faces would break off and float slowly up the chimney. Still kneeling, he would rub his cold hands, waiting for the fragile flame to pop and roar into red life and push the cold smoky air around him away. It was the only heating in the house.

'Is it warm yet Dad?'

It was Bobby. Dressing himself under the blankets.

'Not yet son. Another ten minutes.'

***

In summer it was easy and he welcomed the warm solitude before the world woke up, when he could be still and alone. And today the weather was going to be hot.

He enjoyed breakfast. In the drowsy rooms above they could hear him cheerfully bustling around to the rattling and clinking of plates, bowls, mugs and cutlery. Sometimes he would sing to himself in a warm tenor voice. 'Da da deee…da da da da da deeee da dah da.'

Soon he had shaken a new bottle of milk to distribute the cream evenly before the first rush of cornflakes and to prevent arguments, and was sawing neat slices from a large white loaf. The grill was heating and the kettle beginning to whisper, when he heard the bright clink of the wrought iron front gate. *Someone's early*, he thought.

'Coo-ee. You there?'

He didn't look up.

'Flo-ree, it's Joan.' He aimed his call towards the bedrooms and bathroom.

'Morning Ted. Making breakfast?'

Ted didn't answer directly. Apart from the obvious fact that he was doing just that, he felt a little wary of Joan. It wasn't just her flirtatious ways that worried him (mind you, Cyril didn't seem to mind that much and sometimes he appeared to encourage her, but maybe he had just given up – anything for an easy life). No, it was more than that. Florrie was always on about her and Cyril, about private things, and he didn't want to know about that.

'She won't be long.'

He placed the bread onto the grill. No, it was good really that Joan and Florrie were neighbours; friends. They probably helped each other and were close with their little secrets. They nattered away, the way women do. It was good for Florrie, she was a bit down at the moment – a bit moody, a bit sharp with him. He didn't really know what was wrong with her.

He peered at the bread under the grill. It was browning nicely.

Joan stood in the hallway with her hands clasped in front of her as if she was waiting outside the headmistress's office. She had put on a few pounds in recent years that had curved her beanpole frame slightly. Not generously, but enough for her to drop her neckline by another inch. She liked to share. Joan had also coloured her hair after discovering a single grey hair that she thought shone like a beacon. Maybe she had dyed it too dark, because it now looked at odds with her pale complexion. Black liner accentuated her soft brown eyes and they, together with her full red lips, seemed too big for her face, but in the mirror she could still see Scarlett O'Hara. Unfortunately Cyril frankly didn't seem to give a damn. Maybe it was time for a change, maybe Scarlett was old fashioned now.

She watched Ted in the kitchen, busy but apparently ignoring her. She wanted him to like her as a neighbour – just as a neighbour. Although he did occasionally appear in her dreams. She wondered why he was so cool to her. She had never done anything wrong. She wondered if he fancied her and her stomach fluttered briefly. She banished the thought – he was devoted to Florrie. Florrie was so lucky.

Florrie arrived from upstairs like a whirlwind – grinning and smelling of soap and hot water.

Ted looked up. *Well, Florrie you seem a lot better now*, he thought.

'Morning Florrie.' Joan smiled. Her hands unclasped. 'Do you want to come round? For a coffee? Now…? Soon…?'

The word *please* hung desperately in the air.

Ted crunched into his toast.

'Of course, Joan. Just have some breakfast first. Can't stay long today. Still got to do the shopping.'

'Oh me too. I'll come with you.' Her painted face lit up from within like a lantern. 'Is that OK Ted? Will you be looking after the boys?'

Ted waved a hand, chewing toast.

'OK? See you later Florrie. Bye Ted,' she said, her voice quieter for him.

The front gate gave a clunk as Joan left. It was a different sound from the clink it made when visitors arrived, almost as if it was sad to see them go.

Ted and Florrie stood looking at each other. Ted raised his eyebrows slightly and shook his head.

Florrie retorted fiercely. 'She was a good neighbour when...'

'When what?'

'When you weren't here.'

For a second she wanted those bleak days back.

The gate clinked again. There was a pause and the front door opened, slightly. Joan's eye and some dark curls appeared cautiously around it.

'Sorry, me again. Baker's here,' Joan announced in a singsong voice.

'Thanks Joan.'

'That's alright Florrie. See you soon?'

'Yes. OK. Byee.'

Outside, the Co-op van was waiting – it was early. The large black horse that pulled it, occasionally tossed his head, making the metal parts of his harness sing sharply, but otherwise he stood still, one hind hoof raised slightly, his eyes shielded by thick leather blinkers. A mother held up her small child to stroke the horse's smooth flank and the child started back as the dark skin twitched under the feel of tiny fingers. The horse snorted and now they both stood back, uncertain – mother laughing, child concerned.

'Steady,' the roundsman growled lightly and slipped a nosebag around the horse's head.

'Morning Ron.'

'Morning Mrs T.'

'Cuppa Ron?'

Florrie always invited the roundsmen in. They would sit awkwardly on the creaky high backed chairs in the dining room, wearing their light brown overalls. Leather satchels, containing a weight of coins, would be slung around their shoulders and they carried wallets that would consume pound and ten shilling notes with a fluid twist of their wrists like a magician. They would gulp down their drink as politely as possible, anxious to resume their rounds.

'Not today thanks. Need to get on,' he smiled back.

Florrie passed over her shillings and pence. They had stood on the mantelpiece, waiting patiently, piled neatly atop a scrap of paper marked "Baker" in grey pencil.

'Anything extra today?'

'Think we might have a cake each. Come on boys.'

Ron opened the wooden doors at the rear of the van and released the warm sweet smell of freshly baked bread and cakes. It saturated nostrils, engulfing mouths with a watering frenzy. With the pride of a jeweller, he slid out a wooden tray, full of magical glittering cakes, each jostling for greedy attention. What a deliciously awful, delightfully agonising, impossible choice. Plump golden doughnuts glistened with a white frost and a smudge of darkness that indicated sticky, red jam, waiting to ooze out, giving a moustache of sweetness to lick away and then to lick in memory for hours after.

Jam tarts – round, glossy, red, yellow and green – looked like pools of sweet colour surrounded by battlements of crumbly pastry. Regimented rows of vanilla slices gleamed, each with their secret pattern of icing flowing perfectly across each pale top. And between, a yellow custard wedge, so soft and yielding to a gentle fingertip, that somehow stood firm until you bit into it, causing a desperate yellow custard-slide that covered faces, hands, shirts and sometimes even the tip of a shoe.

Such beauty. Such greed, thought Oliver.

As usual, the boys couldn't make up their minds. Florrie stepped in. 'Five vanilla slices please Ron. Then there won't be any arguments.'

'There you are Mrs T.'

Florrie paid.

'Git up.'

The horse strained forward, took the weight and clattered off slowly, on his own, toward the next stopping point, where he would wait patiently for Ron to catch him up.

Florrie placed two of the slices onto a plate, then into a brown paper bag and announced that she was going to see Joan and that she wouldn't be more than ten minutes. Everybody knew she would.

'What about your breakfast, Florrie?'

'I'll have it at Joan's.'

'But I've got it ready for you now.'

'You have it Ted.'

'Can we have our slices now, Mum?'

'No you can't. They're for tea.'
'Owah.'

The front gate clunked and she took the twenty paces to her destination. It could have been Timbuktu. It might take just as long for her to get back.

Ted looked annoyed, slid her toast onto his plate, poured his tepid tea into the sink and took her cup. He also looked a little worried.

***

'I was sure there was a cake fork at the back of that drawer.'
'Oh don't worry Joan, a normal fork'll do. And a knife.'

Florrie placed her slice in the centre of a light blue plate. It looked so nice there.

'You start Florrie. I'm just getting the tea ready.'

She needed no further bidding. Time was racing on and she hadn't had any breakfast. She stopped occasionally to dab the corners of her mouth, all the while rounding up errant crumbs like a pastry sheep dog.

Joan brought the tea in and sat watching her.

'Aren't you having yours Joan?'

'Later,' she said as a large tear rolled onto her cheek and halted there.

'Joan. Whatever's the matter?'
'Oh nothing.'
'Nothing? It doesn't look like nothing.'
'Oh it's just Cyril.'
'Cyril? What has he done to you?' Florrie pushed her plate away fiercely as she spoke.

'Oh nothing. Huh. That's the trouble.' She laughed strangely and wiped the tear away. 'Sometimes I just don't know who he is any more. You know – moody, withdrawn. Used to be such a laugh. We used to go to dancing at the Pav, every Saturday night… But not now.' She tried to stifle a sob. 'No interest. Not much in me either… you know.' She paused and looked away into her back garden and it became misty again. From inside her sleeve she took a small hanky and blew her nose loudly. The hanky had her initial on one corner. 'And that used to be so good. You know.'

'Yes.' Joan had made little secret of her and Cyril's activities in the bedroom – no explicit details, that would be wrong but lots of saucy innuendo and you could always tell by her jaunty walk and the way her slim hips moved and her eyes sparkled. Florrie always envied her that. She would never tell her, of course. She just grinned knowingly in the right places.

'Oh Joan, I'm sorry.'

'Not your fault is it?' she replied sharply, words aimed at her husband. She sniffed.

'I've asked him if it's me and he says no. You know… quite certain… but I don't know what it is.'

Her scarlet-tipped fingers tucked the hanky away.

'Is it about Jon?'

'Jonathan?'

'Yes. The fact he wasn't here. Couldn't save him. Must have been awful for him. And you know what they're like – men.'

'Don't know. Maybe. We never talk about it.'

'No?'

Oh. Not the only one then, Florrie thought.

Another tear fell and disappeared into Joan's sleeve, leaving a black mascara trail on her cheek as if her dark inner anguish was spilling over.

'Oh Joan,' and Florrie gently rubbed her arm.

Joan dabbed her face smearing it with black smudges. For a second Florrie saw herself sitting on a wall not so far from where they were now, herself holding a handkerchief, streaked with tears and sweat and smoke. What a long way both women had come and yet at times they seemed to have travelled no distance at all, after all that. It's not fair. Not bloody fair.

Joan was speaking but her words slipped past Florrie.

'Sorry, Joan. I was miles away.'

'I said how lucky you are – to have Ted. Even if he doesn't like me,' Joan sniffed.

'Of course he likes you. He's just a bit old fashioned, that's all. Bit shy.'

'Does he. Really?' Joan said, not quite believing, but her watery eyes lit up.

'Course he does. Always saying how nice you look.'

'Really.'

'Yes. Course.'

'He's such a strong man your Ted. A good man. And I bet he's very attentive,' she smiled knowingly.

Florrie felt a shock hit her in the middle of her chest. For a moment she couldn't speak. She took a sip of tea, hoping that its warmth would soothe her and give her time. She hoped Joan hadn't noticed.

'Oh he's alright,' she finally answered.

But he wasn't.

The man that had returned safely from the war was her husband, of course he was, she knew that. However, after the initial euphoria, after she had stopped looking at him in amazement, stopped purring at the sound of his voice, stopped telling everybody she met, even strangers – after that, slowly time had ticked on towards the everyday and she began to realise that her husband was another man, one that she didn't really know, didn't understand and even disliked at times. She had taken him out to meet friends and relatives. She had been so proud with him on her arm as she smiled up at him and felt the strength and comfort of his body brushing hers, but he had been reserved. He had almost been shy in their company and then at times angry, sarcastic at their questions and soon their trips stopped. They rarely went out anymore, and might as well have been sleeping in separate beds. Where had that gentle, strong man gone? He had left one day and never come back. Thank God for the boys.

Joan was drinking her tea. She seemed better now. 'Thank you Florrie. So good to talk about these things isn't it.'

'What we need is a good holiday. Have you ever had a holiday Joan? You and Cyril?'

'No never. Can't afford it. How about you?'

'No. Need to find a holiday where you don't have to pay.'

Both women drank in silence.

'Do you remember that film we saw Joan? 1946 I think. It was about three men coming home from the war – Americans. One had hooks instead of hands. Oh what was it called?'

'Oh yes, I remember. It was on at the Regent. Ted and Cyril didn't want to go... Oh who was in it... You know... er... Andrews. Dana Andrews. That's it. Dana Andrews. Ooh I thought he was lovely.'

'Do you remember when the man with the hooks played the piano? A duet. It was a duet. They were laughing on the screen, but it made me cry.'

'Me too Florrie. Thank God we were in the dark.'

Both women laughed and then sat quietly.

'Do you think that's what the problem is? With Cyril? Joan?'

'What no hands? Might as well be. He doesn't use 'em much!'

'No, not that. But you remember how they couldn't get used to being home – after the war? One of them, the man with the hooks, I remember, was followed by children. Just curious – you know how kids are and he smashes his hooks through a window at them, straight through. He shouts at them to go away. "*Stop looking.*" He's so upset. I've never forgotten that.'

'What did the kids do Florrie? I don't remember that bit.'

'Oh they just ran away. Bit frightened. Didn't understand of course... But do you think that's what the problem is. The war?'

'No, surely not. Cyril came back without a scratch. Same as Ted didn't he? He wasn't disabled. Fit and well and surely they would tell us wouldn't they?'

'S'pose so Joan. S'pose so.'

'You're a good friend Florrie.'

Joan stroked her neighbour's arm.

A loud rumbling crash echoed through the room.

'Quick, coalman's coming. See you later Joan.'

Florrie ran to her house, leaving her own front gate wide open.

'Quickly, move the mats,' she ordered urgently. 'Close the doors and windows. Clear the way. Oliver, count the sacks.'

All hands dashed swiftly to move mats and rugs from the onslaught of black boot prints. Inner doors and windows were closed against the threat of invading coal dust and the top lid to the concrete coal bunker in the back yard was quickly removed. At the same time, the access opening at its base was closed. Oliver stood nearby to watch the spectacle and to count the number of sacks piled empty after each thunderous avalanche into the bunker. It was not unheard of for a coalman to deliver short from time to time.

The coalman was small and wiry. He didn't seem to have the strength needed to lift and then carry the huge sacks of coal. He wore a leather jerkin over a jacket, baggy trousers and a filthy flat cap – all shining with ground-in dust. Every part of his clothing, hands and face were coloured black, right down to his large boots.

By the time he had returned to his lorry from knocking on the front door, turned his back, seized the corners of the open sack with both hands and pulled the enormous shape onto his back, there was no going back. The sheer weight propelled him forward at a quick trot, through the open front garden gate, into the house with a clatter, along the hallway, through the kitchen, through the back door, bearing right and with a deft movement, crashing the open end of the sack into the gaping mouth of the bunker and pouring the contents with a roaring tumble into the blackness. Little plumes of black dust arose from this mighty collision until the bunker was full to bursting. Lumps of black gleaming coal protruded jaggedly upwards.

During this entire time the coalman uttered not a single word, only nodding in response to the 'Thank you, coalman,' that followed his departure, leaving the smell of the mines drifting behind him.

Soon the rumble of coal thunder slowly faded along the road and Ted took a broom and began to sweep up the dust left behind in the yard.

'Morning Ted. Alright mate?' The voice boomed across several gardens.

'Morning Harry. Fine thanks.'

'Florrie alright?'

'Yes. Fine.'

'And the boys?'

'Yes. They're OK.'

'Growing up fast, eh?'

'Certainly are. Oliver's eleven now. Bobby's just eight.'

'Fine boys.'

'Yes… Helen. How's Helen?'

'Yeah she's fine thanks.'

Ted rested on his broom and faced Harry Smith, leaning on their adjoining fence.

Harry was muscular. His receding blonde hair was always Brylcreemed and swept back from his forehead in slick thin comb lines. When he remembered, his hand would slide across them, checking their sleekness and then slip down the nape of his neck for comfort. Maybe he was also looking for new growth. He never found any.

From a distance his pale eyebrows seemed to vanish into his face and his blue eyes, unframed, would advance eerily towards you. His voice was loud, too loud for he joked, cursed and shouted all day with a gang of stevedores and then brought it home with him. This camaraderie and the joy he had for the river and the sea – their smell, taste and moods – were in his blood and had been for centuries ('Plenty of Smiths along with Nelson mate') and his first and only ambition had been to join the Royal Navy.

On his right arm he wore a red heart and blue anchor tattoo ('Did it when I was a lad. Bit pissed') and it wouldn't have mattered except that he had never joined the Royal Navy. He'd been placed in a reserved occupation and had spent the war unloading merchant ships.

Nowadays, the tattoo always remained hidden – it didn't seem right to show it somehow. But he was a popular man and it was to Harry you came if you wanted a bottle of Scotch on the cheap or a few dented tins of pineapple. 'Perks mate.'

Ted had a lot of time for Harry and knew of his ambition to join the navy; knew of his frustration, maybe guilt, and knew of the tattoo on his arm. Ted also knew that he had saved two lives, which was more than he had ever done, although Harry would never have talked about it. Salt of the earth was Harry. In many ways he reminded him of Billy: loud, ducking and diving and strong.

No, there was only one Billy. Billy had blagged his way across Europe, causing chaos to friend and foe alike. Ted tried to remember the nickname that the lads had given him to shut him up? *Oh yes. Nick or Nicks or maybe Nix. No, not Nix, that didn't make sense, although I never saw it written down. You don't write nicknames down, that's their power, they are attached by common consent, carried by word of mouth and once attached are impossible to remove (except by the same common consent) and in this case it was a gentle reminder: Billy mate, we've got you sussed.*

Newcomers – fresh faced recruits – sent to replace the fresh faces now stiff and cold, often made the mistake of addressing Billy by his nickname, just to be friendly. They thought that it was his real name, and were taken aback by the torrent of angry abuse.

'Don't you fuckin' call me that. I ain't no bint.'

The old hands looked on, grinning silently.

'And I ain't no iron 'oof either.'

Billy would either storm off or sit in a rare state of silence, both of which had the desired effect.

The newcomers would be bemused.

'What did I say? What was that all about? Why Nick?'

'Well, it's short for "knickers".'

'Knickers?'

'Yeh, you know. Up and down like a pair of wren's knickers. Up and down – his stripes. Get it? Private to lance jack to full corporal to sergeant to corporal to lance jack to private. Billy's been promoted and busted more times than I've had 'ot dinners.'

Good old Billy. Mind you that was nothing to the language he summoned up on each of the three times he was wounded. Three times – can you imagine? Pity we couldn't have bottled that and fired it back at Jerry.

Ted often called them up – the lads – in his dreams. Two to four, when the night was at its darkest. When his mind slipped its collar, shook itself and wandered off on its own dark journey. He called them up as he had done so many times as Company clerk on an issue of pay or leave or duty. They stood before him, to attention, chests out, shoulders back, faces impassive and thumbs in line with the seams in their trousers. "Yes corporal. No corporal." They never smiled. Why didn't they smile, his ghosts?

Did they blame him for surviving? Should he have done more night patrols? Cleared more shattered buildings, hunted for more shadows that might destroy him? Not known fear? Not wanted to run away? Should he too be cold and unsmiling and drifting in the night?

Sometimes he couldn't remember them all and tossed and turned in his sweaty sleep, in his desperate hunt, mumbling the names out of his brain. Sometimes this dream world turned to blood and he called out desperately. Perhaps he could save them this time. He never could. *But I must go on trying. I must.*

'It's alright love. Wake up. Come on wake up. It's just another nightmare.'

'Sorry.'

He licked his dry lips.

'It's OK now. It's OK. What was it about to upset you so?'

'Can't really remember.'

Pray God it never escapes.

By day, awake, he sometimes saw them: a snapshot in the distance, a sudden reflection flashing in a shop window.

'Dixie. It's Dixie.'

A quicksilver leap of joy. Then the prickle of pain.

No of course not. No. Dixie is still in that trench that took a direct hit. He's in France somewhere. We couldn't find much of old Dixie so we simply filled it in.

And all the while the street crowd moved around him, brushed past him, ignored him, couldn't see him or see into him, didn't understand and couldn't understand. *Better to keep away from them. Have nothing to do with them. Better to count ghosts.*

'Going to the match this afternoon, Ted?'

Harry liked Ted. He also held him in great respect: an Airborne soldier, a war hero. Harry told his mates about his next-door neighbour and they listened respectfully. Okay so Ted was reserved, modest, and said nothing about his experiences and Harry wanted so badly to hear about them, but knew he couldn't ask. Still, it was natural. Now safely home, Ted wanted only to relax, take it easy, get back to normal, and relish his life with Florrie and their boys.

'Who they playing Harry?'

'Swindon Town.'

'No... I've got to look after the boys.'

'Helen'll look after them, she would love that. Oh come on Ted. Do you good to get out.'

Harry was surprised at the prickle of annoyance that flickered over Ted's face. Maybe he was shouting again. Helen was always telling him about it. 'Harry you're not in the middle of the River Medway now, I'm only three feet away.'

'Come on mate.' His voice softened. 'All the lads are going – from work, you know, George and the others. Have you met George? Lives in the next street. Should be a good game and a few pints after. Yeah OK, I know you don't drink but it'll be a good laugh. What yer say?'

Out with the lads again. Harry was a good man but still he couldn't be allowed in. *But out with the lads again?* 'I'll talk to Florrie. When you leaving?'

'Half an hour mate. Half an hour.'

Florrie was sitting in the dining room writing a shopping list.

'What do you fancy for Sunday roast? Another nice piece of English beef? Or English lamb or pork? We haven't had pork for a while. Some nice crackling.'

Florrie always insisted on English produce not on the grounds of flavour or even price, but simple patriotism. We had won the war hadn't we? She might occasionally relent and buy New Zealand lamb - at least they were in the Commonwealth.

'Whatever you like love, you decide. Look, Harry has asked me to go to the match with him.'

She looked up, eyes sparkling. She liked football. She didn't understand most of it, but she loved the energy and passion and colour and noise. It made her grin a lot. 'I'll come.'

'Thought you were going shopping with Joan?'

'Oh we can make do with that piece of beef left over in the pantry – have it cold. Joan won't mind.'

Ted grimaced. 'Yes, but all the lads are going. Harry's mates from work.'

'That's alright. Long as they keep the language down.'

'We'll have to stand.'

Her sparkle began to crystallise. 'Don't you think I can stand up for an hour and a half then?'

'Yes of course. But you may not be able to see very well.'

They looked at each other.

'OK love, you go. You're right, can't have cold beef for Sunday dinner. Enjoy yourself.'

Florrie's face showed no sign of her hurt as yet another drop of cold water dripped into her stomach.

***

Florrie and Joan stood on the platform of the 32 bus as it glided to a halt near the Victorian town hall. Florrie jumped down and turned to help Joan.

'I don't know why you insist on wearing that.'

Joan wriggled up her long pencil skirt, turned and reached for the pavement with one high heel. Scarlett O'Hara had been replaced by Sophia Loren – it had been coming for some time.

'And those shoes.'

'Cost me sixty nine and eleven in Dolcis.'

'Didn't know you had them.'

'Had them for ages but kept them in their box.'

'In their box?'

'Yes. Just liked looking at them – all new and perfect. Not every day you get a pair of new shoes. Wonder who we'll meet,' Joan said, already scanning the crowds around her.

Florrie strode off with her neighbour click-clack-click-clacking beside her. Soon they reached the turning into the busy High Street and, to Joan's relief, slowed against the shoppers bobbing on an incoming tide towards them, past Woolworths, past George Carter's the hatters, past Stones radio shop and the Discharged and Demobilised Sailors and Soldiers Club.

'I've got to get a few things in David Grieg's but shall we treat ourselves first? I'm starving. Only had a vanilla slice.'

'Oh I don't know Florrie.' Joan smoothed her hips. 'Maybe just a cup of tea?'

Florrie smiled to herself. Despite Joan's concern for her figure, she knew she had the appetite of a stoker and could consume copious amounts with little impact.

'Well actually, I was thinking of a nice piece of fried cod or rock salmon with chips and bread and butter with lashings of salt and vinegar and ketchup and a cup of tea or a glass of Tizer along at Whittaker's. You didn't have fish yesterday did you?'

Joan's eyes gleamed and she licked her pale painted lips. 'No, and it would save cooking tonight *and* there's that nice looking waiter in there.'

'What about Cyril?'

'Oh there's always a tin of soup.'

'No. I meant the waiter.'

'What he don't know won't hurt him.'

'Come on then.'

'Can you slow down a bit?'

Florrie enjoyed being with Joan although at times she felt like the older of the two. She was always such fun despite the terrible tragedy that had fallen out of the skies almost thirteen years ago. It was strange how it had selected them – just bad luck really. You could have forgiven Joan for retreating from the world after that and becoming bitter. Many people would. You just don't know how you would react after a thing like that, but Joan hadn't retreated, in fact now she seemed determined to make every day count. 'Oh Florrie, look.'

Ahead of them two young sailors were approaching: tall and bright in their square rig uniforms, faces tanned by overseas duty. They moved briskly, their confidence cutting a bow wave through the grey mass of shoppers. Their youth shone through their tight blue serge jumpers. Around their caps a ribbon read "HMS Daring".

'Ooh daring,' Joan said moving her hand to her hair, licking her lips again, smiling and attempting to wiggle.

Think Sophia Loren Joanie.

The two men smiled back and one of them winked as they brushed past. Joan could smell their freshness and vitality and a stab of excitement caught her as she concentrated hard on not stumbling.

She looked back. She knew she wasn't supposed to. The sailors didn't and she could see them laughing to each other before they disappeared. She knew they were laughing about her.

'Did you see that? The dark haired one winked at me and he was gorgeous.'

'Yes, Joan.'

'What were the two stripes on his arm?'

'Good conduct stripes.'

'Good conduct! No good to me then.'

'Oh Joan. Come on, or everything will be sold.'

Some people were just out for a walk, wandering, seeing what they could see, meeting and chatting. Others moved from shop to shop, queuing and buying, looking for a bargain from the butcher to the baker to the greengrocer, smiling at the pencil stub stuck behind the assistant's ear for additions on a soiled cuff. Some were bustling, concerned about catching their bus home or getting the dinner on: meat and two veg with tinned peaches and Ideal milk and a Wagon Wheel or maybe two ounces of banana splits in a paper bag for the kids. Everybody dressed in greys and browns and black – practical, nothing smart or fashionable because there wasn't much smart and fashionable to be had. The occasional splash of a white collar and the muted reds and blues of shop signs against the tired grey buildings could have placed them all in a huge Kitchen Sink painting.

The two women continued towards Whittaker's at the far end of the High Street. Normally this journey would not have taken very long, but today their progress was much slower. The crowds were larger and Joan's heels were higher. Suddenly, something happened somewhere in front of them. They could not tell what, but the mood that was strolling happily along with them, had taken on a serious face. The crowd, like pack animals, sniffed anxiously on the air and the morning buzz stuttered and slowed. Now the grey masses became silent, flocked together and stared.

There, right before them, and with no warning, blew a gale force tempest of change. They felt its wind strike their eyes and ruffle their minds. Challenge strode there defiant, knuckle-dustered and dangerous. A swaggering sip of things to come, saturated in a crazy palette of colour like a degenerate peacock. Both women stood rooted to the spot, fascinated, and gasped in the moment. It was as if somebody had suddenly splashed pure colour onto their comfortable grey-brown world. They tried hard to comprehend how shocking, how exciting, how ridiculous, how brave, how arrogant, how scary this all was.

He wore a long sky blue drape jacket with strips of black velvet at the collars. His matching drainpipe trousers ended just above the ankle, allowing a flash of shocking pink sock. A pristine white shirt shone from within a brocade waistcoat and a black bootlace tie hung from his throat. Thick black hair and long curling sideburns, shiny and sculptured with Brilliantine, mocked the short back and sides of the onlookers and his quiff bounced gently in time to the soft crêped footsteps of his brothel creepers.

'Don't look,' hissed Florrie as if the Teddy Boy was Medusa. He prowled past like a big cat freed from his cage – fascinating and dangerous. The gawping crowd waited for him to turn and consume them with a ghastly roar, but he ignored them and soon disappeared from their sight into the future.

'Is that wot we won the bleedin' war for? Excuse my French ladies, but I ask yer.'

''E's got medals 'e has.' His wife nodded in her husband's direction. 'Medals.'

The pair moved away, the man still muttering under his breath. 'Wot is the world coming to?'

'They're called Teddy Boys now. Saw it in the paper. Yeah, costs a small fortune, yer know, all that gear. They have 'em made special.'

A younger couple with a small, bored child joined the group still standing where the shocking encounter had stranded them.

'Can cost up to a hundred pounds,' the young man explained.

'A hundred pounds!' Florrie exploded.

'Yeh, they pay it off weekly.'

'How much do they earn? Can't be much. They're not... clever are they?'

'Dad, I want to go home.'
'I don't know. About five, ten pound a week.'
'Dad.'
'OK darling. Nearly ready.'
Florrie shook her head.
'Anyway, got to go now. We're off to Whittaker's.'
'Oh that'll be nice.'
'Yes. Hope we're not too late. Bye.'
'Bye. Bye.'

***

'What *did* he think he looked like? Ridiculous. Did you see his socks? Pink! Bright pink! Men don't wear pink unless…' Florrie leant forward over the Formica topped table. 'Unless they're, you know, a bit odd.' she said with a giggle.

'You mean queer.'

'Shh… Joan!'

'Well, nice to see some colour though Florrie. Everything's so drab.'

'Colour. Colour won't get you anywhere. You have to dress properly to get on: nice pair of grey flannels, white shirt and nice tie – nothing loud and spivvy – and a navy blue blazer, double-breasted, silver buttons with a badge on.'

'Badge? What badge?'

'A badge. A nice badge with gold and Latin. Like my younger brother James.'

'Brother?' Joan looked surprised. 'Didn't know you had a brother?' Joan took a sip from her tea and contemplated the slices of bread and butter waiting on a white plate.

Florrie continued. 'Oh yes, and four sisters, although one's in Australia, so I never see her. Don't see the others much – you know weddings and funerals – keep themselves to themselves, but my brother, yes, he's an officer in the Merchant Navy. Very important. Travelled to Rotterdam the other week. Although his wife's a bit…' Florrie pushed her nose upwards slightly.

'Does he have a blazer then?'

'Joan! Of course he does.'

'Cyril was in the Navy. Yes, an able seaman. An AB. "Able Bodied". Well he was then… Hey Florrie, there he is, the waiter. Look at his eyelashes – they're so long. Gorgeous. Do you think they're false?'

'Don't be daft. Men don't wear make-up.'

'S'pose not. Hope he serves us. He's got lovely hair too, bit like that Teddy Boy. Thick and curly. Makes you want to run your fingers through it,' Joan toyed with her own curls as she spoke.

'Oh Joan. How disgusting. It would be greasy.'

'Well your Ted wears Brylcreem.'

'Yes I know, the older men do. It makes their hair go darker though and Ted had such lovely fair hair once, but not my boys. It would make them look like spivs. No, you need your hair cut short, nice and neat with a straight parting, and you need to be independent. My boys will be. They can already cook and clean and sew and do housework.' Florrie's eyes gleamed. 'That's my job – to teach them while Ted's working.'

'They'll make someone a good wife.'

'That's not funny Joan.' She paused. 'Anyway I don't like your waiter.'

'Florrie, why ever not? He's lovely.'

'He's got his sleeves rolled up *and* his collar turned up.'

'What's wrong with that?'

'He's English. He's not a ruddy Yank.'

'Oh Florrie, really.'

They both sipped their tea.

'Cyril says they have DAs.'

'Who.'

'The Teddy Boys, at the barbers near the Arches. They go there.'

'What's a DA?'

'Don't know. He wouldn't say. Just grinned.'

'Maybe it's a Dreadful 'Aircut.'

They both laughed.

A young waitress arrived before them carrying two plates. 'One rock, one cod and chips.'

'Oh it's you. That's a shame.'
'Pardon?'
'Ignore my friend. Mine's the cod.' said Florrie.
'Anything else? Gherkin, pickled egg, pickled onion?' The waitress reeled them off. Her lack of interest made them seem very unappetising.
'No thank you dear.'
'Vinegar, Joan?'

They both sat for a brief moment and breathed in the hot honey brown fried fish and golden chips speckled with sharp vinegar and salt before crunching into the crisp batter and releasing a drift of pale steam.

'Wonder how they get the money?' Florrie spoke.
'Who?'
'The Teddy Boys. A hundred pounds!'
'Don't know. Must be really important to them though. This rock salmon's good. How's your cod?'
'Fine… They don't know how lucky they are. We had to make and mend. Remember clothes rationing Joan?'
'Certainly do. Nineteen forty-one for eight long years.'

Both women tucked into their meal and filled their minds with the past.

'Too easy nowadays.'

Florrie broke the silence while picking a small fish bone out from between her lips.

'Yes, s'pose so.'
'Think of all those things we had to do.' Florrie's eyes shone at the memory and she added,
'Like unpicking and cutting.'
'Patching and sewing.' Joan joined in.
'Darning.'
'Dyeing. Re-lining.'
'Hemming. Knitting.'
'Re-soling and heeling.'
'Taking in.'
'Taking out.'

'And then when you had grown out of them, you passed them on. Couldn't buy new.'

'No Florrie, but sometimes you have to buy new. Bet you keep your two boys in short trousers far too long. They'll be shaving by the time they get long trousers if you have your way.'

'Oh don't exaggerate. Anyway good to get the air to their legs.'

Both women continued with their meal. Around them the last customers found tables.

'So, what do your boys want to be when they grow up?'

Florrie put down her knife and fork and leaned towards Joan. This was a favourite topic. 'Well of course at the moment Oliver is at secondary school. Just started and top of his form. Learning French.'

Joan's eyebrows rose. Mouth full.

Florrie didn't know if that was actually true, because her pride could deflect the truth at times. 'That'll get him somewhere up there. Somewhere posh,' she said pointing upwards. '*He* won't be working in the Dockyard.'

She spoke with such fervour and determination that for a moment Joan felt sorry for Oliver.

'Yes Florrie, but what does *he* want to do?'

'At the moment he spends all his pocket money on going to the pictures. He says he wants to be an actor or something. Expect he'll grow out of it. Be something important.'

'Like what Florrie?'

'Oh I don't know. Like a… manager.'

'A manager?'

'Yes a manager – someone who runs things, somebody who's in charge. You know, like Ted's boss in the Dockyard. He's a manager and *he's* got an Austin A30, a new one.'

Joan's eyebrows lifted again. She took a sip of tea and put the cup down.

'He can be a bit er… moody at times don't you think Florrie?'

'Who? The manager?'

'Nowah. Your Oliver… seems a bit moody… sometimes.'

'No Joan, he's artistic. Artists are always a bit serious aren't they?'

'S'pose so. And what about Bobby?'

'Oh he wants to be a sheriff.'

Both women smiled. They were used to seeing Bobby galloping around on an imaginary horse, whipping his own bottom to make it go faster. It hadn't been easy to get the cowboy outfit that he wanted so badly. They had found a silver star in Woolworths with the word 'Sheriff' on it. Bobby never took it off. And a black cowboy hat with a string chinstrap and a small silver coloured pistol that could fire caps. After the first few fusillades, they had been banned. Florrie had found an old scarf that acted as a bandana and had taken in a waistcoat that had belonged to John Henry. Ted found an old leather belt and had punched extra holes in it. It still hung down but for Bobby it was perfect, allowing him to practice fast draws although occasionally the pistol fell out onto the ground. Both Ted and Florrie glowed with pleasure at being able to give their son such a gift.

Joan pushed her plate away, sat back and looked at Florrie.

'You went to a lot of jumble sales didn't you, Florrie. You were very good weren't you?'

'Oh yes. Loved them. Still do. I was well-known you know. You don't want that last slice of bread and butter Joan?'

Joan shook her head and thought about Florrie performing at jumble sales. Jumble sales had a mystique, Joan knew that. She also knew that success required tenacious determination, a selective eye, physical strength and a penchant for a good scrap and that Florrie was born for the task. It seemed almost like a calling. Her father's trading blood must have thrilled through her veins because eagle-eyed she slipped through impossible gaps in human walls, seized desirable items with startling speed and then held off the enemy with flashing elbows and icy stares, always searching for a bargain or some treasure that would change their lives forever. She never found it. Others, aware of the demands, approached the problem in pairs: one searching and sifting, the other guarding, blocking and intimidating. But Florrie always went alone and her success soon established a sort of begrudging fame.

Joan would see her returning home, grinning, flushed with victory, carrying her booty like a Viking warrior, only to realise in the cold light of morning that it was of little use and had to be returned to the next jumble sale, but that didn't matter.

'You know Joan, I miss those times.'

'Oh Florrie, how could you? They were desperate.'

'I know, but then I felt like I was fighting for something. We were *all* fighting for something worthwhile, together, but now…'

'Well that's change I suppose. At least our men are home and nobody's dropping bombs on our heads.'

'I don't want change. I want *un*change.'

'Well, I don't want the past,' Joan looked sharply away as she spoke, out of the restaurant and into somewhere within the High Street crowds. Maybe he would walk past. She wondered if she would recognise him. He would have been twenty-nine now.

'Oh Joan,' Florrie said, gently touching her hand.

'It's OK. Just sometimes…'

'I know.'

'You know what Florrie? I know it's horrible killing people and all that, but I think we women should fight wars. We're much tougher really. And when we're finished we can all have a good chat about it and get back to normal.'

The young waiter was smiling and talking to the waitress out of sight of the owner. He ran a finger over her arm. She shivered, but didn't move. Joan and Florrie caught their reflection in one of the several mirrors around them that tried to make the little room larger. Each one bordered by little fishes swimming uphill.

'Lucky cow, I could do with some of that,' Joan said as she coiled a curl with one finger.

Florrie said nothing. She couldn't remember the last time. She had smiled and encouraged him, but he was always too tired or had to get up early and turned away. It was as if he was afraid to touch her. So she had given up and now they shared their bed as strangers with a glacier between them.

Joan was still talking.

'Not much chance though. Even the navy's not interested. You saw that. So did I. No it's alright Florrie. I know. I know. Why on earth do I bother?' she asked and took another sip of tea.

'Why do you do it Joan?'

'Do what?'

'You know, dress up and flirt like you do?'

Florrie expected her to deny it, but she didn't. She put down her tea and faced Florrie with a serious face. 'Cos it makes me feel alive... I know I'm ridiculous, but I need to feel alive.' She turned away and then back swiftly. 'And wanted. OK?'

'OK, Joan.'

'Anyway it's alright for you Florrie, you've got Ted.'

Both women felt the strain that had slipped between them. Joan looked down at her plate for a while and then began to smile mischievously. She turned towards Florrie, eyes sparkling again.

'You could always have George. Oh Florrie, isn't he a hunk? Looks just like Burt Lancaster don't you think?'

'What do you mean George? I haven't got George. I don't even know George.'

'Oh come on Florrie. Yes you do. Harry's friend. He calls round sometimes. I've seen the way he looks at you.'

Florrie glared at her friend.

'No, you're right. I'm only joking. Right, come on we need to get this shopping.' Joan drank the last drop of tea and took out a small mirror and lipstick. Florrie sat and tried not to think about George.

The two women returned along the High Street, past McFisheries, past Lyons, past Victor Values, past Home and Colonial, calling in at several shops, queuing and buying, until their arms strained and their fingers were striped and bloodless under the weight of their bags.

'These bags are so heavy Florrie.'

'Yes. Pity we can't just grow the stuff.'

'What, in pots you mean?'

'No, what we need is an allotment each.'

'Can't see my heels doing well on an allotment.'

'Oh Joan.'

They waited in the queue for the 32 and once aboard, Florrie sat quietly, bag balanced on her lap and thought about her conversation with Joan. She also thought about Ted slipping away from her. Was this simply about the war? Surely not. That had ended eight years ago. What on earth had he seen and done that made him like this? What could have been that terrible?

She had tried to talk to him in the beginning. He had simply smiled and said it was OK and that he was just getting back to normal, but normal never came. Later, when the passion of returning alive died down, he seemed to have no defences. He retreated into his own wilderness, then he evaded her eyes and looked away.

Maybe he was trying to protect her, afraid that fermented pain and horror would pour from his damaged mouth and eyes and ears and drown them both. Maybe he was afraid of losing control, afraid of standing there like a little boy again, his own pants soiled and stinking, lost and ashamed and wanting to run away and hide forever, but unable to move. What if? *No. Can't be.* But a jolt punched her stomach. What if he simply missed it all: the excitement, the status, the importance, the comradeship – the men often talked about comradeship. In a mysterious way she knew that wasn't meant to include her. What if life now, with her, simply paled into insignificance? She felt a shiver run over her.

***

Ted was already home, laying the table for tea. His back was to her as she walked in. She just wanted to hold him and a huge wave of love for this man swept over her. She walked up, put her arms around him and laid her head on his shoulders, wanting it all to be better, as it was before. He recoiled.

'You made me jump. Didn't hear you come in.'

She knew that was a lie. Florrie turned and walked into the kitchen and hid her tears with clattering teacups. 'What was the game like?'

'Oh, good game. We won three nil. That Harry and his mates are such a laugh, especially George.'

'That's good.'

They stood in separate rooms just a few feet apart, but it might as well have been separate worlds.

***

That night, in her sleep, she returned, a child again, to the small Sunday school at the very top of the Hill – nearer to heaven they said. Even now its fusty, dusty smell of fear filled her mind: fear of God, of Hell and Damnation. The teacher had shown them pictures, exhorted them to be good children, or else. One picture had followed her home that Sunday like an unwanted black cat and had curled up in her soul. Often when she was troubled it appeared in her feverish sleep and stared at her. She remembered the artist's name as clearly as if it were yesterday – Blake. Couldn't remember his Christian name. Maybe he shouldn't have had one, he didn't deserve one, Mr Blake. The night before it had reappeared again. This time she hadn't tossed and turned, trying to open her sleep tight eyes and release it back into the darkness. This time she stared back, tried to look deep into it, unafraid, beyond the smoke and flame and writhing naked figures, deep into its pain and anguish, trying to understand, trying so hard to understand, but she couldn't. She awoke in the early morning, exhausted and felt, not for the first time, unloved and unwanted.

***

Sunday

Ted was up bright and early as always. He took Florrie a cup of tea in bed and began to tackle the vegetables. In the dining room the sturdy table flexed mahogany muscles and prepared itself for the weight of food to come.

Soon sprouts had been stripped of their worn outer leaves and bobbed, bright green and cheerful in a saucepan. Nearby lay the King Edwards. Some had ragged holes burrowed into them to remove an eye or blemish and now they were lying quietly like pale yellow wrecks submerged in cold water. Dusty carrots were scraped red-orange and soft sweet green peas, now shucked, flocked naked and uncertain together. Next to them, a proud cauliflower, stripped of its thick outer leaves was cut in half to reveal its architecture of gleaming white tracery.

Ted gathered up the wet potato peelings to boil them up later for the three chickens scratching in the run he had built. He disposed of any other rubbish, wiped the sink area shining clean, put away the kitchen tools and stood back to admire his handiwork. There was an air of satisfaction and expectancy. He picked up the carving knife, opened the back door, stepped outside, sat on a warm step and sharpened the knife against a concrete edge.

The lawn looks a mess with that bare strip where the swing used to be. Not much of a lawn anyway. Never has been. You know, think I might crazy pave the whole lot. Easier to sweep than mow, that's for sure.

Beside him the washing line jingled. He looked up to the top end of the washing pole that stood way above him. From where he sat it seemed to poke into the blue sky like a ship's mast. He wondered if that's where this local tradition had started. Washing lines in the area were originally ship's masts taken from the Dockyard. Problem was, at that height, on a good drying day, the washing vibrated horizontally until the wooden pegs disintegrated and somebody's shirt ended up clinging to a gooseberry bush three doors away. Nobody seemed to mind. In fact, when one of the boys was sent to collect something that had blown away, they would not be allowed to return until full of lemonade and biscuits, clutching the errant item (in a brown paper bag if it happened to be of a delicate nature).

Ted smiled to himself. He loved it here so much. *We may not have a lot, but today we are all together and today we will eat Sunday roast dinner until we burst.*

Back in the kitchen, he opened the inner door and called out. 'Florrie. It's ready. Florr-ee.'

'All right, I can hear you.'

Florrie arrived, checked that everything was in order, pushed Ted out, closed the kitchen door and began to conduct the performance.

Before long, the stench of over-boiled cauliflower began to seep under the kitchen door. The skins of peas, once round and taut, split and their insides collapsed into a sad mush while the other vegetables, once proud and firm, were drowning, swirling helplessly in large saucepans of bubbling hissing water, lids jiggling in protest. The kitchen windows wept streams.

Florrie cut large cubes of soft sticky lard and placed them around the English beef that sat rather majestically in a large blackened tray surrounded by a flotilla of attendant potatoes. She smeared the last traces of lard on the knife across the joint, opened the oven door, turned her frowning face away against the blast of hot air, slid the tray in and slammed the door shut.

'Can I come in?'

'No. Keep out.'

'But I only want a glass of water.'

'Go upstairs then.'

'Muum.'

'Go away. Can't you see I'm busy?'

They waited. Four places had been prepared: knife, fork, spoon and a glass sat neatly around a table mat. Each showed a different London scene.

'What have you got?' It was Bobby, holding up his mat away from sight like an ace.

'I've got the Tower of London.'

'Huh. I've got Buckingham Palace,' Oliver replied, as if in this game that trumped the Tower.

'Behave you two.'

Ted arrived with a large bottle of lemonade.

In the centre of the table was a row of larger place mats, some singed or battered at the corners. Between two of them rested a pair of larger spoons that had been in service for many years. Once bright and ambitious, they now lay dully next to each other, backs curved like elderly lovers. Nearby lay the carving knife with its yellowing ivory handle and its blade, once straight, now worn into a curve. Every week it sliced, cut and chopped, until worn and exhausted. Now stroked back into life it was bright and gleaming, like a sharp smile.

Dotted around were a saltcellar, a small tub of white pepper and a plastic bottle of Sarson's vinegar.

Ted moved the dial to the "Light Programme" station and switched the radio on just in time to hear the remaining three pips and a familiar voice.

'The time in Britain is twelve noon. In Germany it's one o'clock, but home or away it's time for *Two Way Family Favourites*.'

'Dah dah dah, dah dah deee. Dah dah dah, dah dah dah dah dah dee.'

At that moment Florrie burst out of the kitchen, face flushed and carrying a plate of crisp beef surrounded by dark brown roast potatoes. 'Plate's hot,' she said, disappearing again. 'Come on you lot, I can't do it all on my own,' came a shout from the kitchen.

'And now for Corporal William Brown serving with the…'

Dishes of vegetables appeared: sprouts, yellow and bewildered; peas, terminally grey-green; carrots, limp and pale and cauliflower, waterlogged and disintegrating, leaving fragments spread around the plate like a plane crash followed by Yorkshire puddings, exhausted from their unsuccessful struggle to rise.

'Just waiting for the gravy.'

When the gravy arrived, it sat in a blue and white ceramic gravy boat, seducing you with its thick silky brownness and meaty aroma. It was quickly poured, hot and steaming, onto the carved slices of beef that now appeared on each plate, leaving a brown dribble running from its lip. But it hid a secret.

'Looks good love,' said Ted pouring vinegar onto his sprouts in the hope of some resurrection.

'Should do. I spent long enough getting it ready.'

There was silence except for the clicking and scraping of knives and forks and music from the radio.

'Any more beef anybody? Potatoes?'

Eventually, every dish was cleared, knives and forks placed together and plates pushed away in a signal of "Enough, thank you". The gravy left behind on them was now beginning to solidify into thin sheets and in the gravy boat, long-cold, there had now formed a soft crust of beige fat.

'I'll take them,' Bobby cried, picking up the plates and moving towards the kitchen. There, the remains would be scraped into the bin, but he found it fascinating to watch the torrents of hot water cascade from the tap into the sink and magically change the hard fat that he had placed there, into soft sensuous shapes that slowly dissolved and disappeared to clog up some unseen underground artery.

'What are you doing out there?'

'Just filling up the sink with hot water.'

'Leave it.'

They now awaited the highlight of the meal. They would always have to leave room for this. It *might* be a pale suet pudding studded with dark currants. Wrapped in a cloth and bound with string, it was immersed for hours in boiling water, like a body committed to the deep of some bubbling hell. Unwrapped with careful fingers, it first appeared as a huge unappetising stodgy sausage, but once sliced open it revealed itself as a fluffy delicacy. It demanded custard yellow as a field of buttercups, or better still syrup scooped straight from the tin. The boys would watch fascinated as the dark syrup slowly, slowly accelerated from their spoons and then fell sinuously to make shiny, twirly golden rings on the pudding below.

It *might*, however, be a currant pie or treacle tart or, best of all, it *might* be an apple pie. Whatever failings could be levelled at the main course (and nobody dared level them), Florrie's apple pies were sublime.

The table waited again. Large white bowls had arrived and the odd pea that had attempted to escape was brushed away and that small gravy stain in the tablecloth could wait until washday. They toyed with their spoons.

Florrie appeared bearing a large hot apple pie held between a scorched red and white tea towel. She placed it carefully in the centre of the table and stood back. 'Not bad.'

But the delicious smell of crisp golden pastry sprinkled with crunchy sugar disputed that.

Florrie sat down on one of the high backed chairs, puffed cool air over her pink face and pushed her curls away.

They all beamed at each other. Slowly, Ted picked up the knife. The boys watched enthralled, in absolute silence. Like a surgeon about to perform a most delicate operation, he approached and the knife tip crunched through the pastry and tap-tapped lightly on the plate below, releasing the first piece. With it came a steam of sweet and sour apple and summer sunshine.

'Florrie?'

'No, give it to the boys first. I'll have mine later.'

They ate slowly, savouring every taste, every mouthful, saying nothing, lost in an apple pie and custard world. Finally, reluctantly, having scraped up the very last trace and licked their spoons until they could taste metal, they pushed back their empty plates,.

Ted smiled. Oliver and Bobby smiled.

'That was excellent. Thank you love.'

'Thanks Mum.'

They sat for a long time, saying little, looking from one to the other, grinning, knowing that they had to move, but were unable to. The music requests came to an end and Ted switched the radio off. Florrie seemed a little distracted and soon stood up.

'Come on. Let's clear this away. Who's washing up? I'm not, I cooked it all.'

She always said it even though she knew that Ted always did the washing up.

'I'll do it. No, don't need any help.'

He always said that too.

Soon Ted stood in the small kitchen pouring hot water into the sink, surrounded by dirty pans and plates and cutlery, now cold and greasy and precariously balanced. As he organised things, he noticed another smaller pie sitting on the cooker top.

Unusual. Maybe there had been enough pastry left over for one more.

The kitchen door opened and Florrie appeared. She had washed her face, brushed her hair and was wearing lipstick. She picked up the pie and covered it with a clean tea towel.

'Won't be long.'

'Where are you going?' Ted turned surprised, hands wet and covered with soapsuds.

'I'm taking this round to George.'

'George!'

'Yes, George.'

'Why?' Ted turned, quickly wiping his hands and faced her. He looked troubled.

'Because he's our neighbour and he lives on his own.'

'But we don't know George. I've hardly spoken to him.'

Florrie stared back. 'Well, maybe it's time you did. Maybe it's time we went out and met people.'

Ted said nothing.

'Won't be long' she repeated as she brushed past him, opened the back door and walked down the garden path to the back gate and the alley that ran past it.

Ted stood outside the back door and watched her go. Normally she would turn, grin and wave, but this time she didn't.

He stood for a long time after she had disappeared from sight.

SEVEN

Ted, George and an Elm Tree

'Tender-handed stroke a nettle,
And it stings you, for your pains;
Grasp it like a man of mettle,
And it soft as silk remains.'

Aaron Hill

Ted looked through the net curtains. He was careful not to stand too close and be seen from the road – old habits. Florrie was out, somewhere. She was often out these days, doing something. The boys had gone to the river with Harry and Helen. They had no children. Harry had promised to show them the docks where he worked. Wisely Helen had taken a picnic. She knew from her nephews how much one growing lad could consume, let alone two.

They were good boys and Ted loved them dearly as did Florrie. He probably spoiled them a bit, but Florrie kept them level-headed. However, now there was something he had to do.

It was a sunny summer's day and Ted felt the heat strike his face as he left the house. He opened and closed the metal gate with a clink-clunk, looked left and right and set off, face set. Ahead of him, he could see the crossroad at the end of the street. He didn't like crossroads, they made him uneasy, especially as he watched cars speeding towards them in the daylight.

At times the crossroad appeared in his dreams, although he didn't always remember clearly. The dream was confused, jumbled, but in the deep blackness he could hear the whine of an engine slowly approaching. Closer. Closer. He waited. Stiff. Tense. He wanted to shout out, "For Chrissake you stupid bastard. Put your foot down. As fast as you can. They'll hear you coming. They're not stupid. You'll get caught in the middle. Crossed out." He tossed and turned, sticky with fear. He covered his ears, waiting for the explosions, waiting for the awful sound of slicing metal. Crash. There. Jesus, I told you. I told you. Turn him over. Oh Christ, his chest is gone.

Sometimes he would wake up, his pyjama top cold and clammy, and wait, in the comforting light that crept in from the landing, for his heart to stop pounding.

Now, as he approached the crossroad, he turned left into an alleyway. It was a long way round, but he felt safer walking in the narrow space between the fences and walls. There were times when he could hardly be seen. He could think more clearly and decide again what he had to say, what he had to do.

As he approached the small terraced house he noticed its name on a wooden plaque. Dunroamin. *Surely not*, he thought as he knocked firmly.

The door opened, and with it the unexpected smell of baking. For a moment he wondered what his own house smelled like. *Coffee, toast, pain?* George stood there wearing a plain apron. His feet were bare. He looked surprised.

'Ted.'

'Didn't know your house had a name.'

'Oh everybody says that. It was there when I came. Seemed sort of appropriate.' He smiled uncertainly. 'Come on in. I've just been baking some cakes.'

'Didn't know you could cook either.'

He thought about apple pies.

'That's what I did in the Merchant Navy, as a lad. Helped in the galley. Long time ago.' He flashed his large white teeth again. 'Go in the dining room. Take a seat Ted. I'll just sort out these cakes.'

Ted sat down in a small armchair. At right angles to him was a two-seater settee. He looked around. The room was neat and tidy, but sparse. On a polished table, newspapers and magazines were folded and lined up one above the other and above the fireplace, a framed photograph showed a freighter ploughing through some black and white sea. There was only one other photo. It showed a group of people standing together – old and young smiling in the sun.

'Tea Ted?' George called from the kitchen.

'Thank you.'

Ted could hear children next door running down the stairs. An adult shouted something. He looked at the empty settee. Is that where Florrie sat? Did they sit next to each other? Close enough for their knees to brush or did they climb *his* stairs? She first, eager, smiling, looking back, his hand behind?

'Here we are.' George returned. He had removed his apron and was wearing dark red slippers.

'Can you pull that small table out please Ted?' He motioned with his eyes. 'That's it, thank you.'

He put down a silver coloured tray on which he had placed two cups and saucers, each with a spoon, two serviettes, a small teapot, a milk jug, a bowl containing sugar lumps and a pair of tongs. It was a neat arrangement in white ceramic and bright metal. He caught Ted's look.

'I was also a steward for a while. Old habits. Do you take milk?'

Ted nodded and watched George's thick fingers moving deftly and nimbly. His brown hands were flecked with scars, flat and white and his fingernails were cut very short. He wore no rings, but Ted knew about that. They might get caught on something in his line of work – could take a man's finger off.

As George bent close to him, pouring tea, Ted could smell him: soap, sweat, cake and anxiety, all mixed with hot tea. Anxiety, Ted had smelled that before of course. Well, fear certainly. It was strange how senses can become so heightened. Normally they just sit there, ticking over, waiting. Maybe for some people – the placid, the unfeeling, the inexperienced – they waited forever and were never needed, but they were there alright, living in your nose, at the back of your neck, down your spine, waiting for that extreme, testing moment. Ted wondered if George felt them now. They could be two male lions circling each other, watching, sensing weakness and strength. No, Ted smiled to himself. *How could he? What had he ever done?*

Ted looked at his profile and noticed a small puncture. It was just a speck in his ear lobe, as if George had worn an earring at one time. That didn't surprise him – Black George, the pirate. A rampaging, pillaging bloody pirate.

'I've been expecting you, Ted.'

George sat on the settee, two seats away but facing him and took a sip of tea. He replaced the cup slowly, his hand steady, looking down as if thinking about what to say next. 'It's about Florrie isn't it?'

Ted sat silently. Surprise brushed anger away.

'I can imagine how you feel. I would feel the same about her coming here, but nothing is going on, Ted. Really. Nothing. Nothing at all.'

George looked directly at him, dark eyes appealing to be believed.

Ted said nothing because he didn't know what to say. This was not how he imagined it happening. He had thought about this day many times and this was *not* how it was supposed to happen. He realised that George was still speaking, but his voice seemed distant.

'… certainly didn't encourage her. I always asked her "does Ted know you're here?"'

'What did she say?'

George paused, knowing that the words were becoming sharper, more dangerous, likely to cut and hurt.

'What did she say?'

'You didn't mind… care.'

'Care?'

'I told her that wasn't true. Of course you cared. Anybody could see that.'

Ted stared stonily, said nothing and waited, forcing George on.

'She said you were changed. Different. Something like that. I can't remember exactly.'

There was a long silence. George picked up his cup and took a long drink. His mouth had become very dry. Ted sat still.

'Don't forget your tea, Ted.'

'Different from what? When? How different?' Ted leaned forward and looked directly at him.

'She said she thought it was the war. I said, but that was a long time ago.'

Ted sat back again. The bloody war.

'Am I different?'

'Don't know Ted. Didn't know you then.'

'Well how am I now?'

'Now? Well… you're OK. Good bloke. If I'm honest…'

'Be honest.'

'Well, a bit quiet at times, bit sad. But everyone respects you. The lads respect you. Harry and…'

'Quiet? Sad?'

'Yes, not all the time. Trouble is, Florrie's so lively. She's always doing things, dashing about. You know. Can't be easy.'

'You have no idea what it was like.'

'What what was like, Ted?'

'The war.'

'No, well I wasn't in the war. Not directly. But I can imagine.'

'No you can't. You have no idea. What did you do?'

'I was on reserved occupation, unloading ships. That's where I met Harry.'

'Huh. Easy.' Ted gave a short scoffing laugh. 'You had it easy. What, occasional air raid? Bomb dropped two miles away? Home every night? Jesus.'

'Oh come on Ted. I had no choice. I wanted to join up same as you, same as Harry. I wasn't allowed… we all did our bit.' George's voice rallied, rose, and then dropped away.

'Do you know how many of the lads died George? Do you? Do you? You felt every death cut into you like it was you, like it was your brother.' Ted paused and looked away, through the bright windows into his darkness. 'You didn't want to know them after a while, the new ones, or feel their hand on your shoulder. Friendly touch. You know. 'Cos that touch died.' Ted looked down and thrust his hands apart, fingers splayed. 'I don't want to be touched anymore. Not anymore. Cos they go. What's the point in getting close, if they all just go?'

They both sat in silence for a while, George stumbling for words in his mind.

'Must have been awful Ted, but Florrie's your wife.'

'Just go. Why didn't I just go? With the lads. It would be so much easier.'

'Oh come on Ted. It's over now. It's all over.'

'It was never over. It went on and on and on forever. A nightmare. It was only over when you were dead. Then it was over… thank Christ.'

'But now Ted. Now it's over. You were lucky mate.'

'Lucky? Lucky? With my wife running around. Huh, that's my lousy luck.'

'She's not running around Ted. She's just…'

'What.'

'She's just a bit… unhappy.'

'Unhappy. What has she got to be unhappy about? I work hard, put food on the table, pay the bills. Christ. And if she's so bloody unhappy why doesn't she tell me. Talk to me. Why does she talk to you?'

'I don't know. Maybe she doesn't want to upset you.'

'But we're married for Chrissake. There are vows. For better for worse. In sickness and… No. NO. I know what you're thinking. There's nothing wrong with me. Nothing. I'm not mad… It's all the other buggers,' he said laughing at the cliché.

'I don't know Ted. Well, I know you're not mad but…'

'What?'

'Do you talk to *her*?'

'What!'

'Do you talk to her?'

'About what?'

'The war. How it makes you feel. Now.'

'She wouldn't understand. Nobody understands… except the lads. Rich isn't it? You do fuck all and I fight every day. Shitting myself. Waiting to die and you're OK and I'm…'

'No, it's not fair. Of course it's not, but it's over now. You need to move on; put the past behind you.'

'It's not easy. Maybe I don't want to. Maybe I'm...'

'Come on Ted. I thought you were strong. You've got a lovely wife, lovely kids, a good job. What more do you want? If you're not careful you're going to lose her, lose it all.'

'To you I suppose. Lose her to you. I tell you mate if that happened I'd kill you. You wouldn't be the first.' *Safety catch off.*

For the first time George felt a kick of alarm. 'No, don't s'pose I would be.' His forehead was now shiny. 'But Ted, I told you. Nothing's going on mate. Nothing. I swear it.'

Ted looked up sharply.

'I'm not your mate.'

'God, you English are all the same. So buttoned up. Stiff upper lip and all that bollocks.'

'Yes, but that's what won us the war. That's called discipline, duty. We'll never give in.'

George shook his head slowly. 'Yes Ted. Very good. Very good. But it might lose you the future.' He picked up his cup, paused and then put it down again. 'Look Ted, as a friend. If you lose Florrie it will be your own fault. Don't you see that? No matter what happened to you. What terrible things. You owe it her. You need to talk to her, to include her. It's not her fault now is it? Is it? How do you think she felt, waiting? Not knowing? It must have been awful.'

'She never said.'

'No, because she's as stubborn as you... but she is very worried about you. She loves you, you know. You do know that?' He got up, picked up the framed photo and showed it to Ted.

'This is my family, back home, in my country. We talk all the time, all the time. Usually all at the same time.' He smiled at the group and replaced it. 'We also argue all the time. Huh. But we have no secrets.'

Ted felt confused. If only his head would clear. He picked up his cup and drank the tea. It was cold. He didn't notice. He just knew that he had to get back.

He left the small terraced house. Maybe George said goodbye, wished him well, shook his hand. He didn't remember. He walked away, the sun catching his face again. But he felt cold.

This time he walked along the road and not through the alley of trenches until he came to the crossroad. He stood still for a moment, looking at it, uncertain. His stomach winced but he had to know. He stepped off the pavement and strode into the crossroad and stopped, exactly in its centre and waited. He stood there quietly, trembling, trying not to run. He strained his ears, listening for a distant hollow thud and the whistling of metal arriving through the air. He waited for the explosion that would toss him aside, in ribbons. He waited… nothing happened, nothing at all, not a thing. All he could hear was the sound of distant traffic and sparrows squabbling in nearby hedges.

'You alright mate?'

A cyclist had stopped and stood, legs astride his machine, watching him.

'What day is it?' Ted spoke without looking at him.

'What?'

'What day is it?'

'It's Wednesday mate.'

'No I meant what date? Month?'

'It's June mate.'

'Not June the sixth?'

'Almost.'

Oh yes of course. Building up to it.

'An anniversary I suppose? Of sorts,' he continued.

'For a lot of people mate. Yes, it certainly is.'

'For you?'

'Yes mate. For me too.'

'You never forget, do you?'

'No, you never forget.'

'Thanks. Do you think I'm mad?'

'I think you might get run over if you stay there much longer. Bus due soon.'

Ted sighed. He could feel the road surface hot and hard through the soles of his feet. The protective shell he wore didn't cover them.

He thought they were safe. Nobody could get at him through the soles of his feet. Could they? It covered the rest of him though. Black and brittle, it lay just below the surface of his skin. People sensed it and thought it was a bigness, a strength, something mysterious or enigmatic. But it wasn't. The blackness just soaked up emotions and feelings that attempted to enter and stopped any leaving.

'Sure you're OK mate?'

'Yes. Yes thanks... Do I know you?' Ted looked directly at the cyclist.

'We all know each other, don't we?'

'Yes I suppose we do.'

'Sure you're OK?'

'Yes thanks. I'm fine now.'

'OK. Good luck.'

Ted crossed to the pavement and walked back towards his house. As he walked, he left a dark trail on the hot dry pavement as tiny fragments of the shell cracked and broke away from him. They blew away like ashes, though there was not a breath of wind. He turned and looked back, but the cyclist had vanished.

He opened the gate with a click, left it ajar in his haste, pushed the front door open and stepped into the shadow of the hallway. It took a while for his eyes to adjust but soon he saw the yellow sun-hat with the artificial red rose that Florrie had taken with her earlier, hanging brightly on the bottom of the stairs.

'Florrie,' he called urgently.

There was no reply.

He moved quickly to the kitchen and then to the dining room. It was empty apart from Blackie who looked up at him with green eyes. They understood each other, Ted and Blackie. The big black cat had appeared from the shambles of a nearby house whose owners had acquired a menagerie of domestic animals that they did not care for and rarely fed except when they took matters into their own hands and ate each other. Blackie appeared to have avoided the emotional scars of his awful imprisonment with a quiet stoicism, and showed a fierce independence and the certain knowledge that you could not really trust anyone. Despite his ghastly experience, his wretched frame and dull dandruff-speckled coat soon became sleek and glossy with the love, attention and chicken he was offered on a daily basis. He had arrived at the front door in the arms of an RSPCA inspector. He had taken a long green eyed look at Florrie and had decided to stay... for now at least. His deep impassive eyes gave no indication of the horror he had survived, although occasionally he would twitch and quiver in his sleep at some cat memory. Often he and Ted could be found sitting quietly next to each other.

'Where is she mate?'

Ted looked through the French windows to see if she was in the garden. He called up the stairs but his voice was met with silence. And then he heard her, or at least the tinkling of an out-of-tune piano. He opened the door to the front room quietly and stepped inside. It felt cool and musty. Unlike the rest of the house, this room was carpeted and only ever used for best. It was hardly ever heated, not that it needed it today.

Florrie sat at their old second hand black-brown piano. Despite regular polishing, its previous life was evident by the rings of countless beer glasses that still marked its top. A paper guide showed the position of every note, black and white, running the entire length of the keyboard and it had begun to sag and tear in places. It had been repaired but with clear tape which had become yellow and brittle. Ivory key covers, stained like old teeth, occasionally fell off. They were glued back, but remained slightly higher than those surrounding it, which made playing difficult. It may have been for that reason that Florrie now sat playing *Für Elise* slowly and deliberately, her feet on the brass foot pedals worn shiny yellow.

Ted stood silently and watched her concentration.

'Just a moment,' she said without looking up.

She played the last few notes. They were slightly out of tune, but she didn't seem to notice and she sat up satisfied. Discord had become a regular companion after all. She turned towards him and smiled a smile as deep and endless as the summer wheat in the Kent fields, the same smile that had embraced him all that time ago at the church on the Hill. *God where have I been?*

'Have you been for a walk? It's a lovely day.' She closed the piano lid with a careful sound to prevent pinching her fingers. 'We should go for a walk. Up to Bluebell Hill... together.' A cool breeze rustled the summer wheat.

Why had she said that? "Together"' She shouldn't have said that. Testing him again. But she couldn't help it.

She waited heavily for his polite refusal. His excuse.

He smiled back.

'Where are the boys?'

'They're out with Helen and Harry. Won't be back till five.'

'Oh yes. Of course.' He paused. 'OK. Let's do that – the walk. We haven't done that for years. Shall we have lunch first? He wanted his smile to say so many things that he couldn't tell her yet. He hoped she could read the messages that waited there, tangled hopelessly like wild briars. *Please don't give up on me.*

He believed George. People outside must see things so clearly. He realised that now. And he thought he had hidden them so well. He mused on how people never said anything to you, not to your face, and how they never wanted to be straight with you. They said 'Good morning Ted. How are you?' But never wanted to hear his truth: 'Good morning. I'm terrified of living.' To be fair it was none of their business. *It's my problem. My responsibility. My secret.*

Except now it wasn't. Maybe never was.

He felt foolish and confused. But knew he couldn't go back. Not now.

'Why don't we have lunch at that pub on City Way? They're doing chicken in a basket now,' he said. 'I'll pay.' Another piece of shell cracked. He felt it go and hoped she didn't hear it. It felt good. A relief but there was also a cold naked draught.

Florrie wanted to hold him. Have him hold her, but she sat on the piano stool not daring to move.

'We'll never be able to walk after that,' she smiled gently.

'Oh OK. Well, you decide love. Whatever you want. I'll lock the back door.'

'We could have a drink outside in the garden – they have shades.' She sounded happy.

In the kitchen he locked the door and thought again about George. George had been very honest and he hadn't been very nice to him in return. He knew about the blitz on the London Docks – fires of blazing liquid rum and exploding barrels, pepper fires that attacked your face, nose and eyes, ships on the other side of the Thames, far away from the inferno, but still with blistered paintwork.

George might have been sent there. He would have had no choice. Maybe he was sent into hell. Same as me.

Ted could see why Florrie had turned to George. He was strong and not just physically. Maybe George was the old Ted. That's what she wanted. Where the hell was he? He shivered. But they would have talked about me. What had they said? How personal? Maybe George had put his arm around her, to comfort her. Bastard. Perhaps he had made it all up. They had been caught out. He had to say something. No. Calm down Ted. No, it was true what he had said. He knew it really. He had failed her hadn't he? Let her down. And himself. Would George be discreet? *God I can't think straight. These thoughts are all mixed up. Swirling in this dank mist. Looming in and out.* He looked down. He still held the dark door key in the lock. His finger ends were white.

'Are you ready?'

'Coming love.'

Florrie was standing in the hallway, in front of the long mirror, adjusting her hair before going out. He stood behind her and placed his hands on her shoulders, uncertainly, like the first time. In his head he whispered. *Sorry. So sorry.*

Her stomach trembled and a feeling flickered across her mind and then vanished. It was gone very quickly, but for a second it felt like the moment a long illness finally lets go, slipping away, leaving you whole again, but weak and uncertain, still needing a lot of care and sustenance. His hands felt warm and strong and comforting and she placed one of her own on his and spoke to his reflection.

'I'm going to take my book.'

'Book?'

'Yes my book on trees.'

'Trees?'

'Yes. On City Way there are at least one of every English tree growing.'

'Really?'

'Well it's such a long road that the Council decided to grow them. Wasn't that a good idea?'

The shiny words slipped between them, light and smooth like small silver fish moving together in a warm pool. Their eyes caressed each other, shyly, like before.

Ted broke off the look.

'Come on then. Before they close.'

But it was a start.

They walked next to each other. After a while, Florrie slipped her arm through his. It felt strange but Ted did not flinch. Soon they turned into City Way.

It was indeed a long road, part of the main road that joined both towns. Here the houses were large and semi-detached and stood back behind impressive front gardens. In front of them, a wide strip of grass sat between the pavement and the roadway. It was there that the trees grew, neatly spaced. Between them, at regular intervals, pathways of single paving stones shot across the grass from the pavement to access the road. From far above, they must have looked like the rungs of a ladder, or a child's strange board game – a ladder with the foliage of trees between each rung. The whole feeling was one of space and care and tidiness.

Further along the road, just out of sight, was the pub. It was a large modern building with mock Tudor chimneys and white stone mullion windows. There the historical association ended. It had never managed to fool anybody into believing that its drab red brickwork and tiles were steeped in anything but pollution. They had been there many times when they were first married.

'Well I know that one. That's an oak,' Florrie said as she waved around excitedly and started thumbing through pages. 'There you are. Look. Look at the shape of the leaves.'

It was then that Ted remembered the pub name. The George! His mouth felt dry. No she wouldn't do that on purpose. No it had been his idea.

'Yes love, you're right,' he said, barely looking.

'I'm going to tick them off.'

Ted wrestled with his thoughts. *No, it's just a coincidence.*

'Are you alright? You look a bit pale.'

Florrie looked at him, concern on her face and the book in her hands dropped downwards.

'Yes love, I'm fine. Bit warm that's all. You know I don't like the heat very much.'

'Oh I'm sorry. Let's go home.'

'What about your trees?'

'Oh they will still be here. Let's cross over into the shade. You'll feel better then. Come on.' She took his arm and steered him across the road.

They stood in the shade of a tall wall.

'That's why I couldn't stay in the army, after the war. I would have liked to, but the battalion was sent to Palestine. I couldn't have faced that, not with my skin.'

'I thought you left to be with me.'

'Well of course I did love and you couldn't have come to Palestine. You and the boys would have been left on your own again. So I left.'

Florrie looked at him. Uncertainly.

'So what is this tree?' Ted changed the subject.

'That's easy. Look at those leaves. They will prick you. It's holly.'

'Didn't know holly was a tree. Never thought about it really.'

'Oh yes it's in my book. Somewhere. E, F, G, H. Hornbeam,' she mumbled. 'There. Holly. There it is. Page thirty two.'

She turned the pages excitedly now, like a child. Ted watched her enthusiasm and suddenly felt warm inside for her. He smiled – a real smile, not a polite one, a smile that spread so easily, almost out of control and he watched his hand as it moved and touched her shoulder.

'Here we are. Holly. Ilex aqui…aquiflor…um. Aquiflorum.' She smiled, pleased with herself. 'Listen. *Holly berries can be poisonous to humans although deaths are almost unknown. An important source of food for birds and wild animals. After frost and cold weather the berries soften.*' She read slowly and deliberately to make sure she would remember. 'Well, fancy that.' She looked around, her appetite whetted. 'I wonder what that big tree is? Just up there. I'm just going to have a look. You stay here, in the shade. Won't be long.'

It was more of an instruction than a suggestion, but Ted didn't mind. The shade was beginning to comfort him. Around him the pavements and road looked almost white in the heat and the grass verge pale and thin. Further away, the road shimmered and what looked like strips of liquid appeared to glisten and tremble in a mirage. Ahead, Florrie strode up to the tree and was walking around it, hand shielding her face, eyes screwed up, stopping occasionally to check her book. The passenger of a passing car, elbow protruding beyond the wound down window, looked out at her in mild curiosity.

'Can't see what it is,' she shouted back. 'Might be a beech or maybe an elm but I can't reach the leaves to check. Can you come and help me?'

Ted moved somewhat reluctantly into the sunshine as Florrie kicked off her shoes, pulled up her skirt, reached between her legs, grasped a handful of material, pulled, and tucked it into her waistband. For a moment she was back on the Hill, wrestling with the boys.

'What are you doing?'

'Come on. Give me a leg up – onto that branch.'

'You must be mad.'

'You used to like that.'

Ted said nothing. He stooped and she placed one foot into his cupped hands. He lifted her easily upwards. She scrambled onto the branch and sat there grinning down at him, her legs bare and brown and strong. A family out for a walk passed by on the other side of the road. A child pointed at Florrie and turned towards her parents. Florrie waved at them. The mother bent towards her child who waved uncertainly back.

'Come on then. Got your leaf? What is it?' Ted said and looked up.

'Elm. It's an elm tree.' She paused and looked around at the world from eight feet up. 'It's nice up here.' She swung her brown legs. 'Come and join me.'

'Not up a tree.'

'You're not embarrassed are you?' she asked, looking down at him.

He said nothing but looked away.

'Come on love. Let me help you down.'

She turned and gazed through the pattern of leaves, her face still.

'No… I've decided. About us.'

She was no longer smiling.

Ted stood in the bright sunshine and felt his body and mind turn icy cold. *Christ. No. No.* He'd tried so very hard today. George's words hammered into his brain.

'What have you decided?'

Around him, the day stopped moving.

'Florrie what have you decided?'

'Well…'

She looked down at him. A single small cloud began to cross the broiling sun.

'Well. I've decided to join a cub pack. Will that be OK? It should be a lot of fun and we can help the boys learn about trees and nature and lots of other things. Pass on our experience and you can join as well. You have so much to offer and we can go camping and give them discipline and confidence and… what do you think?'

'I'm not wearing shorts,' was all Ted could manage before his frantic heart choked his words.

EIGHT

Hopping, Foreigners and a Ghostly Revenge

> *'There were three in a bed and the little one said,*
> *"Roll over, roll over."*
> *They all rolled over and one fell out.*
> *There were two in the bed and the little one said...'*

Anon

True to her word, Florrie found the nearest cub pack. It was about halfway down the long terraced road. One evening she had arrived there unannounced, grinning madly, and told them that she had come to help, and did they know there was a hornbeam growing outside. The cub leaders looked a little shocked. The cubs grinned back. They understood her. Ted, beside her, looked at the little boys, thought of his own sons and suddenly felt alive – quietly alive, inside.

But before taking that on, Florrie wanted them all to have a holiday – the whole family. They had never had one, they couldn't afford it and Florrie remembered the conversation with Joan about a holiday you didn't have to pay for and then had seen the ad in the local paper asking for hop-pickers.

'It'll be fun *and* healthy for the boys *and* we'll get paid. We certainly could do with the money.'

Ted had smiled and said, 'Good idea, but I won't be able to come with you. Not in September. Used up my leave for this year.'

'Can't you ask for some more? I'm sure they'd understand.'

Ted just smiled and shook his head.

***

Florrie, Ted and the two boys arrived one Sunday in early September, bouncing in an old Austin wagon. Florrie sat in the back, against the cab wall, with her two boys. Precious boys. Her hair fluttered in the vehicle's wake and the man's checked shirt she wore over olive green slacks was opened at the neck to capture the sun's rays, tingling her body like an adventure.

Harry was driving. Being a weekend, Ted could join them and he sat next to Harry, a large map spread across his lap. Their muffled laughter could be heard from the cab as Harry steered with one large hand, fair hair grazing the cab roof at every bump. Both men glanced back and forward, faces enquiring, receiving, then replying, like chatty ping-pong. Ted, who didn't have the insurance to drive, didn't like to ask where Harry got the wagon from or even if he had a licence to drive it. He asked about George instead, quietly.

'George? Don't know mate. He's jacked it in. Probably gone back to his family. Liverpool I think. You know what seamen are like – always restless, can't settle down.'

Ted felt relieved and sad at the same time. He had been trying hard to communicate with Florrie; had not always succeeded, and he was not even sure that was possible. She had never mentioned George's name again and never ever made more than one apple pie at a time, but sometimes she would give Ted a long silent look. Partly accusing. Partly asking. Partly who knows?

'What?' But she just looked away.

He realised that he had come to respect George. Like it or not, here was someone he could actually talk to. He had been forced on him of course, but nonetheless. Maybe he was even a friend. No, he realised that was going too far. He thought how funny it was that confrontation could bring people together, break down barriers and allow septic feelings to escape. They shot out like an angry throbbing boil being lanced and afterwards you felt better. But now George was gone, Ted felt a sense of loss. It was not through death this time and the feeling wriggled in his stomach, uncomfortable and pleasant at the same time.

Florrie had never been hop-picking before and was a bit nervous, but the fat man in the smoky little office where she had signed on had reassured her.

'Nothing to it,' he had smiled. 'You and your hubby?' he had asked, looking at her in an enquiring way.

She had glared back fiercely and he had looked away, his chubby nicotined fingers returning to the paperwork.

'There you are Mrs Tappenden. All done.'

She *had* felt an unexpected stab of pleasure at his interest, but she took the details, turned and left the office without a word, thinking how gross he was, with his fat wet lips. Maybe some women took advantage of being away from their husbands, but not her. She already felt guilty enough going hopping on her own, although she had to admit that it would be a break from the moods that enveloped Ted from time to time and bound him to his armchair. She couldn't be sure that given the opportunity he would have joined them anyway, not because he was work-shy – he certainly worked hard enough for two men – but because of the darkness that could possess him, cloud his words and thoughts as he kept his feelings locked away, buttoned up. There was no doubt it spread a coolness between them at times. *But look, now, he's chattering away with Harry.*

She had still told him that she felt guilty leaving him on his own, but he simply laughed that off.

'Think you'll find it quite hard work, especially with those two young boys to look after. Don't worry love. I'll be fine on my own.'

'Well I hope you're going to miss us.' Her eyes flashed dangerously.

'Of course love. Course I will.'

She felt strange leaving the familiar townscape and venturing into the countryside even though this was Kent, the Garden of England and therefore a huge garden on the doorstep of everybody who lived there, townie or not. Ted, Florrie, and the boys had all ventured to its outskirts many times when Florrie had insisted on long weekend walks. They would arrive hot and flushed at the top of the steep hill named after the bluebells that painted its woodland shadows. Looking down, they were always calmed by the panorama that met their gaze.

'Isn't it amazing?'

What would it be like, she wondered, to wade waist-deep through those sunny patterns and warm colours far below? Through those golds and browns and greens. Would it be like strolling in a huge tufted tapestry?

On excursions to the seaside, they had also seen fields and orchards smeary through grubby bus windows and, on rare occasions, on an expedition by steam train. Then, the train's smutty smoke plumed in white clouds across the sunny landscape, completely obliterating sheep and cows and trees. Craning backwards, the boys would see them reappear through the haze, unconcerned, unchanged as the wispy smoke was sucked away into the blue sky.

However this was quite different. This time they were not just passing through or peering in. This time they had to leave the town forts and become part of the country ritual of growing and gathering, and as the autumn sun fell upon them, they felt a mixture of excitement and uncertainty.

Soon the Austin wagon had turned off the familiar town roads edged with houses and gardens and street lights into much narrower lanes. They were darker, cooled by the foliage of trees above and around. As they looked up, the sun glinted and sparkled through the pattern of branches and leaves, like an upside down green lake as they rattled towards their destination. The boys sat on a pile of potato sacks, holding on tightly, fearful of the lorry's apparent determination to bounce them into the speeding road. Why was it that the grown-ups who looked after them now seemed intent on dashing their bodies onto the hard ground? What would happen? Would their heads crack open like pink eggs and spill out their red jelly brains full of everything that they had taken so much effort to learn?

Soon, they heard the gears grind as the lorry slowed and turned through a large farm gate that appeared around them and then moved quickly away into the distance. They bounced along a sun-hardened track littered with small stones, pebbles and flints and then suddenly, slid to a halt. The handbrake crunched across its ratchets. The engine was turned off and ticked quietly after its long hot journey. For a brief moment, the rhythm and noise of the journey continued to sweep them along and then slowed to a compelling silence. Nobody felt like breaking the spell.

'Here we are.'

The lorry door closed with a metallic slam and Harry's brown smiling face appeared above the tailboard. He always seemed brown, even in the winter. It was a combination of the burnishing sun and strong wind that surrounded him on the river. Small chains rattled, the tailboard crashed down and stiff and uncertain, the boys were swooped down by a strong tanned arm onto a large grassy area.

'Come on Florrie.'

Florrie sat on the edge of the lorry, legs dangling. She felt Harry's hands grip her waist and lift her down, delicately, as if she was something precious. She was surprised how gentle he was.

'Thank you, Harry.'

The boys stood, uncertain as what to do. A gang of children gathered and stared silently. The leader chewed gum. Then, abruptly, at some unspoken signal, they whooped off, arms outstretched, wheeling in unison across the open field like a flock of starlings. Nearby, adults buzzed about, engaged in some important activity and carried with them, a tangible air of experience. One of them approached. His smile revealed a number of missing and stained teeth.

'Just arroived eh? Been ere afore? No? Aye wall, soon get 'ang of 'er. Wots yer name then young un?'

'Robert.' Bobby was always formal with strangers. It seemed proper and, in any case, "Bobby" had to be earned.

'And you son?'

'Oliver.'

'Wall, welcome boys. Now, let's see, where are yer? Let's 'ave a lookeer. Roight. Umm… Thatser. Second from and. Nexter old Mrs Jones. She'll see yer roight. OK?'

'Thank you.'

The elderly man waved and moved slowly away.

'Why is he talking like that Mum?'
'Shh.'

The lorry ride like a long listless journey through space, had dulled the boys' senses but now, landing on this alien planet, they ran riot. Eyes dashed hither and thither trying to grasp the picture around them, fragment by fragment. Noses tried desperately to make sense of new smells, some not entirely pleasant. Ears twitched and struggled at every strange word and new sound. Their minds were being bombarded.

At their feet, patches of bald earth, brightened by yellow spikes of scattered straw, held limp tufts of verdigris grass and the occasional plantain. A grey brown track continued away, its surface rutted by huge tractor wheels. Along its centre ridge, a narrow strip of green was growing safely.

Beside them, the residents of a large duck pond had turned and waddled for the safety of the khaki water, quacking loudly at the intrusion. A cool breeze shivered the pond's surface and tall green plants at its perimeter swayed gently. Scattered in the grass, white dashes of daisies peeked out and above them the rich yellow splashes of dandelion shone. All around, the area was covered with the debris of small duck feathers, long since preened and discarded by their owners. Some sat white and curled amongst the grasses and plants, trembling with each passing breath; others lay sad and sodden in the dark water. The ducks themselves sat dotted about the pond at different angles like toys left on a nursery floor and on one bank stood a large wooden duck house, its door wide open, revealing piles of golden straw gleaming from the dim interior like bullion.

Suddenly, whistling wings beating the air made them jump, as a squadron of brown mallards dropped from the sky into the crowded water, scattering birds in all directions and producing a raucous argument of splashing and squabbling. Peace slowly returned, but not before a *corps de ballet* of preening and stretching and wing flexing, accompanied by a chorus of waggling tail feathers. Nearby, large white Embden geese stood and watched disdainfully, silent as sentinels, their heads turned backwards, yellow bills tucked under warm feathers.

In the distance stood an old red-tiled farmhouse. Its original crisp lines and bright colours had been softened by the passing of time until now it had become part of the surrounding landscape, just like the trees and the clouds. In front of it, just beyond the pond, a group of alders normally bustling with siskins, finches and tits, hungry for seeds, stood quiet and cautious as a black cat appeared silently from the shadows. He travelled low to the ground, body and tail stretched and intent, weaving his way delicately around the clumps of nettles, ignoring the wasps and flies and white butterflies that hovered there. One blink and he had vanished.

A dark eye surveyed them with suspicion. Nobody had noticed. How unnerving to be secretly watched in this world of hunter and prey. The large white mare looked over a sharp edged fence, its grey wooden lengths twisted and turned by sun and rain. The boys moved curiously towards the horse and then stopped, uncertain. A shudder rippled along its flank towards a long tail that swished at a few annoying flies. The dark eye continued to stare. She was silent. Maybe she could sense they were townies. She looked so knowledgeable they half expected her to say "What are you strange boys doing here in my world?" Maybe she would have a strange accent like the old man. They stood uncertainly, not knowing whether to pat her or stroke her or give her an apple.

'Don't touch!' cried out Florrie, reading their indecision. 'It will bite you.'

Shocked at her abrupt certainty, they jumped back and made the horse start, snort and shake her mane. The boys retreated.

Nearby grew twisted gnarled black trees. Fallen crab apples, some squashed by the heavy boot of a passing farm worker, peeked dark red like a blush through the long grass.

Ted looked across from helping unload the lorry. 'You wouldn't want to eat those,' he said reading the uncertainty that was slowly giving way to temptation in the minds of his sons. He laughed to himself.

The two boys looked at the ground embarrassed and wondered how grownups always seemed to know just what they were thinking?

Inside the steamy kitchen of the farmhouse, the farmer's wife bustled about unseen and from a top window drifted snatches of music, tinny from a small record player.

'Look at that.'

Silhouetted against trees, stood a large barn whose vast thatched roof, grey and weathered, appeared to slope almost to the very ground. Spiky ends of thatch protruded over its end walls to allow the winter rains and snows to drain away and tall double doors had been swung open to reveal a cool, cavernous darkness. Scattered around, other small outbuildings stood black and strangely forbidding against the green and blue backdrop of the landscape and the characteristic shapes of two oast houses appeared red roofed above the treetops, each white cowl sniffing out the vagaries of the wind and turning accordingly. Their bases, built in a pattern of grey stone and without windows, were strong and solid and stood closely together like brothers. The eldest was square in construction, but the youngest had been made round.

'Why are they different?' Bobby asked.

'Don't know. You ask.'

'No you.'

Florrie straightened her back from unloading a heavy battered tea chest with the help of Ted and Harry and looked around.

'Look, over there,' she cried. In a gap between a dark mass of trees, they caught their first sight of hop bines, growing along diagonal strings, gleaming in the sun, like the green streamers of some giant maypole, scattered with the pale yellow green of the hop cones.

'Are they hops?' Oliver asked excitedly. 'They look like decorations.'

'That's right,' said a man passing by. 'Ain't you ever seen hops before?' He winked good-naturedly back towards Florrie.

'No. We've never been here before,' retorted Bobby thinking that grownups were a bit stupid sometimes.

'Right,' said the man grinning down at him. 'Anyway, good crop this year.'

'Why is that one round? Why is it different?'

This time it was Oliver, the elder brother, who felt obliged to ask.

'What, the oasts?'

Both boys nodded.

'Well that's where they heat the hops and the old building, the one on the left there, the square one, used to get cold in the corners. Didn't work so well. So the next one, on the right, was built round like that so it got hotter all over. See.'

They nodded again. Confused but happy to talk to such friendly grown-ups and one that at least they could understand. Above their heads a collared dove sat quietly next to one of the rearing Invicta horse shapes fixed to each cowl and watched them.

'Come on you two, give a hand,' called Florrie.

They ran towards the pile of items on the grass, both happy to leave the strange country world behind for a while and to help carry their belongings inside.

The hut was a timber-framed box built on a solid concrete floor, with sheets of black painted corrugated iron fixed to each side and to the top. The only entrance was through a stable door, the top half of which could be opened to let in light and ventilation during the day, but when closed at night, it rendered the inside pitch-black and suffocating. There was no heating, no lighting, no water or drainage and, to their horror, no toilet. There was, however, a wooden frame on which was placed a palliasse of straw that was to be the bed for the three of them for the next two weeks.

'Let's go and look at the huts next to ours.'

The boys returned quickly, excited by their findings.

'They've got real chairs and tables and tablecloths and wallpaper on the wall and funny rugs and lamps and jugs and a budgie in a cage and things hanging from nails. Have we got any nails?'

It all came out in one breathless stream. It turned out that the wallpaper was pinned to the wooden framework that formed the walls, the funny rugs were made of rags and fortunately a previous occupant *had* left six-inch nails hammered into the beams of their hut. Soon their hurricane lamp, towels, sewing kit, first aid box, trays, various jugs and baskets began to fill the empty space. Fold up stools and tables quickly became cluttered with cutlery, plates, cups, saucers, spoons, bowls and saucepans while Florrie directed each new item and found a home for it.

'Where shall I put this Mum?'

'The alarm clock?' asked Florrie, squinting in the gloom even by daylight.

'Yes.'

'On the shelf.'

'And this?'

'On the shelf as well, thank you.'

The "shelf" was in fact one of the horizontal wooden beams that supported the hut and on it now sat the alarm clock, along with a cruet set and various packages and bottles. Pillows and bedding covered their straw bed and they hung clothes from a length of rope stretched across one corner. It was effective but crude compared with their more experienced neighbours who had constructed a shelving system that hung from two nails with the wooden shelves separated and held by knotted rope. Their neighbours had also brought wide-brimmed hats to ward off the sun and rain as well as thick aprons to stop the rough hop bines from scratching them. They had neither, but quickly learnt that old sacks could be worn as aprons or around your shoulders like capes, or could be folded into hats using the sacks' corners. Their neighbours also had strange fire-blackened metal rods, hooks and chains that were soon erected into perfect constructions for supporting bubbling pots above wood fires. Gypsies, who also picked, had dug metal tins into the ground as ovens, surrounded by the heat of glowing embers. There were so many new things.

Ted and Harry had carried all the heavy items to the hut and stood back as Florrie organised the interior.

'Think we need to be getting back now love, but Harry and I will come in a fortnight to take you home again. Harry can't get the wagon again before then.'

Harry grinned and nodded.

The boy's faces dropped.

'Come on, cheer up. I thought you were all big strong men,' Harry said as he leaped forward and grasped the boys' hands, which disappeared into his and shook them exaggeratedly.

They giggled.

'Bye Florrie. Bye boys.'

Harry picked up his coat.

Ted kissed Florrie awkwardly on her cheek.

'Bye love. Bye Oliver. Bye Bobby.'

Ted turned with Harry, stopping just once for a final wave.

Florrie touched her cheek.

They sat and ate the remains of the soggy cheese and tomato sandwiches and drank the now lukewarm tea from their flask. The boys looked a little lost.

'Right. Come on you two. Don't just sit around moping. There's a lot to do and the sooner we do it, the sooner you can relax and have some fun.'

'Have you been here before Mum? To this field?'

Florrie stopped wondering where to store spare underclothes and sat down.

'No, but my parents – that's Tiny Gran and Granddad – met in the hop fields and later they were married in the church at Tudely near Tonbridge, not so far from here. That was a long time ago in 1901 – over fifty years ago, this same month.'

'Did they come from Kent?'

'Granddad did but Tiny Gran came from Ireland.'

'How did she get here?' Bobby asked curiously.

'She came on a boat I expect.'

'On a boat? Gosh that must have been exciting.'

Bobby grinned at his brother and wondered what it must be like to sail the seas.

Soon the hut looked like home and Florrie sent the boys off to explore.

'Don't get lost,' she warned with a serious smile. 'And Bobby... do as your brother tells you, OK?'

'OK,' Bobby muttered back.

They set off, turned the first corner and there, in front of them, stood a row of red brick buildings with proper sloping roofs. The walls were a pattern of red and orange bricks that were punctuated every now and then with blue-black squares. Above them rose tiled roofs, darker in colour and speckled with yellow lichen. Large squat brick chimney stacks appeared above the roofs, with a row of bricks standing out as decoration. The stable doors were painted an ominous black and even when open to reveal their dark interiors, they stood out like rows of black open mouths. The boys stopped and looked at each other, confused. Why were these so different from their simple hut?

'Must be where the guards live.' It was Bobby who spoke. He stood slightly in front of his brother, hands on hips. If he couldn't be a sheriff then a guard might be the next best thing.

'The guards?'

'Yes, the guards.' Bobby was warming up nicely. 'The guards that make us work. Bet they've got whips and dogs.'

'They don't have guards, silly.'

'Of course they do. You don't know everything. Just because you go to a big school. Come on, let's look inside. Dare you.'

Peering inside, they could see dark red tiles on the floor and, in one corner, a blackened fireplace. On proper wooden shelves, white enamelled dishes, slightly chipped with black scars, sat next to their pale yellow cousins and on a brass pot, a straw hat sat at a rakish angle. It had pink and white flowers on its rim and waited patiently for sunshine and its owner. Nearby, there was a small dark wooden table covered with a crisp white tablecloth decorated with blue parallel lines that ran around each edge and somehow collided into dark blue squares at each corner. On the cloth was a pile of blue and white patterned dinner plates, side plates and Dutch style bowls, all waiting to be distributed and a white glossy teapot, its spout protruding from the woolly warmth of a yellow and red tea cosy. A variety of tea cups of differing sizes, designs and colours and a large plate covered with a range of cutlery were laid neatly next to each other, the yellow knife handles worn smooth by the hands of eager eaters. An empty brown beer bottle stood on a shelf and next to it rested a modest wooden frame holding a faded black and white photo of an old lady, smiling at the camera. Nearby, balanced a brightly decorated round tin tray, extolling the virtues of Watneys Pale Ale and from a wooden beam above their heads hung a shiny new hurricane lamp. At their feet the red tiles were scattered with strands of straw and along one wall a dark blue cover lay over the bed with straw protruding from each end like some vast portly scarecrow. Laying on the cover, dressed in a blue top and red trousers, was a golliwog, its arms stretched permanently sideways and its white eyes staring at them. They looked at each other in mute confusion at this relative grandeur as they wondered why this hut, or was it a house, was so much better than theirs?

'That's not fair.'

'I suppose it's because we're beginners, Bobby. Don't tell Mum. She's got enough to do. We'll be alright. Come on, let's go back.'

Bobby looked up warmly at his elder brother and nodded. This would be their grown-up secret. Sometimes, he thought, going to the big school did make you understand things better – especially about adults.

Florrie had gone to collect a faggot of wood and so the boys sat in the sunshine outside their hut to wait for her. Soon she returned, but accompanied by a tiny woman dressed in a long black dress. Her hair was tied back in a severe bun and she peered at them, though not unkindly, through a set of small spectacles below which a semblance of a moustache straggled across her upper lip.

'This is Mrs Jones, our neighbour,' announced Florrie rather triumphantly as if she had just won her.

'Hallo boys.' The voice came large and confident from within such a tiny frame.

To be addressed by a moustachioed neighbour after such an exhausting day was too much for the boys and they looked away towards their boots and mumbled something fairly incoherent.

'What was that,' demanded Florrie fiercely. 'That's no way to treat a neighbour and after all that I have taught you.'

She turned to her new companion in despair.

'Oh don't worry. It's OK. I understand boys and their ways. Should do, I've got four of 'em,' she smiled at them as she spoke, the way adults do when they are thinking one thing and smiling another.

'Mrs Jones has been hop picking for forty years. Even during the war.'

'The war!' The boys cried and looked up in unison.

They knew about the war. They knew that somehow it had been bad although to them it just seemed exciting.

'Did you shoot anyone?' asked Bobby enthusiastically.

'Oh no dear,' she smiled, 'but I was shot at and bombed, but then most of us were.'

'Was it dangerous then?' Oliver continued.

'Well quite often the German bombers on their way back from London would drop their bombs into these fields and the German fighters would fire at the pickers and even at cows and sheep would you believe.'

'Cows and sheep?'

'Trying to damage our food supplies I suppose.'

'It must have been very different then, compared with now.'

'Oh yes Florrie. Before the war, most of the pickers were women and older children 'cos the men stayed behind to work until the weekend, in a factory or the docks or something. Then they would visit us. Yer know. And jobs like pole pulling or measuring was always a man's job. But during the war it all changed. Most of the men were in the army or navy or air force, so us women took over their jobs. It wasn't easy and the Londoners who came down to Kent to get away from the Blitz found it just as dangerous.'

'What's the Blitz?' the boys asked.

'Oh that's when there was a lot of bombing in London.'

They listened, eyes gleaming, fascinated.

The tiny lady continued. 'Most of us carried gas masks with us which we used to hang from the poles and wires, but we never had to use them, thank the Lord.' She hastily crossed herself. 'We were lucky 'cos we had trenches to go to when there was an air raid. They were covered with planks and mounds of earth so that the German pilots couldn't see us.'

'Did you have many air raids?' Florrie asked.

'Oh about three or four every day. Some women took no notice when the sirens sounded. No, they simply carried on picking and when the guns started firing, they just lay on the ground and waited till it was all over.'

'What about the children?'

'Oh they were sent to the trenches. They were safe.'

Oliver and Bobby looked relieved, but worried that you never knew when war might break out.

'Mum, was Dad in the war?'

'Not now Robert.'

'Why?'

'Not now!'

'He was Mum. I've seen his jacket hanging in the wardrobe, with badges on it.'

It was Oliver who now joined in excitedly; he wanted Mrs Jones to know he was proud of his Dad.

'You never told me Ollie.'

'I couldn't Bobby, I...'

Oliver looked quickly at Florrie's serious face and looked away at the ground. He knew that there was something wrong; he felt it inside him but could not understand.

'Oh they're just curious,' Mrs Jones said as she ruffled Bobby's hair. 'They must have been born in the middle of it Florrie?'

'Well Oliver's twelve now. Born in forty two and Robert's just three years younger.'

'You just don't know how it affected them, do you? Lovely boys.'

The boys looked from one to the other again and without speaking decided they liked this tiny lady.

***

That night it rained. The first heavy spatters soon played a thunderous tattoo as they bounced and rattled off the metal roof and dropped in a steady stream onto the sodden ground. Some rainwater found a nail hole in the corrugated sheeting and ran down inside the hut wall in a steady trickle towards a wooden beam before falling into an empty jam jar placed beneath to catch it. To begin with, each drop landed with a crash against the glass before gradually turning into a liquid plop as the jar filled. Every now and then the white beam of a torch would cut through the cold air to check on progress until Florrie, moving carefully across the cold floor, poured the contents out through the stable door. She felt the icy spikes of rain strike her hands and arms and the cold night air shiver her face. She thought of Ted and wondered what he'd been doing. Same old thing she supposed. He seemed to need a routine, but she missed him. Even though things were difficult at times, she still couldn't be without him, she still needed him. Maybe he felt the same. If only he would say so. She shivered and rubbed her arm.

Inside, feeling the chill, the straw bed rustled loudly as the occupants covered by heavy blankets squirmed to try and find a comfortable position and then stopped and stared into the blackness, trying to remove thoughts of the spiders and earwigs they might be sharing with. Outside the shower ceased abruptly and with this came the crystal clear sound of the final drips slapping into the wet soil, magnified by the night's silence. Somewhere nearby, an owl hooted mournfully.

***

The next morning, as first light filtered into the hut, through small chinks in the metal walls, the alarm clock shattered the silence and a warm arm wavered in its general direction before silencing it. Having spent the night burrowing like underground animals into a warm comfortable place within the straw mass, there was a reluctance to leave and the air struck cold and damp on the small part of head exposed. Florrie was up and dressed and wiped a cold flannel around her face to revive it. She opened the stable door top and let in the smell of damp fields and dripping leaves.

'Come on you lot. Up you get. Buck up.'

She looked intently out into the morning and breathed it in deeply.

The firewood and kindling kept inside the hut at night were taken outside and a fire was quickly lit. Florrie buzzed about as both boys stood shivering and feeling helpless. Fascinated, they stood and listened to the fire crackle and pop and hiss as the flames took hold, and watched twigs twist and curl with the heat as if in some desperate and silent death throe. Occasionally the morning breeze would send white wood smoke and a lick of flame towards them, grabbing at their throats and making their eyes smart and water.

They twisted and turned and tried to weave away from its grasp only to discover that in the meantime their pale urban legs had become red and singed.

A large blackened pot balanced precariously on some equally fire-blackened bricks donated by a previous occupant. To their surprise the water soon boiled, allowing hot water for washing and mugs of hot sweet tea that quickly filled them all with warmth and smiles. Around them, neighbours called out cheerily 'Morning. Gonna be a fine day,' peering intently at something in the cool dull sky and sniffing at the messages left by the passing breeze.

'Don't forget your hats children. Don't want to get burnt.'

The neighbours spoke directly to them as grown-ups do when they don't want to embarrass accompanying adults with their advice.

And so Florrie led her troops in single file into the hop fields towards the row designated to them. The air was still chilly and damp from the morning dew and silver drops of the last night's rain sat upon the leaves. In the small valley below, the mist sat around tree trunks teasing the absent rays of sun to chase it away.

'The mist? Ah, no more than a donkey's breath. Soon go,' said a large woman wearing a hessian sack apron and a headscarf brightly printed with flowers of the nearby hedgerows tied tightly around her chubby face. She smiled a twinkly smile. 'Cold son? Yeah. Finger cold this morning. Soon get warm.'

They trudged along with sweaters, topcoats and plastic waterproof macs, and with their trousers tucked into their wellies. The walk across the sodden grass left a dark trail behind them and made their wellington boots black and shiny. The other pickers looked, for all the world, like an army on the move, carrying all that was required for the coming battle: folding chairs for the adults and a couple of empty apple boxes which, when upended, acted as tables or seats for the children; bags full of sandwiches, bottles of lemonade and water, bags of crisps, apples, chocolate; tin mugs, a thermos full of hot tea and a small first aid kit to alleviate stings, bites and the chaffing of soft urban skin against the rough hop bines as well as the burning effect of the sun. All had to be brought with them as the farmer offered only accommodation and the opportunity to work.

Tall grey poles often holding long splits soon appeared and stood before them. At their base, through a tangle of hops, nettles and thistles, a protective dark brown stain peeped out. The poles held a cat's cradle of wires and strings that supported the thick hop bines twisting around them. They spiralled upwards towards the sun and met in the middle to form a dark green tunnel with the lime yellow hop cones peeking through. It felt strange and slightly intimidating to enter this dark, damp world across the rough muddy earth but already, all around them came the sounds of chatter and laughter or the rebuke of a misbehaving child, as their fellow pickers settled down.

'That child is right polrumptious. Need to anoint his bottom, no mistake.'

Nearby large yellow wicker baskets stood next to the sacking trough of their bin that was soon to be brimming with picked hops.

'Come on then,' called Florrie, 'lend us a hand.'

With enthusiasm they all reached up to grasp the nearest bine.

'Careful. Mustn't damage it. Ready?'

The boys nodded.

'Right. Now pull!'

Instantly they were all showered with icy water. It ran down upstretched arms and invaded the warm protection of dry sleeves, leaving clothes cold and clammy. Their shrieks were met by laughter from their neighbours.

'That'll teach you,' they chuckled. 'Need to shake it first. Never mind. Sun'll be out soon.'

And so it was.

They picked steadily and soon steam began to rise from the foliage around them and the early morning mist slipped away, leaving the landscape bright and clear. Now the dawn dankness turned to the smell of drying earth mixed with the bitter taste of hops staining their fingers and the small early orange sun became white and fierce against their skin.

'No dirty picking now,' said Florrie. 'No leaves. Only hops.'

''Ow yer getting on,' said a man picking next to them. He removed his flat hat that had been weathered by sun, rain and sweat, and rubbed flattened greying hair with rough fingertips.

Florrie smiled an OK back at him.

'Good. 'Ot ain't it?'

Around them clothes were being discarded.

Later, when their bin was full, the measurer arrived. He kicked the bin and the large pile of feathery hops collapsed into a smaller heap.

'He's only allowed one kick love. Them's the rules.'

The advice came from their neighbours who although a long way ahead had walked back to keep an eye on things. The measurer ignored them and wrote a number of bushels into a small weary notebook. They had worked all day with hardly a break. Only stopping to grab a bite to eat and for Florrie to dash off to buy ice cream from a visiting ice cream van, which she wrapped in newspaper to try to stop it melting.

'Pick no more bines. Pick no more bines,' came the call and everybody stopped and grinned at each other through sheer weariness and the satisfaction of manual labour and of being together.

Their sandwiches, crisps and drinks had barely sustained them during the day and now as evening approached they were quickly discovering the hunger of physical effort. It gripped their stomachs in painful spasms and weakened trembling bodies. But it was worth it for the smell of lamb, potatoes, carrots, peas and thick gravy bubbling and merging into one tender, rich, unforgettable flavour that tickled their noses with its unbearable deliciousness and made their mouths water until they gulped in anticipation. They discovered the sheer joy of filling their mouths until their cheeks bulged and gravy ran down their chins. They chewed and swallowed as fast as possible in order to fill the demanding void and with never a word spoken. They wiped the last drop from their china plates with thick hunks of bread until they shone bright again and then sat back, stomachs swelled, round and firm, at bursting point. They grinned at each other, satisfied.

'I'm blown out like a kite.'

'That's a pity. We've got milkshakes next.'

The boys looked at each other and then back to Florrie in amazement.

'And tomorrow… roasted jacket potatoes.'

***

Florrie had roasted potatoes before, at the Guy Fawkes night bonfire in her garden, with her sisters and brother. She knew how to roast large King Edwards in the hot embers, turning them with a stick until they were black and then scooping them from the dying fire, blowing on her fingers as they hopped baking hot from hand to hand. She had cut and crunched into their roasted crispness revealing the creamy coloured flesh inside and had watched as each potato sat steaming in the air and rich yellow butter slowly softened and slid across them in a delicious caress.

She had also toasted thick slices of bread, each piece balanced precariously on a pointed stick that had been fastened into the crust for safety. Occasionally they had dropped into the grey ash, which she had simply wiped off. It had been no place for etiquette. When golden brown and hot she had spread the toast with butter, which would melt, soak and drip through onto sticky fingers. Rich red raspberry jam piled on top gave the sublime taste of fruity sweetness, rich butter creaminess and the smoky flavour of burnt chestnut.

Maybe tomorrow we might also have some nice Cox's orange pippins or a juicy Victoria plum, Florrie wondered. 'There must be a shop around here somewhere. If we buy some apples and plums, remember to give me the cores and stones.'

'Why's that Mum?'

'Don't want the farmer to think we've been scrumping do we? Perhaps tomorrow we can also pick some wild blackberries? At least they're free. Lovely with the top of the milk.'

Like other pickers they would, from time to time, hear the honking of van horns announcing the arrival of a local trader carrying milk or bread or joints of meat. 'The baker's here' and the cry would be taken up and passed around the entire site. Florrie would look carefully into her purse and decide whether she could afford it.

'Now ladies, whose first? Alright, don't push, plenty for all. Now, who wants a bloomer? What you're already wearing them missus? Now, now. That's enough of that.'

Also, occasionally, came the sound of the fish and chip van, lurching and clattering over the rough fields, horn blaring, metal chimney trailing the smoke and the smell of appetising hot fat, pursued by a bustling crowd eager for cod and chips sprinkled with salt, vinegar, tomato ketchup and maybe a pickled gherkin or two.

Florrie would unwrap some newspaper and from it, drop a slab of the ice cream into three glasses of cream soda and watch them fizz and bubble and grow a pale froth. It reminded her of the luscious milk shakes that were only available on the screen milk bars of Hollywood, another world away. All the while she wondered what Ted was doing.

***

Ted had enjoyed the peace during the first week and in the evenings he sat quietly in his armchair, staring out into the garden. He watched the light slowly changing on the leaves and slip past. The clatter chatter of the house had dropped to a whisper and new noises surprised his ear. His newspaper pages now turned like a gust of wind shaking the treetops.

As the first weekend approached he began to feel unsettled. Perhaps he *should* try and make his way to the hop fields.

'Harry. Any chance of getting the wagon for Saturday or Sunday perhaps?'

'Sorry mate, it's being used. Don't really know anyone else with a car.'

'Don't worry. Just thought I might surprise them, Florrie and the boys.'

'Can't you go by train or bus?'

'Station's seven miles away. Don't even know if there is a bus service. Certainly not on a Sunday.'

'You alright mate?'

'Oh yes. Fine.'

But he wasn't really.

Ted returned indoors and started to clean. It took two days but when he had finished the house sparkled like a barrack room.

***

Approximately two miles from the hop fields, along a tree-lined lane, was a small hamlet. Nobody seemed to know its name and indeed it consisted of only a few buildings clustered happily around a small area of grass that was tended with care. The sight of this flat, well-tended rug of green appeared out of keeping in a rural setting but it was certainly a pleasant surprise turning the bend in the lane and seeing it appear before you with a smile.

Dominating the buildings was the Bluebell Inn, and "the Bell", as it was familiarly known, was very popular with hoppers who needed to slake their thirst after a hard day's picking or at weekends when the menfolk might arrive from their regular work elsewhere to see their families.

The Londoners in particular were attracted to the only part of the alien countryside that reminded them of home – "the German cruiser" – and here, the landlord, unlike some, was very happy to see his new customers. He was very aware of the considerable boost to his turnover that this annual migration offered him, and he was more than willing to put up with the odd altercation and a few missing glasses. In the Bell the peaceful idyll of rural Kent was sometimes shattered by noisy, laughing, arguing voices and the raucous sounds of *Nellie Dean* and *Won't You Come Home Bill Bailey*. However, good sense and bitter experience had gone as far as a notice fixed to the saloon bar door that bluntly read: 'No hop pickers or gypsies in this bar.' This kept the pickers and locals apart, leaving the locals sulking and complaining into their pints in the saloon bar, listening maybe rather enviously to the joyous sounds reverberating and slurring through the adjoining wall.

'*You're my 'art's desire. I love yer... Nell...ie Dean. Sweet... Nell... ie... Dean.*'

Close to the few red-bricked workers' cottages nearby, stood the village hall. Its walls and roof were completely covered in corrugated sheeting that had been painted dark green. Outside, grew bushes of aromatic rosemary whose green spikes belied the withered appearance of its silver-grey branches. Inside, out of the brightness of the sun, it felt cool and dark and visitors' noses prickled with the spicy mustiness of nests of mice and long forgotten vegetable competitions. The grey wooden floors creaked with every echoing footstep and small coloured flags hung sadly from the roof supports waiting for the next dance or wedding celebration. In one corner stood an old piano, its ivory keys were dusty and yellowing and here and there pieces of veneer had peeled off, assisted maybe by tiny curious fingers. On the walls were two empty noticeboards, enclosed by wooden frames with glass doors. Above them hung a round clock, looking important with its Roman numerals, but which had stopped at twenty past six and now waited patiently to be rewound. But Florrie had no time for this. Today she was heading for the General Stores.

The words "Thomas Atkins and Sons" were painted quietly in faded yellow on the green fascia board above the shop front. The shop window was crammed full of items, but that was nothing to the treat that awaited you once you stepped inside and wiped your feet on the doormat, the shop bell still tingling gently but urgently in your ear. The interior seemed to be in darkness, but as your eyes recovered, they swept and flickered in astonishment across an Aladdin's cave of colours and shapes, stacked and hanging and spilling onto the wooden floor around you, calling out with a cacophony of words and tastes and memories. And the smell – there was no single smell although putting your nose closer to individual items set off their own aromas, each quickly swamped by eager neighbours. The shop smelled of everything – of ham and wood and spices, of candles and apples and pepper; of bread and cake and herbs and tobacco, oil and paraffin – all in one glorious heady mix that you gulped in greedily in case it should disappear.

On the floor, arranged in neat rows, were seven pound boxes of biscuits, some baked by Huntley and Palmer, some by McVitie and others by Crawford. Some offered the pale yellow of custard cream, others the round plumpness of shortbread and some the tang of cheese. Above them, rows of shelves ascended in front of the counter where there were bottles of brown sauce, tins of Oxo, cartons of Bisto, tubs of Bird's Custard, tins of Ovaltine, Izal and Bovril and cans of corned beef. To one side was a yellow mound into which was stuck a tag reading "New Zealand Pure Creamery Butter" and nearby were stacked packets of Robin Starch, Rinso, Oxydol, Recketts Blue Starch and Pearce Duff's pea flour.

At child's eye-level rows of sweets were arranged: glistening Rowntree's fruit gums, thick Mars bars, sharp Sherbet Fountains, chewy Sharps Super Kreem toffee (made at the nearby factory at Maidstone), dark liquorice, succulent chocolate and pretty pink and white sugar mice. They had all been laid out in the hope that the wheedling and pleading would persuade harassed mothers to add to the day's profit.

On rows of shelves behind the counter, stood jars of Robertson's jams, red and purple and orange, next to bottles of fizzy lemonade and sweet Cream Soda and Tizer. Below, were tins of Batchelors peas, Tate and Lyle syrup and rows and rows of cigarettes. Player's Navy Cut competed with Woodbine, Craven A and Piccadilly together with Wills Castella cigars, for that special occasion. Golden Virginia tobacco or the more exotic Addkin's Turkish waited for you to fill your pouch or maybe roll your own with the Rizla cigarette papers that sat waiting nearby. You could then light up using a box from the stacks of brightly coloured and decorative Bryant and May matches. Occasionally advertising cards would peek above rows of products exhorting you to "ask for Players Please" or reminding you that Senior Service "really do Satisfy".

To one side, stood a large dark wooden construction that contained row after row of small boxes, each with its own brass handle. Painted carefully in white upon each, were the names of the seeds the boxes contained: carrot, cauliflower, varieties of cabbage, parsnip and Brussels sprout whilst other boxes indicated varieties and sizes of nails, screws, bolts, pins, fuse wire, string, washers, mouse traps and hinges.

On the floor were large open sacks of flour and rice and sugar with a metal scoop ready to pour into blue or white paper bags that could be then be weighed on the Avery scales that stood on the counter. A small collection of pots, pans, colanders, lamps and carpet beaters hung close by, and, under the counter, available after a brief whispered conversation, were senna pods, cod liver oil and Beechams pills along with bandages, plasters, bicarbonate of soda and other essentials to help soothe the inevitable upsets of hop picking.

In the middle of it all stood Mr Atkins. He was a small, wiry man who only ever appeared from the waist up behind his barricade of groceries. His head was shaved from the neck up to a point just above his ears where the razor stopped abruptly, allowing his greying hair to sprout freely. His delicate hands were always raw from a compulsion to continually wash them. But nothing rid them of the mud of the Somme. Nothing would ever remove the dark brown soup of earth and blood and pulverised young flesh that also stained his sleep. No bratwurst or coal scuttles here.

He wore a brown overall, the top pocket of which was marked by red and blue biros and even on the hottest days, a collar and tie. His trousers and shoes were rarely seen, behind the barrier of his counter, the floor of which was slightly raised like a fire step. From there he would peer through thin wire framed glasses at those who entered his shop. Of his sons there was no sign. Of Mrs Atkins there was no sign.

He was a shrewd trader. For generations before him, there had been a metal grill protecting the valuable goods plus a sign chalked on a child's blackboard proclaiming "Grill will come down when hop picking is finished" – a barely disguised comment on the honesty of hopping customers. But his skill as a shopkeeper was to know exactly where every single item was, to somehow keep a watchful eye on every one, to know how much everything cost and to immediately add the total in his head, even when dealing with several customers at once. He simply did not need the protection of a metal grill.

'Will that be all? That will be nine shillings and tuppence,' came the instant response before the astonished shopper had time to even consider the calculation themselves. Such was the positive nature of the demand that few felt secure enough to contest it.

Now, at the weekend, and with no picking, Florrie left the boys under the watchful eye of Mrs Jones and strolled the two miles, grinning at the dappled sunshine and blue sky flickering between the trees, and at the square of measured green and eventually arriving at the little shop. Soon Mr Atkins had sold her half a pound of sherbet lemons in response to her request for a quarter (to give the little ones a treat) and two packets of Players instead of one (to save shoe leather) and was about to pay when the door crashed open and the figures of a man and woman entered.

'Bleedinell, Rose. Look at this lot.'

'Christ,' replied Rose succinctly.

Fred, Rose's companion, continued to look around. He was a short, thickset man with dark hair slicked back and bushy sideburns that grew from the sides of his sallow face. His blue and white checked shirt, over which he wore a shiny black waistcoat, was opened at the neck, showing a yellowing vest., Crumpling over large unclean boots were his baggy trousers, held up by a thick black leather belt with a worn brass buckle as well as by a pair of dark red braces. His features were dominated by dark, deep-set eyes and a bulbous nose, tinged and veined with red and purple. He smelled of engine oil and stale beer, and walked and talked with a swagger.

Rose followed him. As loud and dark as Fred was, Rose was his antithesis. Pale and thin as a rake, she tried hard to make her wispy brown hair look fashionable, but usually failed and had turned to the bleach bottle instead. The result closely matched the bales of hay in the fields, apart from the dark roots that dared to peek through. But it pleased Fred. She wore a brightly coloured frock covered in large red and blue flowers and white shoes with a significant heel which on the uncertain country surfaces made her totter and sway like some strange exotic plant in a breeze. Her brown eyes darted about the little shop like a frightened animal and occasionally she would point a thin, crimson-tipped finger and sniff. She seldom spoke except to agree with Fred.

Both began to move around the tiny shop, rummaging and peering and poking.

''Ow much is yer cheese, mate?' called Fred over his shoulder to Mr Atkins. 'You like a drop a cheese Rose don't yer.'

Rose nodded.

'I'll be with you in a moment, sir,' replied Mr Atkins, watching them from the corner of his eye and counting out Florrie's change at the same time.

'Blimey, sir is it. That's posh. Never git called sir in Romford, now do I Rose.'

Rose smiled uncertainly. Fred moved towards the counter with Rose glued to his elbow.

'Thank you madam. Hope to see you again soon.'

Florrie smiled her thanks, closed her purse with a snap, dropped it into her bag and turned to face Fred and Rose who now blocked her way.

'Got everyfing luv? Got yer swedes? Mustn't forgit yer bleedin' swedes. That's all they eat down ere yer know. Bleedin' swede bashers. Yer don't need swedes. Yer wanna good bit a meat. Put some beef on those bones.' He stretched and pinched Florrie's arm. 'Know wot I mean?' and he put his grinning stale face close to hers.

Florrie froze, twisted her arm away and glared silently at him.

'Only joking luv. Don't git yer knickers in a twist. Just a larf.'

He moved out of her way.

Florrie left the little shop and walked back to the hut. The sun still beamed upon her but now she appeared not to notice it. 'Common little man. How dare he. Right we'll see about that,' she thought and her back straightened, her jaw jutted and she began to stride forward. Soon a little smile began to play around her lips. By the time she had reached her hut, she had the beginnings of a plan.

She knew that hops had been grown for centuries in Kent and as a young girl she had heard the stories of the many thousands of Londoners that travelled from the East End to the hop fields to help supplement often empty purses. They were tough and streetwise; called "foreigners" by the gentler country folk and such was the difference between town and country that they might as well have come from a foreign land. Inevitably there was friction between the two. Florrie smarted not only because of Fred's oafish behaviour, but also because of his assumption that she was a country yokel. *How dare he.*

But if the Londoners had an Achilles' heel then it had to be their uncertainty about the strange countryside and their nervousness of the blackness that descended over the fields at sunset. Here, there were no street lamps, no lit street windows, no headlights from passing vehicles. As the sun slipped below the horizon, confident

Cockney chatter would slip to a low hum and they would gather together for protection and wish for a full moon.

Inevitably, this encouraged the telling of vivid stories that turned the countryside so gentle and benign by day into a place of terror and unspeakable horror by night. Such stories were often told by the flickering light of a single oil lamp in an otherwise pitch-black hut where you could hide from the hideous creatures that crept silently around you by pulling a blanket over your head and listening to your heart pounding in your breast. Outside, around the dying flames of a fire, you could listen and stare wide-eyed into the glowing embers and start at the sudden crack and movement of the fire and watch the fiery sparks fly away and die somewhere out there in the blackness. You could feel the heat on your hands and face, but at the same time the night crept up behind you and ran its cold fingers down your spine. There was nothing better than being frightened in company.

That night, with the boys in bed, Florrie sat around the fire, and listened.

'It 'appened right 'ere on this very farm, along that very lane.' The speaker pointed somewhere out into the darkness. 'Terrible, quite terrible it was. Yeh... And 'er ghost can still be seen on clear nights. In September. Like now. Like tonight. In these fields. Here. Where it all 'appened.' He paused. ''Cos they never found it you know. Her body... Nah. Just her 'ead. That's all they found... Poor girl... Terrible...'

He shook his head sadly and looked for a long time into the fire. 'Quite terrible,' he murmured to the dying embers.

There was another long pause and total silence. Suddenly his voice rose, more urgently. 'And yer know wot. Yer know wot... It talks, yeh it bleedin' talks. Just er 'ead. On its own'

There was a sharp intake of breath. Somebody cried 'Oh no.'

'Oh YEH. Calls out is name. 'Er lover see. Calls 'is name, ever so softly. 'Enreee... 'Enreee.' He paused. 'Yeh just down the lane.'

A piece of wood, blackened and eaten by the flames, suddenly gave way and fell, sending another shower of sparks. An owl hooted. Woo woo... ''Enree...'

Florrie looked across at Fred and Rose seated almost opposite her and noted Fred's sardonic grin and Rose, pale-faced, holding on tightly to him.

Now her plan was complete.

***

Saturday night, after a long week's picking, would find many celebrating in the Bell. From inside would come the loud warm sound of chatter and laughter, the odour of hop-stained clothes and best bitter, the heavy smell of many cigarettes and pipes and the clink and clatter of glasses. Outside, unnoticed, the dusk quietly gathered and the familiar shapes of trees, fields, fences and pathways quickly disappeared behind a veil of darkness and waited for the dawn to arrive and change them back again. The only light now blazed yellow from the pub windows. Outside, the countryside quietly watched the flickering silhouettes and waited.

'Time… gentlemen… please.'

The heavy brass bell inside the pub rang out clearly announcing that business was over for yet another day.

Fred staggered noisily into the darkness, supported by Rose, and stood swaying and blinking uncertainly at the blackness that now surrounded him.

'Which bleedin' way Rose?' he bellowed.

'This way Fred. Turn right outside the pub an' straight up the lane.'

'Oh yer. You're right girl.'

He lurched into the night.

'Hang abart Fred,' cried Rose. 'Let me get the bleedin' torch out.'

'Come on Rosie old girl, this way,' slurred Fred, heading towards the nearest row of trees.

Rose caught his arm and swung him around and they both stumbled towards their hut two miles away, following the wavering white beam of their single torch.

To begin with they had the company of others and enjoyed the noise and banter of the group, but gradually they were left behind as the amount of bitter and port and lemon they had consumed turned jollity into quiet contemplation and then the desperate need to sleep.

'Gawd, I could do wiv another pint,' mumbled Fred, mouth now bone dry and reeking of beery fumes.

'Keep going,' urged Rose, trying to hang on to him and keep the bobbing torch beam on the track, all the while looking out for ruts, holes and the occasional cow pat.

'Wot a gawd awful bleedin' place to live in,' moaned Fred, now sober enough to realise his predicament. 'Ain't there a bleedin' bus?' He paused. 'Christ I could murder some fish 'n' chips. Yeah, wiv salt an' vinegar an' bread an'…'

'Oh for Christ's sake Fred. Can't you stop moaning?' snapped Rose in a rare moment of anger and frustration, but knowing that the drunken man clinging on to her was still too far gone to give her his usual backhander.

'Can't you stand up? You're so bleedin' heavy.' She moved his arm that was draped around her shoulder to a more comfortable position.

For a while they staggered on past open fields where what moonlight there was vaguely picked out the dark silhouettes of great trees that watched their progress impassively. In the distance they could see the faint glow of the nearest town and that gave them some comfort.

A mile ahead the rough lane left the open fields and passed through a small wood where all light was virtually extinguished by the canopy of branches and autumn leaves. Soon, out of the darkness, came the sounds of disembodied voices, talking quietly as people do when they are surrounded by the black of night.

'What should we do about those two?' whispered a woman as her hand pointed unseen in the direction of Fred and Rose.

'Perhaps we should wait for them?'

'No, they'll be OK and anyway I want my bed.'

'Besides he's such a cocky bastard. You think he'd wait for us? No way. Come on.'

And so they carried on willing their huts to loom out of the darkness.

Gradually, a long way behind them, out of the night, came the sound of just two voices moaning and whining in succession and then a wavering light emerged from the darkness and stopped.

'Gawd it's dark up there Fred. I'm frightened.'

At that moment, the breeze like an accomplice, strengthened and swirled and rustled the thousands of leaves. Unseen branches creaked and moaned.

'For Chrissake woman, keep going, I need…'

'What's that?'

'Wot?'

'That… Listen.'

'I can't hear a bleedin' thing.'

'Listen.'

'WOT?'

A soft voice whispered out of the darkness and swirled around them.

'Henry.'

'That… oh Gawd Fred.'

'Henree.'

The voice was louder now. The sound lingered into the night. The breeze grinned to itself and sent the branches and leaves into a crescendo of sound.

'It's 'er Fred. It's bleedin 'er!' screeched Rose.

Fred felt the hair on the back of his neck leap in fright and he stood open mouthed and speechless. The alcohol that had left him largely incapable now drained from his sodden brain and was instantly replaced like a slap in the face with ice-cold water. He knew that Rose's crimson nails were biting into his fleshy hand, but he felt nothing. A rasping sound trickled faintly into his consciousness and, turning, he saw Rose, mouth open, eyes bulging, face glowing white with sheer fright even in the surrounding darkness.

At that precise moment, it appeared – a head, a head so awful and so distorted, and a face, a grotesque face, flooded in a ghostly aura, hovered bodiless in the surrounding darkness.

Rose screamed.

'Jesus Christ!' Fred's voice was charged with panic.

'Run Rose, fer Chrissake RUN.'

At that moment he felt the flooding wet warmth of his bladder releasing, unable now to withstand the effects of both numerous pints and his physical terror.

'Wait for me!' screamed Rose and their gurgling gasping voices disappeared into the night.

***

The next day the news of Fred and Rose's dramatic encounter spread like wildfire through the huts.

"Ere, did you hear about the ghost last night?'

'No. What ghost?'

'The ghost. Just down the lane. Those two in the hut near Daisy saw it.'

'Not the mouthy one. What's his name, Fred?'

'Yeah that's him, and his tarty missus. Doesn't know if she's on foot or horseback that one.'

'Gawd 'elp us.'

Fred, now recovered, was soon embroidering both the event and his own courage to anyone who cared to listen.

'I stood me ground. Nuffing scares me. Nuffing. Rose was shitting 'erself. Know wot I mean? 'Ad to git her back 'ere didn't I.'

Rose said nothing.

That evening, being Sunday, to round off the week and before the dawn chorus woke them for yet another morning's damp picking, a large fire was built. Everybody contributed something that would burn brightly without billows of choking white smoke and the curses of those who might get caught downwind. Newspaper, dead twigs and dry straw quickly became yellow flames and soon the main timbers and dead branches were roaring with sparks cascading into the coming twilight. The pickers assembled, armed with chairs and stools or an old log to squat on, potatoes to roast, bread to toast, cooking pots for a communal stew (stew was the best and safest description as nobody knew exactly what individuals had thrown in to cook) bottles of beer and glasses, blankets to cover your knees when the flames began to die down and on this occasion, a rather battered and wheezy accordion. They sat and listened to the rhythm of the fire as it popped, cracked, whistled, hissed and roared into the fast approaching darkness. Soon they were all joined as one in the chatter and laughter and shouts, and grinned at each other as they felt the closeness of their little community. The accordionist took one last swig of ale from a large brown bottle, wiped his lips on a dirty sleeve, took hold of the beast with an extravagant movement and squeezed two raucous, spluttering chords from within it. A cheer from the assembled pickers brought a smile to the player's tanned face.

'Bill Bailey!' came a cry.

'On Mother Kelly's Doorstep!' came another.

'We want Nellie Dean!'

The demands filled the air until it was impossible to distinguish them and everybody began to laugh at the nonsense of it all. The accordionist bent his head towards his faithful friend as if whispering encouragement and then notes poured slowly into the night air.

> *'When Irish eyes are smiling*
> *Sure 'tis like a morn in Spring.*
> *In the lilt of Irish laughter*
> *You can hear the angels sing.'*

People began to sing in a mood of quiet reflection as their voices sought the expression of the song. The flames flickered shadows on faces burnt by the sun and wind and people swayed gently in time to the music. They were close to the sun and wind, the rain and dew, the clouds and stars and to each other.

An Irish tenor now took the tune and his voice clear and sweet as a bell cut through the night air.

> *'When Irish hearts are happy,*
> *All the world seems bright and gay.'*

It was at that moment that Oliver and Bobby thought that Florrie was taking a very long time to come back from the hut.

'Don't worry boys. She'll be here soon. You'll see,' Mrs Jones smiled reassuringly.

> *'And when Irish eyes are smiling,*
> *Sure, they steal your heart away.'*

The final note hung in the air before drifting away into the night. There was a moment's silence.

'Sure dat's a foine tune.'

And the chatter and laughter began again.

From the other side of the fire came a movement and a low murmuring.

'Hallo Fred... Rose. What you doing here? Don't often see you around.'

'Is that a problem then?' came the unmistakeable growl.

'Nah, not at all. Just saying.'

'Seen any spirits recently, Fred?' came a woman's voice.

'Only at the bottom of a glass,' cackled another, hidden in the semi-darkness and people laughed, but quietly as if uncertain about the ghostly truth or of the menacing presence of Fred himself.

'You wouldn't a laughed if youda seen wot we saw,' he menaced. 'Looked inta the jaws of death itself an bleedin' stared back I did.'

He looked around in the flickering darkness and gauged that he now had an audience that he could control and his confidence grew and with it the exaggerations.

'Called me name yer know. Called out "Frederick" like me dear old mum called me, bless her soul. Like me time 'ad come. I looked it in the face. It wos 'orrible, like a skull. A talkin' skull.'

'You never told us that before,' called out a voice.

'Were yer there? Were ya?' he snarled. He paused and sniffed. 'I said to it, I said, "Ghosty you don't scare me. If yer want me, come an' bleedin' get me." Them's me very words. Ain't that right Rose?'

Rose, hovering in the shadows with a rug around her looked a sorry sight. Even in the firelight, dark shadows showed beneath her sad eyes and her white-heeled shoes were now scratched and dirty. 'I think so, Fred.'

'Yer bleedin' think so,' and he turned on her but aware of a growing sympathy for Rose, stopped himself, half laughed and returned to his audience. 'Hah. Women eh.'

'Fred.' Rose's voice suddenly called out in a strangled squeak. 'Oh Gawd Fred.'

She pointed, gasped and fell backwards into the darkness.

Everybody turned in the direction of her quivering finger and there no more than twenty feet away floated a distorted ghoulish face flickering in the darkness.

'Jesus Christ. What the hell…?'

There was a mad panic to get away from the now approaching spectre. People clustered together and held each other. Despite the apparition, nobody wanted to leave the safety of the fire, but grouped together on the opposite side of the dying flames. A few men turned to face the monster, uncertain as what to do and a voice was heard reciting The Lord's Prayer.

'Frederick,' said the face. 'Frederick,' it repeated.

Fred fell to his knees and began to cry.

Mrs Jones held the boys protectively. 'It's all right' she said calmly.

Despite the horror that was unfolding, the voice sounded familiar.

'Frederick… you… are… a… lying… cheating…'

The face now arrived at the fireside and removed the black material that covered most it.

'Cowardly… evil…'

The torch held under the face was switched off.

'Pathetic… BULLY.'

There, looking down at the crumbled broken figure at her feet, stood Florrie. Arms akimbo. Feet placed firmly apart, jaw set.

Only the sobbing of Fred and the quiet crackling of the dying fire broke a total stunned silence.

'Jesus,' said a quavering voice, 'it's Florrie.'

'It's Mum,' said Bobby. 'Knew it was.'

'It's Florrie' and the words ran around the fire from mouth to mouth. The relief was palpable.

'Florrie was the ghost.'

They laughed and cried and slapped each other on the back and laughed again until they couldn't stand up. Florrie just grinned and grinned and grinned.

The next day, Fred and Rose had disappeared and Florrie led her small but triumphant army into the fields once more, heads held high.

'Morning Florrie,' called smiling voice after smiling voice. Women came up and hugged her and men touched her affectionately on her arm.

'Well done girl,' and turned away shaking their heads in admiration.

'Have a sweet boys,' and Oliver and Bobby rustled eagerly into crumpled white paper bags and withdrew thick lumps of toffee wrapped in shiny clear film and sucked them noisily.

'Ain't you proud of your Mum?'

The boys looked at each other, smiled, nodded and turned away.

'Oh, don't be shy,' said a large lady with apple red cheeks.

'Oh we're not shy,' said Bobby. 'But it's a secret. On pain of death.'

He turned back to his brother.

'Is it still a secret Ollie?' Bobby whispered, eyes shining. 'Can I tell?'

'Yes, I think so Bobby.'

'Well our friend Mrs Jones and Mum told us the plan—'

'So that Bobby wouldn't be frightened,' interrupted Oliver.

'And you!' Bobby retorted fiercely. Bobby turned back to the large lady. 'Because our Mum will never be in…tim…ulated.'

'He means intimidated.'

'No I don't.'

Oliver raised his eyes skywards.

Undeterred, Bobby continued passionately. 'Good job our Dad wasn't here. He would have shot them. He was in the war. Ollie has seen his jacket – in the wardrobe. He's great, our Dad, and our Mum, aren't they Ollie?'

Oliver smiled and nodded again.

Florrie sat in the sunshine, picked hops into their bin and sang loudly.

> *'When Irish eyes are smiling*
> *Sure 'tis like a morn in spring*
> *In the lilt of Irish laughter*
> *You can hear the angels sing.'*

***

'Bye Florrie. It was good to know you.'
'Bye Ada.'
'Bye bye boys. Look after your mum.'
'Bye bye Mrs Jones.'

They sat quietly outside their now empty hut. Even their straw bed had been taken away to be burnt. They felt different. They certainly looked different with brown faces and necks and hands still stained despite countless washes.

'Scrub harder.'
'It hurts.'

They also constantly scratched itchy scalps.

They wanted to return to the comfort of their home and of course see Ted again, but already Bobby had found a lump of chalk in the nearby field and had carefully and slowly written their names in a wavy line on the back of the hut. The rain and sunshine would eventually dissolve the childish letters into a stain, but it would always be their hut.

The two boys stood next to each other and stared at the writing.

'I feel happy and sad,' said Bobby. 'All mixed up together, like a trifle.'
'A trifle?'
'Yes. I like the cream, but I hate the jelly.'
'We'll come back one day Bobby, when we're grown-up.'
'Is it good to be grown-up Ollie?'

Bobby looked up at his brother.

'Oh I'm sure it will be.'

'Bye Florrie. Bye.'

The pickers waved their grinning farewells.

'See you next year.'

'Here they come,' Florrie said as the Austin wagon bounced off the rough track, drove across the grass and halted before them.

Ted and Harry jumped down, slammed the doors and advanced towards them, both smiling broadly.

Oliver and Bobby ran towards them. Bobby grasped at Ted's legs, making him stumble.

'Mrs Jones looked after us and Mum was a ghost and we haven't washed.'

'Hey careful,' he laughed taking both boys by their hands.

Florrie stood up. She did not smile but waited. Ted placed one hand on her shoulder and kissed her soundly on her cheek.

'Hallo love. Did you have a good time?'

Harry looked on.

The boys grinned.

NINE

Akela, the Concert and a Black Smiling Dog

'To be yourself in a world that is constantly trying to make you something else is the greatest accomplishment.'

Ralph Waldo Emerson

The Committee
Florrie Tappenden: Akela and Chairman
Ted Tappenden: Secretary and Treasurer
Harry Smith: Committee member
Helen Smith: Committee member
Joan Williamson: Committee member
Louis. Cub Scout Assistant: Guest member
Alan Jenner: Guest member

'Come on Louis. You're late.'
'Sorry, Akela.'
Louis arrived and slid onto the remaining chair in a single fluid movement. He looked around, giving a faint smile in mute apology, his pale eyes framed by deep black lashes. Nobody knew if his startling appearance was an act of nature or whether nature had been given some assistance. Nobody liked to ask.

The committee, now complete, sat around an old fold-up trestle table, acquired for free from a local canteen. It was clean, Florrie had seen to that, scrubbing it vigorously with Dettol. But it still bore a faint history of human activity – spilled gravy and custard – like cave paintings.

Florrie sat at one end with Ted to her right. She was busy studying her notes and tapping the end of her pencil on the table. It wasn't for attention, for the other members now sat in silence, waiting. The sound echoed slightly around the large wooden hall.

Her rise to Akela had been meteoric – a mixture of enthusiasm and determination. She was unstoppable really, since that sunny day sitting on the elm tree branch. She was determined that her young cubs would themselves understand right over wrong, freedom over tyranny and strength over weakness and that they would be able to march up their own Hills when the time came. She was firm and fair, she tolerated no nonsense, gave herself totally and the boys loved her. She scared most of the adults.

Ted had stood beside her, well, one step back, supporting, guiding, but always as her consort. While she fizzed around like a jumping jack, he kept an eye on her, never diluting her energy, but at times redirecting it, reining it in. She was happy. And if she was happy, Ted was happy. He knew he couldn't compete and he didn't want to.

They talked more now, not about the war, it had been almost twenty years now since it had ended. He still couldn't do that, but now there were other things in their lives and the horror and guilt had been pushed further away, save for the occasional churning dream.

He had found a space in the garden and planted a small elm shoot – no more than a few inches high. He didn't tell Florrie, although eventually she found it. "Must have self-seeded," he said "but we should keep it. Shouldn't we love?"

"Of course." Florrie would never turn away a wandering soul, especially one that had floated in on the wind seeking her refuge. But *he* knew that it was a reminder – for him. And it steadily grew taller and stronger.

The house, still with the front door on the latch, now received even more visitors as the cubs called in, sometimes on their own, just wanting to say hallo to Akela, or more often, in groups as part of their training. Florrie was very keen that they worked for and be awarded badges, lots of them.

'Gives them self-confidence. Makes them have a pride in themselves. Makes them realise that if you work hard, then you get rewards.'

It also gave her a deep sense of satisfaction – both helping others and being centre stage. Consequently it was not unusual to step over young boys lying in the hallway, covered in mock blood, ghastly white make-up and swathed in bandages or to find Florrie doing handstands as part of the programme to instruct them for their 'upside down badge' or whatever it might be called or to be banished from your own kitchen, dripping with condensation and giggles as the cubs carefully counted down seconds while boiling eggs.

'Guess what I did today Mum, with Akela? I boiled an egg, buttered some bread and ate it for my tea. You have to count the minutes otherwise it goes hard. And I'm going to get a badge. Can I do it here? Please Mum.'

Such was the enthusiasm for acquiring badges that it was not unusual for the boys to run out of black woollen sleeves to display them on. It was little wonder that parents held Florrie in awe.

***

Florrie looked up at the committee and met six pairs of willing eyes.

'OK. Today we have to…'

Ted touched her arm, leaned towards her and whispered. She cocked her head and listened, nodding.

'Yes. Yes. OK. Thank you,' she murmured then looking up. 'Sorry. Firstly, thank you all for giving up your Saturday mornings.' Florrie beamed. Everybody beamed back. 'Also Bagheera can't make it today. Her youngest is down with tonsillitis.'

'Oh no, that's nasty.' Joan and Helen cut in. 'My niece had that.'

'My Jonathan too. In bed for two weeks. Could only take ice cream.'

'Oh dear, poor thing.'

'Yes. Very nasty.'

Florrie tapped her pencil.

'Sorry Florrie, er, Akela.'

Florrie paused. 'Right. So, instead, Louis has volunteered to take her place.'

Everybody now turned and smiled at Louis who moved his head slightly to one side and gently pouted.

'Also, welcome to Alan.' Florrie looked in his direction at the far end of the table. 'You all know Alan.'

Everybody turned again, nodded and smiled. Alan nodded and smiled back.

Florrie continued, 'Alan is Sidney and Alice's son from number fifteen.'

Everybody except Louis already knew that. They also knew that Alan had been Jonathan's best friend and that Alan's hands that now rested in his lap, carried the scars of burns from that awful day. But they didn't mind. In a strange way it bound them together, made them stronger. Life had to go on and it did.

'You alright mate?' Harry's voice boomed out.

Joan started, placed one hand below her throat and made a tiny gasp. She looked around slightly embarrassed, but nobody seemed to notice. They were too busy trying not to laugh. Not at her, but at Harry and his high decibel voice.

She smiled uncertainly. She had been looking forward to meeting Alan again. It seemed impossible that he was a grown man now. Must be getting on for forty. Where had all those years gone to? She had felt quite calm about it. Thought about Jonathan of course but had felt calm; fairly calm.

Helen nudged her husband in the ribs and he half turned towards her. She raised her eyebrows and slowly shook her head. It was a signal that they all recognised. Harry shrugged his wide shoulders and began to trace a cave painting with a large finger.

Florrie continued.

'Alan's going to help us with the electrics.'

'Oh thank God for that. Do you remember last year? With those wave light things?'

'Floodlights Helen, and I'm sure Alan will sort everything out. Now can we get on with the meeting, please?'

Florrie bathed the committee with her cool blue eyes.

Harry, having lost interest in cave art and apparently colour-blind, turned towards Alan.

'You an electrician mate?'

'No. Plumber.'

Joan's look threw out concern and Alan caught it.

'It's OK. Don't worry. Working on the buildings, you pick up a lot.'

Joan smiled protectively at him, maternally. A tiny nerve ticked in her cheek without permission. Jonathan would have been Alan's age now. Married? With children? Even grandchildren?

'How's your little sister. How's Pamela?'

'Not so little now Joan. My *little* sister is twenty eight.'

Joan felt Alan's words throw their arms around her, like her own son would have done.

'Yes, Pam's working in a hospital in Melbourne. Doing well,' he nodded to reinforce her success.

'Melbourne? Christ that's a long way away.'

'Harree.'

'Sorry, but it is. What sort of work she doing, Alan?'

'She works in a specialist burns unit.'

There was a pause that slid into silence. Alan felt something grasp his stomach and twist it. *Oh shit.*

Harry looked down at the table. It was only half a second, but long enough for a thousand hours of thoughts to canter through his mind. Funny how that memory still clutched at him. Even now, after all this time. Sometimes a smell or a sound, a distant bonfire or an aircraft rumbling low, or like now, just a word would bring it back.

Didn't always though. You never knew. Often it caught him unawares. He could pass that very house a hundred times and nothing. Then the hundred and first… there it was. Thank Christ most of the time that memory just sat there, like an unwanted book on the bottom shelf in a library.

He thought how strange life was.

We found a house; looked nice; right price; near to work; nice garden for the kids, but you never know what else you were buying into. What else would come along? No kids for a start. Not for them.

Poor Helen. Not that she ever said anything, but he could see. If they had gone for that house on the other side of the river, then things might have been different: different lives, parallel lives, fate. That's what Helen said sometimes. Nah bollocks. You just had one life. Up to you to make the best of it.

People had said how brave he'd been, that he deserved a medal, but he didn't want any fuss.

Just did it without thinking really. Had to help them.

Maybe he was trying to prove that he was as good as the others. Those he wasn't allowed to join. Maybe.

The only thing that shocked him was the thought that just a few feet away, hidden by smoke, Jonathan had lain blackened and burning. He hadn't known. There was nothing he could have done anyway, he told himself. He hoped that Joan had never seen that. She never said of course.

He looked up again.

Helen and Florrie had looked quickly at Joan, sending a message: *Are you OK?* Joan looked back, said nothing, but raised her eyebrows just a fraction and smiled thinly. *I'm OK. Really.*

It was all over so quickly, so much.

Ted grabbed them back. He had seen their spirit fall away. He understood why and felt compassionate, but at the same time realised with a shock that he was on the outside looking in. He looked around like a stranger. No matter what he or they did or said he could never join them. Not really, they alone would always be bonded by that experience.

God. That must be what Florrie feels about me. He felt saliva gather in his mouth and tried not to swallow nervously. *Come on. Get a grip*, he told himself. 'Time is getting on,' he said softly.

'Yes, Ted's right,' Joan agreed, telling them again she was fine. She was also telling Ted of her admiration for him. Ted didn't appear to notice.

Florrie tapped her pencil. Twice. Louder. The sun came out.

'Right you lot. I've worked out what each of you has to do.'

'Don't we get a choice, Akela?'

Florrie looked at Harry, the naughty little boy. Harry the clown. Cheering them up now.

'Take it that's a no then.' He grinned.

Everybody grinned, even Florrie.

'Right. Now. Joan.'

'Yes, Akela.'

'I want you to look after the costumes. Check what we still have from last year. I think some of the grass skirts for the Hawaiian number look as if they've moulted. And maybe some more costumes. I've got some new ideas. We can talk about that later.'

'Yes, Akela.'

'Louis.'

'Yes, Akela.'

'You help Joan and also help the boys get ready on the night.'

'I'd also like to do the make-up again Akela. I've been practising.'

Harry grinned, but it wasn't a salacious grin. He had told the lads working on the river about Louis and then wished he hadn't, which had surprised him. They had responded with loud crude comments. What did he expect? But he saw the commitment in the young man. He felt Louis' quiet acceptance and at times unspoken anguish. He was also an outsider, like Harry had been.

'OK Louis. Thank you. That's fine. Now, Helen.'

'Yes, Akela.'

'You organise the food and drink. Lots of sandwiches. Cheese maybe, but no pickle. Can't take the risk of it falling out onto the costumes. Can you imagine young Jeffrey Saunders? Nice lad, but there would be pickle everywhere. Lots of biscuits and maybe those mini sausage rolls that we got cheap from the Co-op last year. And we've got that urn now from the jumble sale for the tea.'

'Yes, Akela.'

'Harry.'

'Yes, Akela.'

'You do the publicity and help Ted on the door.'

The two men smiled at each other.

'Contact the local papers. They'll send a reporter and photographer oh and we need some celebrities. The mayor and our MP. What's his name? No, I don't know either. Is he Conservative?

'Yes, Akela.'

'Don't bother then. And footballers. Are they doing well this season? Always helps. Yes? OK, invite the manager of the Gills. And the captain. In fact try the whole team, but not that right half, the short one with the curly hair. Dirty player. Must set an example to the boys. Oh and what about that Mr and Mrs Potter? You know… the ones from Broad Street. They won the pools last week. Anyone famous. Oh and Harry, we need some decoration. We've still got those bed sheets that we sewed together and that big Union Jack for the stage but we need something extra to brighten the place up.'

'OK Akela. I've got a mate in the stores in the Dockyard. He owes me a favour.' Everybody grinned at Harry, each imagining the story of that favour. 'Oh also Akela, there's a ship in next week from Rotterdam carrying tinned fruit…'

'We don't want anything illegal, Harry.'

Harry sat back, trying to look hurt and failing. 'Just perks,' he mumbled.

'Ted. You want to say something?'

'Yes Akela.'

It had felt strange at first for Ted to call Florrie by her title, although he had no problem in referring others in her direction particularly when advising them to 'go and ask Akela'. He was of course no stranger to rank and eventually decided that it really was no different from saying 'Yes Sergeant. No Sergeant.' After all, she was in charge and he needed to support her fully.

He looked at them over the top of his glasses, like a schoolmaster.

'I'm going to be looking after the accounts. We'll be selling tickets as last year, but also it's important that you keep receipts for everything that you buy and let me have them. No receipts, no money back. OK?'

Everybody nodded.

'Will you be doing your adding up trick Ted?'

Ted groaned inwardly. All eyes moved from Joan to Ted and back again as she continued.

'It's brilliant. He adds up all three columns of figures at once, you know. Pounds shillings and pence. Four I suppose if you include the ha'pennies. I've seen it. Perhaps you could do that as an act Ted? Get a big blackboard and get the audience to call out the figures and then add them up, quick as a flash.'

Joan smiled rather nervously. Ted looked back at her over the top of his glasses and said nothing.

'What will you be doing, Akela?'

It was Helen who changed the subject.

'Same as last year. Record the music and prepare the acts. Bagheera and Louis will help with the rehearsals.'

'You could play that new album. The Rolling Stones one. Just come out. Have you seen him? On the box? Mick Jaggers? What a laugh.'

'I don't think so Harry. It's horrible. Can't see the boys prancing about like that. It's… it's disgusting.'

Harry laughed.

'But you're going to do your solos aren't you Akela? Oh you've got to do those. Star of the show isn't she?' Harry looked around encouraging the others to agree with him. 'Isn't that right Ted?'

'She certainly is.'

Everybody smiled and nodded. They meant it.

Florrie glowed.

'Are the boys coming, Florrie?'

'Afraid not Joan. Oliver's working at the theatre. He's going to move to the West End soon. Work with all the big stars.'

'How exciting. And Bobby?'

'Bobby's on a police course at Guildford. CID.'

'CID? But he's still only a cadet isn't he?'

Florrie glared at Harry.

'Pity. They could bring their girlfriends.'

'Not interested in girls, Joan.'

'Oh Florrie. Of course they are.'

Florrie just scowled.

Joan smiled to herself.

'Will we have another meeting Akela?'

Her thoughts re-gathered. 'Er yes. We'll have to meet again to finalise everything. Same time next week. OK?'

It wasn't really a request.

***

The boys, Bobby almost out of his teens now, called in to see Ted and Florrie as often as possible. Ted was very proud that his sons had done so well. They had gone further than he ever dreamed they would and he knew that it was his generation that had given them their opportunity. He certainly loved them deeply, especially as they were born at the darkest, most hopeless time, when he knew he might never survive to be with them. But he *had* survived, to see them grow, gleaming out of that terrible blackness. His boys.

Maybe he loved them more than he did Florrie? He didn't know. It was confusing, he couldn't rationalise those thoughts. He had nobody to bounce those ideas off. Sometimes, he realised that he never told them how he felt. He wasn't able to say those words. *But it doesn't matter, does it? Surely they know? Of course they do.*

When the boys pushed open the front door at number twenty-one, Florrie simply grinned nonstop and fed them. Her boys were back. She tried to grasp what they were telling her, but it didn't really matter. What she failed to take in, she simply embroidered into her own reality and then told everybody, repeatedly.

'You coming to the concert, Bobby? Mum would be so pleased.'

'Sorry Dad, I can't make it.'

'I'll pay for the tickets.' Ted always wanted to pay.

'No, I really can't make it. Got to go to the Training School at Folkestone. Thirteen weeks. Then I'll pass out as a regular copper.'

Ted beamed.

'That's a shame. Oliver can't come either.'

'Yes, he phoned me.'

'How did he seem Bobby?' Ted's voice sounded concerned.

'Oh you know what he can be like. Rabbiting on ten to the dozen. I could barely get a word in and then he'd be annoyed because I couldn't keep up with his great plans. Anyway, he's got this big production on at the theatre. Mind you, I think he might be afraid Mum will ask him to find her a starring role. And he's got a new girlfriend, very keen on her. Er… posh name… and Mum won't like that.'

'Oh he brought her here, to meet Mum and me. Lucinda. Nice girl. Very well spoken. Doesn't come from around here.'

Secretly Ted had always wanted a daughter, someone to spoil. He loved his two boys of course but a daughter – to dress in frills and pinks.

'God, that was brave. What happened?'

Florrie had treated Lucinda with cool suspicion.

'And where did you meet my Oliver?'

'At drama school when Olly was training to be a stage manager.'

'It's Oliver, not Olly.'

Lucinda just smiled.

'So are you a stage manager as well?' Ted asked.

'Oh no. Far too difficult for the likes of me. No, I'm an actress,' she smiled at Oliver as she spoke.

'An actress!' Florrie looked horrified.

Oh no, thought Ted. *Two actresses under the same roof. That's all I need.*

'So are you acting now?' Florrie asked abruptly.

'Sorry.'

'Are you acting now? That funny accent. Or are you foreign?'

Lucinda had laughed. The sound tinkled uncertainly.

Florrie's boys had arrived in the world at the worst possible time. They had been surrounded by death and black uncertainty, so in her mind they were very special. Nobody could ever be good enough for them.

***

Florrie knew there was a lot of hard work to come to make the concert work but she didn't mind. It was for her cubs although she did have to admit a feeling of excitement standing on the stage, in front of an audience, hearing the applause, just for her. Some didn't like it. They felt embarrassed, but she felt like…well, a star. And Ted would help her.

She would have to scour her growing jumble sale record collection for any new material, picking out suitable songs from *Max Bygraves Sings* or *Songs of Sunny Spain* or that Ray McVay record she had. Very early Sunday morning was a good time. Then the house would be hushed and Ted would be stationed in the front garden as she recorded on her battered tape recorder. She didn't want somebody walking in and calling out halfway through *The Gang Show*, or the bus trundling past at the wrong moment. Ted would knock twice on the front room window if all seemed to be clear and everybody held their breath, hoping for silence. Everybody remembered last year when the sound of a phone ringing suddenly appeared in the middle of the Charleston. Fortunately it followed the beat of the music very accurately and not many noticed and those that did probably thought that it was deliberate – the sort of thing Florrie would do.

She had wondered if she should phone and invite her brother James's wife. It couldn't be easy when he was away at sea so much of the time. Mind you, he might have thought he was lucky, getting away from her.

'Hallo. This is Henrietta speaking.'

How did she manage to turn five words into a class statement?

'Hallo Hetty…' She paused. 'It's me, Florrie.'

'Oh Florence dear. I do wish you wouldn't call me that.'

Florrie knew that, but simply ignored her. 'I'm organising a concert in a few weeks time. Wondered if you both would like to come? It'll get you out of the house, should be fun.'

'What sort of concert? Not Brahms I suppose. I do love Brahms.'

'No Hetty. A cub concert. I'll be performing of course.'

There was another pause.

'I really don't think it is our sort of thing, but I wish you well. Bye.'

The phone clicked dead.

'Silly, stuck-up cow.' Why did people think they were better than her?

***

The big day eventually arrived and parents, friends and relatives drifted out of the sunny evening, past the welcoming smiles and nods of Harry and Ted and into the cool of the large hall. They waved and hallo-ed at friends and slowly found their places on the hard seats.

Soon the hall was completely full and laughter and chatter drifted warmly around. Children were settled and quietened, bottoms eased into comfortable positions, eyes turned towards the stage area and slowly, a hum of excited anticipation covered them.

Before them was an area of polished pine floor, beyond which hung a number of large white bed sheets sewn together and suspended from a clothes line which was stretched as taut as possible across the room. Despite that, it dipped slightly in the middle. In the centre was a very large Union Jack and next to it, a much smaller flag of St George that gave the stage area a rather lopsided look. In front, on another line, were hung long blackout curtains. These hid the cast and the backstage area, although occasionally a small face peeped through and grinned at the audience. Across the very front, at the top, hung a number of smaller naval and Commonwealth flags Harry had borrowed from the Dockyard, including a bold red and yellow signal indicating "Man overboard".

The centre of the stage area was empty and bathed in a strong, white light. As the main lights were gradually switched off, the excitement grew and in the semi-darkness the audience grinned at each other and then turned and fixed their concentration on the floodlit area in front of them.

Suddenly, from nowhere, the tinny sound of *Happy Days Are Here Again* burst out and Florrie in full Akela uniform, green beret perched on the back of her dark curls, strode into the centre of the stage, blue eyes flashing and beamed to enthusiastic applause. She held up her hands for silence and it arrived quickly.

'Welcome to the Fourteenth Medway cub scout concert.'

There was a ripple of applause. She held up one hand. The ripple died.

'The boys have worked very hard to entertain you and I hope you enjoy it. There will be a raffle during the interval. First prize, a bottle of Harveys Bristol Cream Sherry.'

The audience oohed good-naturedly. Florrie smiled back.

'Which I know you *will*... *all*... buy tickets for.'

The audience grinned to themselves at the instruction. Florrie turned and marched off, shooing away two cubs straying close to the open stage in their eagerness.

There was a long pause and the audience shuffled in their seats. Off stage came some very audibly whispered instructions and then suddenly the tape recorder burst into life again and a troupe of slightly bewildered barefoot boys danced on, dressed in raffia hula hula skirts, floral garlands, matching bras and wearing red and pink plastic flowers in their hair. The tape recorder now soared with the sensuous sounds of Hawaii and the boys tried valiantly to sway the hips they didn't have. One plastic flower immediately tumbled to the floor and its owner already overwrought by the occasion left tearfully while nearby a floral bra several sizes too large for its owner drooped provocatively revealing a flat white bosom. This encouraged a number of wolf whistles that were quickly hushed by the audience as they strained forward to catch sight of their own tiny family entertainer.

'Look, there he is, next to the ginger haired boy with too much lipstick. Aahh isn't he sweeeet.'

In the meantime, a curly haired baby crawled determinedly towards the swishing skirts gurgling with delight, but was quickly rescued by an elder sister. The first act swayed off, almost colliding with a group of señoritas and moustachioed matadors who, now having caught the spirit of the occasion, were over-anxious to show what *they* could do. There was a lot of stamping and clicking of imaginary castanets (although one pink faced boy shook the real thing after a recent family holiday to the Costa Brava). Red capes were waved vigorously at a whole herd of imaginary black bulls and a number of boys postured proudly in the manner of Spanish bullfighters – all of which was completely out of time to the invigorating sound of Bizet's *Carmen*. The baby, startled by such passion, wailed loudly and was removed outside.

The Spanish act eventually came to an end, shortly before Bizet had intended, and there was a brief pause as Florrie made her first solo appearance. She was now in a tight black dress covered in fringes, red shoes, a sparkly headband, holding a large pink frond and a bright green boa from which a feather occasionally flew off and fluttered to the floor. There was a collective gasp from the audience followed by more wolf whistles from the safety of the darkness. She stood smiling, occasionally looking into the wings, anxious for her music, which then stuttered into life although obviously at a slower speed. Undeterred, she executed an energetic dance while at the same time singing, "Charleston, Charleston," continually, these being the only words she knew. Eventually the music caught up. This received polite applause and was quickly followed by a group of 'schoolgirls,' wearing heavy make-up and school uniforms who sang "Sisters, sisters, there were never such devoted sisters". Delighted by the audience's warm reaction, some of the "girls" who had sisters, wiggled off in a manner far too lascivious for ten year olds, but to great applause. A cub appeared in uniform, holding a large sign that read "Interval" in several different colours. The hall lights went up, a flood light bulb popped into darkness and suddenly the first half of the show was over.

The audience clapped, stood up, stretched, discretely massaged their aching backsides and burst into a buzz of appreciative chatter.

'Weren't they good!'

'So sweet.'

'They must have all have worked *so* hard.'

'Where's the loo?'

Ted, at the back of the hall, groaned inwardly. 'She's mad, quite mad,' he said to himself.

The more experienced reached into large bags and withdrew plastic boxes full of their own sandwiches, cakes and crisps, while others queued patiently for the tea urn that had now appeared and helped themselves to cups of hot, slightly stewed tea, biscuits and warm sausage rolls.

Some of the cubs who had already performed, still wearing their stage make-up, briefly joined their friends and relatives to bask in the warm glow of their praise and to tolerate a wet kiss on the cheek from an emotional grandmother. More importantly, hungry from their physical and emotional exertions, they now needed large slices of chocolate cake and glasses of lemonade to sustain them before slipping away to join their fellow entertainers behind the scenes.

There, those about to perform checked their costumes and jiggled nervously.

Florrie reappeared from changing for her second solo. She checked the tape, then her watch, and looked around. 'Everybody ready?' she whispered.

There was a collective nod, a fist appeared through a gap in the curtains, thumb extended upwards and Ted, waiting for the signal, switched off a row of lights. The audience stopped their chatter, returned to their seats and waited patiently as the room darkened once more.

The haunting notes of *The Dying Swan* unexpectedly filled the air and onto the empty stage flowed the slim figure of Louis. The audience, surprised by the sudden change of style and stunned by the image before them, gasped. Somebody giggled. Louis, oblivious of their reaction, floated before them dressed in a white tutu and matching bodice, flesh coloured tights and white ballet shoes. His slim legs skipped hither and thither occasionally stopping to wobble on his points. His blackened eyes stared impassively from a whitened face and his hair, now swept back, was dark and glistening with oil. A small pink flower sat at each temple. His smooth arms soon became wings in torment as he circled again and again before finally faltering, staggering and sinking to one knee. He looked out towards the semi-darkness, face contorted with anguish. The audience looked back in disbelief. Then with head bowed, he trembled violently and slowly expired.

There was total silence.

He rose slowly, feet turned out, hands clasped before him, face still showing the pain and emotion of the part and bowed.

Somebody coughed nervously. Open hands were raised tentatively, as everyone glanced at their neighbours out of the corners of their eyes, uncertain as whether to clap or not.

In the front row a little girl had watched, spellbound and she now stood alone and clapped, jigging up and down with delight at the same time. The tiny soft sounds slapped into the conscience of the audience and slowly a faltering ripple of clapping spread across them like a revelation. Louis smiled in return. It was a tiny smile, uncertain maybe, but nonetheless triumphant. A start at least and he skipped of the stage.

'Well done Louis,' whispered Harry in the wings.

Most of the audience heard him of course and grinned to themselves in the darkness. But he meant it. *Well done son.* He recognised that courage came in many forms. And Florrie was right. Everything and everybody should have the chance to flourish no matter what. And in Florrie's garden, they did.

'*Baby face. You've got the cutest little baby face,*' burst out and swept away any uncertainty in a tidal wave of crazy jollity as the boys, dressed in oversize nappies and carrying jumbo dummies poured onto the stage. The audience laughed and clapped and then roared at the sight of Harry, wearing a bonnet and apparently little else, being wheeled onto the stage, knees poking skywards from a large Silver Cross pram. Pushing him was an embarrassed looking Alan wearing a blue and green floral dress and matching headscarf plus a large green wig that clashed with his increasingly reddening complexion. His attempts at being a stern guardian, chiding his large charge, quickly collapsed into uncontrollable laughter at the ridiculousness of the situation – a hysteria that quickly spread to the audience. Soon people everywhere were wiping tears of laughter from their eyes and howling at the scene before them. The act came to a complete standstill and the young cubs looked at each other, bemused as to why the adults were behaving like this. Slowly, very slowly the audience recovered and retrieved the situation with loud cries of 'Off! Off!' and the helpless duo staggered thankfully out of sight if not out of earshot.

Hardly had the audience had time to recover when the rousing sounds of Offenbach's *Orpheus in the Underworld* can-can poured over them and with no bidding they immediately began to clap loudly in time to the music as Florrie, resplendent in a green can-can dress and red rose in her hair, burst onto the stage and began her second solo of the night. Her muscular black stockinged legs pumped relentlessly into the air leaving the audience breathless at such energy. What her dance lacked in technique and finesse was more than compensated for with sheer relentless power and enthusiasm. Her petticoats swished as she pistoned around the stage and young men in the audience fired by such athleticism rose and urged her on… 'Go, go, go!' until eventually the music brought her to a reluctant end and she bowed to a wave of applause and cheering.

The stage now stood empty, hungry for the finale. Gradually the entire cast found their positions and grinned helplessly at the audience who grinned helplessly back. Florrie took up her position at the front of the stage and the music swept over them all like an anthem and the cast swayed from side to side.

'*We're riding along on the crest of a wave and the sun is in the sky…*'

Florrie pointed towards an imaginary sun crossing the sky. Some of the audience were already standing and clapping. Others also pointed. There were suns everywhere.

'*All our eyes on the distant horizon look-out for passers-by…*'

Now they had it. They scanned horizons, hands shielding eyes.

'*…We'll do the hailing, when other ships are round us sailing.*'

Everybody now swayed from side to side, some clasping arms around each other.

'*We're riding along on the crest of a wave…*'

Arms now waved and swayed above heads.

'*… and the world… is… OURS.*'

And, for that moment, it was.

There was a tumultuous roar: clapping, whistling, cheering and cries of 'More, more'. The cast waved at the audience. The audience waved back. The lights came on. Everybody stood.

Outside, an old couple walking their dog, stopped, somewhat startled at the sudden noise. They looked curiously from one to the other. The black dog strained towards the hall, light pouring from the windows and it sniffed the emotions floating on the air. The dog turned and cocked his leg against a garden wall. This was worth marking.

Inside, the concert reluctantly came to an end. A gentle buzz floated happily around and visited everybody, smiling at them and listening to their words.

'That was great, Akela. Can we do it again?'

'I am so proud of you son.'

'Harry, you were awful.'

It had not been sophisticated or professional or even very talented and, in fact, the presence of any of those elements would have distracted from the simple fun and honesty of the occasion. Strangers now spoke warmly to each other and those who had been shy and worried about performing had grown. It had been destined to melt your heart or have you falling off of your seat helpless with laughter. What more could you ask for?

In the middle of all of this stood Florrie, the heart and pulse, beaming and soaking up respect and thank-yous. She was the concert and the concert was her. From the back of the hall, Ted watched her for a moment, smiled and slowly shook his head. There she still was, the girl he had met on the Hill, still bubbling and fizzing – the glowing centre of attention, soaking up the warmth and praise as if she couldn't get… A small shiver surprised him.

'She is pretty amazing, Ted.'

Joan stood beside him looking towards the crowd around Florrie, all anxious to say their goodbyes.

'You must be very proud of her.'

Ted smiled. He *was* very proud, of course he was – proud of her enthusiasm and determination, of her ability to inspire, her willingness to knock aside barriers or convention. But he also knew that it all came at a cost.

'We all know how much you support her you know. She couldn't do it without you.' Joan placed her hand briefly on his arm. 'Well, s'pose I'd better go and help with the clearing up.'

'Thank you Joan.'

She turned. Smiled back.

Slowly, still chattering, the audience thronged towards the exit, throwing loud goodnights over and around each other to friends and neighbours as they left the glow of the hall, their smiles bobbing away into the early evening dusk like fireflies. Soon, they had all gone, each warmly wrapped in their own brightly coloured shawl of memories.

The clack of chairs being folded and the rattle of teacups and metal spoons being washed sounded coldly alien in the golden atmosphere. Florrie looked around.

'OK. That'll do. We'll finish off tomorrow. Get your coats on.'

They had all worked so hard, but now the adrenalin was fading and tiredness was waiting. Gold was fading to brown.

'Goodnight Joan. See you tomorrow.'

'OK. Goodnight Florrie. Night Ted.'

'Goodnight.'

'Goodnight Harry. Helen. Thank you.'

'Goodnight Florrie. Goodnight Ted. We thoroughly enjoyed it.'

'Goodnight.'

'Goodnight Alan. Thanks for your help.'

'That's OK Mrs T, any time. Goodnight.'

'Goodnight Louis. You did really well.'

'Thank you very much, Akela. Goodnight.'

Florrie stood in the empty hall and listened to the soft echoes of the evening. She looked around. She thought it was a pity her own boys hadn't been here, her precious boys. But they had gone now, left to begin their own lives without her and she wiped a hand across her brow. Ted stood patiently by the door waiting for her.

'Ready love?'

Florrie took one last look and joined him. He switched off the lights and locked the door.

They walked together along the long road that led to their home.

'It went well didn't it?'

'Yes love, it was brilliant and you were pretty amazing.'

'Really? Was I?'

'Certainly were.'

'I always knew I should have been on the stage.'

'You should take your act around the old people's homes. They would appreciate that. You singing to them.'

'What a good idea. They *would* appreciate it wouldn't they?' She turned to him. Eyes now gleaming. 'Someone semi-professional like me. Will you take me Ted?'

She sounded like the young girl on the Hill again – full of spirit, full of uncertainty.

'Of course I will, love.'

She slipped her arm through his and they walked together, quietly, while she basked in the warmth of his words.

'We make a good team, don't we?' Ted asked.

She failed to notice the query in his voice.

'Oh yes, they all did well. I was glad Alan was there to sort out the electrics this time. It was a bit gloomy last year. Don't you think? I'm sure those at the back couldn't see me doing my routines.'

Ted said nothing.

They walked on for a while, each in their own personal silence.

Suddenly Florrie stopped.

'That's it. That's what we need.'

She turned towards Ted, eyes blazing.

'What?'

'A team of course. A team.'

'What are you talking about love?'

'A team. A football team – for the cubs. Oh why did nobody suggest it? Why do I have to think of everything? Come on. We've got a lot of planning to do.' She pulled Ted along the pavement.

Walking slowly towards them, returned the old couple, still walking their dog. It was a slow meandering process; stopping at every lamp post, inspecting front gardens, peeking through lit windows. It was that time when the day had slowed down its urgency and yawned and stretched before being covered by night.

The couple stopped, surprised, uncertain, as Ted and Florrie approached at speed, swerved into the road around them and disappeared into the gloom. They stood for a moment, saying nothing, just curious.

The black dog looked in the direction of Florrie. He smiled knowingly.

TEN

St Crispin's Day: A Kamikaze Pilot and Steel Ted

'It is not an offence in itself to be in an offside position. A player is in an offside position if he is nearer to his opponents' goal than both the ball and the second last opponent. A player is not in an offside position if he is in his own half of the field of play. If a player is in an offside position when the ball is touched or played by a teammate, he may not become actively involved in the game. There is no offence if a player receives the ball directly from a goal kick or a throw in or a corner kick.'

The Rules of the Football Association,
post 1925

Florrie enjoyed going to the match. She only went to the home games and not when the weather was really bad but on a fine day with the sun shining she would set off, excited by the drama about to unfold. She had to get there early of course in order to get her spot, right at the front, in the corner and against the rail over which she could place her coat. She didn't know why she had to go to the same spot. She had never thought about it really but she did get a good view from there. Even with the terracing she didn't want to stand behind a group of large men and not be able to see anything. And you never knew about the language. Not only that, but it was hard on the legs standing for a couple of hours or more, stamping cold feet in the autumn. At least she could lean on the rail and be right at the front. There she got to know her neighbours. Like her, they usually arrived at the same place. They were nearly all men of course, but a few women joined their husbands. They all nodded and smiled at each other. The women chatted. The men discussed the game, checked the programme and the team for that day.

'Exeter City this week, Jack?'

'Yes. We should win today. Exeter in the bottom half of the table.'

'And that'll be fifty-three home wins for us then – in a row.'

'Yeah, impressive but you never know. We'll need to watch their inside right. Irish international.'

'That's true, Jack. That's very true.'

They were polite and there was hardly any swearing despite any frustrations that might be unfolding on the pitch. Sometimes the men would call to others nearby.

'Oi watch the language mate. There are women here.'

Florrie liked that. That's how it should be.

Once, a newspaper photographer came to their corner, before the match.

'Come on ladies and gents. Big smile now. Look happy while you can. May not be so happy at full time.'

They all laughed and waved at him.

'What paper you from mate?'

'The Standard.'

A few days later the newspaper came out and there she was, on the sports page, smiling out of the grainy black and white photo. *Happy Gills supporters before the game with Bournemouth and Boscombe.* She went to the newspaper office and ordered a glossy ten by eight which she showed to everybody. Even carried it around in her shopping bag between two pieces of cardboard to protect it.

'I'm in the paper. Look,' she would say, proudly pulling out the photograph.

'Oh Florrie. That's so good.'

She would beam proudly.

Inevitably, one corner of the photo caught and bent over.

'Oh no. How did that happen?' she worried and from then on she held it up for people to see. 'No, I'll hold it.'

Eventually everybody she knew or met had seen it. Some several times, and so she placed it very carefully into a drawer, still between the cardboard, with nothing sticking out, where it would be safe. "Might get that framed," she told herself.

Sometimes she went to the match with Ted, but because he often worked on Saturday mornings, it wasn't always possible, it depended on the kick off time. It was OK in the summer when the game started at three, but later, when it went back to two thirty or even two fifteen, it was very difficult. But she didn't mind. It wasn't fair for Ted to dash around and rush his lunch when he had been working all week. So even though he loved the game, he often sat quietly at home. She quite liked being out on her own, stopping to look at things that interested her, talking to strangers, talking to dogs and the occasional cat. She preferred dogs. Cats were too aloof – didn't always come when called.

She liked the ritual of the journey and the reassurance of everything being in its comfortable place: the clunk of the front gate and the walk down the long road past the row of identical terraced homes. She would check her favourite house fronts for any changes. *Mmm new net curtains there. Mind you, about time. Oh look at those geraniums. How wonderful! My favourite colour...* Chatting to strangers.

'Hallo. You're doing a good job there. I must cut mine soon. Grows so quickly doesn't it? I'm off to watch Gillingham play. Yes. Hope so. Must go. Mustn't miss the train. Bye.'

Now the Victorian park should appear. There are the green railings and the open gate. Should see the bandstand soon, through the trees. There it is. Painted in different colours. Why do they do that? Why not leave it alone? It was always just green. Looks like a fancy cake now. What a shame. Anyway, turn the corner and there, cut deep below, will be the railway line, rails shining. Yes there it is. I can see it through the black iron railings. Silly really. Knew it would be there of course.

Keep to this side of the road. Past the little sweet and cigarette kiosk. Between the black taxis and enter the station. It's always cool there.

'Hallo Bert. Return to Gillingham please. Going to see the match... Thank you.'

Now, click down the stone stairs with their metal lips and onto the platform. Right, stand next to the iron colonnade, third one along, surrounded by all that riveted metal supporting the stairway. Further along the sun might be striking the platform, but here it will be quite gloomy. That's OK. We always wait here... Groups of men and boys, some wearing blue and white striped scarves – always do. Expect I'll be the only woman, often am. It always feels exciting. The anticipation. Being together. Sometimes the train's late. I hate that. It's the two thirty two from Victoria. It will be up on the indicator board but I can recite it from memory. Chatham, Gillingham, Rainham... oh all the way to Dumpton Park and Ramsgate. I always wonder what Dumpton Park is like? Sounds quite pretty... The pigeons will flutter away when the train arrives. They make so much mess... Can be frustrating waiting... I always check the ticket in my pocket. Just in case there's an inspector and I can't find it. I forget which pocket sometimes. There it is. Feels sharp when I flick it with my thumb. Makes a little noise. Sounds anxious... When the train arrives, the carriage door should stop right opposite us. Usually one of the men will open the door because those handles are so heavy. I always try to get the same seat, my seat... Those doors slam shut so loudly they always make me jump. Must make sure the windows are closed. Wait anxiously for the whistle and then we're off. So exciting.

Florrie's train, full of eager spectators, would move out, under the stained brick arches and into the first tunnel cut through the chalk. Sometimes the carriage lights failed to work, leaving them sitting in total darkness, but soon they would rush out into the pale daylight of a cutting, shrouded on both sides by trees and ivy. She would watch them flashing past and feel the motion of the train – clickety clack, clickety clack – into the open, crossing the viaduct, looking down now, dirty red rooftops, through smeary windows – clickety clack, clickety clack.

She would crane her head to catch sight of the Hill winding away upwards. It took so long to walk it, but now they would pass it in a moment. She was hardly able to take it all in. They would rush into the next tunnel, darkness again and then out, slowing down to a halt.

Gillingham station was just one stop along the line but within easy walking distance of the ground. The carriage doors would shut in a volley of crashes all around her and she would step down and join the throng slowly shuffling along the platform. At the stairway she would feel for the first step and slowly climb up, step by step by step. Behind, a cry of support. "Come on you Blues". Around her the crowd pressed politely, full of smiles. Ahead, the ticket barrier waited and beyond that, the light of the street. The barrier would turn and the whole mass of supporters would veer left, stretch their legs and move urgently along a long road channelled between two rows of terraced houses.

'They won't be able to get out of their front doors for a while,' somebody would always joke.

'No not with this crowd,' replied a stranger.

They always said that and it seemed to bond them together. Florrie wondered if the occupants of the small houses made special arrangements for home matches or were they simply trapped for an hour or two? Did they rush out at kick off and make sure they were back five minutes before the end of the match? What did they tell estate agents when it came to selling?

She would feel the warmth of the chattering tide around her and soon she would see the stadium. It was always exciting, like first glimpsing the sea as a child on a charabanc journey. Whirr. Clunk. *Through the turnstile, straight ahead and there's my spot. Waiting for me. Ahh.* She could relax now.

Florrie enjoyed the emotions of the crowd. Often thousands of voices would suddenly swell like a choir into one spontaneous roar or groan. Many hands would applaud some action or skill. Sometimes she failed to understand, but when her own reactions burst out in harmony, she felt included and that was wonderful. She absorbed the colour and movement, the excitement and drama, the tension of the clock ticking away and the battle for victory. Like her neighbours, she felt close to the game. It was as if the passion on the terraces spilled over onto the field, galvanised the players and then swept back again. They were all playing together, end to end, and for a while she was back on the Hill, battling away.

If she was truthful, the game was also something of a mystery and she didn't really understand the rules, not all of them, but she pretended she did. She took cues from the opinion shouted out around her and then shouted the loudest.

'Where're your specs ref? That was never offside.'

But that didn't really matter. It was the game that mattered and how you played it. Not the rules. Wasn't it?

***

It had taken a long time to get the cub football kit together. It had been down to raffles, jumble sales, begging letters and imploring phone calls. Finally a local amateur club donated an old practice football complete with pump and adaptor and two linesman's flags. Most of the boys had their own football boots and the rest managed with plimsolls. Socks came in a variety of colours as did shorts and school exercise books made good shin pads but the biggest problem was a supply of matching shirts. To buy new football shirts was beyond their means and so Florrie asked each parent to supply a white shirt of some description which she promptly dyed her favourite colour. The result was a variety of reds, sometimes on the same shirt.

'Bloody 'ell,' said Harry. 'It's Mottled United.'

Florrie dived into her new role with her customary enthusiasm and soon small boys were to be seen jogging around soggy fields, their pale stick-like legs protruding from baggy shorts, thin arms pumping energetically and their boots gradually amassing a weight of wet mud and blades of grass. They ran forward and, under Akela's command, occasionally backwards. She had seen the latter on the telly and although she had no real idea as to its purpose, was determined to introduce it. However, as most of her young stars managed to tread on the player behind them with a lot of yelping and pushing, this was quickly discontinued.

Ted, being the only person with any real experience of the game, was wise enough not to take control, but instead made the occasional suggestion to Florrie, who after some consideration issued it as her own.

'OK boys, one at a time. I want you to practise dribbling and kicking the ball with Mr T. Jeffrey. Jeffrey Saunders. You go first.'

Meanwhile the committee, who had come to watch the Saturday morning practice with some enthusiasm, soon recognised the task before them and gradually excused themselves for more pressing engagements leaving just Ted on duty along with Louis, who, although he wasn't playing, had arrived wearing the briefest shorts.

Unabashed, Florrie pressed on.

'When can we start playing, Akela?'

'When you are fit and strong. When you have big muscles.'

The boys stopped briefly to compare biceps and quadriceps, but finding none, kept running.

That night, they felt tired but went to bed eager to experience the next stage in Akela's plan for success. Trouble was, Akela didn't really have a plan.

'It went really well didn't it? I think we're going to win.'

Ted, aware of how young most of the cubs were and the alarming lack of talent and understanding in the team, tried to divert her.

'We need, er *you* need to decide who is playing in each position and then maybe you can tell them at the next cub night. Maybe then we can practise as a team. You know, try out some corner kicks and passing. I think Big Billy Butler would be good in goal, he's certainly tall enough for the high crosses and quite intimidating to an attacking forward.'

Florrie had never thought about high crosses. She wasn't sure any of her players could lift the ball more than six inches off the ground. In any case it didn't matter.

'Don't think there's much time for that.'

Ted looked bemused. Florrie continued.

'I've arranged a game for two weeks time, twenty-fifth of October, against the seventh cub pack.'

'But we're not ready and the seventh have been playing for at least a year.'

'We will be. I'll see to that. I'll talk to the boys. Now let's arrange this team.'

Ted was worried. He had the greatest admiration for his wife's fearless fighting spirit but you needed more than that. You needed planning and organisation and practice and teamwork without which you were bound to lose. That's what he had done in his playing days. And when she had lost, what then? Days of black despair *he* would have to deal with. He also couldn't bear the thought of her being made to appear ridiculous in front of the others when she tried so hard. She deserved more than that. But she was *so* stubborn.

'Perhaps we can postpone it, love. Play later when we're really ready. Beat them easily then. That would be good wouldn't it? Eh? Don't want the boys to be discouraged. What do you think?'

Florrie looked at Ted. It was a look of scorn. Almost pity. It was a look that said *don't worry. I have courage for both of us.* Ted knew that look well. Knew it couldn't be changed. He sighed and looked away.

'OK love. Cup of tea? Sandwich?'

As Ted prepared the supper, Florrie thought about her strategy. She had watched many matches and yet her eyes remained fresh and unblinkered. Unhampered by knowledge and understanding, she was able to see the game's very essence – its beating heart stripped bare. So, she simply ignored convention and conceived a plan that was breathtaking in its simplicity and directness and which, in that moment, looked into the future. She simply moved away from the rigid structures and roles of the time. Who said that you had to have a two, three, five formation? Who said that each position had but one role? No, her plan involved multi-skills, overlapping play, fluidity and, above all, determination, shock and disruption. She would talk to her cubs, inspire them, ignite their imaginations, put fire in their little bellies.

When we attack their goal everybody charges together. Pin them in their goal mouth until we score. If they attempt to attack our goal you all run at them and stop them. Except you Billy, you had better stay in goal. Yes, that would be it. It will be brilliant.

Ted arrived with a tray. On it he had placed a plate of cheese and tomato sandwiches, some crisps and a cup of tea.

'There you are, love. I've sugared the tea. If you want any more just let me know. OK?'

'Thank you Ted. You're very good to me.'

She lifted one sandwich. He watched her. A small piece of tomato fell out. She picked it up and toyed with it, thoughts elsewhere.

'Do we have a whistle?' She placed the tomato segment in her mouth. It tasted sharp and sweet at the same time.

'A whistle? Why do you need a whistle?'

'I'll need it when I'm referee.'

'Referee!' Ted gasped. 'You're not…?'

'Yes. I'm going to referee the game. These sandwiches are nice.'

'You *can't* be referee.'

'That's what the seventh said. Can I have another one? Please.'

'Yes. No. Yes. In a moment. You can't referee your own team.'

'Why not? It's not the Cup Final. It's only a cub match.'

'But the referee has to be impartial and not only that, you don't know the rules.'

Florrie threw the remains of the sandwich onto her plate. It bounced off onto the floor.

'Are you accusing me of being a cheat?' Her voice shook.

'No of course not but…'

'But what?'

Ted said nothing.

Florrie bent down to pick up the sandwich. It had left a greasy mark on the carpet. 'Now look what you've done!' She straightened up and her anger flared again. 'You're the same as all the others.' The words spat out and she threw the sandwich remains at him. They hit him on his chest.

He sat there shocked but silent.

'I'll get you another one.' He spoke softly.
'Don't bother.'
But he had left the room.

***

The day of the match arrived bright and sunny although there had been some heavy October rain leaving the pitch wet and muddy.

'Going's a bit soft,' muttered Ted.

'Is that good?' asked Florrie.

'Could work to our advantage.'

'How's that?' Florrie sounded eager.

'Might slow down the skilful players.'

'What ours?'

'No. Theirs.'

'Oh good. That's OK then.'

The air buzzed with expectation. The word had got around and quite a collection of friends and relatives had assembled. The cubs had already changed into their kit and were thrilled and proud to feel like real players in a real team. Fathers knelt to tie bootlaces, then stood, a damp dark patch on one knee, hand resting protectively on a small shoulder.

'Go on Jimmy. Show 'em what you can do son.'

'Be careful James. Try not to fall over. There's a good boy.'

'Oh Mu-um.'

Florrie and Ted had arrived with the committee and all the equipment required of the modern footballing age: a first aid kit, a bucket half filled with cold water, a large sponge, a whistle, a watch, bottles of lemon squash and a number of oranges ready to be sliced for half-time. The sponge fascinated the boys.

'What's that Mr T?'

'It's a magic sponge.'

'Magic?' They looked at him.

'Yes. Takes away any knock you might get.'

'Does it?'

'Oh yes,' he said, knowing that the shock of ice cold water being placed on a kick and then being squeezed down a hot neck was enough to make you forget anything. Not that he would do that to the boys of course.

Florrie was resplendent in full Akela uniform: dark green skirt and neatly pressed blouse covered in badges, neckerchief and woggle placed precisely, dark leather belt snapped tight around her waist and a green beret perched on dark curly hair. Looking at her watch she waved the two captains towards the centre spot. A coin was tossed. There was a short discussion and both teams took their places. Some of the seventh players in their pale blue shirts, jogged on the spot like professionals did, keeping their young muscles warm, anxious to start. Florrie's team crouched like athletes waiting for the crack of the starter's pistol, faces intent. They looked as if they were waiting to go over the top. It should have been a warning.

All eyes now turned towards Florrie. She surveyed the scene, looked at her watch again, raised the whistle and, like a mighty general sending troops into battle, she blew a long, piercing blast. It had started.

Immediately all of her players shot forward and swarmed after the ball like demented bees with a focus that was extraordinary. Little legs kicked out at every opportunity – at the ball, at shins, at knees and very often at thin air. Lumps of dislodged mud flew in every direction like soggy shrapnel as the ball ricocheted two and fro around the centre of the pitch. Every time an opposing player in a blue shirt received the ball, he was immediately surrounded by ten grimly determined mottled redshirts snapping at his heels. The referee tried not to smile. Even when the ball had left the confines of the pitch it was still hotly pursued by a gaggle of panting pink-faced boys who like puppy dogs escaping their leash had to be recalled and restrained. The seventh looked startled. They had no idea how to cope with this blitzkrieg.

On the touchline, mothers called out in small voices and fathers bellowed. Ted looked amazed. Young brothers and sisters just wanted to go home. Both goalkeepers looked cold and miserable and Big Billy occasionally ran towards the melee looking for a gap to kick in before Ted's shouts sent him scampering back.

With so few opportunities for tactical play or even just passing the ball, the merest chance to break out of this surreal struggle sent the crowd into paroxysms of excitement. Florrie's centre half suddenly found himself with the ball at his feet and in space. Nobody knew how this had happened, but the spectators, excited by this rare chance, yelled conflicting advice from every part of the ground. Looking up, the centre half could see at least a dozen arms waving frenziedly for his attention and hear screams to receive the ball. Completely bewildered by this situation he froze and was quickly flattened by a number of players including some of his own. He rose shakily to his feet to hear the groan of disappointment from around the ground.

Suddenly, this war of attrition was interrupted by the sudden appearance of a small brown terrier who bounded gleefully onto the pitch, bouncing high into the air to collect the ball and then dribbling with enough skill to warrant a ripple of appreciation.

'Dog's better than this lot.'

'Shut up Alf. They'll hear.'

The terrier growled menacingly at anyone brave enough to approach for the ball. Akela strode towards him.

'Sit.'

The dog sat.

Akela retrieved the ball and curtly summoned the dog's owner who led the terrier away, straining at his leash, constantly looking back, until becoming bored, he turned his attention elsewhere. This seemed to be a good point to stop and the half-time whistle blew, with the score still standing at nil-nil.

Ted and the committee, friends and family crowded around the cubs. Somebody mentioned Dunkirk. Brows were mopped. The magic sponge was applied to battered shins. Oranges were sucked and noses wiped. Mothers fretted and fathers swelled with pride as the boys rested, bloodied and muddied and more than a little weary. Some boys, however, paced around, anxious to continue the battle, electricity still coursing through their bodies. Florrie hovered around the centre spot.

'Isn't Akela coming to see us Mr T?'

'No. Because she's the referee she has to be impartial.'

'What's impartial?'

'Means she's not on anybody's side.'

'So she's not on our side anymore?'

'Have another piece of orange.'

Florrie of course wanted desperately to be with them; to praise and encourage, but she knew she had to remain separate. That's what Ted had said – be impartial. Well, that was the loneliness of command she supposed. Somebody strong had to take that responsibility and that was her. She looked towards Ted and caught his eye. She grinned. He grinned back, trying to forget the sandwich situation. She knew she was so lucky to have him.

Ted was pleasantly surprised at how well she had refereed – firm and fair and with no contentious or biased decisions. True, she did have two of the fathers running the line to help her, but then so did professional referees. Maybe he had underestimated her, and he felt a little guilty. And her tactics? Well, they may not be pretty but at least they were not losing and her ability to inspire her young boys was remarkable. Mind you the game wasn't over yet and he noticed the huddle of light blue shirts and fathers engaged in earnest conversation.

Florrie looked at her watch, lifted her whistle and blew for the teams to return.

The second half was to bring a few surprises.

The seventh prepared to kick off with their centre forward standing very close to his inside right. The atmosphere had become tense. The fairground hullabaloo of the first half had been replaced with an anxious expectation and the touchline was quiet, save for a single cry of support. 'Come on Blues!' The cry sounded uncertain.

Florrie looked again at her watch and waited. Every eye was upon her. She raised one arm, waited… and blew. There was a roar.

The Blues' centre forward tapped the ball to his inside right but as he did, the Reds charged. The Blues' inside right, aware of the horde now bearing down upon him, turned to pass the ball a long way back to his right half who was a large boy with strong legs. So, that was their plan; to lift the ball over the red masses and sprint to attack. But the inside right had been nervous. He could hear the approaching thud of muddy boots. The pass was slow, too slow. The right half hesitated. Leading the Red charge was Jeffrey Saunders who approached with the tenacity of a Kamikaze pilot. The right half swung a large leg. The ball shot forward and hit Jeffrey in the stomach with a loud thud. In slow motion he doubled over and exhaled a long strange gasp. The whistle blew. Everybody stopped.

'Are you alright Jeffrey?'

'Agghh.'

Florrie waved to Ted to come on. He placed a blanket around the young boy's shoulders and helped him off the pitch.

'I... stopped... him... Mr T... didn't... I?'

'You certainly did Jeffrey. You certainly did.'

'Do I get the magic sponge?'

'No not today. Come and sit here for a while. On the touchline.'

Florrie blew her whistle.

'Drop ball. Here,' she commanded and the battle continued.

Weary legs and sore lungs were now allowing the stronger and fitter boys to break free from the general melee and to begin to threaten the goals more seriously. A sudden attack down the left flank by the Blues' left-winger looked dangerous. He was an energetic tall boy whose pace was leaving the nine Red defenders doggedly chasing him, increasingly far behind. Lofty had had that look about him from the beginning. His football strip sat comfortably on his young body. His physique was fashioned by many hours chasing a football around the local park and his skills had been honed by constantly kicking a tennis ball against a back street wall. He had already shown some thoughtful and delicate touches in the first half, which had completely bewildered both the opposition and his own teammates leaving him frustrated, but now his moment had arrived. If *his* surge was not danger enough, the Blues' centre forward, unnoticed by anybody, had now occupied the huge gap left by the absence of the entire Red team so determined were they to halt Lofty's threat. Even more alarming was the knowledge that the centre forward was known to have the unusual ability of being able to kick the ball in the direction that he intended. The sense of danger was everywhere.

Jeffrey, who had been sitting talking to his goalkeeper Big Billy, immediately recognised the threat and ran onto the field. At that moment Lofty looked up and selected his target. With a flash of his left boot, the ball arced its way beautifully and accurately across the sky towards the lone centre forward who waited hungry as a wolf.

Blue fans leapt in excitement. 'GO ON! GO ON!' they screamed.

Red supporters were clutched with an icy fear.

Mothers held their hands to their faces in speechless horror and grown men turned away in despair. In a flash, the centre forward bounded past Jeffrey, who promptly slipped over. Big Billy stood transfixed, open mouthed. It was an open goal. Suddenly the shrill blast of a whistle snapped everybody back into an electric silence. All eyes turned towards Florrie. Her voice rang out, clearly and confidently.

'OFFSIDE!'

Spectators looked at each other open mouthed.

'Never. That was never offside. Was it?'

They turned to each other.

'RUBBISH DECISION. NOT OFFSIDE. NEVER. BLOODY STUPID WOMAN.'

Heads turned.

The voice came from a short man standing alone on the touchline. He wore a long black coat beneath which a red checked shirt and mustard waistcoat snarled at each other. Nobody knew who he was, but he had spent the match shouting from time to time, but not in an encouraging way. The drama of the referee's decision now spurred him on.

'RUBBISH. WHERE DID THEY GET HER FROM?' He turned and appealed to those nearest to him but they looked away.

Ted was standing on the opposite side of the pitch but he had heard every word. So had everybody else. He stepped onto the pitch and began to walk steadily towards the man. All eyes watched him. There was an eerie silence.

Ted felt strange. Coldly separate from his self as though he had absorbed his own shadow. He was surprised that in his nostrils he suddenly smelled pine and the tautness of danger. He sensed men around him, the lads. Ahead in his mind, he saw lines of barbed wire, dark against the gaps in trees and then shambling figures, dead eyes, piles of bone and rag with skin stretched taut. There, two small emaciated children, huge eyes, sat holding hands on top of a pile of naked rotting corpses. *Jesus Christ what is this place?* A man had strutted towards him wearing a black leather coat that flapped against immaculate jackboots. A small slapping sound – the only sound. At his waist was a holstered pistol. The man had stood, hands on hips and harangued Ted in fluent English for his inferiority, stupidity and, all the while, his arrogance and hatred swept over Ted in sickening waves. Ted had drawn his revolver. The German had scoffed at his impudence. Ted stepped forward and looked unblinking into his enemy's eyes. They were blue like topaz, but hard and cold and empty. On his forehead was a livid scar. Ted said nothing but looked deep into the man, searched for the man's soul in the inner darkness, but found nothing. There were no words, only the will of both men. His enemy suddenly stiffened. Fumbled with his holster. Ted pulled the trigger. The scar disappeared.

'That's my wife you're talking about.'

He spoke softly, each word encased in steel. Striking the man, bruising him. Ted's eyes drilled into the spectator but *this* man's arrogance was flabby and weak. Ted's stare frightened him.

'I'm sorry. I really didn't know.'

Maybe that will be enough.

'Doesn't make any difference. You don't speak to women like that.'

'No of course not.'

He wanted desperately to avoid the stare.

Around them people watched in awe.

'Apologise.'

'Yes I will. Of course.'

'Now.'

The two men walked across the pitch, Ted slightly behind, like a guard, towards where Florrie stood, looking severe, ball under her arm.

'I'm sorry referee, deeply sorry. My words were rude and offensive. Please accept my apology.' He looked uncertainly at Ted. 'I really don't know what…um.' He waved his hands, now at a loss for words, just wanting to be allowed to go; afraid of Ted.

He looked down.

'Now go.'

'Yes sir.'

The man walked briskly towards the playing fields gate, anxious to disappear. There was a ripple around the pitch.

'Thank you Ted.'

Florrie gently touched his arm.

'Bloody 'ell Ted. That was amazing. Why didn't you just deck 'im mate?'

Ted smiled at Harry.

'Florrie alright Ted?'

'Fine thank you Joan.'

Florrie looked at her watch.

'Right. Now. You lot. Off my pitch.'

She put her whistle to her lips and blew long and loudly.

'Game's over.'

Everybody felt very relieved.

The Akela of the seventh came to speak to Florrie.

'Many thanks Florrie for organising this and for volunteering to be referee. I must say your husband's quite some man. You must be very proud.'

Florrie grinned.

'I wasn't quite sure about the offside decision although the referee's decision is final of course.'

'Oh it's quite simple really,' Florrie said with the authority of ignorance.

'You see Jeffrey, my cub, came back onto the field after being injured, without my permission and that is an offence and as he wasn't technically there that made your centre forward offside when he received the pass, you see. I would have dealt with Jeffrey and awarded you a free kick but we ran out of time. I know it seems complicated but you have to know the rules and in any case the boys enjoyed it. Nobody lost and it's the game that really counts isn't it.'

'Of course it is Florrie. Of course it is.'

Florrie gathered her boys together and told them how well they had done and how their determination had meant that they had not been beaten although battling against superior odds. She told them of the Hills they would have to climb and how proud she was of them.

'I'm very tired now, Akela.'

'Of course you are. That's because you have been trying so hard. Now you can go home, have a nice bath and a nice tea.'

'Do we have to have a bath, Akela?'

'Whatever your Mum says.'

They all gathered their belongings together and made their way slowly home. The boys with heads full of glory, legs full of lead and covered in drying mud stretching their skin.

'Bye Akela. Bye Mr T. Bye.'

Eventually Ted and Florrie found themselves alone.

Florrie grabbed his arm.

'Thank you for what you did today. I've never seen you like that. You were very powerful. You scared that man didn't you?'

'Well nobody should behave like that and get away with it.'

'Was that the war Ted? Made you like that? There's a lot I don't know isn't there? I'm really sorry if I don't understand. Can't you tell me?'

'Don't worry. As long as we're together.'

He gripped her hand.

They walked along together in silence. Ted suddenly stopped and turned to face her.

'How did you know about that rule?' He stood upright as if quoting from a rulebook. "Irrespective of whether the ball is in play or not, only the referee is authorised to allow an injured player to re-enter the field of play". Or something like that. How did you know?'

'I didn't. Just made it up. Thought it had to be something like that.'

Ted stopped and laughed aloud. The sound shocked Florrie. She hadn't heard his laughter for such a long time. It was the sound of their courtship and early married years, of fun and freedom and warmth. It was there then, but when he came back from the war, it had been stolen and she had never noticed. How could she not notice? Oh God. Poor Ted. She smiled and hoped it hid her guilt.

They walked along together, Ted occasionally chuckling then growing quiet and thoughtful.

'I've saved up quite a bit. From all that overtime I've been doing. Thought we might have a holiday. We've never had one. Well not a real one. Only hop-picking that time, for you, when the boys were small. What do you think love?'

'A holiday? Ooh how super,' said Florrie, mimicking her sister-in-law's posh accent.

Ted looked a little hurt.

'No, I'm serious. We've got enough to go abroad somewhere.'

'Abroad! What outside England?'

'Well yes.'

'Thought you never wanted to leave England again?'

'Well I never want to go to France again. Once was enough and certainly not Germany. Seen enough Krauts to last me a lifetime but the Co-op are doing these special package holiday things to Spain with big discounts, Costa somewhere or other. Thought it might be a nice change.'

'Will we go on the Golden Arrow? I've always wanted to do that.'

'No, don't think that goes to Spain love. No, we'll fly.'

'Fly?' Now it was Florrie's turn to stop. 'Fly!' Her eyes sparkled. 'I've never been in an aeroplane.'

Ted smiled at her infectious innocence and enthusiasm.

'Well,' he said ruefully, 'it's pretty exciting, especially when they don't have any engines.'

'Ours will have engines though. Won't they?'

He smiled again. 'Oh yes. Ours will have engines.'

ELEVEN

The Allotment: an Uncertain Hero, the Irishman, a Bullfight and a Piece of Metal

'My genial spirits fail;
And what can there avail
To lift the smothering weight from off my breast?'

Samuel Taylor Coleridge

Florrie approached the challenge of the back garden gate with her usual determination. It stood tall before her, taller than her stocking-footed five feet four and a half inches, and it growled at her intrusion in a darkly creosoted sort of way. A large, black metal bolt that stubbornly refused to budge until you had tugged and struggled and cursed it to hell for a good while, secured it. Suddenly, slyly, the bolt would release its hold and slide open with a vicious clank hoping to remove some skin from an unwary knuckle. The gate was high, but it served as little deterrent because the adjoining fence was low enough for the averagely athletic adult to step over into the garden. Maybe the original intention had been to build the fence to the same height, but somehow that had never happened and now, over the years, a comfortable resignation had set in. And so the gate stood, fiercely resistant, until time gradually ate into its structure, causing its original spirit-levelled uprightness to sag, leaving one bottom corner now resting on the cold concrete step below. Despite its perverse attitude, there were times when

Florrie felt sorry for its deterioration and wished for the return of its sweet pine youth.

She took a deep breath, grasped a convenient wooden crosspiece with one hand and lifted the gate bodily upwards, while tugging the stubborn bolt open with the other. Pulling the protesting wood towards her, it scraped along the dark scar already traced on the concrete. Hinges cried out against the strain and threatened to pop but suddenly she was through, leaving a trail of rotten wood particles behind. She could have stepped over the fence of course, although she was probably too short to manage this elegantly and in any case fences were not gates, as gates were not fences.

Picking up an old garden fork and a battered shopping bag, she tugged the gate closed and set off for the allotment a short walk away. She wore an old pair of lime green corduroy trousers tucked into a pair of dull black wellington boots and a sleeveless yellow blouse that showed off her toned arms. The trousers had seen better days (in fact she was pretty sure that she had worn them hop picking) but were perfect for the task in hand, even if they now required a small silver coloured safety pin to hold the exhausted zip together.

'Why buy a new pair of trousers when, with a bit of effort, these will still do the job,' she said. 'People can think what they like.'

In her bag were all her requirements for the coming day. Although her hands were hardened by her labours, she still carried a pair of old gardening gloves encrusted with dry soil plus a tin of Elastoplast. In addition she had a packet of ten Players, a box of matches, a thermos flask full of hot sweet coffee, a small bottle of Scotch, a lump of Cheddar in a brown paper bag and a bright red apple that she had shined vigorously on her blouse. These would sustain her for now.

'Has to be a red apple.'
Ted had heard this many times before.
'Why?' he would reply rather wearily.

'Because they're the best, the sweetest. They're red. Red apples are always the best. Stands to reason. Everybody knows that.'

Occasionally Ted might attempt to dismantle her colour coded logic.

'So does that mean that red buses are better than green ones?'

She would look at him as if he was crazy. 'Of course not. Now you're being ridiculous.'

She clumped off along the alleyway that ran the length of the back gardens, stopping only to balance on one foot against a convenient gatepost to remove one wellie and retrieve a black sock that had already worked its way off her foot. Around her neck she could feel a chord pulling and occasionally chinking. From it dangled the two keys needed to open both the entry gate to the allotment and the padlock that secured the ramshackle shed that she had built with Ted's help. He had worked hard and enthusiastically.

'There you are love. Just what you need.'

'It's for both of us.'

'Of course. But you're the gardener. The expert.'

Well of course she was and she had settled for that, but sometimes she felt it was built to get rid of her. When these thoughts came into her head, she pushed them out again, *No. He was just supporting her. As he had always done. That was it.*

Her ten rod plot was identical in size to that of her neighbours, but there the similarity ended as every plot took on the personality of its owner as well as individual cultivational choices. For Florrie the heart of her kingdom was a place where all could live and be nurtured and grow in abundance. Everything was allowed to flourish. Thinning out the weaker plants to allow the stronger to thrive was not permitted in her caring society. She had already seen too much of that played out on the battlefields of Europe. Even the odd dandelion, struggling on the edges of the bare pathways that surrounded each plot, was invited onto the rich soil and celebrated for its sunny flower. Other immigrants, arriving by chance on a warm breeze and finding a spot to settle, were welcomed and treated with curiosity and respect as their green shoots developed. However, those that attempted to invade were ruthlessly eradicated, not only the brambles and deadly nightshade but also the bindweed that smothered the black iron railings surrounding the allotment with its mass of tendrils. Passing children, innocent of the true nature of this aggressor, only saw the white bell-like flowers and would pop them onto the ground and sing.

'Granny, granny, pop out of bed.'

But still the bindweed remained strong. Occasionally it would attempt to infiltrate a row of runner beans or sticks of peas, wrapping a choking coil around them and then climbing, seeking the sun and domination. Florrie would pull it from the ground and leave it to wither and die as a dire warning to others.

In one corner of the plot, closest to the communal water source and balanced precariously on two piles of crumbling red and yellow bricks, sat an improvised water butt made from an old leaky cold water tank, long since removed from someone's loft. Two sheets of plywood, now black and curling, rested on the open top in an attempt to keep out leaves and insects. Around it nettles grew strongly, attracting both butterflies and the concerns of passing fellow growers.

'You need to get rid of those Florrie,' they said, picturing their Savoys riddled with holes.

'Why?' she replied fiercely, hands on hips.

'Well, they attract butterflies.'

'Good. I like butterflies,' she retorted turning to watch a Red Admiral float past exactly on cue.

'Yes, but their caterpillars eat the cabbages.'

Nearby a duo of Cabbage Whites danced together above a large group of brassicas.

'Well, they have to eat something, don't they?'

It was usually at this point that the growers withdrew, somewhat bemused, and decided that they could after all cope with a few lacy cabbages rather than encourage conflict with their eccentric neighbour.

Nearby an old metal bedhead had been sunk into the ground and now acted as a support for succulent peas. On sunny Sunday mornings, sitting on the back door step, the pods would be shucked by hand and a pile of green peas would steadily grow in a yellow metal colander slightly chipped around the edge.

Next to the bedhead, cloches had been made from old window frames resting on thick wooden boards sunk into the ground. The boards had become warped by rain and sun and most of the frames still had their original handles and in one case the original hinges, metal twisted and dark brown with rust. Over a number of seasons the paint on the frames had curled and peeled, revealing layer upon layer of colour. Once, each colour had been carefully chosen and applied with loving care, but now it flaked off and blew away, tiny coloured memories of somebody's home.

In the centre of the plot stood a line of slim dark-brown chestnut palings, cut from the local woods, lashed securely together and protruding from the soil as inverted Vs, and supported by a central spar. They stood quietly, some with their summer string ties now having turned grey, moving gently in the breeze. They resembled a skeleton, waiting to be covered once again with a cloak of green, spiralling upwards, flecked with red and white flowers and carrying scimitars of juicy green beans.

Florrie's allotment was an extension of the small back garden and even smaller front garden that she also ruled over. Those approaching the front door would be pushed off the path by a huge bush of lavender, releasing a delicious fragrance and often some mildly irritated bees. Visitors would arrive indoors with mud on their shoes and lavender fragments on their clothes and in their hair, smiling but equally irritated. Occasionally, Ted, exasperated, would attempt to prune this bear of a bush and would grab an oil can and a pair of rusting shears, only to be met with wails of anguish from Florrie.

'Ted stop it. Leave it alone. You'll kill it.'

Kill it? It would take a nuclear device to kill it, Ted thought to himself.

The back garden was even worse. Every plant was left to grow wild. Every shoot, briar, branch, flower and leaf entwined around every other in an amazing tangle of greenery and colour, all growing ever skywards like a manic magic fairy story. Even the weeds that grew at the base of the garden fence and were normally removed by gardeners as social outcasts, were heartily welcomed and flourished in large bunches.

Ted found himself caught in a dilemma between his support for Florrie's eccentric gardening extravaganza and an urge to conform. All around him gardens were tended. Plants were fed and watered, shrubs pruned, lawns mown, fruit sprayed, tomatoes staked and in the middle of such neat discipline erupted this jungle of nonconformity, this liberal self expression. Not being normal was such bloody hard work. He sighed, snapped the shears shut and returned to a tearful Florrie, made her a nice cup of tea and sat silently with her and waited patiently for her sad face to recover.

Gradually, the back garden also became full of figurines collected from numerous jumble sales. These withstood the attentions of dogs, cats and heavy frosts, the latter splitting and cracking them and gradually removing lumps of faces and limbs like some awful predatory disease. Still they stood stoically, their expressions unchanged.

As the years went by, so the plants grew thicker and wilder and new ornaments were introduced. Nothing was rejected on grounds of aesthetics, size, appropriateness, beauty, colour or downright ugliness. The little pond, which had become the centre of this society together with its surrounding rockery, became a mecca for the unloved and unwanted – a symbol of a multicultural society before we even knew what that meant. Nothing was abandoned. Nothing was unloved. All were welcome.

The garden shed however, seemed to be outside of this sanctuary. Maybe Florrie was uncertain about the purpose and importance of the large number of strange tools and pieces of equipment that it contained – many rusted or covered in oil and grease.

'What are those, Ted?'

'They're mole grips love.'

'Mole grips?'

'Yes. Mole grips.'

'Oh.'

She remained confused but thought it better not to ask why on earth anybody would want to grip moles. This was part of a man's strange world. The shed was declared an exclusion zone from her botanical aggrandisement.

But the shed was much more than that. Maybe it was an unspoken monument for the Anderson air raid shelter that had originally been dug into the ground at that spot, or maybe it simply hid its memory. Maybe there was simply nowhere else to put it. Whatever the reason, the shed and its several successors never moved position remaining there, full of rubbish, for decade after decade. They did however act as a barometer of change.

The original shelter was sold for scrap immediately after the war and nobody was sorry to see it go. After all, all around them, signs of destruction were being removed and a new order introduced. And so, a new shed arrived, still made of corrugated iron but now painted a delicate shade of green as if to indicate the arrival of a new spring and a fresh beginning.

But the fresh new beginning took a while. It was a few years before a windowless wooden replacement arrived. Painted brutal brown, it was stark and soulless and sullenly watched the 1950s come and go.

Later, as things improved, white clematis started to grow over the brooding monster, adding a little more hope and finally, in the next decade, there arrived a neat four-windowed construction with a felt roof and shiplapped walls. This delicate creature received neat curtains at each window, and a white trellis, over which red roses joined the clematis. It was as if the world had eventually returned to normal after such a dark time. Prosperity had increased and with it new adventures such as chalets by the seaside and travel to exotic places, although there was of course nothing quite as exotic as Florrie's gardens.

Florrie opened the allotment's iron gate with a squeak, entered, and stopped briefly to relock it behind her. It was early Saturday morning and so far, she was alone. It was almost ten years since they first took over the plot and she had loved every moment of it. It had been perfect for her cubs – growing things, learning about nature, taking responsibility. She stopped for a second, closed her eyes and took in a deep breath, tasting the warm air mixed with the flavours of soil and plants. She breathed out slowly and made her way towards her home-built shed.

Sturdy rough timbers, which threatened the unwary with splinters, formed the basic structure. Onto this, old doors had been fixed to act as walls, one of them still opening and closing as a door once again. They stood there in a variety of colours – white, green, blue and yellow – with their locks and handles removed, leaving holes like dark wounds. One door still had a tarnished brass house number hanging helplessly upside down below its faint shadow. A former front door acted as the only window. Its frosted glass section allowed a dim light into the interior and, where a pane of glass was missing, chicken wire had been tacked over the gap from inside. White corrugated plastic sheets had been placed onto the walls to act as a roof and were held in position by a number of balding black car tyres. Despite their weight, the brisk winter winds could cause the plastic edges to flap frantically and occasionally pieces would snap off and fly dangerously away, leaving an even more distressed feel to the building.

Florrie unlocked the large padlock and stepped into the gloom. She placed her fork against one wall, put her bag onto a paste table that stood with two tea chests on the hard packed floor and withdrew her flask, Scotch, packet of Players and matches. These she placed alongside an old stained white enamel mug and a black ashtray full of charred matches and cigarette ends tipped with lipstick. She poured herself some hot sweet coffee, added a slug of whisky and sat down on a tubular picnic chair whose red, yellow and blue canvas stripes offered the only colour in the monochrome interior.

On a long wooden shelf sat a fat ball of brown string – with one loose end dangling – a gardening knife and several opened packets of seeds, their ends tightly screwed up with elastic bands. A faded gardening calendar, showing a snowy January landscape, hung from a rusty nail. Next to it, stood an equally rusty hoe, its split handle held together with black insulation tape, a grey metal watering can, some yellow bamboo poles and, at their feet, a dibber with its blunt end hewn from some former spade handle. In the dark corners, away from the entrance, hung thick cobwebs and across the chicken wire window, a spider had spun a trap and waited patiently for the flies that buzzed carelessly around.

Below, a metal tray emblazoned with the symbol of Guinness, was jammed against a rotten gap caused by the wind and rain, in an attempt to prevent field mice from entering and seeking shelter and a large galvanised bucket stood with a trowel handle poking out of the top. The shed smelled of dust and earth and rot and tobacco, but despite its ramshackle appearance it offered a retreat. A place of peace and reflection… Florrie closed her eyes, settled into her chair and slowly felt her body soften and drift. Around her a breeze whispered drowsily through the broken window. Outside, a fork clinked against a stone.

'Hallo Florrie. Are you there? It's only Morris.'

Florrie awoke with a start. She had been dreaming, only minutes, dreaming of being trapped alone in a dark place, unable to escape, with silent faces looking in at her through many small windows. The dream had been very vivid and she was relieved to find herself safe with the sun now flooding through the half-opened door. She quickly refreshed her dry mouth with the tepid coffee and whisky and mentally shook off the terrors of her dream.

'Come in Morris.'

The door moved very slowly and cautiously the shape of a short man appeared, darkened against the morning sunlight. He stood nervously in the doorway.

'I do hope I am not disturbing you.' His voice was clipped but not in a sharp way, he merely allowed the minimum of expression needed to communicate. His words were perfectly pronounced with an accent that appeared to come from a more upper class background, but which occasionally allowed the sounds of the local streets to creep in. Their sentiment, as always, expressed politeness and good manners. Once again Florrie found herself wondering as to who this man really was but, as always, there were no chinks in the barrier he wrapped around himself.

'No, of course not, Morris. Come on in. Take a seat.'

'Thank you, Florrie. Only I didn't see you outside and I wondered…'

Florrie felt disinclined to reveal she had been asleep and looked across at the dapper man now seated on the edge of another multi-striped picnic chair, his legs closed together and his hands resting in his lap. She could smell the brilliantine that darkened his fair hair and saw the parting incised with surgical precision on the left side of his head and the straight white strip of his scalp. His small moustache was also clipped with the same care, such care that it appeared at times to be unreal and to have been carefully positioned and stuck on that morning

'I was only resting,' she smiled.

He made no response. In the silence, Florrie wondered again about Morris. She did know that he was the epitome of tidiness and neatness and that even in the summer heat he always wore a dark tie clipped with a silver tie pin against a white shirt. His black blazer was always carefully brushed and buttoned and often showed the tip of a white handkerchief peeking from a top pocket. His matching trousers held razor sharp creases and his black shoes were polished like mirrors. He only ever arrived at the allotment on Saturday mornings, riding a large clanking bike, his trousers held neatly by black bicycle clips and a shiny attaché case fixed firmly behind his saddle. No matter how many times he arrived, as he stepped carefully over the rough ground to avoid contact with his sparkling shoes, his appearance always raised heads. But nobody said a word.

'Would you like some coffee, Morris?'

'Er no thank you Florrie. Just called in to say hallo. Just to be neighbourly, you know.'

'That's kind of you.'

He smiled and looked towards the floor. He had his own routine of course and tea for him was always at 10.30 am precisely. *Everybody needed a routine didn't they?* When he arrived at his shed, he would remove his bicycle clips and place them in the right hand pocket of his jacket, which would then be carefully hung on a wooden coat hanger. His shiny shoes were placed perfectly together in their allotted position on a low shelf and he would put on a pair of polished black boots, first the left one and then the right. He would then open the small attaché case and place the contents next to his shoes. First, a honey coloured clothes brush, then a black nylon comb, then a yellow duster neatly folded into a square, followed by a tin of black boot polish, and a shoe brush strangely stamped with a set of numbers. His delicate fingers would carefully move each item until they were perfectly spaced apart and at the same distance from the shelf edge. He would stop and turn his head at an angle to gauge the effect and stand for a moment feeling a sense of satisfaction. In the world outside he would hear the murmur of voices as people arrived to work on their plots and he would turn to check his appearance in a small mirror pinned to the shed wall.

'OK Morrison. On duty.' He spoke the words like an order.

His plot exuded discipline and attention to detail. He had first dug the soil and broken it down into small pieces with the back of his fork. Then he had sieved it, removing any stones or pebbles or twigs until it was flat and even. It was then raked, again removing oversize pieces of soil or small stones and then sieved once more until it resembled a smooth flat beach with the marks of the rake at right angles to the plot edge and parallel to each other. The other plot holders looked on in astonishment. After all that effort, it seemed a shame to then spoil the effect by planting at all. But he did, with seeds held between a pair of tweezers, dropped in individually at measured distances apart. His neighbours only hoped that the plants would grow to identical heights.

Florrie felt concern as she looked at Morris. She realised that this was the longest conversation they had ever had.

'Is everything alright at home, Morris?'

'Yes thank you, Florrie. Mother is well now. Had a touch of the old flu at the beginning of the year but…' and his voice trailed away as if he was saying too much or betraying a confidence. 'Yes everything is fine thank you Florrie.' He looked away.

At the window, the spider moved quickly from the shadowy corner to the centre of its web and started to bind a hapless fly.

Florrie knew he lived alone with his mother and he appeared to be a devoted son. He never spoke of any brothers or sisters and she assumed that he had decided for some reason to look after the old lady. As he must be now approaching his middle years, she wondered if he had ever regretted that decision. He wasn't married or at least he wore no wedding ring and never spoke of a girlfriend or any friend for that matter. Maybe the decision had been forced upon him. He never spoke about it – the problem that had to be faced up to. Maybe he had done so reluctantly. Maybe with dread or even anger as his life and dreams were taken away from him. That would be a normal human reaction. But he gave no indication. Maybe he had no dreams. Who knew? But there was no doubting his sense of loyalty, his sense of duty. Although sometimes he would leave the allotment hurriedly and nervously and Florrie wondered about that too.

'Are you going already, Morris?' Florrie would say.

'Yes must go. Mother will be waiting,' he would reply cheerily, but his eyes showed his discomfort.

Morris wanted to leave *now* but he also wanted to stay. He felt comfortable with Florrie, but at the same time he could feel her gaze gently searching his features.

'And how are things at work, Morris?'

'Oh very well thank you Florrie. Yes very well.'

His face brightened and he sat up and faced her again.

He worked from Monday to Friday as a clerk in an insurance office somewhere, maybe even in a fairly senior position. Florrie was never sure about that, although he often gave that impression.

'Yes, they are very pleased with me. My manager said so in front of the others. I was an example to follow he said. Hinted that I was chief clerk material. It's the discipline you know and seeing things through. Youngsters just don't have it.' He stopped as if surprised at his enthusiastic outburst and sat for a moment smiling to himself. He looked up. 'Well, must go now. Lots to do.' He rose and moved towards the doorway but then stopped and turned. 'Thank you Florrie.'

The sunshine that poured through the door placed his face into shadow and Florrie was unable to see his pale eyes moisten. She smiled her reply.

Outside, Morris moved slowly to his adjoining plot, picked up a shiny fork and drove it fiercely into the dark brown soil. Below the surface, one of the fork's tines struck a jarring blow against a black and white flint he had missed. He felt the collision ringing along the handle into his soft hands.

'Damn,' he muttered.

He looked around. Fearfully. But nobody seemed to have heard him.

'Damn, damn, damn.'

***

Exactly one week later, Florrie peered through the veil of rain that flowed down the windows of her back bedroom and forced her eyes to focus on the soaked allotment in the distance. She realised the plants growing there needed the life-bringing rain, as did her make-do water butt, but it was frustrating to be indoors. She loved to be outdoors, feeling the sun and wind on her face and the satisfaction of physical effort. As she turned away, a flash of light on the allotment suddenly caught her eye and she turned back and scanned the area intently. *That's odd. No, nothing there. Can't see anything. Must have been my imagination. No. Wait. There. There it is.* A pale yellow light was wavering through the lashing rain. Her first thought was that vandals had set fire to one of the huts and she felt anger rise into her breast, but as a sudden gust of wind beat a fierce crescendo against the glass, she realised that was unlikely. So, who was out there in this foul weather? It was then that she realised the light was coming from Morris's shed.

'I'm just going out Ted.'

'But it's raining cats and dogs!'

'Won't be long.'

And she was gone with the wind threatening to wrest the bucking umbrella from her hand and the rain gradually soaking her trouser legs and running into her wellington boots.

It wasn't until she arrived at the allotment that she realised her curiosity and concern had blinded her against the possibility that whoever had lit the lamp that now flickered more brightly through the shed window, may have had other motives. She paused. *Surely a burglar wouldn't light a lamp would he? Wouldn't that betray his presence? Is that the correct word? Do burglars only burgle houses and not sheds? What do you call people who...* and suddenly she caught sight of herself standing there, alone in the pouring rain, and shook herself. *I must be mad.* She paused. *OK Florrie, you can do this* and she took a deep breath, pulled a nearby metal stake from the mud, approached the closed shed door, and placed a wet ear against it. Nothing. All she could hear was the rain striking wood and glass and the wind scattering wet leaves. She raised the metal stake and rapped loudly against the door.

'Hallo. Who's there?'

'Who's that?'

The words from inside were loud and clipped.

'Morris. Is that you? It's me. Florrie. Open up. I'm getting soaked.'

The shed door opened and there stood Morris, dwarfed in an old tartan blanket and wearing a black balaclava from which tired pale eyes peered. His moustache normally so sprightly, seemed to droop.

'Florrie! My goodness. Do come in. Such fearful weather.'

They both stood facing each other, uncertain of what to do next. Morris was unable to look Florrie in the eye, like a child that has been caught out being naughty.

'Morris, what are you doing here?'

There was a pause.

'Morris, it's been raining heavily all night.'

Florrie spoke kindly but her words quietly demolished the pretence. Morris's body, always so upright, now suddenly slumped as if the tension that had held it so taut for so long had snapped like an old spring. He turned and sat wearily on a small wooden chair and placed his head in his hands. He looked up.

'I used to be in the Army once.'

He knew she would be surprised. Why shouldn't she be? 'Look at me, hardly a soldier.'

'Yes, I thought you might have been.'

'You did?' And he looked up, eyes shining. 'Really?'

'Yes, I did.'

'Oh... Well, I was in the Royal Army Service Corps. Corporal.' He hesitated slightly as if uncertain. 'During the war of course.'

The words began to tumble out, nervous but excited, like prisoners escaping from their incarceration, looking around, uncertain, but not wanting to go back. 'Best time of my life.' His words roared out quietly. Tears filled his eyes and spilled out to be soaked up by the black wool of his balaclava. He wiped them away. Fiercely. 'We were all mates. All together you see,' He wanted Florrie to see so badly. 'Once our convoy was bombed. I was so scared Florrie. So scared, but then so was everybody.' He paused. 'My pal, Stanley – Stan – he died in my arms... He held me so tightly... So tightly. Nobody has...' and his voice faltered. 'Then he died, very gently.' He paused again. 'I was surprised it was so gentle.' He looked up at Florrie to share that surprise. 'I didn't know what to do but the officer shouted at me and said that I was now the corporal in charge and to get the convoy moving again. And I did,' his voice rose. 'I shouted orders at them and they obeyed me.' He paused and shook his head slightly as if puzzled. 'Later of course they said that I was to be a private again. Not really NCO material you see. But I did it Florrie, on that day I did it.' His eyes shone again, 'And it felt so real... Not like now.' He slumped again, exhausted, and looked at the floor.

'Why are you here, today Morris?'

'It was easy during the war. We were all mates together and we helped each other. I felt like I belonged. When it was over, well, I just went back to mother. She was so proud of me. Told everybody of course, but after a while it just went back to normal.' He paused. 'It wasn't easy you know,' and his voice flared up as if he knew what Florrie might be thinking. 'It wasn't easy to get work. After the war.'

Florrie moved and sat on the edge of a narrow table and looked down at the crumpled figure.

'I know Morris,' remembering the struggle Ted had faced before the job in the Dockyard.

'And I couldn't let her down, could I? What was I supposed to do?' His face pleaded with Florrie. 'So I told her I'd got a job as a clerk in an insurance office.' The words blurted out sodden with emotion. 'I lied.'

The rain pattered heavily onto the roof and in a corner an alarm clock ticked loudly.

'So that's why you come here dressed so smartly.'

'Yes,' and he pointed limply at the shelf with its orderly parade of brushes and cleaning items.

'And that's why you spend so much time tidying yourself up before you leave?'

'Yes. Every trace. I don't dare leave a single trace. Same at the cemetery. I have to get rid of every piece of grass, even check my turn ups.'

'Cemetery?'

Morris pulled the old blanket tightly around him and mumbled into it.

'During the summer I cut grass at the local cemetery. Monday to Friday I cut grass. Rest of the year I'm a labourer, a garden labourer.'

'And Saturday. When you come here?'

'I don't work at the cemetery at weekends and so I told Mother that I worked in the office on Saturday mornings. I don't know why. Maybe I thought that it would give me some time to myself. Time to think.'

Outside the rain had eased and the light grew stronger through the small window. Florrie got up and extinguished the oil lamp. It felt as if a long dark night had passed and the morning had arrived at last.

'You won't tell anybody,' Morris's voice pleaded with her.

Florrie stood in front of him.

'You have to tell her Morris. You have to tell your mother. You've nothing to be ashamed of. She will be proud of you no matter what you do. You fought for your country remember. You *are* a hero.'

'Oh no, hardly,' and Morris's voice began to regain its clipped authority.

'To her you are Morris. To her you are.'

Florrie turned, picked up her umbrella still shiny with rain, pushed the shed door open and peered outside. The rain had stopped and the weak sunlight was attempting to bounce its reflection off the many silver puddles that now dotted the brown muddy allotment. She stepped outside.

'Good luck Morris.'

She thought she heard him give a muffled reply but it could have been the sound of a man sobbing.

Ted was waiting for her.

'Where on earth have you been?'

His voice sounded both concerned and annoyed.

'On the allotment. That's all. Thought I saw a light but it was nothing.'

'Nothing? Must have been something.'

Ted had met Morris briefly on his visits to the allotment. He hadn't been very often. Florrie had unusual ideas on cultivation. Florrie had unusual ideas on everything, ideas that couldn't be changed. Best let her get on with it.

'It was just Morris.'

'Morris! What was Morris doing in all this rain?'

'He was talking to me.'

Her voice rose slightly. Ted looked away.

'Listen, he told me he was in the army during the war. Thought he was. Something about him. Royal Service Unit or something. Had a bad time. Sounded awful.' She felt her words immediately carve a space between them. Perhaps Ted would fill it? Bridge it with his own words. His own experiences. Clamber over it to meet her.

'Probably a fake.'

'A fake?'

'Yes. Some men pretend. For the glory.'

'Glory! Thought you said once there was no glory.'

'There wasn't.'

She waited for more. Ted looked at her with his lost eyes.

'I don't think he's a fake,' she said softly.

He turned away. *Sod Morris. Why should Florrie give him any sympathy when he got none? Royal Army Service Corps. OK. Everybody had a job to do but there was just no comparison. If she only knew.* It still burned inside him. 'Well, bloody lucky to come back then.'

'Oh Ted.'

The following Saturday, Morris did not appear nor on any Saturday that was to follow and soon his plot was completely covered in weeds, smothering any trace of him. One morning when Florrie arrived at her allotment shed, she found a brown paper parcel, perfectly wrapped and tied with white string, propped against the door. On it, written in tiny neat letters were the words 'To Florrie. Thank you.' Inside, she found a well-used shoe brush with what appeared to be an Army serial number stamped on its back.

'Hallo. *I* am Marjorie Goodfellow and *I* am the secretary of the Allotment Association.'

Florrie stopped digging and stared at her. A faint spark of recognition tickled her memory. The woman that stood before Florrie was quite short and fat, although the male plot holders might consider her to be voluptuous. Aware of that distinction, Marjorie wore dark orange trousers that gripped her ample thighs tightly and an equally tight blue and white checked shirt. This she unbuttoned one or even two buttons more than necessary, displaying the undulating landscape of an ample bosom, constantly straining to break free and smother the nearest male.

'You must be Florence,' she smiled coldly, knowing perfectly well who she was.

Florrie winced at the sound of her full Christian name. She much preferred Florrie but never Flo, the sound of which would turn her into a fizzing, fighting fiend. *My name is Florrie. Do not call me Flo! Why do people think they can take liberties with something as personal as your own name?*

'It's Florrie.'

'Of course dear, but I do think that Florence is such a superior name, classical even.' Her eyes framed by dark brown hair and enlarged by large powerful pink framed glasses, darted about like a pair of frantic black mollies in a fish tank. 'I am concerned about Mr Kellagher who has now taken the vacant plot next to you.'

'You mean Patrick.'

She swept the clipboard, which she carried at all times, upwards from her side with the exaggerated movement of one not used to authority. Her fishy eyes swam around looking for a name. 'Er Yes. Kellagher. Patrick Kellagher. Well… Mr Kellagher seems to have a rather unconventional view of the purpose of allotments.' She spoke like a set of regulations and lightly jangled the army of keys that hung around her chubby neck like an ancient badge of office.

Florrie's heart sank slightly. In the short time since Patrick had arrived at the allotment, she had struck up an easy friendship with the small, wiry Irishman, although her own dubious claim to also be Irish, like her mother, had been met with a wry smile and a twinkle in his pale blue eyes.

'Away with yerself Florrie. Is it Dublin yer from?'

'He's Irish. They have different ways over there. He'll soon fit in.'

The mollies stopped swimming for a moment and stared earnestly at Florrie, who stared back. The keys rattled briskly, thoughtfully and Florrie noticed a line of perspiration on Marjorie's top lip.

'Very well. Thank you Florence. I knew I could count on you.'

She turned and walked briskly away, eyes now scanning the surrounding plots. All around her, other plot holders moved silently into the shadows of the nearest shed or quietly merged into the camouflage of their runner beans and stood there, quite still, hardly daring to breathe, until the threat had passed.

Florrie watched Marjorie's large round rear retreat and thought of pumpkins. *How could somebody with the backside and brain of a pumpkin know anything about the true role of the allotment?* She knew. All around her she could see the benefits they brought to people. Families and children could play and enjoy nature. Workers could leave the strains of the office or the factory and find relaxation – it was amazing how ten minutes of heavy digging could heal the frustrations of everyday labour. The unemployed and not so well off felt a sense of community and inclusion as well as the chance of cheap food and immigrants began the process of integration. The disabled were welcomed and shed their loneliness and the elderly simply felt fulfilled. It was a place of trysts and friendships, of reflection and self-knowledge, and she thought for a moment of Morris and mentally wished him well. The allotment welcomed everybody and offered them healing as well as potatoes.

It was then that she remembered. Marjorie; of course, it was Marjorie Truman! Chubby, tubby, goggle-eyed, bossy boots Truman. The teacher's pet, who thought she was so superior because her father owned an old Singer car when the rest of us had to walk. Suddenly she could hear Marjorie's young voice echoing in her head, bouncing around, loud and superior, and she could see the children, clear as day, running around the playground, calling out in their sing-song way. 'Large Marge! Large Marge!' and Marjorie, her face red with anger and moist with tears, storming off to tell a teacher. Florrie was defiant, but the other children were fearful of the punishment to follow and Marjorie would smirk, just out of reach. *S'pose thinking back it was a bit cruel. No. She deserved it. Children can also be very perceptive can't they? Mmm. So, here we are. Truman to Goodfellow. How odd.* At that moment another image slotted into her mind. It was faded around the edges, but she knew that it had come from the Hill, in her father's yard. She could see his cart and his horse standing nearby, tossing his head and mane and tail at the irritating summer flies. 'She's a horse fly,' she mumbled aloud and turned and looked in her direction and thought only of swatting her.

'Was dat yer auld biddy Pudfellow herself?'

Patrick had appeared from nowhere.

He was a wee leprechaun of a man with hands that obviously belonged to somebody else. They protruded from the frayed sleeves of his dark jacket, far too large for his body and hung self-consciously at his side, calloused and darkened by labour and their lifelong contact with the soil, through many inclement seasons. He wore no rings, certainly to protect himself from injury, but maybe because he had nobody to wear them for. His fingernails, cut short, still always seemed to contain a black line of dirt the same colour as the large boots he always wore. His grey trousers were held up by a wide leather belt above which an old white collarless shirt peeked out from behind a waistcoat, shiny with age. He never wore a raincoat or an overcoat, only a shapeless grey jacket whose bulging pockets contained many mysteries, including his battered tobacco tin. His thin face was as gnarled and leathery as his hands but from below bushy greying eyebrows, his blue eyes danced and twinkled, as clear and warm as a summer's day. On his head he wore a flat cap of indeterminate colour that he was never seen to remove. As time slipped by, Florrie realised how it was an integral part of him, pulling it between finger and thumb whenever he met her, tipping it back sometimes in exasperation or pulling it down firmly in an attempt to ward off the cold wind or autumn showers that dripped from its peak. Occasionally he would lift it back to mop a perspiring brow revealing a strip of skin that gleamed white against his dark weather-stained face. Florrie came to believe he actually slept in it.

'Yes Patrick. She's complaining about you again.'

'Oh for the love of Jaysus, what does she know? What a lot of blather. Oim just after der diggin. Is dat a crime now?'

His twinkle died away for a moment. It was true that Patrick had few interests in life but those that he had, he held dearly. He would often arrive with a well-thumbed copy of the *Racing Times* protruding from one jacket pocket and regale anybody who cared to listen of the sleek power, beauty and sinew of the racehorse.

'Now Tulyar, dat was some horse.'

He would sigh wistfully, look into the distance and the liquid silver of his voice would summon up the thunder of hooves over the green turf at Clonmel beneath the Comeragh Mountains or of the Kerry hospitality that went on for days in the hot sun at Tralee. Sometimes, he would leave early with no farewells and make his way with his winnings to the King's Head where he would sit in blissful solitude dreaming into a few bevvies, only stopping to frequently relight his straggly hand rolled cigarette.

'I suppose you drink Guinness,' Florrie had once asked.

'Guinness! Jaysus Florrie,' he said as his eyes had clouded and looked into the heavens. 'Dat's cruel mean stuff you have here. Oi won't drink dat. Not here. No I won't.'

He became unusually morose at the thought of how something so revered, something of such national and cultural importance could have been prostituted by the cynical English across the water.

'Jaysus, haven't they caused enough problems already?'

His mood lasted only for a second as slowly into his mind flooded salivating thoughts of the silky black stuff back home – the real stuff, black as the bowels of a thunderstorm, round and creamy as a ball of butter and as smooth as a colleen's thigh. *Ahh. Now dat's a foine pint and no mistake.* He smiled and wiped the imagined creamy froth slowly from his lips with the back of a calloused hand.

'Now back home. A quart every mornin'. In a jug by me bed. Ready an' waitin', the little darlin.'

'A quart! Isn't that two pints Patrick?'

'Yer right there Florrie.'

Florrie found it difficult to imagine anybody having two pints of Guinness for breakfast when they could have egg and bacon. While she mulled over these thoughts including those that were now bordering on disbelief, Patrick turned, crossed to his plot, picked up a spade and started to dig.

Patrick had inherited an affinity for the soil as others would feel the call of the sea or the power of the word or the thrill of the musical note. It was in his blood and generations of his family had used their muscle and skill to reshape the face of the land around them. Their sinew had moved hills, cut canals and dug roads and in doing so had perfected man and spade as one, into a perfect digging machine. It was handed down, father to son. And so his alert eye would scan the ground before him and determine its content of wet clay or dry sand or flint or chalk thus recognising the ease or difficulty of the task before him. He would prepare his back and stomach muscles for the gut-wrenching pull of heavy clay or his joints for the jarring ring of hidden stones and just occasionally his eyes would sparkle as his spade bit joyously into the perfect soil. He felt the need to feel the sun on his back and the crispness of frost crunching beneath his boots. He needed the feel of hickory in his strong hands and the spade's metal edge against the sole of his boot. To watch Patrick digging was to witness power and grace. He was the Nijinsky of the allotments.

Soon, however, he stopped, held his back, stood up and looked around cautiously. Nobody was looking and he quickly and vigorously rubbed his back and left knee. Early mornings now arrived with aches and pains as his bones and joints called out for some respite and refused to cooperate as he struggled, cursing aloud from his bed.

'Come on now Patrick Kellagher. Get down on yer knees an tank God dat you're still on yer feet.'

But later he had looked quietly at his thin pale reflection in his bathroom mirror and knew that the time had come for something easier. Did he not deserve it? Had he not traipsed from site to site on this God forsaken island looking for work? Had he not spent his life there – hard, demanding and at times dangerous places to be? Had he not felt the hot sun burn his neck red and the wicked cold freeze his fingers numb and make his nose run? Had he not felt the pelting rain dripping from the peak of his cap onto the chalky slurry that cracked the coarse skin of his fingers wide open to the white bone beneath? Had he not been jaded and hungry with hardly a copper to buy himself a drink? Boys oh boys he had. Now he deserved a rest, that was for sure and what better place than this allotment with its soil dug and double dug by generations of gardeners and its clay broken down and its stones removed. Here he could spend his retirement gently digging, stopping for a rollup when he felt so inclined, choosing the weather, doing the horses, dreaming of home. The only problem of course was Goodfellow. And he spat into the soil and cursed her.

'May she be afflicted with the itch and have no nails to scratch with.'

Within a week, Patrick had dug the entire plot twice, stopping occasionally to puff on his cigarette or to share a cup of coffee with Florrie plus the cheese sandwiches she brought him every day.

'You don't only have to have cheese Patrick. You could have something else. A nice slice of ham maybe or tinned salmon.'

'Tank yer Florrie but oi loike a nice piece of der cheese,' he said, breaking off a piece of crust for some bold sparrows nearby. 'Does yer husband not loike to join yer? Help yer wit der diggin loike?'

He squinted at her.

'Sometimes. But he works Patrick.'

'So where is he now? On a Sunday?'

'At home. Getting dinner ready.'

'So he does der cookin and you do der diggin? Sure but dats back to front.'

Yes, we've been back to front and upside down for a long time now.

'Oh Jaysus. It's dat woman again.' Patrick pulled down the peak of his hat as if that would hide him.

'Mr Kellagher, I need to speak with you. Mr Kellagher, I have tried to give you the benefit of the doubt, but I need to inform you of the regulations pertaining to the use of allotments.' Marjorie's voice had taken on the official tone she had been practising alone in her small bungalow. Her husband, Geoffrey, would have known how to handle this situation but Geoffrey was no longer with her.

'Sure dat's very kind of yer.'

She looked up from her clipboard unsettled by the affable reply. Wasn't this difficult enough without this Irish person making it more so? *Come on Marjorie old girl. Duty calls.* Geoffrey's voice echoed around her anxious brain.

'Mr Kellagher. I am bound as secretary.' She paused and her bosom, buttoned away from view on this serious occasion, swelled slightly. 'I am bound as secretary to inform you of section one of the allotment regulations.' She licked her lips and continued. '"The tenant shall use the said allotment garden wholly or mainly for the cultivation of vegetable or fruit crops for consumption by the tenant or the tenant's family and shall not use the said allotment garden for the purpose of a trade or business."'

'Oh to be sure, dere's no business here. What do oi know about business?'

'I know Mr Kellagher. I know that, but all around you people are planting and growing crops. While you…' she paused in exasperation and her cheeks flushed pink. 'You… Are just DIGGING!'

The word exploded from her and echoed around the now silent allotment.

Patrick cocked his head to one side like a terrier.

'And what's wrong with de diggin may oi ask?'

'You have to plant and grow AS WELL!'

The pink turned to a light red and a small ball of spittle flew from her open mouth. The keys around her neck jingled nervously and she jabbed furiously at her clipboard. There was complete silence. Patrick scratched the side of his head and looked very thoughtful.

'Sure dat's a powerful ting. Growin'. A powerful ting.' He shook his head at the very thought of it.

Marjorie stood speechless, impotent. This was not how it was supposed to happen. She had fired the lightning bolt of officialdom. It was supposed to consume the ignorant and the ungodly in its terrible white heat of power but somehow it had gone out with hardly a fizzle.

'He *is* going to plant and grow.' Florrie's words cut through the swollen air like a whiplash.

Marjorie's clipboard fell to the soil. The pages rippled in the slight breeze and small pieces of earth rolled onto the allotment regulations.

'He's going to plant potatoes of course. What else would he plant?'

'It's too late for potatoes now,' and the words *isn't it* hung in the air. 'Shouldn't they have been planted by April?'

'These are Irish potatoes. They go in later,' Florrie continued. Florrie managed to maintain her glare and raised her eyebrows. 'Everybody knows that.'

Patrick looked at Florrie in admiration and said nothing.

Marjorie stooped with some difficulty, picked up the clipboard and brushed it clean. Patrick grinned at her. Florrie's blue eyes bored into the pink rimmed glasses and the mollies swam away. Marjorie turned, her heart still thumping under her ample bosom, and began to walk away. She stopped, looked at the regulations and looked back. *One last shot Marjorie old girl. No retreat.*

'I hope so. Otherwise he will have to leave.'

Patrick still grinned. Florrie still glared. Marjorie walked away feeling slightly more in control now and undid another button on her blouse.

'Ahh BeeJazus. De gob on dat woman an her as fat as a bishop. Face on her loik a bag a mickies. Sure the bleedin tide wouldn't take her out.'

'Patrick. You will have to plant something or they *will* get rid of you.' Florrie's voice was tender but insistent.

'I know. I know.' And Patrick slowly turned, picked up his spade and started to dig but with little enthusiasm.

Patrick did not arrive at the allotment for the next few days. He sat in his small room, stared into the distance and sipped the last drop of the Jameson that his most recent big winnings had supplied.

'Dis country is no good for der loikes of meself,' he mumbled. 'No good at all. It's toime to go home.'

He put on his cap and coat, locked the door to his room and made his way to the bookies in the next street. He had come to the same conclusion many times in his life but had never quite managed to save the travel fare and even when he had got close, he'd found himself in the King's Head or somewhere similar and had woken the next morning, bleary eyed and broke.

An hour and a half later, the two thirty at Doncaster had seen the outsider Paddy's Joy beat the favourite by a short head, coming in at ten to one and Patrick now looked at the bundle of notes nestling crisply in his hand.

'Jaysus,' was all he could say. 'Jaysus.'

He went back to his digs, polished his boots, put on a clean white shirt, placed his belongings in a large paper bag and left with never a backward glance. Soon the London-bound train was passing towns and countryside. Patrick sat and watched houses, fields and trees flash past and thought. *Perhaps cousin Declan would put me up for a few days, if he's at the same address of course. Aunt Molly must be dead by now poor soul. In any case, there's Liam. Never got on with him. Probably wouldn't be welcome. No... And my little sister Kathleen. Now in New York these past forty years. Forty years... Jaysus it's hot. I feel trapped in this metal box.*

He took a large white handkerchief, mopped his brow and waited uncomfortably for his destination to arrive.

He could feel the perspiration sticking his clean shirt to his back as he descended from the train and made his way through the ticket barrier. Ahead of him he could see a bar and he headed straight for it. His mouth felt dry and he needed a quick one. In any case there was plenty of time to catch his connection.

'Yes sir. What can I get you?'

'Point and a chaser if yer will.'

'Right. Will that be Irish? The chaser?'

'To be sure. Jameson if you have it.'

'OK.'

'There you are sir.'

'Bless yer.'

It was cool in the bar and not too crowded. Patrick found himself a corner table and drank his beer greedily. He lifted the glass of whiskey, looked at it fondly for a second and then swallowed it in one practised gulp.

'Jaysus dat's better.'

He felt the spirit spread and console his body. He wiped his mouth on a sleeve of his coat, sat back in his chair, looked at his watch and pulled the paper bag at his feet closer to him.

It was dark when he stood unsteadily in front of the bar for the last time.

'You alright Paddy?'

The barman's concern was not for the plight of the man in front of him but because he wanted to close the bar on time and get home early if he could. The last thing he wanted was to have a drunken Irishman taking off his jacket and rolling up his sleeves.

'Oim foine, jusht foine. Tell me, do oi have enough for a bottal of der Jameson?'

He leant against the bar and held out an open palm on which rested a few coins.

'Sorry, sir.' Best to be polite now. 'There's not enough. Maybe you should go home now. Do you have a train ticket or something?'

'Oh to be sure.' He produced his return ticket from a top pocket and began to move slowly out of the bar and towards the ticket barrier he had passed through earlier that day. His paper bag remained resting sadly against a table leg.

***

Florrie sat rigid in an armchair. Despite the brightness of the early day, she had pulled the curtains roughly, almost closed, and now sat in the gloom. She stared at the floor, white hands tightly gripping both arm rests. A single chink of light slanted through into the room and stopped just before her foot as if it dared come no further. Her features were fierce and dark as if the complexion of her Irish ancestors had swarmed to the surface looking for a fight. But the light that normally poured from her blue eyes had been switched off.

'You can't look after every lame dog love.'

Ted sat on the arm of a nearby chair, looking down at her. His voice was tender and pleading. He loved her dearly, always had. He admired her willingness to help others even though he recognised it was also something that she needed for herself. *Wish I could give you what you really want. But I don't think I can. I'm not really sure what that is anyway.*

She had a desperate need for something. Still, he never stood in her way. He'd always supported her and he always would, that was his duty. He would stand by those sacred vows at all costs. There was never any argument about that, never any wavering.

'First Morris and now, what's his name?'

She turned and looked at him and said nothing. Her eyes were darkened by confusion and depression. She wanted to blame him. Blame anybody. That would explain it, justify it.

'Is that what this is all about?' Ted said.

He sighed. The sound lapped up against the brittle wall surrounding Florrie. 'Come on love, let's have a cup of tea eh?'

He didn't know why she behaved like this – one minute wild and extravagant and the next in despair. There was neither rhyme nor reason, but her behaviour *was* beginning to worry him. Maybe he should see a doctor about her. He knew that old Doctor Green would see him, have a chat… *No. She'll be alright. She'll snap out of it. Probably a bit tired that's all. She's always had her moods, but she'll be OK.*

'Right I'll get the tea. OK?'

Florrie stared at him silently, unblinking. Sometimes those looks almost frightened him. They seemed so… unnatural. God it was like walking on egg shells. Why be like this when she could be so sunny, so uplifting, so amazing, so feisty and yes it was true, so scatty. In the kitchen he leant both hands against the cooker and stared down and saw and heard nothing until he was roused by the sound of the kettle boiling.

He returned with the cup of tea. The cup, saucer and spoon rattled lightly in the crisp silence. Florrie looked up at Ted, face still dark as if her mood was staring at him through her flesh.

'I don't want your tea.'

The rejection cut Ted. 'What do you want then?'

'You never do anything.' The voice was hardly hers. The words squeezed out without her lips apparently moving.

'What do you mean, "never do anything"?'

'You never take me out. We never go anywhere.'

'I have to work love.'

'Not all the time. Not all the time you don't. You never take me on holiday. We *never* go on holiday.'

'We went to Spain.'

'Spain!'

She sneered and leant forward and he thought she was about to charge from her chair.

'Spain. Huh. That was years ago… Spain.'

'What's the matter love?' She was scaring him.

'Nothing. You. You're the matter.'

She looked up at him. Her eyes were still wild. But also moist.

Ted felt helpless. It was true of course. They rarely went out together any more. But that was after Spain. Spain changed everything.

***

Florrie had been like an excited child, grinning and talking to everybody.

'We're going to Spain. On holiday. We're flying, in a plane. I've never been on a plane before. My husband has. He was in the war.'

She had held his hand tightly as the engines roared and the aircraft shook with the power surging through it. Suddenly it lunged forward, racing towards the end of the runway, bumping and rumbling.

'We're up. We're airborne.' Ted's voice had sounded strangely muffled in her ear.

Florrie had looked down upon the roofs and fields below and then back at Ted with an incredulous grin. They were on their way.

Theirs had been a simple clean room with shuttered windows that kept the interior cool and dark. They had been concerned to begin with, until the porter had pushed the windows open and let the shimmering light and warmth flood in. Ted had tipped him far too much and then he and Florrie, side by side, had looked out upon warm terracotta tiles and a cerulean sky sliced by the dark darts of swooping swallows. They had smiled at each other.

Later they ate strange oily versions of English dishes, longed for a cup of tea and wondered how the boys were. Bobby the youngest, was twenty one now, too old and independent for a family holiday. Later, they strolled in the soft evening warmth, looking forward to the day of the champagne festival and a mock bull fight. They had never tasted champagne before, but certainly they didn't want to see a *real* bullfight.

'I can't believe these nice people would allow such a thing.'

Florrie glowered at everybody with a dark complexion who passed by.

'No, not real bullfight. Nobody be hurt. It will have fun,' the waitress had reassured her. 'And the champagne, it is free. Much champagne.'

And there certainly was.

They had sat in the shade of the trees at long wooden tables. In front of them had stood a half bottle of champagne each and a plastic cup. Other bottles were stacked waiting nearby.

'Are you sure this is free?' Free was not a concept Florrie was used to.

'Si señora. It is free. It is to celebrate the champagne harvest this year. Very good. Come. Drink. You try the porrón?'

Soon Florrie's bottle was empty.

'Are you not having yours Ted?'

Ted had had a sip and decided that champagne was highly overrated.

'I'll have yours then.'

'Think you've had enough love. Don't you?'

'No, of course not. We're on holiday.'

She grabbed the bottle and drank from it. The champagne frothed up, ran down her chin and dripped onto the table. She attempted to stand but sat down abruptly.

'Come on. Let's sing. When Irish eyes are…'

A tannoy drowned her voice.

'Señoras y señores. Bienvenidos. Ladies and gentlemen. Welcome to our festival. We hope you enjoy yourselves. Please make your way now to the bull ring where our matador de toros awaits you.'

'Florrie. Florrie. Wait here. OK? I have to get the camera from the coach. Wait here.'

Florrie's eyes were having trouble focussing. She looked at Ted and said nothing. When he got back she had gone.

Ted scoured the crowds without any luck and finally found himself inside the small bullring looking down upon the circle of yellow sand. He felt angry and concerned and used his height to scan the eager faces in the crowd around him. Below him the master of ceremonies stood beside a matador wearing knee-length pants, white stockings and black slippers, his black montera in his hand. The sun caught the heavily embroidered gold of his silk jacket. Nearby in a special box sat a Spanish señorita in a bright red flamenco dress, her black hair pulled tightly back into a bun beneath her mantilla, a red rose behind her ear. The master of ceremonies lifted his microphone and began to speak. Ted heard the sounds of his words but not their meaning as he craned anxiously seeking Florrie.

'Ladeez and gentlemen.'

Where the hell is she?

'Welcome.'

Never again. Nev-er again.

'Today we have a special matador.'

Perhaps she's collapsed? Been taken to hospital?

'What is your name señora?'

How the hell do I get there?

'Florree? Si. OK. Now. Ladeez and gentlemen. I present to you. Señora Florree.'

What!

'Señora Florree will fight the bull.'

What!

There, below him, in the centre of the ring, stood Florrie, waving and grinning at the applause of the crowd. She crouched and adopted a boxing stance. The crowd howled. The matador, laughing, handed her a red cape and stood behind her, holding it with her.

'Now. Ladeez and gentlemen. In a few moments the fierce bull, el toro, will come through those gates.' The master of ceremonies pointed to one side of the ring. 'And the brave Señora Florree will face him alone.'

The matador stepped away.

Jesus Christ.

The crowd hushed, uncertain. *Surely not?* they all thought. Suddenly there was a long drum roll, two assistants pulled the large wooden gate open. There was a pause, and then a huge black beast appeared shaking vicious curved horns. Florrie flinched and then crouched, stern faced, ready to do battle. The beast stopped, turned and retreated, its udder flopping under it.

'It's a cow. It's a bloody cow.'

The crowd went wild.

The master of ceremonies lifted his microphone again.

'Brave Señora Florree. She faced the bull.'

The crowd started chanting. 'Floree. Floree. Floree.'

Florrie waved and grinned and clenched her hands in victory.

I'll give her brave Florrie when I get hold of her.

He waited beside the coach until she appeared, staggering slightly, grasping a half-empty bottle of champagne and a red rose. Beside her well-wishers clapped her on her back and smiled.

'Well done Florrie.'

She didn't appear to notice them.

'Where did you get to?' she slurred. 'Some husband you are. I fought the bull. Come on.' She pushed her way towards the coach steps, slipped and was helped on.

By the time the coach pulled into the hotel approach, Florrie was snoring, still clutching her bottle, the front of her dress sodden with sticky champagne. The rose had fallen to the floor somewhere. For everybody the euphoria of the occasion mixed with copious amounts of champagne had slipped away, leaving a flat, uncomfortable reflection.

'Do you want a hand mate? Bit of a handful you got there.'

'No thanks.' Ted smiled weakly at his neighbour across the coach aisle. 'I'll manage.'

I always have to.

Ted half carried, half walked her into the hotel foyer, trying to ignore the looks and praying that the lift was working. Florrie moaned loudly.

In their room he half laid, half dropped her onto the bed and stood back damp with sweat. Florrie rolled onto her side and vomited over the bed and floor. The stench made Ted gag.

Damn you. Damn you. Why do you do this?

He picked up a heavy ashtray and flung it against the wall. It thudded to the floor spraying cigarette ends and showering grey ash. The smell of stale tobacco now mingled with the stink of sick.

Never again Florrie. Never again.

***

'Don't you want your tea? It'll get cold.'

Florrie looked at the cup as though unaware it was there. She made no attempt to lift it but seemed calmer.

'Thank you.'

'How are you feeling now, love?'

Before she could answer they were both startled by a loud and insistent knocking on the front door. They looked up, uncertain. The front door was always left open. Friends and neighbours simply walked in and called out their arrival. Nobody knocked unless…

'I'll get it.'

Ted marched towards the continuing rat tat tat.

Marjorie Goodfellow stood before him. Her face was red and damp with exertion and she struggled to calm her gasping lungs.

'Florrie,' she spluttered. 'Is Florrie there?'

Florrie, following, now peered around her husband's frame. Marjorie's face lit up and her hands fluttered in front of her.

'Oh Florrie, oh dear, come quickly, it's Patrick. Help.'

The words shot out in a tangled bundle ending in a breathless squeak.

'Patrick?'

'Yes. Yes. He's... DEAD!'

The word exploded from her and her plump frame shivered with an involuntary sob.

'Dead?'

'Yes, he's in a hole and he's... he's... dead.'

Marjorie gulped and looked helplessly from one to the other. That word had been bouncing around blackly in her head. Now, actually hearing herself utter it, it did seem rather final. These were words she normally avoided. They were not very nice words. Certainly not the words you would use in polite company. A chilly thought suddenly clutched at her breast. What if she was wrong? She had to admit that she had never seen a dead body before, not in real life, only at the cinema, when Geoffrey had taken her to watch the Westerns he liked so much. Then, after the gunsmoke had cleared, the shot cowboys seemed to look the same as when they were alive, except with their eyes closed. Oh dear. How was she supposed to know these things? But she was the secretary of the allotment association after all and with that came responsibility. People expected leadership and direction. Geoffrey had always said so, although she had to admit she found such responsibility difficult. Oh why couldn't she just be normal like everybody else? Everyone else seemed to know what to do. How did they know that?

'At least... I think he's dead.'

'I'll go. You stay here Ted.'

Florrie pushed past them both and strode off grim-faced with Marjorie half walking half running behind her. Ted watched them disappear, amazed and angry at Florrie's sudden revival. *She'll behave for everybody else. Not for me. Oh let her go.*

He closed the door, returned to his armchair and sat with his head in his hands.

A small group stood in a ragged circle on Patrick's plot, looking intently downwards. Nearby, a young child wriggled, protesting, as his stern faced mother restrained him. On the nearby metal railings a large black crow watched. Marjorie stopped, gave a weak smile and stopped near the mother for comfort. Florrie marched towards the circle, all of whom stood back as she approached. In front of her, she could see a rectangular hole about the length of a man, with earth piled on either side. She stepped onto the mound and balancing carefully, she peered downwards. A few pieces of earth that had been disturbed by her climb tumbled downwards and fell softly onto the figure lying prostrate below her. Patrick lay on his back with his hands folded neatly in his lap. His spade lay by his side like a faithful pet. His eyes were closed, his face deathly white and his lips had a noticeable blue tinge. There was no movement and no sound save for the flapping of wings as the crow flew lazily away towards the coming night.

Florrie felt in one single moment, a kick of shock followed by waves of sadness and then clawing anger. Her emotions, unbottled, ran uncontrolled through her, flooding her eyes with hot salty tears. One fell like a message and soaked into the dry soil beneath her. Slowly, sadly, she knelt on the broken earth and felt the cold shadow below shiver her flesh.

Oh Patrick. You idiot! What have you done?

She looked up at the small group.

'What happened?'

A man slowly shook his head and the others stood in an uncomfortable silence uncertain as to what to do and unwilling to make any suggestion. Florrie looked down once again at the sad shell below her when suddenly, unexpectedly, loudly, the body stretched out there broke wind. There was a shocked gasp around her and she sat back, startled. What was happening? In a split second her brain hurtled through millions of dusty cells full of information seeking some sort of reference. Some sort of answer. A corpse. A bloated corpse? So soon? Full of fetid air and wind? And then in a flash it struck her.

'Patrick!' She shouted loudly. Angrily. 'What on earth are you doing? Patrick, get out of there.'

The body below stirred slightly. One arm moved painfully, slowly, rubbed his mouth, and a slit of an eye barely opened and looked up at the bright light of the sky and the strange silhouettes looking down at him. A ragged voice forced its way out.

'Jaysus. Can't yer turn dat feckin loight off? What yer gawking at?'

A white-coated tongue appeared and licked dry lips.

'Oh oive got a powerful troat on me.'

'Get him out of there.'

Ted appeared beside her. He couldn't stay behind. Despite her strange and difficult behaviour he had to help her and, with the group's help, he hauled and shoved and pulled until Patrick sat in a sad dishevelled heap on the ground. He seemed to have shrunk.

'What on earth were you doing?'

Florrie's voice still betrayed shock and anger but she knelt beside him and gently touched a bony shoulder.

'I taught me toime had come.'

She looked at him in disbelief.

'So did you dig this hole, this... grave?'

'Oi did. Not many people can say dat now.'

A grin appeared on his grimy face and he jutted out his chin and stroked the white stubble that grew there.

'Come on.' She helped him to his feet. 'Come on, to my shed. You can have a hot cup of coffee and wash your hands and face.'

'Ah oi need a jar Florrie. Oi'd rather go to de pub.'

'COME ON.'

He followed her meekly.

'What are we going to do with him Florrie?'

Marjorie stood beside her. She had abandoned her clipboard. In fact she had mislaid it in all the excitement but it didn't seem very important now. She had wiped the tears from her puffy eyes, buttoned up her blouse, tried to tidy her hair and gain some composure. She had completely lost control of the situation – panicked. She'd not known what to do and she knew it. To make things worse she had heard a voice in her head. *Must do better than that old girl. Oh do shut up Geoffrey.* She turned towards Florrie. Concern in her voice. 'Mr Kellagher, er Patrick. What do you think we should do? He won't be able to stay will he?'

'Give me a week. Just a week before you do anything. OK?'

'OK Florrie.'

Marjorie walked away, grateful that somebody else was making a decision.

Patrick returned the next day, filled in the hole under Florrie's stern gaze and carried on digging his plot whilst she desperately racked her brains for a solution.

'What are we going to do Ted? What are we going to do?'

Five days passed and an uneasy peace had settled over the allotment. Patrick continued to dig but with far less enthusiasm, often stopping to look up and peer intently somewhere beyond the horizon as if searching for the first signs of the oncoming storm. The other plot holders greeted Florrie with their normal cordiality and bright smiles but their eyes too were clouded with concern. Despite the warm sunshine and the bright cheeping squabble of the sparrows, a chill had descended.

Florrie sat again on her back doorstep and looked distractedly for a long while at the pile of sleek plump pea pods she had picked. What to do?

Of Marjorie there was no sign.

Patrick sat in the afternoon sun. He took the *Racing Times* from his pocket, unfolded it and considered the runners and riders at Chepstow. For a while he found himself engrossed in the details of form, but then stopped and looked at the white clouds moving slowly and silently across the sky. As a child in Ireland he had often sat on the green hill near his grandparents' house and looked across the valley. In the distance, the hills were washed with blue and purple and he pondered why *he* wasn't surrounded by blue grass and purple trees. He really didn't know. Sure, it didn't really matter. He would lay back and look up into the sky, select a single cloud and watch it drift away until he could see it no longer. Until it looked down on places he could barely imagine. He always wanted to sit in the middle of its fluffy softness and arrive… well he didn't really know where, just somewhere new and different, where life might be better.

He looked up again. *Time to catch another cloud.* He sighed.

The final day of the week had arrived and Florrie had retreated to the shade of her shed and was sitting, desperately thinking and watching the smoke of her cigarette lazily float above her in the bright shafts of sunshine. Suddenly a sound pierced her senses, a familiar sound, a ticking, a regular ticking, a mechanical ticking. It was getting closer. She hastily stubbed out her cigarette into the black ashtray and sat up waiting. There was a gentle knock on the half-opened door.

'Hallo Florrie. Are you there? It's me. It's Morris.'

'Morris. Come in.' Her voice sounded delighted and she heard the slight bump as Morris rested his bike against the shed wall. 'Come on in.'

The door opened and Morris stood there. The same old Morris except that he seemed even smarter and held a large bunch of red, yellow and pink flowers that glowed in the shed's shade.

'For you Florrie.'

He sat and told his story. How his mother had cried and held him close and told him all was well. How the shackles that had held his mind and soul and body and which he wasn't really aware of, had shattered and turned to dust, leaving him scared but free.

'And you know the way things happen to you, good things, when you're positive.' He hadn't known of course until now.

Florrie smiled at his new found enthusiasm.

'Well, the foreman at the cemetery is retiring and they said I could take his place, if I wanted to. More money, but more responsibility.' His face clouded for a moment. 'I wasn't sure, but they said they needed somebody with my experience. Someone disciplined, reliable, like the army. You know. Strange how things work out.'

He looked up and beamed.

'That's wonderful Morris. You deserve it.'

A thought dashed excitedly into Florrie's head.

'Do you need any more labourers… gravediggers?'

'Oh yes. They're always coming and going. Hard to find good people you know.'

Florrie related Patrick's strange story.

Both men left Florrie that day with a smile and a handshake,

Patrick quoting something in Irish she did not understand and telling her "'twas a grand day'. She was left buzzing and triumphant.

She returned to her shed and sat for a long time in silence, thinking, smoking a Players and drinking a little whisky in celebration, until the sun began to dip away, taking its healing heat and light somewhere else.

The other plot holders gradually packed up and made their cheery way home but Florrie stayed on her own with just her thoughts. She had done well. She knew that, but still she felt unsettled. Why couldn't it always be like that, all the time? Why did it have to be taken away? The stage so full of drama now seemed very empty. Just shadows where the players had been; applause, an uncertain echo. Outside the dusk settled onto the heated land, calming and soothing it like a balm, but in the shed a heavy black curtain slowly came down and began to cover her. Florrie tried to push it away, but its weight bowed her mind onto the ground and held it there. She looked up at the shelf covered in gardening bits and pieces and caught sight of the edge of a small square of dull, twisted metal. It was always there, although oddly she didn't always see it. She couldn't even remember who put it there. It must have been her she supposed, long, long ago. She stood up and reached for it, half tucked away behind the fat ball of brown string, sat down again and weighed it in her hands. It felt so light and unassuming and she rubbed her fingertips over this fragment of the enemy aircraft. It was still so clean. Not rusted or corroded since it had fallen in flames from the torn sky that terrible September day. It lay there so easily, so quietly, almost innocent. A fragment of something strong and powerful, a piece of her life but a piece that unlike her was unchanged by the many passing years. As she continued to watch, it began to move – almost imperceptibly at first, just a tremor and then, to her surprise, it began to tremble and she felt beads of cold sweat beginning to form on her forehead.

'God. What's happening? What is the matter with me?'

The metal bounced on her palm.

'NO!'

Her voice rang out angrily and she grasped the metal fragment fiercely, desperately, feeling it bite into her flesh, hard, as hard as you can. Feel the pain. Feel alive. Feel the fear. Feel the rage… Feel.

'Ted. Help me. Please.'

Her voice sobbed and she flung the metal against the shed wall from where it fell to the ground and continued to watch her, glinting dully.

She slumped trembling and exhausted back into her chair and stared for a long time at the red marks bitten into her palm.

'Florrie. Florrie. You there?' It was Ted. 'You alright? I was getting worried.'

Florrie stood and flung herself at him.

'Oh Ted. You do love me don't you? You do?'

'Of course silly. Come on let's get you home.'

In the darkness outside a black dog waited. Ears alert, it moved closer.

TWELVE

The Letter and Florrie Becomes Her Garden

*'Today I felt pass over me
A breath of wind from the wings of madness.'*

Charles Baudelaire

Florrie sat alone in her back garden. She felt strange; troubled. She had often sat there before of course, at peace, eyes closed with the sun caressing her face and a milky coffee with a drop or two of whisky by her side. She had marvelled at the shapes and textures and colours of nature jumbled before her, particularly the colours. She loved colour. Not so much when it occurred on a dress or as a photograph or in a painting (other than her own), but the colour before a vivid sunset or a carpet of nodding bluebells. She stood, smiling, trying to articulate the feeling of joy that overwhelmed her, but being unable to do so.

She did, however, paint in her own Florrie style. She never sketched beforehand, but placed the paint directly on the canvas as she saw the vision she carried in her mind. It seemed strange that she never used a large, wide brush, which might have been a more suitable tool for her – more vigorous, more outgoing. Instead she spent ages choosing a smaller sable, sucking the brush's hairs to a perfect point. Then she would sit, totally absorbed in her art. The rattle of ferrule against glass would be the only sound as she cleaned her brush in an old jam jar, which sent swirls of colour drifting through the water, slowly changing the pure and clean into something murky and tainted.

Her finished pieces were placed unmounted into whatever jumble sale frame almost fitted and hung together from the picture rail in the front room. Some were glazed. Some were not. Some squeezed into their frame. Some were lost. Occasionally a painting slipped at an odd angle. This never seemed to worry her. After all it was content that mattered, not presentation.

Her paintings displayed a simple, naïve view and were only ever intended for praise – never for critique. They lacked perspective and any basic rules and often shocked with colour straight from the tube. She never mixed colours. That felt like dilution and she wasn't one for dilution. However, the results had an immediacy, an individuality, an honesty. They also simply ignored convention. They were Florrie.

Now Florrie sat alone in her back garden feeling strange and troubled. The sun burned her face and her coffee had gone cold.

As a child she had travelled all the way to London on a Sunday school trip. The teacher had told them about the Abbey, shown them wonderful paintings and enthused about history and grandeur. Florrie thought that it would be higher than the sky, wider than continents and filled with gleaming jewels... It wasn't. Now she looked around her garden. Where were her gleaming jewels? Her wonder? Who had switched off the blazing light and crunched her world into a small, terraced back garden?

The mad confusion of plants and hotchpotch collection of figures before her, she had wanted to represent a sanctuary; a place of freedom and choice. Now she saw they were none of those things. Now, in horror, she saw a heaving mass of tormented vegetation: some strong, some weak; some throttling; some suffocating silently and some pale with approaching death, but all struggling for survival.

A flurry of wild rose flowers eyed her accusingly. A single petal fell like a ragged pink tear, then another and another until the whole bush wept.

In front of the plants stood her figures: plastic, cement and plaster, mute, staring, imprisoned. She had ignored their ugliness, their kitchness, their garish coats and their shocking disfigurements and had offered them a refuge. But she hadn't understood, she'd been selfish. They had stood there mutely, frozen by ice, faded by the sun, displaying their disabilities for all to see, to be mocked and scoffed at, to suffer everlasting pain, just to satisfy Florrie. And why did they all seem to have Ted's face?

She was afraid that they would shout out at her – plants and figures. 'What have you done to us?'

'I only wanted to save you. To give you refuge. To let you flourish. Like I want. Like I need.'

But there was silence, except for the breeze sighing sadly around them.

Florrie struggled hard to understand, but the same twisting tendrils were growing in her brain, blotting out her memories, strangling her reason, overwhelming her control. Noises filled her and drowned her. It had been like this for some time. Some days she awoke feeling normal. *There. Knew it was my imagination.* On others a dark bile seeped from her brain and frightened her. She tried to think when this had started? *Oh yes. The letter.* And anger twisted and filled her. It had arrived out of the blue one Friday morning. *Yes Friday.* She remembered that. Just a normal day. Just a normal white envelope but with the Scout motto in one corner. She had put on her glasses, torn it open excitedly and read.

Dear Florence

I am writing to confirm that your position as Akela will terminate on May 9th 1976 in accordance with the regulations regarding compulsory retirement.

May I take this opportunity to thank you for the outstanding service you have given the organisation over many years and to wish you all the best for the future.

Yours...

'No. No. They can't…'

She had sat down abruptly, hot tears falling onto the letter and had shaken uncontrollably. Without anaesthetic, her baby had been torn away.

Ted wrote of course, appealing to them to reconsider, telling them how much it meant to her, how much more she had to offer, but they politely refused. He then wrote and resigned his own services in support of Florrie. Harry, Helen and Joan did the same. All their positions were soon replaced. Florrie increasingly sat at home with the curtains drawn, hands gripping the arm rests, staring at the floor, slowly becoming one of her garden figures.

Ted was left with the problem of looking after her. He tried hard to cope with the shopping and cooking and washing and housework. Once he had been a fit, strong man; very fit, very strong. But the years had slipped past and dried the hot juices that once pounded through him. The years had bent him, wearied him. He knew the boys would help but he didn't think that was fair. They had their own lives, their own problems. He would do it. At least he was retired now.

He lit another cigarette and his hand trembled slightly.

Ted got off the bus at the end of his road carrying a large shopping bag. He liked going shopping at the Co-op in town. If he was honest he liked to get out; away from the shivery darkness that spread from Florrie some days. It was like standing in front of a fridge full of tears. It was good for him to get out and he enjoyed going back to the Co-op office where he had worked after he had left the Dockyard. He had been chief clerk. Yes, he had done well. Most of the girls in the office didn't know him now, but he always called in. A few of the older ones were still there.

'Hallo Mr Tap. How are you?'

'Fine thanks.'

'And Mrs Tap?'

'Fine. Mad as ever.'

He soaked up the initial smiles, but as heads turned away back to their work, he knew it was time to leave and head back to the bus-stop, where he would stand, hoping the bus would be late, delaying his return home.

He clicked through the front gate and opened the front door. He would be glad to put this lot down. His forehead felt clammy and he rubbed a dull ache away in his chest.

'Florrie. You there?'

There was no answer.

Probably asleep. Better have a look. Make her a cup of tea if she's awake.

The third stair from the top creaked loudly and had done so for years. He would fix it one day when he had a moment. He smiled at the thought of it. The boys used to pull themselves up onto the bannister to avoid it when they got home too late. He knew they did it because he always lay awake waiting for them to get home safely. He never let on.

The landing was quite dim and so he didn't see it at first. The blood red smear on the white bathroom door and the mark of two fingers.

'What the hell?'

The words gasped.

Now he could see the dark drops on the landing carpet leading to the bedroom. His heart froze and he leant for a second against the wall. There was no sound.

'Oh no, Florrie.'

He pushed the bedroom door open, slowly, and stepped inside.

Florrie was lying on her back on the bed, both arms outstretched. Her hands and arms and clothes were soaked red. A smudge of colour around her nose. A streak slashed across her throat. Her eyes closed. Behind her the wall was smeared and splattered crimson.

Ted recoiled as the violent scene screamed into his senses.

'Jesus Christ.' And hot tears flooded into his eyes. Then he realised something about the smell.

This wasn't blood. He knew what blood smelled like, lots of blood. And the colour…? He moved beside Florrie and placed his fingers on her neck. The pulse beat strongly. Beside her on the bed lay a tube of paint, cap missing and a worm of colour squeezed out. There were others on the bedside table and a large bowl of thin red water. Some had spilled onto the floor leaving a dark puddle. Beside the bowl, a shiny saucepan contained a red solution. Much had run down its side. The pillows, sheets and furniture were spattered with hundreds of spots and splashes. He stood back in horror. She had put the paint on the wall with her hands and fingers, scratching, sliding, smearing a mass of tormented writhing shapes, her painting pad too small to contain her anguish.

The hairs stood up on the back of his neck.

THIRTEEN

Breaking Point and the Listening Tree

'Alone, Alone, all, all alone,
Alone on a wide wide sea!
And never a saint took pity on
My soul in agony.'

Samuel Taylor Coleridge

'I'm going out.'
 'What? What are you doing now?'
 'I'm going out.'
 'Christ not again.'
 'I'm going out.'
 'But you can't love.'
 'Why can't I?'
 'It's the middle of the night.'
 'So?'
 'It's three o'clock in the morning.'
 'You coming with me?'
 'Of course not love. You need to sleep. Come on, get back into bed.'
 'No. I'm going out.'
 'You can't.'
 'Why not?'
 'I've already told you.'

'You're so weak. A weak little shit. Always have been.'
'Get back into bed love.'
'No!'
'You can't go out like that anyway.'
'Why not?'
'You're not dressed. You can't go out in your nightdress and bare feet. You'll get arrested. Bloody put away.'
'You wouldn't care would you?'
'What's wrong with your ears?'
'Nothing.'
'Why are you holding them?'
'They're full of racket that's why. Why do you think?'
'Calm down.'
'I won't. You never go anywhere with me. You're pathetic. You've no interest in me. Nothing. You and your bloody bridge. WHAT ABOUT ME!'
'Stop shouting love.'
'No. I'll shout if I want to.'
'You'll wake the neighbours.'
'Fuck the neighbours.'
'That's not nice, Florrie.'
'I bet you have haven't you? Fucked that skinny tart next door. What's her name?'
'Don't be ridiculous.'
'Joan. Tarty Joan. I know about you and her. You bastard.'
'Calm down please. Come on, take one of your pills.'
'I don't want a pill. What pills? They're not mine. Stick it up your arse… Is that what you did with her? Is it? You dirty bastard. I'm going.'
'No you're not.'
'I am. Let go of me. Let go! I'll bite you.'
'Calm down love. Please.'
'Let… me… go or I'll kick you.'
'Calm down.'
'I hate you! I hate you!'
'Now you've knocked the lamp over.'

'I don't care. Let me go. You're hurting me.'
'Not until you calm down.'
'It's all your fault.'
'What is?'
'Everything.'
'Are you going to sit down now?'
'No!'
'Come on sit down.'
'Don't do that. Don't touch me. I'll spit in your face.'
'Please don't do that.'
'I will.'
'Right. Here you are. Take this. Come on. Open your mouth. Open it!'
'No.'
'Come on. Open wide. Careful, you're spilling the water.'
'I don't care.'
'Come on. You'll feel a lot better.'
'Don't want to feel better.'
'Come on. That's it. Bit wider. Aggh. Jesus! You bit me.'
'Said I would. You keep away from me.'
'You hurt me. It's bleeding.'
'Good. You deserve it you miserable little shit. What have you ever done for me eh? Nothing. You never take me anywhere. Never say you love me. Never kiss me. Save it all for fancy knickers next door. Cow. I hate you.'
'For Christ sake sit down or…'
'Or what? Or what big man. You think you're so big don't you? But you're useless. Fucking useless.'
'Shut up. Shut up!'
'I won't.'
'You bloody will…'
'Stop it. You're hurting… you're choking me… Ted. I can't… Don't…'
'Oh God…'
'You hurt me.'
'I'm sorry love. So sorry. Don't cry.'

'You hurt me.'

'I'm sorry. Please don't cry.'

'Why did you hurt me?'

'I'm sorry. I'm...'

'Why did you do that? You frightened me... You still love me don't you?'

'Yes, of course I do.'

'Why don't you ever tell me?'

'Come on. Sit down. Please love. Sit down. I'm sorry.'

'I don't understand...'

'I know. Come on take a tablet. Please... the doctor said... That's it. Well done. Let me wipe your mouth. There, now back into bed. Come on now. Try and sleep.'

'I'm tired now.'

'Yes of course you are. You sleep. I'll look after you.'

'Yes... I need you... Don't understand.'

'Shh. Go to sleep now. That's it. Go to sleep.'

'Kiss my head. It feels funny.'

'OK... There.'

Ted stood beside the bed. Below him Florrie curled like a child. Black and grey curls resting on the white pillow. The drug began to seep into her brain, forbidding her nightmares for now.

He fell into a bedroom chair and covered his face, trying to rub the horror from his head. Stretching out his hands he could see teeth marks and a smear of blood on one finger. It throbbed painfully. *I deserve that don't I? Don't I? How could I do that? Christ this can't be happening.* Tears dared to fill his eyes. *Jesus what am I going to do? How long...?*

He shouted silently at the night. The night turned its head away.

Shame sucked away at his strength and he sat, trembling, surrounded by the debris of himself. A dull pain crossed into his chest.

He staggered up, moved to the window and carefully moved the curtain. He looked outside. There was nothing. What did he expect? *At least we haven't disturbed anybody*. As he went to close the curtain he thought he saw something at the end of the street. It looked like a dog sitting in a dark shadow.

Florrie was breathing evenly now. She might be asleep. But she might wake up in ten minutes. Maybe twenty. How was he to know? She might smile sweetly at him, unaware, without any memory and tell him he looked so tired these days. Maybe she would ask him if he was he overdoing it. Or she might start again. Launch another ferocious attack. If only he wasn't so tired… Joan had noticed it.

'Is everything alright, Ted? With Florrie I mean.'

'She's fine, Joan.'

'Only she doesn't seem herself these days.'

'She's OK.'

'And what about you, Ted? Are you OK? You look tired. Miss your nice smile.'

'I'm fine thanks.'

'OK. If I can help…'

Ted had gone home and looked at himself in a mirror. He never did that except when he was shaving and then he didn't really see himself only the path of the blade travelling neatly through white foam. The deep lines that curved downwards either side of his mouth shocked him as did the dark smudges under his limp eyes. He tried to smile. *OK, try again… OK, well, think of some happy occasion. Like a… wedding group with the photographer calling out like they do. Remember. Big smile now everybody. Cheese.* He grimaced. *No, well maybe not a wedding,* but he couldn't think of anything else. There must be a smile switch somewhere in the happy zone in your brain. His was just switched off. He stared at the tired old man before him. He had tried so hard to rid himself of the demons of war, for Florrie, for him, for his family. He had almost succeeded and now this. *Christ, I'm so tired.*

Ted moved cautiously around the room and sat very gently on the bed. He turned and looked at Florrie. She didn't move. Carefully, he raised his legs, swung and lowered himself until he was looking at the ceiling, which seemed to be moving slightly. The bedclothes were wrapped around Florrie and he knew that he daren't try and unravel them. He lay there rigid, knowing he couldn't sleep in case she got up again.

That's OK Ted. You've done that before. In the darkness, absolutely still, listening while your comrades slept all around you, relying on your vigilance, your discipline. You can do it again. Of course you can.

But the weight of sleep pushed upon his exhausted eyelids.

He kept the bedside light on and continued staring upwards, through the ceiling and beyond. Now his brain throbbed like an ugly abscess, threatening to burst, and spray and splatter his desperate thoughts across the bedroom walls, like a crime scene. *Oh God. Just like Florrie. Desperately spattering her blood-red anguish.* Within him, some of those thoughts leaped and flopped and squirmed like dying fish. Others raced ragged and jostled screaming at each other, contradicting, punishing, churning, pain and then… *Jesus what is happening to me? Why can't I think straight?*

Now he seemed incapable of doing the simplest task. He heard words sharp and clear, but they mocked him and sent misleading messages. When he went back to check, to see how he could have got it so wrong, the same words stared back at him, insolent and laughing. He felt inadequate, pathetic and useless.

He wondered if perhaps it *was* all his fault. He had made mistakes, of course he had. He knew that. Didn't everybody? He was only human after all. *That's what they said didn't they?* But perhaps his mistakes had been really bad? Had they triggered all this? He struggled, but he couldn't remember. He couldn't remember anything, not clearly. And now this, this terrible thing, with these hands. How could he? Around her throat. If only he could go back. Back to when…. His soul wept and he fell asleep.

He awoke suddenly, in a panic, face and neck wet and slimy. Twisting he failed to see Florrie immediately. Yes, thank God there she is, cocooned in blanket and sheet, still sleeping. He looked at the alarm clock. Six minutes had passed. He looked at her again. Her breathing was so shallow that for a moment he thought she had died. Maybe that would be better? *Oh for Christ's sake Ted.*

He had had a bad dream – yet another. He'd found Florrie climbing up inside a chimney, just her bare legs showing, smeared with soot. He had tried to grab a foot, but she had wriggled free and disappeared from sight into the black, suffocating void leaving him in helpless terror. He sat on the edge of the bed and wiped his face with a hand, then wiped his hand on his pyjama trousers. What had she been trying to tell him? Was she aware of what was happening to her but was too frightened; too confused to say? Was he helpless to save her? Was she slipping away into…? He realised he probably had had vague warnings, snatches of dreams that crept quietly into his waking thoughts and left sooty traces, words and behaviour that itched on the periphery of his awareness. Like comments made by a boring guest at a party when your mind is elsewhere that lodge, but don't register until later. He quietly left the bedroom and went to wash his face. Acid rose from his stomach and threatened his throat. He swallowed uncomfortably and reached for the tablets he always carried these days. *Bloody indigestion.*

He had seen the doctor, on his own, about a week ago.

'I'm just going to see the doctor. About this indigestion. Will you be alright on your own love?'

'Of course. Why shouldn't I be?'

'Do you want to come with me?'

'There's nothing wrong with me.' She had looked at him with fierce eyes and he wondered whether that was fear hiding behind the fierceness?

But he knew Florrie wouldn't come. Anyway perhaps there was no need.

Maybe it would pass? Get better? She had always been highly strung. Had her moods. God don't I know it. They came and went… But never as bad as this. Never as bad. But we'll sort it out ourselves won't we? Like we always do. No need to involve others. None of their business… But Florrie won't talk about it. And I can't really. I mean where do you start? 'I think you're going mad Florrie?' No couldn't do that. That would be so… Jesus I'm so confused and tired and… frightened if I'm honest. Yes that's the truth. Bloody frightened… It takes a lot to scare me but this, and what I did. Terrible. So terrible. So ashamed… What if I do it again? No never again, never. I'm already at rock bottom. Can't get any lower… Christ I wish I wasn't so tired… Come on Ted. Be a man. Be strong. You have to protect her. Help her. Like you've always done. Get through it. But this… God this is so awful. Awful. And it's not fair. Just not fair… What have we ever done…? I have to see the doctor. I know. But it frightens me. What will they do? Take her away? After all we've been through together. No, I couldn't bear that. And, it's like telling tales behind her back; letting her down, a betrayal. That's what it is. What it feels like… And what will people think? They won't say anything of course. Just whisper on street corners. Oh who the hell cares? I have to see him. Get some help. Maybe I'll just ask about this bloody indigestion. Not talk about the other… Maybe. She'll be alright for a while on her own. Seems calm this morning.

Ted didn't tell him everything, he couldn't. But Doctor Green had known Ted and Florrie and the boys for most of their lives and he had become a family friend. Not one you invited around for birthday parties, but one who knew you well and you could trust. What Ted didn't tell him he simply read in the lines on Ted's face – the weariness in his eyes, the quaver in his voice.

'How long has this been going on, Ted?'

'Oh quite a while now. Well, not too long.'

'All the time?'

'No, worse when she's at home. Just the two of us. Tends to take it out on…' Ted stopped and looked away.

David Green had seen the whole gamut of human emotions and behaviour in his long career and Ted was right at the end marked "Strong, dutiful, loyal but private, very private and stubborn." Didn't make his job any easier. Stiff upper lips were notoriously difficult to treat.

'You have to have standards,' Ted had once told him. 'You are nothing without standards.'

Ted found it easy to talk to the doctor. He trusted and respected him. Had no time for those who tried to force their position down your throat. *Bugger 'em.* For Ted, respect had to be earned, always. Didn't happen very often.

'At any cost Ted?'

'Yes, whatever the cost.'

'Are you a religious man Ted?'

'Hardly. Makes no sense. Not after what I've seen.'

'Yes, I can understand that.'

David Green looked at the man sitting opposite him. He rarely saw him in his consulting room and as far as he could remember, never on his own. He had visited the family home of course, which he recalled was number twenty one, but again not often, usually for childhood illnesses. Never anything trivial and he had always been thanked for coming out. 'Just doing my job,' he would say. But of course both Ted and Florrie would remember ill health in the days before the National Health Service. They never took him for granted. *If only some of his other patients...* Anyway now Ted needed help, more than he probably realised. How would he, the medical professional, balance all the necessary balls in the air? More to the point how would Ted?

'You understand that I can't prescribe for Florrie without her being here.'

'She needs help.'

'I can give *you* something...'

'I'm OK.'

'Yes, well, you don't look too well.'

'I came here to get help for Florrie. If you won't...'

'I *am* trying to help Ted. Both of you.'

'Just help Florrie.'

'OK. Look. Just hear me out. This prescription will help you relax and sleep better. If Florrie was here I would probably give her the same. OK?'

'OK. Sorry.'

'That's alright. Now listen carefully. Without the opportunity for a diagnosis, I don't know what Florrie's problem is, but from what you say, and don't say, I think you are going to need help. I can refer Florrie for specialist treatment and care...'

'Care. You mean getting other people in?'

'Well, maybe. It depends.'

'No. I'll look after her. That's my job. In sickness and in health. Till death us do part. That's what I promised and that's what I intend to do.'

'I understand how you feel Ted, but that doesn't mean you have to do it all on your own. That vow means you will get the best care for her.'

'No. I don't want anybody else interfering. It's not right. Not what I promised. It's my responsibility.'

'What about your own health, Ted?'

'What about it?'

'What happens when you become too ill to cope? What happens then?'

'That won't happen. I've been through more than this believe you me.'

'I know, but what if it does. You were much younger then… Promise me you'll come and see me again if that happens.'

'I'll be OK. I just thought you could give her something.'

'Florrie has the right not to accept any medical treatment and there's nothing I can do about it.'

'That's crazy. She needs help!'

'Try and convince her to see me or call me out.'

'She won't do that.'

'Is there anybody else you can talk this through with? A relative or a close friend? Or somebody who has had the same problem? It does help to talk, Ted.'

'No. Don't think so.'

'Well, try and find somebody if you can and let me know how things develop. Come back and see me. Promise?

'OK. Thank you Doc.' He had promised the doctor, but he didn't know if he could keep it.

Ted quickly washed and dressed. Quietly, he peered around the bedroom door. She was still asleep, good. She was always calm after a good sleep and there was something he had to do. He wrote a note for her and propped it on her bedside table. *GONE SHOPPING. BE BACK VERY SOON. TED.* Should he add a couple of kisses? No. They never did that. No need.

Soon he arrived at the long tree-lined road that led to the city and started searching. His stomach turned.

What if he couldn't find it? For goodness sake Ted. Calm down. It's only a tree. But what if it's been cut down? Why should they cut down a perfectly healthy tree? It might be blocking a view. You know how people get upset about their views. What. A view of the road? Hardly. Is that it? No. It's not here. Yes it is. Look – there. Oh thank goodness.

Ted arrived at the elm tree and touched it. He was sweating and his heart was racing.

He didn't really know why, but he felt compelled to be there and he felt a little foolish now. It wouldn't have worried Florrie of course. She would cheerfully have spent ages walking round and round it, staring up, grinning, admiring its structure and colours and textures, marvelling at its sheer presence and then having long conversations about it with the first complete stranger who happened to be passing. Maybe that was part of her problem? Her lack of inhibitions had now got out of control. Maybe that was it? Maybe that explained the long hours of abuse, the violent outbursts, the childish behaviour and the slumps into despair.

His lucid thoughts lightened his mood. He knew it would help him, the tree, this particular tree. He didn't understand why, but it seemed to be acting as a focal point. Something that helped him clear his mind. Something he could talk to. *Christ, listen to me. Talk to? What the hell am I on about?*

Now he was turning into Florrie. Maybe that was not such a bad thing. Maybe if he looked up he would see her again, sitting on the branch, swinging her legs, smiling down at him. But no, she wasn't there, just the branch – a little thicker, a little older. No, Florrie was at home and that's where he should be right now. He touched the tree again and left.

As he approached number twenty one, he passed the terraced houses of his neighbours and saw the lacy net curtains that hid them from view. They were in there alright, vague shadows, playing out their lives, their dramas secretly hidden from view, just as he was of course, except when Florrie shouted out in the night. But nobody said anything. They never would. They just got on with it and let others do the same. Just as it should be. Just as it should be.

He half expected Florrie to be looking out through her own curtains, worried by his absence, but she wasn't. You never knew what mood to expect. He unlocked the front door, felt his stomach churn and stepped inside.

'Hallo. Florrie. I'm back. Are you there love?'

There was silence.

Not the stillness of somebody asleep in an armchair or the quietness of somebody engrossed in a book but the brittle silence of an empty house.

'It's me. It's Ted.'

He quickly went from room to room. Downstairs. The back door was still locked. Upstairs. She wasn't there. He looked at the clock. It showed a quarter to one.

Jesus. Where is she? Where the hell is she?

Panic began to swirl through his body. He came downstairs, stopped, placed his hands on the hallway wall, leant his head forward and closed his eyes. *Keep calm. Think.* A tiny black spider was making its way up the hallway wallpaper, in a straight line, purposefully, as if it was aware of the drama vibrating around it and had chosen to ignore it. It had other things to do, and it crawled determinedly past Ted's hand. Ted suddenly stood upright, rage and frustration clenching at him.

'Damn you!'

His fist smashed violently against the wall, crushing it. The echoes shuddered guiltily in the stillness of their home.

'Damn you,' he sobbed.

Then he saw it. Stuck to the inside of the front door. Written in large bold letters. On his original note. Over *his* words.

Ted read in disbelief.

> *GONE OUT FOR MY DINNER*
> *Florrie*

FOURTEEN

A Bus Ride, a Right Hook and Ted Is Taken Away

'*Invictus*

Beyond this place of wrath and tears
Looms but the Horror of the shade,
And yet the menace of the years
Finds, and shall find, me unafraid.'

William Ernest Henley

Florrie sat on the bus, picking at the small hole in the sleeve of her pale blue cardigan. Occasionally she stopped and rubbed her ears but the noises continued to smack and slam, like a pin ball machine in the arcade of her brain. She turned and looked around threateningly for the cause of this din, but everybody else was looking straight ahead, like rows of silent dummies.

Reaching up she touched the small metal badge she had been awarded and which she proudly carried everywhere. It felt cool and reassuring against her hot fingertips and the touch calmed her. God knows how many thousands of blood red poppies she had sold over the years and how many November ceremonies she had stood at, feeling the late autumn chill catching her nose and fingertips and toes. Ted had stood quietly beside her, his head full of desperate thoughts and damaged memories that she could barely imagine. She had done it for him and for their generation, for those whose lives had ended without warning and for those left behind to sort out the mess. She had also done it for her young cubs, also standing beside her. So their generation would never forget. Never.

Now, she was wearing what she always wore these days, every day. The same lime green trousers that used to accompany her to the allotment, "used to" for there was no allotment now. With the same safety pin still holding the same exhausted zip. Her blue cardigan was stained in places and her grey streaked hair was ragged and unkempt.

Turning, she looked at the shapes and colours moving quickly past the grimy bus window. She tried to focus on them, but the effort was too much and she let the blurry shoals rush on by. She felt dark and strong, almost powerful, for deep inside her, a hot feeling of discontent smouldered and threatened to spread, sending liquid fire along her veins and arteries, charring calm and reason. Sometimes, when the fire raged she probably needed to gulp down calmness and clarity like a medicine. She couldn't see it herself, but that's what Ted said. 'Pity you couldn't bottle it.'

No. No need. A large whisky in my coffee. Just once a day. Better than all the medicines in the world. Mind you, it doesn't stop the racket in my ears.

She sat on the rattling bus and vigorously rubbed the pulse throbbing in her temple, hoping to rub it away, rub it better, like her mother had done. 'That's what she used to say.' She spoke aloud and smiled for a moment at some distant memory.

She suddenly realised that a large woman was sitting next to her. She hadn't been aware of the woman's arrival and she disliked her – didn't know why, she just did. She could smell her perfume, but couldn't remember if that scent was roses or lavender. Whatever it was, it filled her nostrils and stomach and suffocated her with its stench. She pinched her nose and held it there, making small gasping sounds through her mouth. The woman looked alarmed but didn't move. On the other side of the gangway a man turned, curious about the strange noises. Florrie glared at him. He turned away quickly.

Florrie looked down and stared for some time at the large woman's tweed skirt pulled tightly over plump thighs. They had definitely strayed over the edge of the seat – into *her* space. She couldn't have that. She leaned against her large neighbour and pushed. The woman turned startled.

'You're in my space. Move over.'

Florrie's eyes bored into her. Daring her to retaliate like blue lava about to erupt. The woman shuffled as far away as possible, cheeks flushed.

'Sorry.'

At the next stop, the large woman stood in slow motion, hoping that would make her invisible, moved to another seat and sat looking fixedly out of the window.

Florrie grunted and returned to the busy shoals. The bus rattled on.

She had travelled on this bus before, the 29, there and back, on her own. She couldn't remember when now, but she knew she had always had this seat. This was *her* seat. Out of the drafty concrete bus station filled with petrol fumes they would go, gears grinding, past the dark shops and streets, stopping and starting, starting and stopping, gradually clearing the sad traffic and picking up speed. Then, toiling up the hill named after the bluebells towards the bright quilt of countryside resting between the stains of the towns. At the summit, released from the town's grasp, the bus would rush recklessly downwards, bright flashes of green and blue and yellow punching between the silhouettes of trees. Florrie would always smile broadly and turn to share her joy with the other passengers.

On arriving at her destination, she would make her way to a small café, smiling at people and at their children and babies, at dogs and cats and flowers and at the river moving languidly by. At the cafe, she always ordered a large milky coffee, although she disliked the froth – she didn't like the name for a start – it sounded weak, strange. FROFF. Certainly the word didn't sound English, more Chinese or Japanese or something from "over there". English would be stronger, more dependable. She tried out a few possibilities aloud.

'FRITH, FRAM, FRANG, THROTH. No. THROTH. As in BETROTH.'

That would be better, much better, and in any case you never have a real English word with two Fs like that, even the caff where she was sitting right now wasn't its proper name. Its proper name was French – French! Nobody liked the French, they had surrendered, no guts. Maybe that's why it had this more popular name – a double F name – to upset them. Anyway what was wrong with everybody? Why can't we just have good English names?

And not only that, the froth stuck to her upper lip like a pale moustache, like scum, like the scum that bubbles up when you boil potatoes and who wanted scum stuck to them? *What was the point of that? Why have it at all?* she wondered.

The waitress would bring her the coffee and smile at her. They were used to this strange lady by now and knew to smile. Florrie would smile back and then carefully remove all the froth into the saucer a spoonful at a time, every drop. Then, when satisfied, she would drink a large mouthful, remove a half bottle of Scotch from her bag and add a liberal kick of whisky, just to keep her warm, just to keep her well. Best medicine in the world, that's what the doctor had said. She was sure of it.

She would finish her laced coffee and look at the small gold coloured watch on her wrist. Time to catch the 29 back. Maybe there would be someone nice to talk to, although most were reluctant, faced with her wild looks and the smell of whisky on her breath.

Today, however, was different. Today her journey was much shorter.

As the bus stuttered through the traffic she wondered what Ted was doing. He had gone out too, somewhere. She tried to remember if she had left him a note, but couldn't. Anyway he never came with her, not on the 29. 'No, you go on your own love. You enjoy it on your own. I'll stay and get the dinner ready,' he would say and so he would. Well he wouldn't have to today. She would look after herself.

There were times when she felt he didn't want to be with her any more. When her head was clear she tried to understand why this was, but often the noises tangled and confused her. But she *had* worked out the reason and had tucked it away somewhere in her brain, if only she could find it. *Yes that was it.* She remembered now. Yes, he was a good man and she was sure he loved her, although he never showed it, but he had done. She was sure of that and that she hung on to. Now he simply needed his own time and space to be alone with his private thoughts, to talk about them with… who? She didn't know, but it wasn't her. She wanted to help him but somehow she couldn't. And now she felt confused and maybe even got angry sometimes. She couldn't really remember, she didn't really understand.

Poor Ted. She missed him even when they were together. The woollen hole got bigger.

She got off the bus and walked the short distance to the Victorian facade. She viewed it from the other side of the road. 'Used to be smart,' she sighed, seeing the odd mindless scribble and new notice boards, like eczema on its pale stone skin. Looking up she could see the words "Post Office" skilfully cut by the mason's hand. Once, those words represented civic pride. Now they looked sad, out of place, like an old friend – once the belle of the ball, but now, old and forgotten, overtaken by time, but still keeping her ball gown in a musty wardrobe to look at from time to time.

She wondered if the building remembered the taste of envelope gum and the busy buzz of people anxious for stamps and postal orders and wedding telegrams in large gold coloured envelopes. She still had theirs, faded and creased now.

'Why can't they leave things alone?' she said aloud.

She didn't know who *they* were, except their numbers seemed to be growing and *they* were trying to change everything, including her. *They* were telling her what to do, what to wear, what to eat and drink; telling her to behave and that she wasn't as young as she used to be.

Inside the former post office was a charity offering care to the elderly, giving them a meal and playing bingo to exercise their minds.

'Bingo,' she spat. That was for old people, not her. No way. What they need is a good old knees up. A good sing-song. 'Knees up Mother Brown,' she hummed to herself as she pushed the heavy wooden door open and stepped inside.

She stopped humming. The space before her was cool and musty and dimly lit. She was confused by its emptiness. Where were the counters? Where were all the people? Where was the big clock?

The door closed with a loud thud, rippling the space around her. She stood still for a moment, breathless, like a naughty child caught doing something wrong. *I didn't mean to. It was an accident.*

The ripple slipped away into silence and she tried hard to remember. But there were only fleeting fragments of colour and movement and unknown faces mouthing silent words, slipping past, all torn randomly from her memory like pages from an old battered sketchbook.

'Knees up Mother Brown,' she said softly.

On the oak floor, darkened by a million footsteps, she could see lighter marks where the counters had been, like scars; organs cut away by the surgeon planner. She touched them with the tip of her shoe. Maybe if she shut her eyes…

'Under the table you will go,' she said louder. 'Ee-i-ee-i-ee-i-oh,' she said louder still. Her voice echoed and she grinned to herself. When had she last sung that? Must have been when she had visited the care homes. She had volunteered of course. The nurses hadn't minded – anything to wile away the long hours. So she would sing to the old people, try to cheer them up, try to get them to join in, but often they just sat there in their armchairs. Maybe they clapped in time to the music or waved their hands. But they often seemed to be somewhere else. The nurses smiled of course. Some of the old people smiled. Florrie smiled back.

'Come on now. Everybody. Let's give Florrie a big round of applause.'

The nurses applauded vigorously. The old people applauded slowly as if it was an effort. As if they were now running out of applause, running out of everything.

Her stomach rumbled and she remembered how hungry she was. She was looking forward to the meal. She wondered what it would be – succulent roast beef and fluffy Yorkshire pudding, crisp roast potatoes and greens and hot gravy, maybe jam sponge and thick yellow custard plus a nice cup of tea – and her mouth watered at the thought. As long as it wasn't fish and chips, she was always having fish and chips these days, or toast and jam, or biscuits, lots of biscuits.

In front of her were two further doors and on one was fixed the name of the charity. She pushed it open and stepped into a large, brightly lit room. It must originally have been a sorting office. She had often wondered what lay beyond the counters. Around her were a number of small tables at which sat two or three or four elderly ladies and a sprinkling of elderly men. From somewhere came the smell of cabbage and disinfectant, mingling with the chatter. Some of the ladies looked up and smiled at her. Florrie smiled back. She liked smiling.

At the end of the room a middle-aged woman was serving cups of tea from a bright metal urn perched on a wooden trolley. Florrie heard her sharpened words.

'Tea Marjorie? Yes? No? Come on dear, make up your mind. Can't stand here all day.'

The woman looked up and surveyed Florrie suspiciously through heavily made-up eyes set in a powdered face. She had a large aquiline nose which was impossible to miss.

Right away, Florrie didn't like her either, not many people did. It was certainly unfortunate that her nose dominated her features, squashing her eyes and mouth into whatever space was left. It gave her a strange, haughty, unsettled look. No, it wasn't that. That would be unfair, although Florrie did feel a strong urge to comment on it, loudly, in front of everybody.

No, it wasn't her features. There was something else that caught your attention, even deflected you from her nasal misfortune. Florrie recognised it instantly. It was obvious really. It was her enthusiasm for both patronising and repressing the old people who attended each week. It was that which shone through. She had started doing this as soon as she had first arrived and she had been encouraged by the warmth of the smile given to her by the manager. It was not a smile he gave to everybody. It was certainly a smile of approval, maybe more. She hoped it was more. She stopped serving tea, attempted to straighten her shiny plastic apron and approached Florrie.

'Can I help you?'

A cool wind blew.

'I've come for my dinner.'

'Your dinner?'

'Yes, my dinner.'

There was a pause and the chatter around them subsided. Heads half turned. There were small secret smiles and tiny nods. This could be interesting, a change to the same boring old routine. A card game now continued in silence, like a strange mime, eyes flicking from the eight of hearts to Florrie and back again.

'I'm afraid we don't have lunch for you dear.'

'Why not?' Florrie's smile slipped away like a hand wiping a veil of steam from a mirror.

'We don't just accept anybody dear. You have to *apply* to come here and we have a *very* long waiting list.' She spoke loudly, emphasising the words as if speaking to a difficult child.

'Huh.' Florrie dismissed the regulations with a toss of her head. 'Well, I'm here now so I want my dinner.'

'Wait here.'

The Nose held up a palm to emphasise her instruction as if communicating with an imbecile or a foreigner. Johnny Foreigner, *Me no speek Eengleesh*.

Florrie stood, legs slightly apart, arms at her side, fists clenching and unclenching and stared at the retreating apron strings as they disappeared through a door marked 'Private. Office.' Inside her, the smouldering, fanned by this malevolent breeze, began to catch alight.

'Don't take any crap from her.' The voice came from an old man hunched over a cold cup of tea. A sodden biscuit was slumped in his saucer.

'Eric, I do wish that you wouldn't use that language,' a small white haired lady on the same table said without looking in his direction.

'Well,' the voice growled, 'thinks she's Hitler and you know what we did to 'im.' Eric slowly turned his head. His pale rheumy eyes surveyed Florrie. 'You stand up to 'er love.'

For a second Florrie felt a shock of confusion as she saw Ted sitting there, where Eric had been, smiling warmly at her.

'What are you doing here?' she said.

'I'm always 'ere love. Bleedin' live 'ere.' It was Eric who replied.

'Eric. Please. The language.'

At that moment the door to the office opened abruptly and the figure of a thickset man appeared, closely followed by the Nose. Some of the tea drinkers looked nervously away into their cups. Oh dear, the Manager. The heavy brigade had been summoned to deal with this strange interloper. No matter how determined she was, surely she would be routed, forced to withdraw, but you never know. Just maybe. Wouldn't that be wonderful? And elderly hearts quickened.

'I'm afraid you will have to leave.'

'Who are you?' Florrie demanded. It felt like "Who the hell are you?" or "Who the hell do you think *you* are?" or even "who the fuck are you?" although Florrie never ever used bad language, not that she could remember. The impact, however, was the same. A daring, determined raid on the soft underbelly of the enemy, unexpected, spreading confusion, sowing seeds of doubt and his advance, arrogant, assured was unexpectedly halted.

'I'm the manager.' The words came out softly, quieter than he had intended. And he felt annoyed for allowing it. He wondered how it had that happened. He was in charge. He looked away for a second to avoid the intense blue and to regroup and muster his forces. But her strange, unfathomable smile was like the smile of a gladiator about to strike, about to lay down their life if necessary – knowingly, without feeling, willingly, more than you will it said. The smile said, "I have the moral superiority, fuck you." Behind him the Nose shivered slightly and rubbed her hands over both arms.

Florrie took in his square jaw, broad shoulders and close-cropped hair. Inside her she felt the fires burning. She felt their heat begin to scald her bloodstream, begin to melt her brain tissue and to scorch reason and restraint. Suddenly she was fifteen again, on the Hill. Around her, rough boys jostled and pushed and challenged each other. She in turn challenged them. Why not? She ran with them, she was part of their gang. She faced them, daring them, awkwardly trying to copy their fighting stance. They had laughed at her and slapped her head through the gaps in her guard. But her brother had shown her. She had seen his silver cup and read the inscription: "HMS Fisgard. Catch weight. 1936." *He* knew what to do and he had taught her.

Florrie focussed her eyes, placed her left foot forward, crouched slightly, turned her body and brought her fists up into a boxing guard, left hand leading and right cocked and tucked in front of her chin. She was ready.

Jesus. What the... What's she doing? Silly old fool. Now, what to do? Training. That's it. Remember your training. Try and mollify her. Distract her. Smile. Humour her. A myriad of thoughts flashed to and fro across the manager's mind. In the room around them, old eyes became desperate to focus. Old hearts, worn and weary, felt an unexpected rush of blood like a fond memory.

'Well, I've done a bit of that in my time. In the ring. Yes, I was pretty good,' the manager said as he brought his hands up, palms open and faced Florrie in mock combat.

Oh what a man. The Nose's thoughts ran naked through her mind and swooped tingling into her loins. She felt her neck blush a pink rash of desire and for a moment she didn't care. How she admired him, wanted him, dreamed of his body crushing hers, wanted his... *Oh my God.*

A red flame burnt through the last string of constraint and Florrie's right hook exploded in the direction of her opponent's left ear.

All those years ago, on the Hill, the effect would have been shocking and stinging and, above all, accurate but now the drip drip of time had slowed her reactions. In addition, her opponent really had done a bit in his time. He had trained hard, pushed his aching body and felt sweat soak his thick hair into wet curls. However, despite his efforts, he had not been very good when actually facing skilful jabs and cunning one-twos. *Story of my life really. I try hard but... well, that's why I've ended up here, wiping noses and working out budgets for biscuits and toilet paper.* But his brain had not forgotten. It had been waiting patiently all that time for the chance to show what it had been taught and now, and without apparently thinking, he ducked. Florrie's fist grazed his temple, flew over his shoulder and stopped abruptly two inches away from the Nose's most prominent feature.

The shock and expectation of imminent pain caused her to fly backwards, open mouthed, striking the solid shape of the tea urn with a dull thud before landing on her back, legs askew. Florrie's opponent had, in the meantime, managed to avoid the full force of the blow but had spun on the shiny lino, lost his footing and had landed face down, between the Nose's now exposed lower thighs. For the briefest moment she felt a wave of repressed excitement. Were they not alone on a deserted beach? Was that not the roar of the surf crashing around them?

'Bloody marvellous,' Eric said and his voice rose above the uproar.

Somebody screamed. The Nose realised it was her, stopped and hastily pulled her skirt down.

'Bloody bleedin' marvellous.'

A cup teetered on the edge of the trolley, fell and smashed followed by an avalanche of biscuits and teaspoons. Somebody laughed hysterically.

The manager scrambled shakily to his feet. The Nose remained sitting on the floor. It was safer there, despite the elderly eyes now looking gleefully down at her. Somewhere a frail voice kept repeating, 'Oh dear. Oh dear me. Oh dear.'

Florrie stood, witnessing the scenes of mayhem and grinned.

'Get out. You're banned. Come back and I'll call the police. You're mad.'

Florrie raised her arms in victorious salute, acknowledged the cheers, turned and left. What a victory. What a victory. Ted would be proud of her. She had shown them. That little shit of a manager. You had to battle and she had always battled, all her life and nobody was going to stop her now, nobody.

The inner fire soon died down into a warm glow. She felt content and pleased with herself and with no misgivings or second thoughts about the assault she had just committed. That was nothing. *What are you? A man or a mouse? Huh. Pathetic.*

She walked along the crowded streets smiling to herself, talking the whole incident through again and again, oblivious of the other world around her. It was a surprise then, that when she looked up, she realised that she was walking back towards her own house. Well, it was a nice day to walk home and she increased her pace briskly, soon passing the familiar park with its bandstand before turning into the long road that lead to her home. She wondered how many times she had walked this road – hundreds, maybe thousands. Her stomach now complained loudly and reminded her that she had missed her dinner. *Stupid man! What a stupid man!* And the fire flared for an instant. *Anyway, soon be home now. Hope Ted's got the tea ready. I'm dying for a cuppa.*

As she turned into the road where her house stood, she immediately saw the white shape of an ambulance pull away. A small group of people stood uncertainly.

'Oh my God, must be Joan,' she murmured. 'Hope she's alright.'

Suddenly a pang of fear gripped her, almost squeezing the breath from her body.

Many years ago in that autumn of 1940, catastrophe had missed her by two houses. Now it had returned with deadly accuracy.

'Florrie. It's Ted.'

Suddenly Joan was at her side, her large eyes smudged dark with concern.

'He's been taken to hospital. Think it's a heart attack.'

She felt Joan's thin hand grasp her own.

'Oh Florrie. I'm so sorry.'

'Oh no! I've got to go with him.'

Florrie began to half walk half run, waving wildly.

'Stop. Wait for me. Ted, wait for me!'

The ambulance raced on.

'Florrie. Wait. Wait.' Joan and Helen caught up with her.

'Let go of me.' Florrie tried to wrench their hands away. 'Let go!'

'Florrie. Wait darling. Wait. It's too far. Come on. It's too far.'

Their words tried to reason. Calm her madness. Their own eyes, startled and pained, tried to look into hers and make contact with her. Desperately she looked over and around them, her frantic eyes leaping to see the ambulance. But it had gone, leaving just the trail of its siren growing fainter and fainter until there was nothing left but silence and stillness.

'Come on Florrie. Come on. Let's go back to the house. Come on darling. Come here.'

The three women stood on the pavement and held each other.

***

Joan stayed with Florrie that evening and made her sandwiches and cups of tea that she hardly touched. Florrie had cried out pitifully; frantic to see Ted, but her friends had looked into her wild eyes, heard her desperate words and knew she had to remain safely with them.

Joan was shocked at the state of the house. She had not been inside for some time now, not since the front door had become locked. Before, it had been neat and tidy. Before, you could smell the tang of bleach, the comforting aroma of furniture polish and the fresh air seeping from crisp laundry. Now it was dirty. Now you could only smell the sweet decay of the rubbish bin and layer upon layer of dust catching at the back of your throat. *Oh Ted. Why didn't you say?* And there was something else. Something dark and malevolent glowering from the corners as if some terrible crime had been committed and the body parts and splashes removed, leaving no trace except a terrible mute echo. The house was silent; silent but watching fearfully.

'I'll wait for him. Like I did before.' Florrie sat upright in the armchair, trying to smile. Her fingers stroked its smooth arms, back and forth, back and forth, slowly but frantically.

'Do you remember when we used to go shopping, Florrie?'

Florrie smiled back gently, eyes wild.

'Do you remember? We used to go to Whittaker's for fish and chips. Always fish and chips. I used to wear those shoes from Dolcis with the big heels. God I must have looked a sight… I loved those shoes.'

'Where is he? Where's Ted?' Florrie's words battered Joan's attempted jollity. She leaned forward and gently touched Florrie's hand.

'He's in hospital. Ted's in hospital. Cyril and Harry have gone to see him. They'll be back soon.'

'Hospital?'

'Yes darling. Don't worry. Ted'll be fine. They should be back soon. Don't worry.'

Joan tried to sound positive, but her words hid behind each other once out in the open.

'I'd like another cup of tea please, with some whisky.'

Joan ignored the whisky.

'You haven't finished that one yet Florrie.'

'Oh.'

Joan looked at the figure lost in the armchair. She knew that this must have been a great shock to Florrie – her beloved Ted. Although Joan had noticed that Ted hadn't looked too well recently, tired and grey. She had mentioned it to him, concerned for him, but he had brushed it off like he always did. He always kept her at arm's length. After all this time… That's why the house was such a mess. Ted always did the housework, but he had been unwell. Couldn't do it properly and he wouldn't let anybody else do it. He was too proud, just like the rest of them.

She looked again at Florrie, who looked old and small. Her clothes were creased and stained and she noticed a hole in one sleeve of her cardigan and a button missing. Her hair seemed dull and matted and she wore no make-up except for some red lipstick which had worn off like red paint on an old wooden door. Suddenly Joan felt alarmed.

'Are you sure you'll be alright tonight Florrie? I can stay.'

'Oh yes. I'll be fine. Ted'll be home soon. Must have missed the bus.'

Joan gasped inwardly. Her mind fluttered for words. At that moment there was a loud knocking at the front door. Joan leapt up, relieved.

'I'll get it! It must be the men.'

Harry breezed in.

'Florrie. He's alright. Ted's alright. Just a mild heart attack. Nothing serious. He should be back tomorrow. They are just keeping him in overnight. He's OK. Strong as a bleedin' horse. Hallo Joanie. Oh Cyril's just putting the car away.'

***

Florrie awoke much later, aching from sitting in the armchair. Her mouth tasted awful and her stomach ached from hunger. She rubbed her head and tried to remember when she had last eaten, but couldn't. The noises smacked and slammed. She knew Ted wasn't there but she knew he was safe. She knew that, but she couldn't remember where he was exactly, but she remembered somebody, maybe Joan, saying that he would be back soon and not to worry. Things were so hard to remember. She pushed herself out of the chair with difficulty and moved stiffly towards the darkened kitchen. The neon tube flickered slowly into cold light. *We must get another one.* She looked around. It looked different – clean and tidy with all the washing up done. She thought that perhaps Ted had done it. *Where was he? Oh yes. Out somewhere. But he was safe.* They had told her he was safe. In the distance thunder rumbled and slowly grew nearer.

***

Ted arrived home the next day, thanked Cyril for the lift, unlocked the front door, wiped his shoes, wet from the heavy storm and called out.

'Florrie. You there?'

He found her asleep, sitting hunched under the stairs, sheltering from the thunderous sounds of air raids and the electric white flashes of explosions.

FIFTEEN

The Reunion, A False Eye and Romany Truth

'We few, we happy few, we band of brothers.'
                        Henry V by William Shakespeare

Ted certainly recognised them, the voices. One was steady, professional, touched with concern. The other was slower, gruffer, less articulate and full of fatherly pride. Both were relentless, so relentless. Sometimes they spoke separately, sometimes together, each shouting to get their point across. Their voices rose and fell like the volume on a radio – up and down until they became mis-tuned and collided into a terrible screech. Every so often his frustration spilled over and he shouted aloud at the voices arguing in his head, without realising it. *Christ now I'm shouting. Am I going barmy as well?*

Duty Ted. Duty son. I have always told you to say God save your Mother and Father. Fight for everything in life worthwhile. God made living for: wife, parents, freedom… Very noble Ted, very noble I'm sure, but not at the expense of your own health. Your own life.

'Own life! That's going a bit far isn't it?'

I'm a doctor. I've seen it happen. And you have a weak heart… No you're strong son – mentally and physically. You've faced up to terrible responsibilities before and you can do it again. You must not let her down. You're a man of honour… No, Ted just flesh and blood. You must seek medical help. Nobody is that strong.

'But I did it before. It was terrible but I did it didn't I doc?'

You had no choice then Ted. Now you have a choice... No son, you made those vows before your family, before me your father, before God... But God will not approve of you sacrificing yourself Ted. God will want you to help yourself and Florrie.

'I don't believe in God. Why would a loving God let this happen?'

Then believe in Florrie, Ted and help her.

'I am helping her aren't I? Of course I'm helping her, but I can't bear the thought of sending her away, not after all these years. I can't.'

That's right. You made a solemn promise son. You cannot break those vows... But she needs help Ted.

"I know. For Christ sake don't you think I know? Nobody knows what it's like. Nobody.'

Then share it Ted. I can help you professionally... No, you can do it son. Just give her love.

'I can't.'

Why not? Too proud? Too frightened? Too embarrassed? There's nothing to be ashamed of. I see many patients with these problems.

'I'm not frightened of any bugger.'

That's right son. You fought for your country. Destroyed the enemy. That's courage... Then why not use that courage now Ted?

'I don't know. I have to deal with this myself. I don't want anyone else involved.'

So how well are you doing Ted?

'OK, I'm getting there.'

That's right, you'll get there son. You'll get there. Never give in... Getting where? Where are you getting to Ted?

'Oh for Christ sake shut up. Both of you. This shouldn't be happening to us. Not after all we've been through. Not us. JUST SHUT UP!'

But they wouldn't.

During the day, the voices waited patiently. He tried to keep them out by flooding his thoughts, but with the merest relaxation they kicked the chink open and burst in like thieves plundering his mind, over and over and over again.

At night, when the bustling distraction of day slipped away, the voices simply stepped from the shadows and wrestled endlessly, long and sweaty. *Christ will day never come? I'm so tired.*

Beside him Florrie lay silent, rigid with tension. He could feel it freezing the room solid around her.

Ted sat alone in the front room smoking a cigarette. He was losing weight, but he never felt hungry any more. He looked around at the room and its familiar objects. Once they'd been alive and pulsed with their own life force but now they sat still and silent, waiting. There was that clapped out old piano he'd got from the Co-op club. They'd wanted to sell it, but he'd persuaded them it was worthless and they'd delivered it to him free on the back of a works lorry.

'Didn't know you played, Ted?'

'No. Not me. It's for Florrie.'

She had played, picking out the notes, tuned and untuned, slowly and deliberately, like the day they had met the elm tree, her face a picture of concentration. But now Florrie was still in bed. Sometimes she spent the whole day in bed, not eating or drinking or washing. He constantly checked on her of course, but she refused to talk to him. She just lay there, silent and sometimes weeping.

He stubbed out his cigarette, got up and tried to concentrate on something else in an attempt to switch off this awful radio – Radio Ted.

He knew he shouldn't be smoking. The doctor at the hospital had made that quite clear, but he needed them now more than ever. He took out another cigarette, lit it and inhaled deeply. The smoke was warm and comforting.

I'll stop or at least cut down as soon as all this nonsense is sorted out, as soon as Florrie is well again. And if they kill me, well, so be it. Maybe that would be for the best. Who cares anyway? Oh come on Ted. You don't mean that. Do you? That's the easy way out. I just want some peace. Stop feeling sorry for yourself. I'm so tired. Get a grip Ted. If only I could see things clearly.

A long section of grey ash fell onto the carpet unnoticed.

Sleep came just before dawn shook him awake. Ted had been dreaming. His dreams normally edged into nightmares but now, awake, he lay there strangely positive, almost excited. He had been standing alone on a large parade ground, to attention. He'd felt the beret on his head and the rough texture of the uniform against his hands. A column of men three abreast had marched on, arms swinging and boots crunching together onto the hard ground. There were no shouted commands, but they had halted together, turned as one and crashed to attention facing him. He knew them by their insignia. It was the lads – all of them, but he couldn't recognise any individuals. Where's Billy? Where's Darkie? They had stood in perfect lines, waiting silently. Directly in front of him was a space. A man was missing. Something was wrong – you can't do that. You can't parade with a man missing. Unless? Of course…

He had never wanted to go back before. Revisit those painful memories but now… He swung out of bed and sat on the edge. They'll tell me straight. Why didn't I think of that before? He stood with difficulty, knees complaining and moved clumsily towards the bedroom window and the early morning sky.

Thank you God. If you're really there.

Hope was struggling free from the darkness like a fragile butterfly. Its wings trembled nervously.

***

Ted sat forward in the taxi, anxious to recall landmarks, but there were none.

Well what did you expect? It must be forty years at least. Strange how you see things change around you, but forget they're changing everywhere else at the same time. Life moves on. Certainly does. Gathers speed and you get swept along until one day you find yourself about to go over the thundering falls into… what? He had thought a lot about that recently. *But that's OK. Can't be any worse than sitting helplessly in a plywood glider, door open, watching red hot tracer slice through the wings, moving towards you. As long as it's quick and dignified.*

Anyway he'd had his time, his terrifying, glorious time. Strange how something so awful could shine so brightly and give him so much pride. It was probably to do with being tested so severely and being found strong. You never knew, never knew. Some had come apart like poor Tinker. Some had run away – couldn't face it. Couldn't really blame them, but some had to stand and fight, and he had stood.

And of course it had been so very important. It had made the history books and films. They had come to him, years later, when history was ready to be written, to interview him at number twenty one – the historians, the writers, the film-makers, the press. His name was secure in the history of his country. He smiled and sat back in the cab.

It was in June 1940 when he'd first stepped down from a steam train at the station. He couldn't remember the exact date. He'd remembered it for years and had it written down somewhere. It was one of those dates you never forget, like when he was called up and joined the war. Except now he'd forgotten it. When they flicked through the thousands of days that made up his life, it would still jump out, underlined in red. He had a few like that. Many men would have none. They had birthdays and anniversaries of course, but not days that changed your life and the world. He had been lucky he supposed, or very unlucky, it depended how you looked at it.

He'd also written it down when he'd swooped out of the darkness into Normandy. First Allied unit to land in France you know, the very first. He had carried a small Bible and had written the time on the inside front cover. Maybe he had a sense of history even at that awesome moment. Maybe he carried the Bible just in case there really was a God. But he'd seen no sign of him. The taxi weaved its way expertly through the traffic.

He thought about Florrie and the boys, well hardly boys, not anymore. They were grown men now and living away. He hadn't told them about Florrie, didn't want to worry them. They had their own lives to lead and, in any case, it was his problem, his responsibility, his duty.

They visited of course, when they could. He tidied up as best he could and watched anxiously, but Florrie rallied when they arrived, put on her best things, basked in their sunshine and was as crazy and eccentric as ever. They laughed with her, noticed her memory, her grasp, slipping, but that was all. That was to be expected. She was getting on. Quietly they spoke to Ted.

'Everything alright Dad? You look tired.'

'Oh I'm alright thanks. Had a bad night.'

'About time you decorated the front room isn't it? Want some help?'

'No thanks.'

'Sure?'

Florrie was dancing and singing and trying not to spill her whisky mac.

'Come on you lot. Get up. When Irish eyes are…'

Ted looked towards her. 'Just take her out and shoot her.'

The boys just laughed. Family joke.

He never knew if he meant it. He thought of the enemy soldiers, mortally wounded, in terrible agony. A single shot of mercy. But Florrie? No. He couldn't, it was just weariness and frustration. The boys smiled. They knew she could be a handful. They never knew about the continual worry and fatigue, the nocturnal rages and bizarre behaviour, and Ted's sense of helplessness and disaster – not until it was too late.

Wish I could remember that date.

Ted had stepped down from the train, carefully, trying not to aggravate his knees.

Look after your joints boys, look after your knees.

It was the same station. Well, it was the same place at least. He knew that much, but he had recognised nothing, although he knew he'd been there before as a young man. Of course he had, rubbing his scuffed shoes nervously on the back of his trouser legs, pushing his fair curls out of his eyes. Soon *they* would be lying on the camp barber's floor. Long time before he saw those again. But now, he had no complete memory. More a feeling, a feeling of a memory perhaps. Of somewhere he had been before. Now he had stood to one side for a moment, away from the busy travellers flowing in and out, had looked around and felt a little disappointed. There had been so many things to write home to Florrie about back then, but now those memories had gradually been stripped away and lost.

The taxi moved steadily through the streets with the surety of practice. Finally it waited, indicator ticking, before turning left through dark green gates into a large square and stopping.

'Here we are. Slade Barracks,' the cab driver announced and peered into his rear view mirror.

'Yes, I know. Been here before.' Ted gathered up his bag and top coat.

'Right. Back for a reunion are you?'

'Yes first time back.'

'First time eh?' The driver turned and spoke directly to Ted. 'Ox and Bucks isn't it? I recognise the tie.'

'Yes it is. D Company, Second Battalion. We took Pegasus Bridge.' Ted was surprised at his words. He never spoke to strangers about that. It was too personal, too important for strangers. He felt slightly annoyed with himself and made to leave the cab but the driver replied too quickly, too enthusiastically.

'Really! Pegasus Bridge?' The driver's eyes shone and Ted suddenly felt at ease with the young man.

'Yes. In glider one. I was the radio operator.'

'Not the one that sent the signal.'

Ted nodded.

'What Ham and Jam?'

'Yes that was me.'

'Really? I've read about you. Yes. Well well. Would you believe it? In my cab too. Huh.' He paused and looked away for a second. Then looked back. 'Sorry mate. I can't remember your name.'

'Ted Tappenden.'

'That's it. Ted Tappenden, and in my cab. Fantastic. Wait till I tell the missus.' He paused again and his words softened. 'My father was in the First Battalion you know. That's why I know the tie. Yes. Killed at Caen. Never knew him of course.'

'Sorry. Lot of good men didn't come back. I was just lucky.'

'Yes. Guess so… Anyway, let me help you out.'

'No, I can manage.'

But the driver was out, had opened Ted's door and was looking to take his bag. Ted stepped out as sprightly as his joints would allow. The driver smiled at him, held out his hand and grasped Ted's firmly.

'It's been a pleasure to meet you.'

This was not a sentence the driver had ever used before and it sounded strange on his lips, but he spoke genuinely, almost emotionally to the man who could have been his father. Ted felt the goodwill of the stranger, the contact of his hand and was shocked at his need to hug him.

'How much do I owe you?'

'Oh nothing mate. I won't take a penny off you.'

Normally Ted would have insisted; he never owed any bugger anything. But on this occasion he knew not to argue, he knew this was important to the driver.

'Thank you.'

'My pleasure. Have a good time with your mates. Bye.'

The cab drove away with one last cheery wave.

Ted stood alone. The sky around him seemed to lighten.

He placed his overnight bag on the ground, adjusted his regimental tie for the hundredth time, buttoned his black blazer with the badge on the breast pocket, smoothed his hair back, stooped awkwardly and picked up his bag. He'd been affected by the taxi driver's interest. He had forgotten what that was like to be recognised; to be the centre of attention. He stood still for a moment and realised how used he'd become to the dead feelings of alarm and dread that daily turned his guts over. But this... this warmed him, sparkled and bubbled through him, almost urgently, like the moment before a first kiss. First kiss... and he thought of Florrie and of their passion, long ago.

He had arranged for Joan to stay with her overnight. Said that Florrie was not too well at the moment – maybe a touch of flu – and that he didn't want to leave her, but that he had to go to this reunion. He would phone tonight.

Joan had looked at him with eyes that softly disbelieved, touched his arm gently and said nothing other than not to worry and to go and have a good time.

Good time?

Well, he had no idea what to expect, but for now he pushed Florrie away into the back of his mind and set off, shoulders back, marching as best he could across the empty parade ground. Left limp, left limp, left limp.

Ted pushed open an outer door and found himself in a corridor. Despite the dim lighting, the floor beneath him shone as brightly as the moon on a calm night sea and the whole area reeked of neatness and floor polish. Somewhere a door crashed shut and footsteps echoed sharply. It was a place of decisions and orders and discipline. Ted felt that instantly. *Nothing's changed there then.* As he moved along the corridor, he passed framed photographs of groups of men. Some were standing to attention, some sitting in front of them and all faced the camera. Nobody smiled but they looked positive, determined, all together, like a family. Ted was home.

Suddenly, in front of him, a door swung open and a dark figure shambled towards him. It stopped. Peered at him through thick glasses.

'Fu–ckinell. Ted! You old bastard. Thought you were dead mate.'

'Hallo Billy. Not quite.'

Billy Kite stood in front of him. He seemed to have shrunk. Never the smartest soldier, he had tried hard for the occasion. Individually everything he wore was clean and tidy but somehow when put together, they could only manage to be dishevelled. For Ted it was wonderfully reassuring that he hadn't changed.

Billy took Ted's right hand in both of his and shook it vigorously.

'Good to see yer mate. Good to see yer.' Billy spoke softly, affectionately, like a former lover from a lifetime ago.

'The major here, Billy?'

'Yes mate. He's here.'

'How is he?'

'Like us mate. Bleedin' old.' His voice rose. 'Right. Come on then Ted. The lads are in 'ere.'

He pushed a door open, strode in and bellowed. 'Look 'oos bleedin' 'ere.'

Ted stepped through the door into a large well-lit room that sparkled and smelled of beer. Around several dark coloured tables sat a number of elderly men, most of whom wore black blazers. Every eye swung in his direction.

'Well I'll be… Ted. It's Ted.'

Several men struggled to their feet, some grabbing at walking sticks, cursing under their breath. Soon he was surrounded by smiles, by men shaking his hand, slapping his back.

'Ted it's so good to see you mate. How are you? It's been such a long time. Where you been hiding?'

From the direction of the bar a voice called out. 'Hi Ted. What you having? Billy's paying.'

'I bloody well ain't. I'm *not* buying *any* corporal a bleedin' drink.'

'Mean sod.'

'What you having Ted?' asked a voice at his side.

'Oh hallo Johno. A small sherry please. I'll pay.'

'No you won't mate. You can get the next one. You sit down. Take the weight off. Sid. Sid. While you're there, Ted'll have a sherry. What? Can't hear you mate. Oh. Sweet or dry Ted? Dry? OK. Dry Sid. Yes Dry. So… what you been doing Ted?'

It was as if time had never passed.

The major sat with the other officers. He was white haired, slightly bowed and a thick walking stick sat beside him. A look of joy crossed his face as he saw Ted.

'Ted. Ted.' He called him over with a wave.

'Hallo Major.'

'Ted. It is so good to see you again. How are you? How's Florrie? Sorry I can't get up.'

The two men grasped each other's hands and smiled at each other.

They sat talking for a while, just chit-chat between two men who had spent the war fighting for each other. There was no need to say much.

Ted looked at the men around him, drinking their pints and whisky chasers, laughing, chatting and arguing. Inevitably the stories of their shared past poured out. Their own individual versions of history. Their own interpretation of the fog of war.

'Jerry was in that church. You remember the one right on the corner. Kept us pinned down. Ain't that right Sid?'

'No mate. It was a different church. Further on past the crossroads. The one the Sherman cleared. Took the steeple right off.'

'No, not that one. That's where Dawson was hit.'

'In the arm.'

'No, the hand. Took three fingers off.'

'Never played the piano again.'

'No, but at least he could still stick up the other two.'

Funny, ironic often irreverent, always argumentative, but never dark or desperate, with only the occasional quiet pause for reflection at a memory too painful to relate before the banter quickly returned. Despite the arguing, warmth, affection and respect spread from them in soft waves.

Time had taken its toll. Most of them had already lost a limb or an eye or hand and now were also suffering the slow torments of ageing. Strokes and shrapnel, baldness and bullets, hypertension and high explosive; men or officers – it made no difference. Their bodies bent and pausing for breath but in their eyes, deep within, they were the same. There they hadn't changed. There the fire still burned.

Ted wasn't sure his did. He had come through it all unscathed – not a scratch. So lucky and just for a moment he envied them their wounds, their evident badges of courage. But that was ridiculous as he knew that many of them had suffered pain from that day to this, every waking and sober moment. They lived on a diet of whisky and painkillers. Poor sods.

He counted them in his head. Just a few left now and at that moment he loved every one.

'Did anyone ever find out what happened to Darkie?' Ted addressed the table.

'Darkie?'

'Yes. Darkie Mace. You know. The boxer.'

Darkie. Dear Darkie.

'No. Thought Darkie bought it in Germany.'

'That's right. Missing believed killed along with Paddy Hennessey. We found Paddy but never Darkie.'

'He was handy with his mitts.'

'Who? Paddy? Paddy was a wild man, always in trouble. All that bleedin' red hair. Affected his brain.'

'No, not Paddy. Darkie Mace. Flyweight wasn't he? Such a tiny bloke. So fast.'

'Pity we don't know what happened, cos at least we'd have a new story. Look at Billy up there. Every time he tells that he adds a bit, I swear.'

The beer continued to flow and a haze of cigarette smoke hung over the room. The men's voices became louder and more confident, much louder than at home talking to the wife, the neighbour, the shop assistant, because in some way they really were at home here. Not only together, but back to their wartime ranks: Private, Corporal, Sergeant Major.

'Right, come on you idle lot. Whose round is it?'

'Yours Smudger.'

'I just bought one.'

'Well, get another. You can afford it on a sergeant's pay.'

A tall man stood slowly. He wore a dark three piece suit with a regimental tie. His hair was white and tidy and he carried a slim white moustache. He tapped the edge of his glass with a coin. The thin sound penetrated the room's thick buzz.

'Quiet. It's the Colonel. Quiet there.'

Orders rapped out. The room became instantly silent.

'Thank you.' He cleared his throat. 'Thank you. Well, it's extremely good to see you all once again. Some old faces of course, but also some new ones. Good to see you Ted.'

'Thank you sir.' Ted spoke softly.

'None of us are getting any younger.'

There was a murmur of assent.

The Colonel smiled.

'And I regret to tell you of the death of Sergeant Dawson last year after a long illness. I have sent our condolences to his wife Emily and their family.' He paused. 'So...' the Colonel stooped to pick up his glass. 'So, as our tradition, let us be upstanding and raise our glasses to our friends and comrades no longer with us.'

Some men struggled to stand up. Some helped others.

'To absent friends.'

'To absent friends.'

In the brief silence that followed, thoughts flashed from happy times to terrible times and back again.

'OK.' The Colonel waved for them to sit down. 'Just some admin now.'

The men groaned. He smiled.

'Just need to remind those of you staying over tonight of the Remembrance service here tomorrow. We parade at ten hundred hours on the square and then march to the memorial. Medals will be worn. Jimmy Ritchie will be in charge. Any questions see him.'

Ex-Major James Ritchie waved a hand from his seat.

'OK. That's all. Have an excellent evening. Thank you.'

There was polite applause and the buzz resumed.

'You staying over, Ted?'

'Yes. Too far to travel here and back in one day and...' He stopped himself and for the first time that evening, thought about Florrie. 'What about you Johno?'

'Yeh. Hard lines though. Hope my old bones will take it.'

Ted finished his sherry, rubbed both knees and stood up.

'Have one for me, Ted.'

Ted smiled and moved out of the room. It wasn't the toilet he wanted.

The corridor felt cool. Behind him, he heard Billy Kite's voice above the others, but slowly the noise of the men receded. He needed some fresh air, fresh air and time to think.

The parade ground was lit by floodlights, which gave it a harsh eerie feeling and the November air was chilly. Without his top coat, Ted shivered. He took a packet of cigarettes from his pocket and looked inside. Only two left and that was a full packet when he'd arrived. Mind you he had passed them around a few times. He looked out across the parade ground and was about to turn away when his eyes caught a movement at the main gate as a shadowy figure passed through and walked briskly into the light towards him. Better late than never. But he had seen this slim figure before.

'Jesus Christ.'

There, fast approaching him, was what was left of Darkie Mace.

'Ted!'

'Darkie!'

Ted grabbed Darkie's right hand and felt something cold and smooth.

'I thought you were dead.'

'Can't keep a good gyppo down. Let's go in Ted. It's freezing out here.'

In the reception area where they now stood was a table and two chairs.

'Let's sit here,' said Ted.

'Aren't we going to see the lads?'

'In a moment Darkie.'

'OK Corporal,' Darkie grinned.

'So what happened?'

'Oh I missed the train. Only by a few…'

'No. Not that. What happened in Germany? Everybody here thinks you were killed.'

'Do they? Yeh well. S'pose they might.'

Ted looked at Darkie. If anything he seemed thinner than before and his face was dark and gaunt. He wore a brown threadbare mac and thin scarf and his hair, once deep black, was now grey and straggled over his ears. His right eye remained motionless, as if somebody had stuck a large marble in the socket.

Darkie placed his right hand onto the table with a clonk. 'Good to see you Ted. If only out of one eye,' he smiled.

'What happened mate?'

'Well. We were on patrol. Bloody freezing it was and we ran into a large group of Jerry. Most of the lads fought their way back, but me and Paddy… you remember Paddy? Paddy Hennessy? Yeah, well me and Paddy got cut off, surrounded. They kept telling us to surrender. You know all that "kamerad" stuff but we kept going until we ran out of ammo and then fixed our bayonets. Don't think they fancied that, so they threw a stick grenade. Landed right beside me so I picked it up to throw it back but the bloody thing went off. Bad timing eh Ted,' he laughed. 'Made a mess of this hand, took out an eye and most of one ear. Didn't mind about the ear. Never liked them much anyway. Last thing I remember is Paddy throwing stones at them. They were bouncing off the trees. They kept shouting at him and you know he didn't like being shouted at. So he picked up his rifle and bayonet and charged at them, screaming horrible obscenities, like a madman. So they shot him.'

'He was a mad bugger.'

'Yeah, but brave as a lion. Anyway, when I came to Jerry had patched me up. Kept patting me on the shoulder and offering me cigarettes. Silly sods. I ended up in one of their field hospitals. They took off what was left of my hand and sorted me out, but they were very jittery. Retreating by then, and it wasn't difficult to escape. Met up with the Americans, was shipped home, got demobbed and that was that.'

'Nobody knew.'

'Well, there was so much confusion.'

'So what do you do now?'

Darkie squared up. One fist flesh and bone, the other plastic; one eye sightless glass, the other warm and glinting.

'I help train young lads at my local gym. Doesn't pay. Not qualified but I get endless cups of tea and it's warm. I really enjoy it.'

Ted looked at this man who had lost a hand, an eye and an ear. He looked thin and undernourished. He was wearing shabby clothes, but he was still battling, still giving and Ted felt inadequate.

'You married Darkie?'

'No. Who would have a bloke who looks like this? No. Never married… Hey. Do you remember that night we went to rescue Billy from that pub? What was it called? The Moon and Stars or something like that. You know the one? Yer, I often think about it Ted. I remember how brave you were that night and how you stuck by your mates.'

'Me, Brave? No you were the one who sorted out those three Canadians.'

'Canadians were they? You know all these years and I thought they were Yanks. Canadians eh? Anyway, doesn't matter. No, it was easy for me. I had them laid out in my mind as soon as we walked into that bar. But you didn't know that. You didn't know I was a boxer, and good. Well I was then… But *you* mate, you could have taken a beating, but you still went in there. You know Ted, I've never said this before but you and me are very similar. We both believe in the same thing. I was an orphan. You remember that? Yes, well I'm also a Romany. Means I have a big family – a big Romany family. If I get stuck, I know they'll always look after me. You do the same. Look after your family whoever they may be. For us family and honour are everything. Everything.'

Ted sat back. He had never ever heard Darkie say so much and his words swept away the doubts burning in his brain. Now he knew what he had to do.

***

Much later, some of the men had slipped away in taxis or were picked up by family or friends. The rest now stood in a long row in the communal washroom, dressed in white vests, stomachs overhanging striped pyjama bottoms. They chattered, called and complained while washing faces and cleaning teeth, some of which had been removed for that purpose. Simple green canvas camp beds had already been laid out in neat rows in a barrack room, each with a single blanket and pillow and, eventually, and often with much difficulty and cursing, each had an occupant. Beside many beds, a walking stick or crutch or even an artificial limb was laid with a clatter, like a faithful dog, waiting patiently for the morning to come.

The orderly sergeant of the barracks appeared in the doorway and stood to attention before them with his shiny peaked cap pulled down over his eyes, red sash across his khaki chest and boots gleaming.

'Right you lot. Lights out.'

A click sent the room into darkness. But not into silence.

'Bleedin NCOs.'

'Ain't you going to tuck me in Sergeant?'

'Jesus this bed is uncomfortable. Wish I was home.'

'Don't we all.'

'What? Wish you was home?'

'No. Wish you were.'

'Bollocks.'

'Goodnight everyone.'

A series of 'goodnights' some clear, some mumbled, came back in reply and gradually the chatter subsided. Slowly, slowly came the sound of gentle and regular breathing. Finally, at last, peace had returned. But not for long. Suddenly the peace was shattered by a

gasping desperate snore that ripped from somebody's throat like a starting pistol, immediately setting off all those waiting in the dark. As one settled into a desperate din, others took up the challenge and added their weight to the swelling discordant choir. In the middle of the nasal cacophony came the occasional unintelligible fragment of speech thrown in to add some extra texture and mystery. The bass section was not forgotten as farts burst powerfully and explosively.
'Jesus,' came a bewildered voice from the darkness.

In the morning they fussed around each other, straightening ties, checking berets like so many concerned wives before slowly setting off through the crisp air, each bent and lurching step making their medals jingle lightly.

It was a small service, conducted by the local vicar at the war memorial near to the barracks. A small cohort of his choir wearing sparkling white surplices over black cassocks chattered and jiggled in the cold air, squinting into the sunshine, thankful for the hidden, thick jumpers. Around them local dignitaries smiled and nodded and rubbed cold fingers while behind them, a few members of the public had assembled, some of whom stood silently and seriously, backs straight and hair cut specially. Before them, parental hands on their shoulders, the children waited, every now and then turning, looking upwards to ask a question. Nearby, Salvationists stood quietly, solid in their dark uniforms, fingering their gleaming instruments, keeping brass and fingers flexible and next to them, an army bugler stood quietly, resplendent in his dark green uniform. Ted and his comrades lined up and shuffled to ensure their three ranks were straight and true. Like always.

'Let us begin our service with the first three verses of the hymn... O Valiant Hearts.'

A mellifluous harmony poured from cold metal, cold lips and warm hearts. The men sung strongly, not always in time or tune but ensuring their presence.

'Let us commemorate and commend to the loving mercy of our Heavenly Father, the Shepherd of Souls, the Giver of Life Everlasting, those who have died in the service of our country and its cause.'

The silver bugle snapped to the bugler's lips and the haunting sounds of the Last Post pierced the watching sky.

> *Day is done.*
> *Gone the sun*
> *From the lakes*
> *From the hills*
> *From the sky.*
> *All is well*
> *Safely rest.*
> *God is nigh.*

Silently, men's hearts bled tears. The final note drifted away into nothing.

'They shall not grow old, as we that are left grow old. Age shall not weary them nor the years condemn. At the going down of the sun and in the morning, we will remember them.'

'We will remember them.'

A silence hung heavily over them, turning their thoughts inward. Barely noticing the sounds of everyday life around them. The small children fidgeted.

From within the three ranks came the sound of sobbing. Heads remained forward, but eyes glanced sideways.

'Steady there. Steady in the ranks.' Ted's voice called out. Quietly, but firmly.

'Steady now.'

The sob turned into a sad whisper.

Later that day, Ted shook hands with every one of his former comrades. Firm strong handshakes, each looking the other directly in the eye.

'Bye Ted. Look after yourself mate. See you next year.'

He left Darkie to the end. Shook his prosthetic hand deliberately. *Doesn't worry me mate.*

'Thanks Darkie. Thanks for everything.'

Darkie looked confused.

'For what Ted?'

'More than you know mate. More than you know.'
Darkie smiled.
'Good luck Ted.'
'Good luck Darkie.'
They never spoke again.

SIXTEEN

Killed in Action Aged Eighty Four

'We are all tattooed in our cradle with the beliefs of our tribe; the record may seem superficial, but it is indelible'

Oliver Wendell Holmes Snr

'One life is all we have and we live it as we believe in living it. But to sacrifice what you are and to live without belief, that is a fate more terrible than dying.'

Joan of Arc

'Every man prefers belief to the exercise of judgement.'

Seneca

Ted lay on his back in the semi darkness, like a turtle cruelly flipped over and left on a deserted shore. He was confused and in pain. Lifting his head he could just see vague outlines and murmurs of pale light, but felt no wind or speckles of rain. There was no sound other than within him, because, trapped in his chest, an intense pressure was building and broiling like a massive thundercloud and the top of his head stretched and throbbed in protest. He wanted to call out, but knew he couldn't, mustn't – it might give his position away. Slowly he raised himself into a sitting position. The thundercloud still swirled and grew.

Suddenly, out of the blackness, vivid flashes filled his eyes. *Jesus. That sound! That awful sound. Like ripping cloth. Maschinengewehr 42. The Bonesaw.* His mind ducked but his body was unable to move. He tried to call out. *Must tell the others. Take cover lads*, but he was caught, frozen in the open. Long fingers of red hot light poured towards him, at startling speed. Straight through him and his chest exploded in pain. He slumped back. Words gurgled in his throat.

'Florrie! Dad!'

From somewhere a machine called. Faceless figures moved around him urgently, came and went, came and went. There was a warm hand pushing on his chest, but he felt so cold, icy cold. His body jolted. Again. He moaned but it was not over.

Out of the tightly screwed up corners of his mind he felt cracks appearing and spreading across the walls and floor and ceiling and through the turbulent snarling air between them until suddenly, ferociously, and with a ghastly roar, a river burst in from all directions and he was swept bodily away and tossed helplessly and violently into black putrid waters. The foul water filled his nose and lungs and brain, gagging and choking his thoughts and his eyes stared, wide open now, raw and weeping and his fingers and fists clawed and punched vainly into the darkness.

The waters quickly filled the room up to the ceiling and he was swept crashing and helpless past pieces of furniture that loomed dimly, past windows and open doors. Helpless to stop, helpless to speak, trapped in this maelstrom for what felt like an eternity. He looked down and saw his heart exposed. It was smaller and darker than he had imagined and heavily scarred. It fluttered for a while and, as it did so, the waters that held him drained away.

He felt tired now, desperately tired. He wanted to sleep, but he forced the tiredness away. *Mustn't sleep. Must keep fighting.* He forced himself to look around.

He lay in a barren landscape that stretched away into a brooding, dirty, purple haze. Close by, on either side, trapping him, huge vertical black cliffs rose jaggedly into the sky with grey clouds swirling and dancing around their tops. He felt nothing except for his weariness and a stale taste of fear in his throat – a taste he recognised so well and which he knew he mustn't lose. On his cheeks he could feel rivulets of salt, caked dry and tight and a hospital gown, which for some reason he wore, was crushed and lifeless with fatigue and pain and pulled apart.

Cautiously, he raised himself onto an elbow and looked around. The river now ran as a mere trickle nearby, its liquid tinkling showing it to be at rest. Shakily and stiffly he raised himself to his feet and moved slowly and stealthily away, fearful he might rouse it.

Somewhere in the very distance, he could see tiny pinpricks of light twinkling in the haze, seeming to beckon him. He slowly rubbed his eyes and the lights reappeared, sparkling brighter, warmer. He felt a sudden sharp surge in his chest and his exhausted heart beat stronger for a moment and with some small hope, he stumbled slowly across the empty cold desert.

Suddenly, out of the corner of his eye, he noticed a movement and turning, he saw the long, thin shape of the river moving parallel to him, following him like a black snake, moving slowly across the rough ground, over and down and up and around and ever forward, matching his own steps.

He knew it was watching him, waiting, ready to engulf him again. Somewhere he felt his pulse slow and stutter, barely and the black waters began to grow, quickly covering his feet and ankles.

He sat down. He felt nothing, neither heat nor cold, nothing except a huge weariness. He had done his duty, he knew that.

Sorry Florrie. Sorry Oliver. Sorry Bobby. So sorry.

But the lads would be proud of him. Had not given in. Name, rank and number only. He could have done no more. Could he? Now he just desperately wanted to sleep. He lay down, closed his eyes and gave out a long sigh.

'He's gone.'

'Time of death 19:44.'

SEVENTEEN

Kidnap, A Sunday Roast and The Care Home by the Sea

'Remember me when I am gone away,
Gone far away into the silent land;
When you can no more hold me by the hand,
Nor I half turn to go, yet turning stay.
Remember me when no more day by day
You tell me of our future that you plann'd:
Only remember me; you understand
It will be late to counsel then or pray.
Yet afterwards remember, do not grieve:
For if the darkness and corruption leave
A vestige of the thoughts that once I had,
Better by far you should forget and smile
Than that you should remember and be sad.'

Christina Rossetti

In the days that followed, the sun rose black and hung heavily in the sky, casting a shivery shadow over those that knew and loved Ted. Florrie, engulfed, wandered in and out of reality, sometimes appearing to understand, often clouded with confusion and at times in complete denial.

'He'll be home soon. Don't know where he's got too, he's not usually this late.'

Ted had been to see David Green. He told him he intended to look after Florrie and then had gone into hospital for a check up, just a check up. He had died a few hours later of a major heart attack. The shock waves had torn through family and friends leaving them shaken and bewildered. Dozens of people knocked on the front door. Many of them Florrie didn't know or couldn't remember and she stared or grinned at them uncertainly. At night, in the house, blazing with light, she wandered, looking for him.

The boys, Oliver and Bobby, immediately stepped in. They were shocked and angered at what they found.

'Why didn't he tell us? Why did nobody let us know?'

Oliver stormed and paced frantically around the front room, waving his arms and pointing wildly.

'Why Bobby? Why? Why? Why?' he shouted and turned and hammered his fists on the dividing wall.

A small framed photo of Ted and Florrie fell onto the floor.

'Calm down Oliver, for Christ's sake calm down. What's wrong with you?'

Bobby bent and picked up the photo. He spoke firmly. 'All I know, is that *we* have to sort it out.'

In the kitchen, Florrie sat, empty and bewildered.

Fiona was small and wiry and feisty. She had an accent that lingered somewhere between Glasgow and London and Florrie loved her. Whenever she appeared Florrie grinned madly and put up her fists.

'You alright hen? She thinks she's from the Gorbals this one,' she would say before giving Florrie a big hug.

As a care manager she had a reputation for being a scourge of the system, working hard for her clients and telling them straight. The boys were shocked at what they heard.

'Social Services will provide care, but they will want the house in return. Not yet, not while Florrie is living in it, but as soon as she leaves and you do know that will happen don't you? – you will have to sell it to pay them back. And you will have to sell it quickly or else they will do it for you and they won't care how much they get as long as it pays off your debt. And don't even think about caring for her yourselves, it will destroy you.'

'But they lived here all their lives. It was important to them. It was intended for their sons *and* they paid taxes, national insurance and even fought for their country's survival.'

'Aye I know. You have my sympathy but I can only give the facts, cold and hard as they are. I'm sorry. All I can promise is that I will do my best for her.' She smiled. 'She's quite a character.'

Oliver took the opportunity to look at the upstairs rooms. The front bedroom had been Ted and Florrie's, although at some point Florrie had taken to the back bedroom. He entered cautiously, as he had done as a child, even though now it was empty. It was still their private room and he could count on the fingers of both hands the number of times he had been in it.

The room was sparse and full of ghosts who watched silently. It was also dirty and threadbare and the bed had not been made, sheets and blankets just thrown back for the last time, an indentation still in the pillows. On a bedside locker stood an alarm clock and he recognised it as a present given at Christmas or a birthday many years ago. The clock was silent.

> *Ninety years without slumbering.*
> *Tick tock, tick tock,*
> *his life's seconds numbering,*
> *Tick, tock, tick, tock,*
> *it stopp'd short – never to go again – when...*

The room smelled stale and sharp. Against one wall stood a homemade wardrobe and the flimsy doors wobbled as he slid one open. Inside it was almost empty: a dark suit, his black blazer, a jacket, two or three shirts, some ties and a pair of grey flannel trousers. On a shelf sat his maroon beret, a regimental tie neatly rolled and some underwear slightly yellowed with age next to some grey socks. A pair of smartly polished black shoes sat on the floor. At the back of a shelf he saw a dark bundle wrapped in a cloth. It was surprisingly heavy. He unwrapped it and found himself looking at a pistol, a German pistol. There was nothing else.

He sat on the edge of the bed. Behind him the wall was smeared with a swirling stain that was slightly pink. He looked around. Is that it? Is that all there is after a lifetime of toil? Is that all there is supposed to be? You enter with nothing and you leave with nothing. Was that it? Perhaps he was happy with that, just a few familiar items. But no, this was empty and sad. Not sad because he was gone. Of course that was sad, but shouldn't you smile through the tears? Shouldn't you feel the warmth of his presence surrounded now by his things? Things that were important to him, things that pulsed in your hand with memory? But this, this was like being in… in a cell. A cold cell. And why the pistol?

He looked down at the floor. Beside the bed the grey carpet had become thin with time and the tread of feet. Where the threads had parted he could see something beneath. He knelt down and pulled them apart. There it was. The brightly coloured bold patterns of lino from his childhood. Cheery, fun, laughing. He could see Ted smiling and Florrie laughing. It was as if all this joy was now hidden by this dirty grey shroud. This wasn't right.

In front of the windows stood a dressing table. It had always been there. *Why go out and buy a new one when this was quite adequate, did the job. Some people have more money than sense, and besides, it was a wedding present.* He could hear them.

On it was a black comb, a wristwatch and some loose change. Oliver wondered whether Ted had forgotten the watch when he went off to hospital or if he had left it behind deliberately. Sometimes things went missing in hospitals. Or… *No, surely not.* Without thinking he picked up the comb and ran it through his fingers. Did Ted know he wouldn't be coming back? His fingers were slippery with hair oil. He rubbed them together, slowly. Did he know somehow, but say nothing? That would be typical. Typical Ted and he felt an anger boil inside him. *Why did he do that? Why couldn't he just ask for help? Did you ask him? Of course I did. Really ask him or just accept his inevitable answer? Did you talk to the neighbours? His GP? No, not really. But he wouldn't want that. He was proud, stubborn.*

Had his standards. Bloody standards! You should have taken control. I couldn't. I couldn't. He was my father.

A breeze blew through the open window. He shivered, but not because he was cold. He stood and opened the drawers to the dressing table one by one. They appeared to be mainly full of papers and a few coins, keys, paper clips, cigarette papers. As he opened the left hand drawer he saw it right away – a long, buff coloured document. On top of it lay a piece of blue paper folded neatly in half. It partially obscured the document but he still read the words 'and Testament' and below 'of Edward Mark Tappenden.' He had left it to be easily found. He must have known or maybe he was just being prudent. *Was he? Jesus do you think? No that's too awful. Do you think… he'd had enough?*

He placed the will on top of the dressing table and unfolded the blue paper. He recognised the strong neat handwriting immediately. It was the handwriting of a clerk completing a ledger. It was written in sloping capital letters as if the message was particularly urgent and anxious to be found and read.

> TO WHOM IT MAY CONCERN.
>
> PLEASE DO NOT GRIEVE FOR ME. I HAVE HAD A GOOD LIFE. A LUCKY LIFE.
>
> I HAVE HAD TWO THINGS WHICH WERE SO IMPORTANT TO ME. FIRSTLY PEGASUS BRIDGE OF WHICH I AM SO PROUD AND SECONDLY A WONDERFUL WIFE AND TWO WONDERFUL SONS. NO MAN COULD ASK FOR MORE.

Underneath he had signed his name. '*Ted 'Ham and Jam' Tappenden.*'

Oliver sat down on the edge of the bed holding the letter from his father.

***

'All you've got to do is get her there. Best of luck.' Fiona strapped on her seat belt, checked her mirrors, waved cheerily goodbye and drove away, muttering under her breath, 'You're going to need it laddy. Sooner you than me.'

The specialist care home was two hours drive away. Oliver had agreed to take her, with Bobby following later with her possessions, including Blackie the big black cat. Florrie had not been told in case she simply refused to go and decided to fight everybody. The weather and traffic were also unpredictable. There was probably only going to be one chance of success. It felt like a cross between D-Day and a kidnapping.

'I'll pick you up on Sunday. We'll go for a drive. Have a spot of lunch. OK?'

Her blue eyes sparkled.

The weeks and months after Ted's death had been bleak and worrying. Florrie had daily support, but she became increasingly difficult, refusing to cooperate and offering to fight her carer on a regular basis to settle arguments. She was back on the Hill. Fiona gently pushed the boys towards the thought of a care home but that would be like losing both parents in just a few months and to be fair there were still days when Florrie was lucid and coping, but not many.

'We will Fiona. When the time comes. But this is her home. She's lived here all her life.'

Fiona looked at their tormented faces and waited, hoping this wouldn't end in disaster. She didn't have to wait long.

It was a Sunday. A sunny Sunday and Oliver, who lived nearest, drove to number twenty one to see if she was alright. He drove slower than usual, almost reluctantly and after he had parked outside the house he waited for a moment, looking at the house he knew so well. Everything appeared quiet and normal, but you never knew what you would find inside. As he opened the door, he was met with a strong smell of gas.

Oh no she hasn't.

He felt panic rise into his throat. He pushed the kitchen door open fearing what he might find but she wasn't there. A gas ring was hissing loudly. Placing one hand over his mouth and nose he quickly turned it off and opened the outside door and windows.

'Mum. Where are you? Mum.'

'Who's that?'

He found her in the front room. She was on her knees, a cigarette protruding from her mouth, shaking the contents of her handbag onto the carpet.

She looked up at him.

'Have you got a light? I can't find my lighter anywhere.'

He looked down at her. She looked so tiny. Her bony arms were protruding from her sleeves and her clothes, dirty and dishevelled, hung from her. Her hair was thick and matted from her refusal to wash it or have it washed and her face was dark and lined. Only her blue eyes still sparkled. She was still battling. On her own. As she had always done, but this was one battle she could never win.

He felt a sob rise in his breast as he realised he had let her down.

***

Normally their trips out involved a drive through the Kent countryside, trying to vary the routes as often as possible, not that Florrie minded. She sat, hunched in the back of the car smiling at the same panorama of fields and trees and sky and clouds and flint walls, scowling darkly at every vehicle that overtook them.

'Bloody idiot. Why does he have to go that fast?'

Occasionally they would walk slowly along the riverbank and find a vacant wooden bench. She would sit on a sheet of newspaper, brought to avoid the white spattering of seagull droppings, and face the river. Sometimes it flowed brown, sometimes grey, sometimes green or blue, depending on its mood. The boys quietly watched her, relieved at her calmness.

Around them, nylon rope chimed noisily against metal masts, like a child with a noisy toy and the wind would slap sharply against the canvas of sails. The bright sky tingled the water's surface and threw cranes and masts and spars into dark silhouette. The smell of mud and tar and rotting seaweed wafted over them.

They wondered what her exhausted mind made of it. Would the pitch-blacks and trembling greys that could overwhelm her turn the sunny river into night? Probably not, because she sat smiling, occasionally closing her eyes. Did the hellfire that could also consume her, fleck the azure sky and silver shimmering water with slashes of red and orange like a Fauvist palette? Who could tell?

Nothing was said. It wasn't necessary. It was as if she had finally descended from the Hill to the eternal twisting river below and now she sat, breathing in its sights and sounds and smells, and its timelessness. They watched them endlessly flow past, around a bend and disappear.

These trips normally took about an hour, there and back, and it was about that time she started to complain. She looked forward to going out, but once out she was equally concerned to get back. Only this day would be her very last trip. She would never be coming home again.

'Where are we going?'

'Don't worry. It's a surprise. We'll be there soon.'

'Huh.'

Her face appeared in the driving mirror, becoming concerned, agitated. The master plan was unravelling. *Don't panic.*

The country pub, enticingly rural and traditional, arrived at exactly the right moment.

'Look. The Groves Arms. Shall we go there?'

'Oh yes. Very posh.'

As they entered, the smell of Sunday roast and alcohol mixed with the warm bustle of chatter and laughter, changed her mood and drew her in. She grinned wildly at everybody.

'This is my son,' she announced loudly to the family at the nearest table. They nodded, smiled politely and turned away. Oliver found a corner table and sat her with her back to the other customers and next to a window to distract her. So far so good, but for a moment he felt a pang of conscience, not for the devious plan, but for the other customers who sat and stood and chattered and smiled and felt relaxed with friends and family, completely unaware of the time bomb in their midst. He felt like a sort of proxy suicide bomber.

'What's that?' Florrie prodded a parsnip suspiciously with her fork.

'It's a parsnip.'

'Why's it that colour?'

'It's been roasted.'

'Why?' She turned her attention to the parsnip's neighbour. 'What's that?'

'Broccoli.'

She wrinkled her nose in disgust. 'And what are all of those black bits?'

'That's chopped mint. Like you grow in the garden. It's very nice.'

She sat back and pushed the plate way. 'I'm not eating that muck.'

Her words were loud and vehement like a difficult child and for a moment Oliver wanted to slap her legs and send her hungry to her room. The family at the nearest table half turned and stared for a second.

'Well put what you don't like onto my plate and eat the rest. Would you like a drink?'

The question had the desired effect. She looked up sharply from her culinary assassination and regarded him shrewdly, a little smile playing around her lips. She knew full well she was normally steered away from the potentially pugilistic effects of alcohol. A cold hand gripped him and he wondered whether she was suspicious.

'I'll have a whisky and ginger. Large one.' She looked like a naughty child, deliberately pushing the limits.

'OK, as it's a special occasion.'

'What's special about it?' Her eyes narrowed suspiciously.

'The sun's shining. That's special isn't it?'

She smiled and nodded. In her darkening world that was very special. So many things had been taken away from her or lost. The vast warehouse of her mind, filled with a lifetime's treasure of memories was being ransacked. It was growing dim and fusty, covered with the mildew and the rust of age and time. The lights were gradually going out one by one, but from the increasing gloom she still managed to drag a few cherished friends. The warmth and light and hope of sunshine was one.

She ate her meal in silence, ferociously intent on the task before her. She did not slow, her face was red with the effort as if she hadn't eaten for some time or maybe didn't know when she would eat again. Finally, she sat back and surveyed the plate before her, a trace of gravy around her mouth. The edge of her plate now carried neat piles of rejected foodstuff: white fat cut from beef, every scrap of roasted colour from potatoes and parsnips and the dark green specks of mint that had floated in the gravy. She swallowed the last drop of the single whisky before her, sat back, toyed with the now empty glass and stared quizzically at Oliver.

Suddenly music crashed loudly around them. Florrie started at the unexpected sound and a barmaid dashed away to deal with the over enthusiastic volume.

'What's that racket?' Florrie demanded very loudly.

The family group nearby turned in their direction and grinned. Somebody sniggered.

'OK. Let's go now,' Oliver said.

Danger signs were flashing everywhere.

'That's not music.'

'Let me help you with your coat.'

'Bloody racket.'

She got to her feet just as the music abruptly stopped. Oliver hastily picked up her coat but she was too quick and moved with amazing speed, face flushed with the effects of alcohol. 'This is music.' And she grabbed at the arm of a stout woman passing by, who stared at the wild looking figure with a mixture of alarm and sympathy. 'Come on. Knees up Mother Brown...' and despite her meal, Florrie started to pump her legs. 'Knees up Mother Brown. Knees up Mother Brown. Under the table you will go ee-aye ee-aye ee-aye oh.'

Her voice cut through the lunchtime babble. Heads turned, some pointed, some smiled and others laughed. 'Hey, she's a fit old girl. Is she pissed?' A group of young people cheered her on. 'Go on granny.'

A young woman in the group turned to them, a look of concern on her face. 'No, don't.'

They turned back towards her. 'Aah.'

A middle aged couple eating in silence, stared, disapproving, looking up, looking down, still chewing. Voices from somewhere shouted 'Off, off!' The stout woman, still smiling, started to dance but with far less exuberance than her partner. She pulled away, fanning her face, breathing heavily. Undeterred, Florrie made a grab at a passing man carrying three pints between his hands who swerved playfully but spilt some beer.

'Shit.' He scowled to himself.

'No dancing in here,' an authoritative voice called from the direction of the bar.

People turned and looked undecided as to the rights and wrongs of such a command.

'We don't have a license,' the now less authoritative voice mumbled to no one in particular.

Florrie stopped, arms akimbo and looked towards the direction of the bar. Her eyes glinted and her jaw jutted menacingly.

Oliver grabbed her arm. 'Come on, let's go.'

Oliver half dragged her to the door and as he fumbled to open it one-handed, she turned and waved at the grinning faces. The pub door slipped and crashed shut and he hunched, counting the split second before he expected the glass panels would shatter. They didn't.

Thank you God.

They drove off, quickly.

'I was just beginning to enjoy myself.'

Oliver realised how fast his heart was beating. D-Day *must* have been easier than this.

***

In the rear view mirror Oliver could see Florrie's eyes closing and her head begin to nod. Cautiously he turned the car heater on slightly. Soon the combination of food, alcohol, frantic exercise and warm air had the desired effect. She fell asleep. He pushed the accelerator and prayed that she would not wake up until they had made their destination.

His heart leaped at the sudden brightness of the sky and then a silver glint of sea. *We're nearly there. Thank God.* His mind repeated the directions over and over again as if doing so would make them materialise.

Please no red lights. No traffic jams. We mustn't stop. We need the lullaby of motion. The gentle drumming of tyres on tarmac to keep her slumbering. Just drive slowly. As slowly as possible. Don't think about the traffic now crawling behind you. There! From behind a group of pedestrians a street name slowly appeared. Yes. That's it. Just in time. Turn left, slowly. This is it. Now. Look left and right. The number. The name. There it is. There. We've made it. We've made it. Now park. Don't worry about the yellow lines. Fuck 'em. Just park. Slowly. Smoothly. Don't brake too hard. Gently. Stop. We are there.

His hands trembled.

Florrie woke at that precise moment. 'Where are we?'

He had rehearsed a number of scenarios. Just in case.

'At the seaside. A special trip. Come on, let's get a cup of tea.'

Reluctantly she followed until they stood outside the entrance of the care home. It seemed like just any another house in a terraced row. Oliver hid the sign that would have informed her that this certainly was not a tea shop.

She stopped suspiciously. 'Take me home.'

He rang the doorbell.

'Take me home.' Her voice became louder, demanding. She looked around as if to escape, her face covered with concern.

Oliver felt his heart start to bleed. He pushed again. Longer, but the seconds passed with the pace of a summer holiday. *So slow. Come on. Come on.*

'Oliver. Take me home. Please,' she said and a slight sob entered her voice.

Perhaps this was the wrong address. The wrong day. For Christ's sake. Hurry up.

'It's OK Mum. It'll be OK.' He wanted to cry.

At that moment the door opened and a woman appeared. She quickly looked at them both, beamed and opened her arms wide in welcome.

'Florrie, darling. We've been so looking forward to meeting you.' She embraced her like a long lost friend. The woman stepped back and took Florrie's hands. 'I've heard so much about you. Come on in.'

Florrie's dark anxieties instantly slipped away. This is was what she had always wanted. It wasn't much to ask, just love and affection and attention.

She grasped the woman's hand and together they entered the building. At the last moment the woman turned, and smiled gently at Oliver. It was a smile that spoke of many, many things. The door closed with a click and he was left standing on the pavement.

EIGHTEEN

Revenge and an Empty Envelope

'Women do most delight in revenge.'

Sir Thomas Browne

Mrs Thomas smoothed her starched white uniform before easing her large crisp body into the chair opposite. She looked up and smiled. Her look made Oliver feel vulnerable and he wondered if she always did that. Gave that searching smile, searching for clues, like policemen and priests. Maybe she had been trained to do it, perhaps she'd been to a nursing seminar. *This morning we are going to look at body language...* Maybe it just happened after years of practice and experience. In any case why should he feel uncomfortable? Unless he felt guilty about Ted and Florrie. *Tries hard. Can do better.* Sometimes those thoughts did keep him awake. But *he'd* never been to a seminar.

What you should do with your parents when they get old and frail and sick and say they can cope when they can't and never talk to you about it anyway?

He'd done his best. Done his duty. *Ah. There was that damn word again.*

The office was small and tidy and smelled of air freshener and plastic and, occasionally, the predominant ingredient of the dish of the day. Outside the office the odour of old people hung in the air. Oliver wondered why it was that buildings that housed babies and the elderly smelled of the human condition? Was it that babies hadn't yet learnt to hide their natural odour and old folk had forgotten or didn't care or simply couldn't manage? Or was it another smell? A final smell. He shivered.

On the wall were several posters promoting healthy living, which seemed strange as normally only health professionals ever used the office. He knew that by the nameplate on the door. Perhaps health professionals were like artists, happy when surrounded by paintings or like singers surrounded by the sound of music. Perhaps the posters just reassured the occasional visitor or simply filled an otherwise empty wall.

Next to them was a drawing, curling at the corners, of a woman's figure depicted simply in red, green, yellow and blue. Beneath the drawing was written the word "Nana" plus two large shaky kisses as if the artist had tried hard to get them perfect. *Perfect kisses for my Nana but I can't quite control the pen yet.*

'You will love,' Nana would have smiled.

The simple shapes and colours sang out in the muted surroundings. Perhaps that's why it was there – to remind everybody in this place that life starts out hopeful and joyous and that's how it should end, full of colour, a celebration, not monotone, no greys and blacks. There were enough of those along the way. He was realising that. Perhaps Mrs Thomas was also "Nana" and he wondered if she watched the child with the same searching eyes.

She pushed a green folder between them. Even upside down it was easy to read the name typed on its white label. She smiled more broadly. On her lapel she wore a name badge. It read "June Thomas". Her smile was now more June than Thomas.

'Thank you for coming. Do you mind if I call you Oliver?'

'No, of course not.'

She smiled as if he had got the question right.

'You have to travel quite a long way I believe.'

He nodded.

'Well I hope we won't keep you long.' She looked down at the file. 'We are a little concerned about Florrie. Something we don't understand. Perhaps you can shed some light Oliver?' Her words were soft but precise. 'She had a visitor. Not long after you brought her here.'

***

The young nurse had found Florrie on her own in the communal lounge, sitting in an armchair, facing a large picture window, Blackie asleep at her feet. From there she could see the street outside and the occasional movement of people and vehicles, their colour and light and she could taste the salty air drifting through an opened top section. She had been bathed and her hair washed, cut and set. She wore a new brightly coloured floral dress. Her own old clothes (the lime green trousers and blue cardigan) being beyond salvation had been burned. She felt warm, well fed and safe. She had to take tablets these days and no whisky. She had complained about the whisky. Told them that a doctor had prescribed it although she couldn't remember who. They just laughed. 'Not here Florrie. Not with these tablets. We won't be able to wake you up at all.' It was true, she was certainly sleeping better than ever and she felt calm, so calm. It was as if the inside of her body and head had been cleaned out. As if the darkness that had eaten her reason, had been cut out like a black maggot from an apple. And today her mind felt clear – fairly clear.

'Hey Florrie. You've got a visitor.'

'Who is it? Is it Ted? Or Oliver? Robert?'

'No, your sons are coming at the weekend. It's your sister-in-law. Come to see you. Isn't that nice?'

'Who?' The word exploded from Florrie. The nurse looked uncertain.

'Your sister-in-law. Come to see you.'

'Shit.'

'Florrie!'

She had had many visitors. Friends and relations and strapping young men with their girlfriends and wives who she had guided as cubs and who had never forgotten her even if she couldn't remember them.

'Hallo Akela. It's Jeffrey. Jeffrey Saunders. Don't you remember me?'

'Of course I do. Who is it?'

'Jeffrey,' the young nurse bent and whispered into her ear.

'Oh, Jeffrey.'

But this was a bolt out of the blue. Her sister-in-law, Henrietta, Hetty. Who always sent her Christmas and birthday cards from Harrods when Woolworths was good enough. *Still, lucky to get anything. Didn't she once refuse to come to one of my concerts? Silly mare. Silly stuck up mare.*

Looking around the nurse she saw a figure standing hesitantly in the entrance to the room, a nervous smile on her face. As she saw Florrie's face appear, she waved weakly. Florrie shot back into her seat. She curled up her mouth in distaste and looked at the nurse for help.

'Good job I never swear... Can't you get rid of her?'

Despite the sunshine, Henrietta was wearing a lightweight blue coat with large white buttons and a white brimmed hat decorated with a blue band and small artificial flowers. Over her arm she carried a white leather handbag that matched her sensible shoes. In one hand she was carrying a parcel wrapped in silver paper with pink bows and in the other a pair of white lacy gloves.

Florrie slumped.

'What does *she* want? She looks like she's going to Ascot.'

'OK Florrie?' the nurse smiled down at her.

Florrie nodded slightly.

'Hallo Florrie. How are you my dear, you're looking so well. Isn't it a lovely day, can I sit here?'

The words, over-rehearsed, gushed out. Henrietta sat down on a nearby wooden chair, her hands, gloves and parcel in her lap, knees tightly together.

Florrie looked up slowly with a quizzical look on her face and said nothing. She turned and continued to look blankly out of the window.

'We've been very worried about you.' Henrietta hesitated for a moment and then moved slightly closer and whispered conspiratorially. 'You know, with all your problems. Aren't you pleased to see me? I've put off my whist to come and see you.'

Florrie slumped deeper into her chair.

Henrietta tried again. 'Oh dear. Look. I've bought you a little present. Not much, just a pretty scarf, but it is cashmere, quite expensive you know.' She looked around to see if anybody had noticed her generosity, but they were alone. 'Anyway do open it. I'm sure you will like it.'

She placed the parcel carefully onto Florrie's lap.

Florrie looked down at the parcel and then up at Henrietta, her face a picture of incomprehensibility. 'Do I know you?' Her voice was low and vague and her words were slow and slightly slurred. 'Who... are... you?'

Henrietta gasped and placed both hands over her mouth. An icy chill ran through her. 'Oh Florrie. It's me. It's Henrietta. Your sister-in-law. Don't be silly. Of course you know me.' Her words stumbled free, but stood there uncertain, even frightened.

'I don't have a sister-in-law.'

'Of course you have, silly. It's me, your little Hetty. Jimmy's wife. Your brother.'

She leaned forward, took Florrie's hand and squeezed. The hand was smooth and cool and lifeless. The parcel fell to the floor.

'I don't have a sister-in-law,' whispered Florrie turning her face slowly, eyes sad and vacant, towards the distraught Henrietta.

Her eyes closed. Her mouth fell open and she started to breathe strangely.

'Oh my God. Oh no. Oh no,' gasped Henrietta, tears now running down her carefully made up face in a trickle of mascara. 'Oh no.' And she staggered to her feet and fled, leaving her present where it fell.

Moments later the duty nurse hurried in, alarmed at the sudden and tearful departure of Florrie's visitor.

'Are you alright Florrie?'

'Yes fine thank you,' came the bright reply. 'Enjoying the sunshine. Has she gone?'

'Yes she has. She seemed very upset. What happened?'

'Oh nothing happened. She's always been rather delicate. That's what comes of having a privileged life – makes you soft and selfish.'

'She said you'd had a stroke.'

Florrie grinned. 'Does it look like it?'

She reached down and picked up the silver parcel.

'Would you like to have this?'

Blackie looked up, stretched and curled back to sleep again.

***

'So you see there was nothing wrong with Florrie, apart from being very naughty. Just families.'

Mrs Thomas looked straight at Oliver, with that same searching smile and said nothing.

'Well, rather wicked maybe. Pretending like that...'

He felt uncomfortable again and slightly embarrassed.

'Thank you Oliver. I'm glad that's been cleared up. Would you like a cup of tea? Before you see Florrie.'

'Yes please. How is she?'

She picked up the phone, held up her hand for a moment and then pushed a button.

'Oh she's fine. Settled in very well. Hallo. Susan? Susan it's June. Hallo. Can I have one cup of tea please. Milk? Sugar?'

'Milk. No sugar please.'

'Milk. No sugar and do we have any of those nice chocolate biscuits left? You don't mind a biscuit do you?

'Thank you.'

'Helen. Oh you heard. Thank you.' She replaced the phone. 'No she's settled in extremely well.'

'Not wanting to fight everybody or dance and sing on tables then?'

'Oh no. Not anymore.'

She read Oliver's face.

'Oh we don't drug her to make her sleep all day, just enough to calm her and make her behave normally.'

Oliver's mind raced.

Normally! No more putting up fists. No more Knees up Mother Brown. No more When Irish Eyes Are Smiling. No more jutting chin. No more dancing on tables, accosting strangers, flashing eyes or grabbing life by the balls. Has the system caught up with her at last? "Normally"? Who wants normally?

'She still sparkles. The nurses love her. She's still fun. More than anyone else in here. Most have given up, but she hasn't. OK, some days she's lucid and others she can be confused. She's just very tired now. Deserves a rest, and of course she has Blackie with her. He helps keep her calm.'

Oliver smiled to himself at the memory of the big black cat. Bobby had transported him in a cardboard box that he'd closed to stop him escaping. After a while with a lot of scratching and heaving, the lid had burst open and his head had appeared. Green eyes had surveyed the scene before he settled down inside the box again. Blackie knew all about imprisonment.

Mrs Thomas continued, 'You did the right thing for her, bringing her here. You simply couldn't have looked after her.' She smiled. This time a smile of understanding. 'Come on. I'll fetch your tea through.'

Oliver walked into the lounge and looked around. An old man was sleeping gently, the newspaper he had been reading around his ankles. Opposite him a frail elderly lady looked up at Oliver. *Are you my son? Oh, I do hope so.* The lady, confused, smiled hopefully. Oliver smiled, nodded in return and moved on to where Florrie was sitting in the same armchair as before under the same window, wearing the same floral dress. She was also asleep. Her mouth was open slightly. At her feet wrapped in himself, Blackie was dozing. *Cats never really seem to sleep*, he thought, *just constantly nap, one eye always metaphorically open, watching, waiting.* Oliver thought that perhaps he was guarding Florrie, her guard cat. Oliver knelt and stroked the cool smooth fur and Blackie stretched out, watching Oliver with one eye closed. Recognising him, the big black cat stood, stretched upwards with a shiver, returned to the carpet and curled up again. Florrie had not stirred. Oliver stood and watched her for a while. He wondered what was passing through her mind, but then looked away again, feeling slightly uncomfortable at invading his mother's privacy.

On the small table beside her was a cup of cold tea and an envelope. It had been torn open but it was now empty. He picked it up and read the postmark – Bootle. *That's strange. We don't know anyone in Bootle, do we?* He replaced the envelope carefully.

He met June Thomas on his way out.

'She's fast asleep. I don't want to disturb her.'

'She'll be very disappointed.'

'Best not to tell her. She wasn't really expecting me anyway. I'll be back again shortly.'

June looked at him kindly. She had seen it many times. Relatives rushed to get here, blurted out their news and then found they had nothing else to say in this place outside the spinning world, where time stood still. How often can you ask "Are you OK? Is there anything you want?" to which the real response it "Yes. The last fifty years back. What do you think?"

'You will have your cup of tea before you go? Don't want to upset Susan.'

'Yes. Thank you Mrs Thomas.'

'Please, call me June.'

'June.'

'Why don't you sit with Florrie while you finish your tea. Just in case. She would love to see you.'

Oliver quietly returned and sat with her. She must have done the same with him and Bobby when they were very young. Just sat and watched them the way parents do, praying and hoping and wondering about their child's future. Now it was his turn.

NINETEEN

A Sing-Song and the Final Hill

'I stood upon the hills, when heaven's wide arch
Was glorious with the sun's returning march,
And words were brightened, and soft gales
Went forth to kiss the sun-clad vales.
The clouds were far beneath me; bathed in light,
They gathered mid-way round the wooded height,
And, in their fading glory, shone
Like hosts in battle overthrown.'

Henry Wadsworth Longfellow

It was a long journey but Oliver's eye was enchanted, travelling once more through lush countryside, past lazy green-glazed meadows and regular worked fields. Here and there, cows chewed and stared and swished their tails languidly. Maybe in some distant memory they recalled the same fields wreathed in the white smoke of passing trains. *Probably not.* Nearby, groups of pine trees formed ranks, tall and upright, regimental, with dark shaggy tops like bearskins. Others threw massed branches upwards and outwards, etched dark against the azure sky. In the distance, low hills were smudged, blue-brown.

The road twisted and turned, rose and fell and drops of light splashed onto its darkness and flickered over the speeding car as it plunged out of bright sunshine into cool, leafy tunnels. From the corner of his eye, colours and shapes flashed frantically like speeded up film and then, suddenly, at the top of a long winding hill, he emerged onto an open plateau where the entire landscape unrolled before him and stretched away to the wide hazy horizon. Dark barns, small white cottages and red-bricked farmhouses were dotted here and there like children's toys scattered on a huge green carpet. He wondered about the people who lived there. Were they happy and secure? Were they at peace with themselves? He had been happy – or at least occupied – moving the car expertly around the twisting road, but now the serenity began to overwhelm him. All around, the land dipped and rolled and climbed into the sky in a silent eternal majesty, as it had always done, as it always would, forever, through light and dark, heat and ice, rain and drought – unlike him and unlike anybody ever born. He felt cold sweat suddenly prickle his body. He wanted to get away from all this, to run away and forget, to lose himself. He pulled off the road suddenly, viciously, without signalling. He switched off the engine and sat, head back, staring at nothing and breathing heavily.

He knew he had to arrive on time, but he couldn't move. Duty sat beside him, but this time said nothing. *Not now. Come on. Breathe deeply. Calm down.* He looked around. Had anybody noticed? He was alone and for a moment his mind lifted up into the sky and looked down upon himself, a tiny speck. And all around him stretched the timeless landscape: Spring, Summer, Autumn, Winter. That was the natural order of things. He knew that. Of course he knew that. But with every turn of the wheels, he also realised he was travelling towards an end.

Come on Oliver. Get a grip. What would Ted do?

He started the car and drove off again.

The car crunched across the gravel driveway and stopped outside a large red-bricked building. Oliver looked at its impressive exterior, so different from the simple rather sparse home that Florrie had been moved from.

'She is deteriorating Oliver.'

June Thomas looked gently into his eyes and touched his arm.

'The time has come to move her. To a specialist home that can care for her now.'

Oliver got out of the car. *Maybe this was just part of the process of dying. From the simple to the grand to the gates of paradise.*

He stood in front of the building for a moment. The sun had soaked into its clay and stone so that it glowed contentedly. You wanted to feel its warmth, to press your cheek against it.

He listened intently for any sound, but the world barely whispered, hardly spun and part of him wanted to stay there, in that bubble. The other part wanted to fire the ignition and drive quickly away.

The porch was fashioned in a brick perpendicular style and its shade was a shock after the heat drifting outside. A large round Victorian bell-push shone in the dim light and a nervous prod produced a disappointing buzz instead of the anticipated resounding dinner gong. A shadowy fragmented shape gradually filled the door's frosted glass before the door opened and a young man dressed in a nurse's white coat, trousers and shoes appeared. He appraised Oliver coolly before speaking. 'Ooh. Are they for me?'

The flowers were a gift of colour and love he hoped would lift Florrie from the troubled world she now inhabited. Oliver ignored him.

'I've come to see Florrie.'

The young man sniffed and pointed in the direction of the rear of the house.

'They're in the garden. Can't miss 'em. Just follow the sound of singing. If that's what you call it.'

The house was darkly furnished and unloved. Years of lost hope had soaked into its wooden panels and cheap carpet leaving it smelling of sadness and urine. It belonged to nobody, but also to everybody who had ever been there and so its spirit had splintered.

From the garden behind the house drifted the sound of music and desultory singing. A single female voice led the entertainment in a loud confident voice.

'...There'll be bluebirds over
The white cliffs of Dover...'

Her microphone crackled slightly, but it didn't matter much. Before her a number of elderly people sat slumped in plump armchairs that almost enveloped them. They might have been small children sitting on adult's chairs, except that a small child would be bursting full of tomorrow and these people were in danger of disappearing forever down the gap between the seat and the back.

Despite the hot sunshine, many were covered with hairy grey blankets and around them sat friends and family. Most looked lost.

Nurses and helpers moved around, crouching at each chair, encouraging them to sing. Bring back memories, enjoy and have fun.

Florrie looked at the flowers as if she had never seen flowers before and then grasped them fiercely to her. She said nothing to Oliver.

'Oh what lovely flowers, Florrie.' The nursing sister smiled and her dark eyes flickered professionally over Florrie. 'She's not so good today. She let Blackie out yesterday. Her cat, you know?'

He nodded. He knew very well the large animal that appeared to control humans, other cats and small dogs with indifferent ease.

'Well, he hasn't come back. That may have upset her. Difficult to know.'

So what did he know, this big black cat?

She spoke kindly, but as if Florrie wasn't there and indeed it was difficult to know exactly where she was.

'Shall I take your flowers Florrie? Put them in water for you?'

Florrie looked at her darkly, suspiciously, maybe trying to comprehend but making no effort to resist. *Do what you like with them. What do I care?*

He sat for a while with her, silent and uncomfortable, as if with a stranger, listening to the sounds she may have thrilled to, danced to, smiled at, but which now seemed shut out. A young nurse moved around trying to encourage residents and visitors to join in. She moved her hands gently in time to the music. Her eyes met Oliver's. *Join in* they said wordlessly. *It might even do you some good.* He mumbled the next line.

'Tomorrow, just you wait and see.' But tomorrow frightened him.

***

The following evening, Florrie demanded her supper, loudly and fiercely. When it arrived, she complained even louder.

'What's this muck? I'm not eating this muck.'

'Come on Florrie, be a good girl.'

'I don't want to be.' She retired to her small, sparse room, undressed with the help of her nurse and got ready for bed.

'Where's Blackie? Where's my cat?'

'He's gone out.'

'Huh. Got nobody to talk to.'

'You can talk to me.'

'It's not the same.'

'Shall I turn the bedside light out for you?'

'No thanks, I'll do it.'

'OK. Goodnight Florrie.'

'Goodnight.' Florrie turned and smiled. She lay there, looking at the shadows sitting in the corner of the room. Suddenly, she thought about Ted with a clarity that surprised her. 'Where have you been?' She paused. 'I'm glad you're back.' She turned and switched off the light.

She dreamed she was at the top of a hill. She was breathing heavily from the climb, which had been steep and long and arduous and had dragged at her limbs and lungs and spirit. But she had made it, and now, before her, an endless landscape of lush fields and meadows and silver streams, stretched away into a shimmering golden haze. She smiled and felt a breeze kiss her warm cheek. There was no other sound, just utter peace. Slowly, she drifted into a deep sleep.

She had battled all her life against war and separation; against social injustice; against the controls and demands of society; against her own demons and on behalf of many, many people. Perhaps it was only fair that she was let off this one final battle.

She never awoke.

TWENTY

The Photo Album and Florrie Attends Her Own Funeral

'No legacy is so rich as honesty.'

William Shakespeare

It was a silent drive to the cemetery. Inside the car, the air was thick with thoughts that even the open window could not whisk away.

Around them, the world carried on normally, cruelly oblivious of their feelings and they watched it with a strange curiosity as if they had never really noticed its importance before. They longed for it again – just turn the clock back. *This time we will use it better. Every second. Promise.*

The car drove on, obeyed the road and its demands for mile after mile, but they barely noticed.

Florrie sat with them, a different Florrie for each: Florrie laughing, Florrie singing, Florrie dancing, Florrie misbehaving, Florrie in the sunlight, Florrie in the shadows, but Florrie gone forever. They said nothing, but their feelings wailed.

Suddenly, at the brow of a slow hill, a silver sky towered around them, glinting off the metal and mirror and leaving them squinting into its brilliance. Below them they could see strips of sparkling light dancing and rippling as they passed between the dark silhouettes of imposing Edwardian houses.

'Look, there she is. The sea.'

The sea filled their minds. It was powerful, mystical, whispering and restless. Is that where she was? No candy floss and ice cream this time.

They arrived very early, parked at the sea front, found a seat and sat in nervous silence. The day was fresh and sunny and each breath tasted of salt. Nearby, seagulls cried pitifully and waves broke with a gentle roar, endlessly moving shingle in a slow rough caress. On a dark headland a tiny window twinkled in the sunlight.

'Want another sandwich? There's just one left.'

'No thanks.'

'How are you feeling Ollie? You lost weight?'

'I'm OK... Weight goes up and down a bit. No... Working on a new play.'

'Good. And how are the kids?'

'Kids? They're OK. Saw them last weekend. Miss their grandparents of course, especially Dad who doted on them. Mum tended to boss them about. Thought she was still an Akela I think. And how are things with you Bobby?'

'Oh very well thanks, very well.'

'Have you seen these?' Oliver took a buff coloured envelope from an inside pocket.

He had found an old photograph album at number twenty-one, its outer cover a mottled brown leather, its edges and corners scuffed lighter. Inside, thick black paper displayed pages of photographs. Each page smelled of time, old time, time spent, time drifting mustily away.

Some were unknown portraits – strangers smiling out at strangers. Others were grinning groups at play, often by the seaside. Looking at them, the brothers remembered distant cries of laughter, cool sand between their toes, a faint smell of bladderwrack and hot dogs.

Some photos had slumped as the corners that had held them straight and true, had become brittle and fragile. Others were just empty gaps with a name beneath, a faceless name, like a war memorial.

Oliver sat and thought for a long time. The album spoke so much about life. Every new second, minute and hour can be so fresh and tasty, at least for a while. Then they die away, like the flavour of chewing gum does. But there will always be more to follow. Until one day you run out of gum.

He had selected just three photographs. The first showed a young slim woman smiling out of a faded black and white studio photograph. She stood wearing dark coloured plus fours above tartan socks and cycling shoes. That her world was still young could be seen in the slight smile that played around her lips, the positive set of her head and the light that shone from her eyes. Ted stood strong beside her.

'They had a tandem Bobby. Used to cycle to Southend and back. In one day.'

He tried to imagine them cycling together. Was Florrie in front, wind in her face, forging the way and Ted behind, powerful and supporting?

'When was this?' Bobby asked.

'Turn it over.'

Few of the photos had anything written on the back and were just blank. *Shame. Just a few words, that's all it takes to give history a little nudge.* But this was different. It read "Sunday morning. 7 October 1934," written in pencil.

The looping handwriting seemed to invite you in and the years had rubbed against the grey words making them soft and smudged. Had Florrie written those words? Carefree Florrie or Ted, a different Ted, a Ted in love. Before? Taken a pencil stub, licked the end and carefully written them. And *Sunday morning!*

'You can sense that Bobby, can't you? The empty streets in the early morning. Just the church bells and their bicycle wheels clicking the way they do. The only sounds. You can picture it.'

'Can see why you're the playwright.'

Oliver smiled. He felt more than that. He felt the warm embrace, saw a love letter in just two words.

'I wonder how many people have touched this? Seen this? Wonder what they felt?' Bobby paused. '1934. Just five years. I don't suppose they had any idea what was about to happen to them. But then none of us does.'

He returned the photograph.

'This one is very different.'

Unlike the carefully posed one before, this had the immediacy of a snapshot.

The scene showed the entrance to an extension of a house – number twenty-one. It was open, leading to a yellow kitchen door, beyond which only cool, dark shadows could be seen. Frosted-ribbed glass made up the extension's main structure and through it could be seen the indistinct shapes of boxes, umbrellas, plants and a watering can. To the left and tightly cropped within the photo, stood a middle-aged woman wearing a cream dress and matching shoes, both bleached by the sunlight and indifferent exposure. She was pretending to strum a guitar. The fingers of her left hand were flexed tautly as she stretched to reach the guitar string. Her face was partly obscured by an oversize bronze wig, on top of which was perched a dark green Mexican sombrero encircled with yellow zigzags. A dark red chinstrap was hanging over her left shoulder. Between her teeth she gripped a pink plastic rose and, despite the physical demands, she was still managing a manic grin. There was no logical reason for this charade, simply the joyful madness of doing so. Beside her, a young grandchild looked on smiling but bemused.

'Grandma is funny. Why is she doing that?'

'Because Grandma is bonkers, that's why.'

Florrie must have felt a giggle bubbling up inside her. *How crazy, how wonderfully crazy. How wonderfully, hysterically crazy.* Then, she must have felt her life to be secure with her beloved family around her, allowing her to flourish and blossom, to be the centre of attention. People would point and laugh and shake their heads in disbelief. 'Oh Florrie what a riot. Oh Florrie what a character you are. Oh Florrie what *will* you do next?'

'Hey Ollie. Look at Dad.'

Ted was standing near to her, grinning but unwilling to join in the madness. He was there watching and waiting. Allowing her freedom, self-expression, but ready to step in.

'Do you think he struggled with her?' Oliver thought of the desperate bedroom. He had taken the pistol and told nobody what he had seen. What he had felt. Only about the letter.

'What physically?' Bobby asked.

'Well no. Not really. Just struggled to cope. Can't have been easy.'

'No. Don't think so. He would have said. Wouldn't he?'

'Don't know. He often looked tired, and sad.'

'Well he did have heart trouble.'

'Yes, but I'm sure he already knew that. There must have been signs. So why didn't he say something?'

'Oh you know what they were like and their whole bloody generation – independent, stubborn.' Bobby shook his head slightly as he searched. 'Er... proud. The war I suppose.'

'Yes. S'pose so. But I still feel guilty. And angry.'

Bobby turned, surprised. 'Guilty? Angry? About what? You did all you could.'

'Did I? Doesn't feel like it.' Oliver looked out towards the horizon.

'Come on big brother. You can't be responsible for their lives. At the end of the day that's up to them isn't it? And they were also protecting us, remember? At least Dad had no doubts about what to do – his duty, his standards – no doubt at all. I admire that. Remember *his* standards? Hope I'm like that – a real man.'

Oliver smiled to himself. 'Well, must be wonderful to always be that certain.'

'Yes. Almost like a religion wasn't it? Although he wasn't at all religious. Not after the war.'

'Well, worse than that really. He had no choice. It was built into his bones. Probably never knew he was conditioned.'

'Conditioned! No. Do you really believe that? But we're not like that. Well, I'm not. Do you think we're like that?'

Bobby stretched his legs nervously. A nodding pigeon pattered cautiously around them.

'Locked in our DNA? Maybe. I guess you never know until you're in that situation.'

There was a long pause.

Oliver broke it. 'Do you think they talked to each other? You know, really talked.'

'Don't know... But it's not always necessary to talk. I know that. Sometimes you just know.'

Oliver looked sideways at his brother and saw, for the first time, Ted's profile. 'This is the last one.'

He passed the photo to Bobby.

The photograph showed a large sitting room. The room was darkly lit and comfortably furnished. A large, central picture window was the only source of light, subdued by the lacy net curtains that swept theatrically upwards towards the centre. Framing the window on either side hung dark curtains, secured by tiebacks and elaborate tassels. The room was empty save for one person who stood centre stage, looking directly at the camera and crouching slightly. She was wearing a simple blue floral dress and trainers and her sleeves were rolled up to the elbows, allowing you to see her bare arms and her fists tightly clenched in a boxer's guard. Her left leg was sprung forward with the right planted firmly behind for balance. Her head was cocked to one side with her chin tucked in and her face displayed a determined grin, eyebrows arched in anticipation. Florrie was ready.

'I've never seen this. Where was this taken?' Bobby asked.

'Don't know. But quite recently.'

'Typical Mum. Always looking for a fight.'

'Maybe. I'm not sure.'

Bobby looked at his brother. 'What do you mean?'

'Maybe she was trying to defend herself.'

'Against who?'

'Not sure it was a who, except maybe herself. She must have known there was a problem.'

Bobby turned away from the mesmeric sea. 'But never let on? Did she ever tell you?'

'Never, just battled away, on her own. Until it became impossible.'

Oliver took the photo back and looked at it again. Florrie still appeared to be strong and determined, but around her, dark shadows seemed to be creeping from every corner. He wondered whether she had she been aware of that happening. *Maybe, maybe not. Maybe those shadows seemingly so dark and threatening were simply patches of colour to her – red, yellow, blue – splashed there, like her own paintings, straight out of the tube of life, normal in her mind, not fearful at all. Was that it?*

For a second, Oliver thought that the photograph might come to life and the heavy curtains close, leaving her in darkness, squaring up to her fears and demons alone. *God, I know about that.* His fingers trembled as he quickly put the photograph away before that could happen.

Both brothers sat quietly, their thoughts washed by the sound of the sea. The shadow of a swooping gull passed over them.

'Do you believe in ghosts, Bobby?'

'No, not really. Memories, resonances maybe. The imagination spiked by emotions.'

'I just feel she's still around. Here I mean. I think I'm going to bump into her at any moment.'

'Well, it wouldn't be the first time she's been a ghost. Remember when we went hop picking?'

'Oh yes!' Oliver exclaimed. 'Do you really remember that Bobby? You were very young.'

'I remember her grinning for a week.'

Both men paused.

'I can still feel her around me. Didn't feel that with Dad,' Oliver spoke to the concrete floor.

'Yes, well Dad's funeral was different – flags flying, drums beating, that sort of thing. You knew he would be on parade as ordered. With Mum you never knew what she'd do.'

Bobby laughed.

'Yes but she wouldn't want to miss this – her own funeral. Centre of attention. I'm surprised she hasn't contacted the vicar to arrange her singing spot…'

'… and to decide on the hymns,' Bobby joined in. 'The first hymn will be "When Irish Eyes are Smiling."'

'And the congregation doing "Knees up Mother Brown" as they bring the coffin in,' Oliver added.

Both brothers smiled broadly. Oliver looked at his watch. 'Come on. Time to go.'

***

Two miles away, on the outskirts of the seaside town, Florrie sat on a wooden bench, in the cover of an elm tree. She wore pressed lime green trousers and a clean blue cardigan with a metal badge attached. Her hair was dark and curly. Around her, neat red and yellow flowers spread out on green leaves and glowed in the shade. She smiled at them and then squinted up at the hot sun. She had no need to squint or even sit in the shade, as she could feel neither heat nor cold, but these were habits of a lifetime. She looked around. She had always liked cemeteries. Well, not at night of course, although she *had* walked through one at night. As a young girl, on her own, just for a dare, but that was a long, long time ago. But here, now, on a sunny September day, it was so well tended, so green and peaceful and dotted with colour and thoughts.

She had heard Oliver and Bobby talking. She knew they were on their way, but there were no signs of any cars, certainly no big black cars. *There will probably only be one.* She frowned. She had always expected more than that, an entire cavalcade and the entire street… *Oh well. Anyway, plenty of time yet.*

She thought about her sons' conversation and it worried her. She hadn't always got it right and neither had Ted. You can get so wrapped up in your own life, your own problems, that you forget how much you influence those tied to you, umbilically. Was there such a word? Well it sounded right. Look at Ted. Rather kill himself than give in. I never wanted that. *You wait till I see him.* She looked across the tranquil cemetery. *Strange that. It's just a big garden really, but it changes people. This is the very place to come if you have a problem. Maybe marriage guidance offices should be built slap bang in the middle.*

She thought about Ted again. She knew he would be there, wherever *there* was, knew he was around somewhere. She could sense him. In fact all of her senses seemed to have sharpened, not only her hearing, but also her memory. All that material that had been stored away in an increasingly dark, misty place was now fresh and sharp and clean and filed for instant access. So it had been worthwhile, all that remembering. That pleased her.

She selected a picture of Ted in her mind. It *had* been a black and white photo, taken on leave, before D-Day. Taken with a Brownie and slightly out of focus and faded. Now it appeared in colour. Mind you, that might not be so strange. Before, she had always watched films in colour and dreamed of them in monochrome. Anyway there he was, in uniform, smiling, happy, handsome and holding Baby Oliver. *Oh I wish they wouldn't call him Ollie. And Bobby. It's not Bobby. It's Robert.* Anyway, there he was. Ted, still full of hope. Not knowing his mind would soon be pierced with a thousand red hot screws that would turn forever and be borne in silence. *Poor Ted.* There must be a million words waiting to gush out now it was over. She laughed silently at that thought. All those words flying continuously out of his open mouth: big ones, small ones, red ones, black ones – like a coloured cloud of little birds blinking nervously and flapping around, escaping at last. Well at least now she and Ted could both sit down together and talk about everything. Like she had with Morris that day in her ramshackle hut on the allotment. Morris had been saved that day... *Fancy saving it all up until now.* She wondered if every word spoken and heard in a lifetime was recorded on some giant tape recorder. Gosh, that would take... well a lifetime. Still, she had plenty of those now.

Relatives and friends and neighbours were arriving to see her. There was Sarah Jane and John Henry. *Mmm, I'm surprised he was there. Thought he might be thrown out for some dodgy deal, caught trying to sell pairs of left-handed wings to angels. Angels. Now there's a thought.* She wondered if there were any and her mind clicked back to the Sunday school on the Hill. To those pictures on the wall and in the books they had to read. Trouble was they all seemed to be male angels or at least androgynous-looking with short blonde hair. *No that can't be right. That can't be fair. No, maybe you have to audition.* Well, she had all that experience with her cub concerts. Perhaps she could organise an angelic concert? And she wouldn't have all that bother of finding costumes.

There's Harry, but no Helen, not yet. Harry was mouthing something, mouth wide open, but fortunately she couldn't hear what he was shouting. That was a relief. *Perhaps you could switch it off? Oh and there is George. Sweet, handsome George with his deep dark eyes and flashing teeth, so attentive, always the perfect gentleman... Well almost.*

They kept drifting past, all those who had gone ahead.

Now dear Edie. Her tall mother-in-law. Always worrying about something. Florrie remembered those Sunday dinners when Ted was away. She closed her eyes and breathed in the scent of lavender and freshly brewed tea. She opened them again suddenly as the thought struck her. *I hope you can still get a decent cup of tea.* She closed her eyes again... *Edie, do you remember the day the bomber fell from the sky? What a day that was. Ruined a perfectly good hanky not to mention a fence and several rows of beans.* She had always thought of that whenever she had eaten runner beans afterwards. Also destroyed Jonathan of course and Joan really. Hey. Her eyes opened wide. Where was Joan?

'Hallo Florrie.'

'Joan! What are you doing here?'

'I wanted to come and meet you.'

Joan stood before her dressed in a long tight pencil skirt and white high heels. The sun, behind her, caught her brown hair making it glow. She hitched up her skirt, lowered herself carefully next to Florrie and crossed her legs.

'Not very appropriate for a funeral Joan. *My* funeral and you still can't walk in those heels.'

'I always loved this look... La Lollo.'

'La what? Oh never mind... Lovely to see you Joan.'

Joan gently touched her hand. 'Hey Florrie, do you remember when we used to walk up the High Street?'

'Walk! Wiggle in your case *and* ogle young sailors.'

Joan smiled to herself. 'Did I ever tell you I met one?'

'Met one? What a sailor?'

'Yes. He was gorgeous. Asked me to go for a drink with him. Said he fancied older, experienced women.'

'You didn't?' Florrie sounded astonished.

'No I didn't. Told him I was married. Ran up the High Street and caught the first bus home. How pathetic.'

The two women looked at each other for a second and then burst out laughing. Around them the air remained silent.

'Oh Joan.'

The women sat quietly for a moment, immersed in their thoughts. Florrie turned towards her friend. 'Is Ted there?'

'I haven't seen him.'

'Why didn't he come to meet me as well? Is he angry with me?' Florrie frowned.

'No, why should he be? In any case anger soon disappears here. Not much point really. He's probably organising a celebration for you, a street party or something. They're very popular at the moment *or* he might be on Clarence duty.'

'Clarence?'

'Yes. Well that's not the proper name of course but that's what everybody calls them. Like the guardian angel, in the film. You know. With James Stewart. Oh he was lovely. Still is.'

Florrie looked at her friend in astonishment.

Joan uncrossed her legs and pushed both hands down against the bench.

'They've arrived. They're all here,' she said softly.

Florrie stood. 'I know.'

'Are you going to join them Florrie? Is that why you're here?'

'Couldn't miss a good sing-song now could I?'

'Come on then.'

They both linked arms and walked in silence towards the chapel. After a while, Florrie stopped. 'How do I get *there* Joan?'

'There?'

'Yes, you know. *There.*'

'As soon as you are ready you'll know. Don't worry.'

They stopped outside the small chapel. A hymn was just starting and the organ pounded out the introduction.

'All things bright and beautiful, all creatures great and small...'

The singing was ragged. One beat behind the organist, but they heard Oliver and Bobby, singing powerfully.

'They are such good boys, Florrie.'

'Jonathan would have been the same, Joan.'

Joan smiled.

'I hope they're going to be OK, Joan. I really do. I don't know what sort of legacy Ted and I have left them. Have they got everything they need? Do you think they have been infected by us? You know, carry our bad bits as well as the good? It does worry me.'

'Oh come on Florrie. You did your best. They will battle through any problems just as you and Ted did. Listen.'

The unusual sound of laughter came from the chapel, so normally veiled in whispers and tears. Oliver was speaking. 'She might have been an acquired taste but she was always an individual in a time of conformity. Full of fun and adventure and determination.'

Bobby took over. 'Every year she would take her cubs out onto the streets to sell poppies. She wanted to support those servicemen who protected her country and wanted the young to understand their sacrifice. Eventually she was awarded a badge in honour of her own service and she always wore it. She was so proud of it. I bet if she's looking down on us now, she'll be wearing it.'

'And it was usually freezing. I bet he'd get a shock if he knew how close I was,' said Florrie stroking the badge fastened to her cardigan.

'Oh Florrie. You can see the legacy you've left behind. There is nothing to worry about.'

'But people always say nice things at funerals.'

'Doesn't mean they're not true though, does it?'

Nearby, one of the cemetery gardeners was slowly approaching, pushing an old wheelbarrow. Its misshapen wheel turned lumpily and threatened with every revolution to part company with the rest of its battered body. It should have squealed in protest, but somehow it moved on silently. At an angle in the barrow, the handle of a spade protruded, its wooden surface shiny with use. The gardener touched his flat cap in a gesture of polite welcome.

'Sure dey seem to be having a good toime.'

'Yes. Looks like it.' Florrie turned her blue eyes, smiling, towards him. 'You work here?'

'Aye. Sort of. Came in today. To make sure der gardens were perfect. For someone special.'

'Oh yes, they certainly are.'

They stood together for a moment in silence until the last chords of the final song ended and hung resonating in the still air. *'Sure, they steal your heart away.'*

'Now dats a beautiful song.'

'It's perfect,' Florrie smiled. 'But I must go now.'

The gardener said nothing, but with the fluid skill of someone who had performed it over many, many years, took an old battered tobacco tin from his frayed jacket pocket, removed the lid, took out a rolled up cigarette, placed it in his mouth and snapped the lid shut.

'Are you away den?'

'Yes, I have to go now.'

'Me too. Before de boss catches me having a sloy smoke.'

'Is he that bad, your boss?'

'Ah no. He's foine. Apart from being English.' He spat a loose strand of tobacco from his lips, 'and ex-Army. But apart from dat he's foine.' He looked at her kindly.

'I have to go. Meet my husband. I'm very anxious to see him.'

'Well dats a powerful ting.'

'Thank you. And you, Are you staying?'

'Oil stay here for a whoile. Tending der gardens and watching der clouds go boy.'

'OK. Good luck to you.'

'Siochan leat.'

She turned, but Joan had gone. Florrie wasn't surprised. Now she knew where to go. She took one last look across the garden, swung around and nearly bumped into a young man standing patiently. He was tall and athletic, with a wave of fair hair flopping over laughing blue eyes. He was smiling lovingly at her.

TWENTY ONE

Epilogue

A year later, in the summer of 2001, the family decided to hold a memorial service for Florrie and Ted. It seemed only right to celebrate them together. After all, they had been married for sixty-two years when Ted died.

There were few of their relatives left and even fewer able to make the journey. However, friends and children, together with former cubs and their families, swelled the numbers.

Helen Smith (Ted and Florrie's next-door-neighbour at number 19) was now in a care home and suffering the torment of Alzheimer's disease and of course had no children to invite in her place. Harry, her husband, had died shortly after Ted which had left Helen completely alone and in a difficult position when trying to offer neighbourly help to Florrie as both their mental health problems increased. For a long time this seemed to torment her, until her own disease swept away all her memories. Helen had always been quiet and gentle, unlike Harry. Even when a crane wire had snapped in a dockside accident and had dumped him into a hold, he hadn't been cowed. However, to everyone's surprise he had taken early retirement announcing that being a stevedore was a dirty and dangerous job and he didn't miss it. Maybe he could see the changes happening in Helen. In the local streets he was always the hero who had saved lives the day the bomber crashed.

Sydney and Alice Jenner at number 15 had moved away some years before. Alan, their son, still bearing burn scars, had also moved to the North of England, where he worked as a director of a building firm. Joan, secretly, always missed him. Pamela, his sister, had returned to England from Australia, but only for a brief visit before returning to take up a senior position in the Australian Institute of Health and Welfare. She never returned to her home country. The Jenners never seemed to get over that tragic wartime day and were unable to remain living locally. None of those involved realised at the time the significance of 15th September 1940 (later to be known as Battle of Britain Day) as the turning point in the battle for supremacy of the air. To them it was just another awful situation to deal with.

Cyril Williamson was a year younger than Joan (she always had a weakness for younger men) and had survived her. Normally he kept himself to himself, but that changed at the party held after the service. A combination of old age and navy rum and coke encouraged him to tell Oliver and Bobby exactly what he had heard night after night, through the thin walls of Ted and Florrie's home. The brothers were deeply shocked. Cyril was whisked home.

George had also moved away after the confrontation with Ted. Possibly back to the port of Liverpool where he still had some relations. He wrote once to Florrie. She never replied.

Louis arrived at the reunion with his wife and four children.

Henrietta and her husband James (Florrie's younger brother) were away on a cruise in the Caribbean and couldn't make it.

However, June Thomas and her husband made the journey from the care home in Bexhill. That was a very pleasant surprise for everybody. Nobody expected them to make such a long trip, but Florrie had weaved her magic and June was pleased to say a few words in her memory. She was also very jolly on the dance floor.

The Scouting Association was not invited. Oliver and Bobby could still remember the pain of Florrie's enforced retirement.

Representatives of the local branch of the Royal British Legion were present. It was this branch that Florrie had supported so loyally and had also supplied flag bearers at Ted's funeral. Two of the three original flag bearers attended, both wearing their medals and sat quietly in one corner, downing pints all evening. Sadly this was the only direct reference to Ted's military career as his own comrades were no longer alive or too frail to travel.

Darkie Mace had been demobbed from the Army due to his wounds and had returned to the only other family he had known. He met and lived with a Romany girl, Mirella, living off his war pension and typical gypsy business initiatives. He never married and had no children. In 1946 Darkie, like many others up and down the country, placed half of his savings on the grey Airborne to win the Derby. The horse was a rank outsider, but somehow won at fifty to one. He never knew that his good fortune was also the cause of the collapse of Ted's family business. With his winnings he bought a half-share in a small boxing club in South London which he ran and where he lived "above the shop". Mirella decided to stay with her family. Darkie's enthusiasm and reputation as a boxer and war hero, helped the business to be successful, but in 1982 the club was gutted by fire. Darkie escaped unhurt, but found his business partner had not insured the building. With everything lost, Darkie then moved to Bermondsey where he rented a small flat. In 1985 he met Fred Johnson (Johno) an ex-Army pal, in a pub in Southwark, who invited Darkie to help young boxers at a local club. Although now very elderly, he still attends the club on a regular basis.

Billy Kite was demobbed in 1946 and returned to the market stalls of Deptford. A year later he married a local girl, June. They had two girls who Billy doted on. With his eye for opportunity, Billy soon established a business selling electrical goods and by 1966 had become a successful local businessman. It seemed natural to then turn his ambitions towards local politics where his persuasive tongue and acute political sense quickly made him equally successful. In 1972 his name was linked with handling stolen property, but this case was never proved and far from damaging his reputation, seemed to enhance it. He retired in 1980 as a Labour Councillor. Both his daughters went to University, a fact that Billy never stopped talking about. Although he lived close to Darkie, he never made contact.

Oliver left college and decided on a career in the theatre, initially as a stage manager. It was there he met Lucinda, who went on to become a very successful stage and television actress. She never witnessed any of Florrie's performances (much to Florrie's disappointment), but she did encourage Oliver to become an actor himself, which he did with varying degrees of success. They married and had two children, Florence and Mark. Ted and Florrie attended the wedding of course. Florrie spent most of the time telling the guests that it was the worst day of her life.

In 1977 Oliver was diagnosed with bipolar disorder, a condition that on occasion added an intensity to his performances as an actor, but which also caused considerable private stress. The signs had been there throughout his life but had been missed, in many ways like those of Florrie. Maybe they had been passed on from mother to son? Maybe it was no coincidence that they came to a head a year after Florrie had received the disastrous resignation letter, at a time when her own problems were growing out of control. In 1980 Lucinda left, taking the children with her, unable or unwilling to cope with the deep depressions or extreme excesses. Bobby, appalled at her desertion, never spoke to her again. However, for Oliver, it acted as a spur and he accepted proper treatment in order to control the condition. Lucinda and the children visit Oliver on a regular basis and he now works as a successful playwright. Currently he is working on a play based on the issues that each generation passes on to the next. He hopes that Lucinda will accept a part.

Bobby left school and joined the police force. His keen sense of duty and determination ensured a rapid rise through the ranks and he soon established a reputation as a tough, plain speaking and loyal policeman. As a senior officer his "honest bobby on the beat" background made him very popular with both colleagues and subordinates. In the late 1970s as a member of the Surrey Constabulary he was a natural choice to assist in Operation Countryman, the operation to investigate corruption in the Metropolitan Police. He never married, has no children and recently retired with the rank of Chief Superintendent. He is currently writing a book about his father's life.

GLOSSARY

Chapter One
Coal carman
Somebody who delivered coal by horse and cart.

Ten bob
Ten shillings.

Dullahan.
A headless creature riding a black horse with his or her head under their arm.

Whisky mac
A cocktail made of Scotch whisky and ginger wine.

Landaulette
A car body style similar to a limousine with a convertible top, often used for formal occasions.

Chats
Chatham.

Chapter Two
Jildi
Anglo-Indian military slang often used as a command for 'Hurry up' or 'Quickly'.

Forage cap
A side cap. A foldable military cap with straight sides and a creased crown.

Webbing
A series of belts, straps, pouches and packs for carrying equipment and ammunition etc.

Gaiters
Leggings strapped around the ankles.

Button stick
Used to slide around buttons for cleaning whilst protecting the uniform.

Housewife
Military clothing repair kit.

Blanco
Cleaning and colouring compound. Also 'to blanco'.

Ammo boots
Black hobnailed leather ankle boots.

Chapter Four
Flak
Ground anti- aircraft fire.

Tracer
Ammunition that lights up when fired, which is used to indicate targets to others.

Jeep
Small, reliable four-wheel drive vehicle.

Naafi
Navy, Army and Air Force Institutes. A shop selling goods to service personnel.

Chapter Five
D plus one
D-Day plus one day. i.e. June 7th 1944.

Chapter Six
The Andrew
The Royal Navy.

Gone outside
Left the Royal Navy.

Chapter Eight
Polrumptious
Kentish dialect for 'badly behaved'.

German cruiser
Cockney rhyming slang for 'boozer' i.e. 'public house'.

Chapter Nine
Bagheera
Black-toned Indian leopard in Rudyard Kipling's Mowgli stories in The Jungle Book. *Also Wolf Cub leader rank.*

Chapter Eleven
Montera
Fur hat traditionally worn (as in this case) by a bullfighter.

Chapter Fifteen
Hard lines
Basic sleeping accommodation.

Chapter Sixteen
Maschinengewehr 42
German machine gun noted for its very high rate of fire, which gives off a ripping/sawing sound.

Chapter Twenty
Siochan leat
Peace be with you.